D0067172

Prize Stories

1997

The O. Henry Awards

Edited and with an Introduction
by Larry Dark

ANCHOR BOOKS
DOUBLEDAY
New York   London   Toronto   Sydney   Auckland

AN ANCHOR BOOK
PUBLISHED BY DOUBLEDAY
a division of Bantam Doubleday Dell Publishing Group, Inc.
1540 Broadway, New York, New York 10036

ANCHOR BOOKS, DOUBLEDAY,
and the portrayal of an anchor
are trademarks of Doubleday,
a division of Bantam Doubleday Dell Publishing Group, Inc.

Permissions begin on page 473.

Library of Congress Cataloging-in-Publication Data

Prize stories. 1947–
New York, N.Y., Doubleday.
v. 22 cm.
Annual.
The O. Henry awards.
None published 1952–53.
Continues: O. Henry memorial award prize stories.
1. Short stories, American—Collected works.
PZ1.011   813′.01′08—dc19   21-9372
MARC-S

ISBN 0-385-48361-9
Copyright © 1997 by Doubleday, a division of
Bantam Doubleday Dell Publishing Group, Inc.
All Rights Reserved
Printed in the United States of America
October 1997
First Edition

10 9 8 7 6 5 4 3 2 1

Publisher's Note

WILLIAM SYDNEY PORTER, who wrote under the pen name O. Henry, was born in North Carolina in 1862. He started writing stories while in prison for embezzlement, a crime for which he was convicted in 1898 (it is uncertain if he actually committed the crime). His writing career was short and started late, but O. Henry proved himself a prolific and widely read short story writer in the twelve years he devoted to the craft, and his name has become synonymous with the American short story.

His years in Texas inspired many lively Westerns, but it was New York City that galvanized his creative powers, and his New York stories became his claim to fame. Loved for their ironic plot twists, which made for pleasing surprise endings, his highly entertaining tales appeared weekly in Joseph Pulitzer's *New York World*.

His best known story, "The Gift of the Magi," was written for the *World* in 1905 and has become an American treasure. Dashed off past deadline in a matter of hours, it is the story of a man who sells his watch to buy a set of hair combs as a Christmas present for his wife, who in the meantime has sold her luxurious locks to buy him a watch chain. "The Last Leaf" is another O. Henry favorite. It is the story of a woman who falls ill with pneumonia and pronounces that she will die when the last leaf of ivy she sees outside her Greenwich Village window falls away. She hangs on with the last stubborn leaf, which gives her the resolve to recover. She eventually learns that her inspirational leaf wasn't a real leaf at all, but rather a painting of a leaf. Her neighbor, who has always dreamed of painting a masterpiece, painted it on the wall and caught pneumonia in the process.

His work made him famous, but O. Henry was an extremely private man who, sadly, preferred to spend his time and money on drink, and ultimately it was the bottle that did him in. He died alone and penniless in 1910. O. Henry's legacy and his popularization of the short story was such that in 1918 Doubleday, in conjunction with the Society of Arts and Sciences, established the O. Henry Awards, an annual anthology of short stories, in his honor. At the end of the century the short story continues to flourish. Styles have radically changed and there can be no greater evidence of the evolution and high achievement today's short story writers enjoy than the contents of this 1997 editon of *Prize Stories: The O. Henry Awards* selected and compiled by the series's new editor, Larry Dark. Anchor Books and Doubleday are proud, with the seventy-seventh edition of the series, to continue the tradition of publishing this much beloved collection of outstanding short stories in O. Henry's name.

Acknowledgments

Thanks to Tina Pohlman, Martha Levin, Charlie Conrad, Arabella Meyer, Jennie Guilfoyle, Betsy Lerner, Alice Elliott Dark, and my first readers—the devoted editors who spend long hours reading the stories submitted to the magazines consulted for this series.

Contents

Introduction

THE 1997 VOLUME of *Prize Stories: The O. Henry Awards* introduces several major changes in this longstanding series, among them: a new look, a shift in publication from spring to fall, and a new editor: William Abrahams has retired after editing this series for a remarkable thirty years. As new series editor, I have significantly expanded the list of magazines consulted, which resulted in my reading more than three thousand stories for this year's collection—an average of six or seven a day. Canadian magazines and writers were made eligible for the first time, a change that has had immediate results: the inclusion of Alice Munro and Carol Shields in this volume. I've also added a listing of 50 Honorable Mention Stories, with brief summaries, in order to honor more deserving stories, authors, and magazines than can be encompassed by the selection of only twenty O. Henry Award winners each year.

Perhaps the most significant change is that a jury of three writers will now bear the responsibility for choosing First, Second, and Third Prizes. *Prize Stories* was fortunate this year to have Louise Erdrich, Thom Jones, and David Foster Wallace fill this role. The institution of a prize jury is actually not an innovation for the series; during the 1940s writers such as Eudora Welty and John Marquand served as jurors. Ms. Erdrich, Mr. Jones, and Mr. Wallace, who read the stories blind (i.e., not knowing the names of the authors or the magazines), lent themselves to the endeavor of determining the top prizes with all the seriousness and soul searching and wrestling with intangibles that are intrinsic to the task. I thank them for their conscientious and enthusiastic participation. I expect the prize jury will remain an integral feature of the series for the foreseeable future.

Starting with this edition, an O. Henry Award will also be presented to the magazine found to have published the best fiction by U.S. or Canadian writers over the course of the reading period. This year's winner is *Epoch,* published by Cornell University and edited by Michael Koch. Four stories originally published by *Epoch,* more than any other magazine, are featured in this volume—those by Arthur Bradford, Andre Dubus, Robert Morgan, and Patricia Elam Ruff—and another story is listed among the fifty chosen for honorable mention. The five issues of *Epoch* I read included an exemplary range of stories. Additionally, a feature called *"Epoch* Introduces" showcased the work of up-and-coming writers. It is quite extraordinary for a small quarterly literary magazine to publish such outstanding work on such a consistent basis.

What isn't new is that *Prize Stories: The O. Henry Awards* will continue to sift through the year's published writing (in the present case sixteen months' worth, because of the shift in publication) to come up with a collection of the most riveting stories around. Are these twenty stories absolutely the "best"? I'd hesitate to claim that in any absolute sense. There's certainly no calculus by which the excellence of a story can be assessed in purely objective terms, so to a great degree any judgments made are going to be subjective. And though it's tempting to sum up, to identify trends, to make connections, the results of a process such as this defy easy characterization. These writers sat alone in their rooms writing their stories and any influences upon them were distinctly filtered through their individual sensibilities. After months of virtual nonstop reading, what I ultimately picked were the stories that affected me most deeply, stayed with me the longest, and held up best to repeat readings; the stories that staked out a space in my brain or heart or guts or wherever such spaces are staked out and that, when I reread them, got to me again, and kept offering more.

I wore two hats as I read, though perhaps two pairs of glasses would be a more fitting image. Part of me remained a pure reader, a consumer of narrative out for the kick of total absorption, seeking to be so taken into a story that my consciousness was superseded by it or to be so engaged and stimulated that the orbit of my thoughts was temporarily altered by the stronger gravitational pull of the author's. Alongside that impressionable, wide-eyed reader sat the part of me trained to function more selectively as an editor, a deconstructor who weighed and measured and studied and analyzed so that I could intelligently explain to myself the technical reasons why one story worked better than another. But in the end, the technical reasons didn't suffice as an explanation; I read a lot of well-constructed, interesting stories that I didn't find compelling. They lay on the page, never transcending the basic fact of their making. In the best stories, when I am able to find and pull the string that unwinds the sweater the writer has so carefully knitted together, what is revealed is not so much how the story was made but the flesh beneath the sweater, what *we* are made of. These twenty stories, for all their differences in technique and style and subtlety and meaning, break out of their boundaries to make a connection between author and reader; they tell tales that make that mystery happen.

As I continue to read hundreds of magazines and pore through thousands of more stories for next year's collection, I feel sustained in the belief that the writing and reading of fiction are two of the highest human endeavors. Sometimes I think I wouldn't know anything outside myself without fiction—I'd only know what went into and came out of me, the spaces my body moved through and a little something about the few other bodies I brushed past and up against. What a good short story does is open up experience exponentially. The world of fiction is bigger than the world of reality, of science, of time and space because it encompasses everything possible and a hell of a lot that isn't. As a narrative form it has journalism, history, memoir, biography, and every other nonfictional genre beat because they, at best, can only tell the truth, whereas good fiction gets at Truth with a—do I have to spell it out—capital T. These may be pretty lofty claims, but I believe every last one of them. My hope is that you'll read these stories and see just what I mean.

❑ ❑ ❑ ❑

What follows are comments on every story, including remarks from the jurors, that will, I hope, go some distance toward explaining why the stories chosen stood out above the rest. Mentioning every story is not, for me, a perfunctory exercise but a way of giving each its due and of shining the spotlight, momentarily at least, on each writer. It's difficult to speak of the stories without giving away some of the plot details, so those who would like a purer reading experience may prefer to return to these entries later.

The First Prize winner, "City Life" by Mary Gordon, is a window into a squalid shack at the end of a dirt road and into a character who escaped—or thought she escaped—from just such a place. David Foster Wallace said: "It raised hair on parts of my body that don't even have hair. The creepiest story I've read in a long time, and creepy in what seems a totally real and true way, which of course makes the creepiness all the creepier." Thom Jones called it "a story told with great assuredness and verve. It was utterly convincing and its details haunted me long after I finished the piece."

The Second Prize story, "The Falls" by George Saunders, finds humor in the solipsistic musings of two self-absorbed losers as they walk along the banks of a river, in the middle of which a runaway canoe carrying two young girls is heading inexorably toward the falls. David Foster Wallace said of this story, which also received votes from the other two jurors: "I think Saunders is the most talented and interesting new U.S. writer in a long time. And 'The Falls' shows his genius for talking about old-fashioned moral stuff in ways that are funny and human and real and about as far from preachy or PC-gooey as you can get. I voted for it because it was the funniest story in the stack and also because of its moral nerve. A little like Flannery O'Connor on acid, maybe."

The Third Prize story, "The Talk Talked Between Worms" by Lee K. Abbott, is memorable not only because of its description of one man's encounter with what may be a crashed alien space ship outside of Roswell, New Mexico, but also because of the way this event resonates through the life of the narrator, the man's son. Louise Erdrich said of it: "This profoundly unsettling psychological mystery also grabbed me emotionally. As the best stories do, it haunted my thoughts for weeks after the reading."

John Barth's "On with the Story" is a brilliantly constructed metafiction with a narrative surface like a Möbius strip. And in delineating the movements of its characters through time and space so exhaustively, the story breaks out of its fictional construct, reaching into the world of the reader.

Alice Munro's novella "The Love of a Good Woman" is overtly structured around a murder mystery. Along the way, Munro also manages to give a detailed sociological portrait of a small Canadian town and a brilliant exploration of conventional morality. The part of the story where the three boys who find the body return to their respective houses is one of the most incredibly deep and detailed pieces of writing I have ever come across. Louise Erdrich said: "I loved this story for its meticulous observations and sly, incremental structure. Somehow Munro builds casually to a fever. And what an extraordinary grasp of 'boylife.' "

Carolyn Cooke's "The Twa Corbies" presents an unforgettable character in Tad—the childlike, chain-smoking, chocolate ice cream eating, brain-damaged, sixtysomething brother of the narrator.

"Catface" by Arthur Bradford is simply and matter-of-factly told, but the amusing quirkiness of the characters and the seeming randomness of events carry with them a deeper sense of mystery. Who are these freaks, you want to know, and what makes them so compelling and unforgettable?

Andre Dubus's "Dancing After Hours" is a beautifully structured and told story about a waitress who has settled for a life of scaled-back ambitions and forsaken hopes until an encounter with a quadriplegic customer shows her that the possibility for a modest form of grace still exists.

In "The Royal Palms," Matthew Klam exposes the ominous undercurrents circulating between a husband and wife on a Caribbean vacation. The wife is not, as the husband thinks, no longer sexually interested in him because she's self-conscious about the size of her ass but because he's so unselfconscious about how big an ass he has become. Klam not only turns a big ass into a double-edged image, he also deftly manages to make transparent to the reader what remains opaque to the protagonist without condescending to either.

Kiana Davenport's "The Lipstick Tree" paints a vivid picture of tribal life in New Guinea, rife with observations that, beyond their particularity, apply to the lot of women and indigenous people everywhere. "The story had a magical effect on me," said Thom Jones. "I was impressed by the protagonist's dream of a better life and her ability to go to the furthest extremes to make it come true, knowing fully well that the prize of freedom would be mitigated with grievous loss, that it would be a bittersweet victory at best."

"The Red House" by Ian MacMillan is thoroughly steeped in the protagonist's stream of consciousness, offering the perspective of a teenage boy from a brutal and impoverished background who is just awakening to the pleasures of language and, rather uncertainly, to his own sexuality.

Anyone familiar with Mary Gaitskill's fiction won't be surprised to find that her story "Comfort" is really about discomfort, about feeling ill-at-ease in even the most intimate of relationships. One wonderfully excruciating scene takes place in a hospital room where, in the presence of a woman's adult son and longtime ex-husband, a doctor callously examines her, exposing intimate areas of the helpless, immobilized woman's body. It had me squirming as if I were there.

What's gripping about "The Balm of Gilead Tree" by Robert Morgan is the twists and turns it takes you through as a reader. First you think the narrator is rushing to the scene of a plane crash to help out. Then he starts to loot—rifling through burst luggage and broken bodies—and you are repulsed by his behavior. Somehow, though, the action pulls you over into the story's skewed moral universe, reestablishing a strong identification with the protagonist.

"The Final Inning" by Thomas Glave is an uncommon story about an all-too-common occurrence, the AIDS-related death of a young black man. Glave reveals the homophobia endemic to the story's Bronx milieu through an angry confrontation among friends and through the unspoken thoughts of a husband and father struggling to keep a lid on his own confused sexuality. Louise Erdrich cited the story as: "Eclectic, funny—sorrowful language with a ferocious intimacy."

Deborah Eisenberg's "Mermaids" uncovers the unseemly side of adult behavior as viewed through the eyes of a child, without assuming the posture that children are morally superior to adults or more blessed in their purported innocence.

The title character of Susan Fromberg Schaeffer's "The Old Farmhouse and the Dog-wife" is a woman suffering from the Alzheimer's-induced delusion that she is a dog. Just as the woman's husband has, the widowed farmer on whose property they show up comes to accept her odd behavior, and her presence causes him to reexamine his past relationship with his own wife.

Patricia Elam Ruff's "The Taxi Ride" is a quiet story about gentle characters struggling in the face of a not-so-gentle world. When a Washington, D.C., cab driver gives the elderly female narrator a ride in the front of his cab and their conversation continues on as he picks up and drops off other passengers, the story achieves the equivalent of an elegant, cinematic montage.

Carol Shields's "Mirrors" concerns a couple who have long spent their summers in a vacation house without a single mirror. Thom Jones called it "a keenly observed story. I was impressed by the author's technical skills and her ability to compress time and deliver a theme of high velocity in just a few pages." David Foster Wallace said of it: "Two things made this story haunt me. The first is that it's so quiet and unassuming and laconic and you don't realize until the next day that it's about absolutely everything important in the world. The second is that it uses such a heavy symbolic device—the mirror—and puts it in the title and weaves it through the whole story and yet never makes it seem heavy or hoary or hackneyed."

"His Chorus" by Christine Schutt is memorable for its beautiful, dense language and dreamlike quality. It's a portrait of a young man who lived on life's margins that provides some of his deepest, most essential aspects, while artfully omitting obvious, reassuring details, creating a compelling mystery that resonates beyond the page.

The focus of Rick Moody's "Demonology" is ostensibly on the narrator's sister. The details of her rather ordinary suburban existence are both particular and generic, managing not so much to capture her as perfectly circumscribe her space in the world. But though the narrator gives practically nothing of himself, the story, a prism through which he views the world, ultimately serves to characterize him very deeply.

Deep characterization, evocative language, visceral detail, emotional acuity, and the intangible qualities that bring fiction to life, translating it from an encryption of experience into something far deeper—these are what make the twenty stories in this collection tick, hum, whisper, shout, and linger.

—LARRY DARK, 1997

Prize Stories 1997
THE O. HENRY AWARDS

Mary Gordon

City Life

From *Ploughshares*

PETER HAD ALWAYS BEEN more than thoughtful in not pressing her about her past, and Beatrice was sure it was a reason for her choice of him. Most men, coming of age in a time that extolled openness and disclosure, would have thought themselves remiss in questioning her so little. Perhaps because he was a New Englander—one of four sons in a family that had been stable for generations—perhaps because he was a mathematician, perhaps because both the sight of her and her way of living had pleased him from the first and continued to please him, he had been satisfied with what she was willing to tell. "My parents are dead. We lived in Western New York State, near Rochester. I am an only child. I have no family left."

She preferred saying "I have no family left"—creating with her words an absence, a darkness, rather than to say what had been there, what she had ruthlessly left, with a ruthlessness that would have shocked anyone who knew her later. She had left them so thoroughly that she really didn't know if they were still living. When she tried to locate them, with her marriage and her children and the warm weight of her domestic safety at her back, there was no trace of them. It had shocked and frightened her how completely they had failed to leave a trace. This was the sort of thing most people didn't think of: how possible it was for people like her parents to impress themselves so little on the surface, the many surfaces of the world, that they would leave it or inhabit it with the same lack of a mark.

They were horrors, her parents, the sort people wanted to avert their eyes from, that people felt it was healthful to avert their eyes from. They had let their lives slip very far, further than anyone Beatrice now knew could even begin to imagine. But it had always been like that: a slippage so continuous that there was simultaneously a sense of slippage and of already having slipped.

It was terribly clear to her. She was brought up in filth. Most people, Beatrice knew, believed that filth was temporary, one of those things, unlike disease or insanity or social hatred—that didn't root itself in but was an affair of surfaces, therefore dislodgeable by effort, will, and the meagerest brand of intelligence. That was, Beatrice knew, because people didn't understand filth. They mistook its historical ordinariness for simplicity. They didn't understand the way it could invade and settle, take over, dominate, and for good, until it became, inevitably, the only true thing about a place and the only lives that could be lived there. Dust, grime, the grease of foods, the residues of bodies, the smells that lived in the air, palpable, malign, unidentifiable, impossible to differentiate: an ugly population of refugees from an unknowable location, permanent, stubborn, knife-faced settlers who had right of occupancy— the place was theirs now—and would never leave.

Beatrice's parents had money for food, and the rent must have been paid to someone. They had always lived in the one house: her mother, her father, and herself. Who could have owned it? Who would have put money down for such a place? One-story, nearly windowless, the outside walls made of soft shingle in the semblance of pinkish gray brick. It must have been built from the first entirely without love, with the most cynical understanding, Beatrice had always thought, of the human need for shelter and the dollar value that it could bring. Everything was cheap and thin, done with the minimum of expense and of attention. No thought was given to ornament or amplitude, or even to the long, practical run: what wouldn't age horribly or crumble, splinter, quickly fade.

As she grew older, she believed the house had been built to hide

some sort of criminality. It was in the middle of the woods, down a
dirt road half a mile down Highway 117, which led nowhere she
knew, or maybe south, she somehow thought, to Pennsylvania. Her
parents said it had once been a hunting lodge, but she didn't believe
it. When she was old enough to have learned about bootlegging,
and knew that whiskey had been smuggled in from Canada, she
was convinced that the house had had something to do with that.
She could always imagine petty gangsters, local thugs in mean felt
hats and thin-soled shoes trading liquor for money, throwing their
cigarette butts down on the hard, infertile ground, then driving
away from the house, not giving it a thought until it was time for
their next deal.

Sometimes she thought it was the long periods of uninhabited-
ness that gave the house its closed, and vengeful, character. But
when she began to think like that, it wasn't long before she understood that kind of thought to be fantastical. It wasn't the house,
houses had no will or nature. Her parents had natures, and it was
their lives and the way they lived that made their dwelling a mon-
strosity.

She had awakened each day in dread, afraid to open her eyes,
knowing the first thing they fell on would be ugly. She didn't even
know where she could get something for herself that might be
beautiful. The word couldn't have formed itself in her mind in any
way that could attach to an object that was familiar to her, or that
she could even imagine having access to. She heard, as if from a
great distance, people using the word "beautiful" in relation to
things like trees or sunsets, but her faculty for understanding things
like this had been so crippled that the attempt to comprehend what
people were saying when they spoke like this filled her with a kind
of panic. She couldn't call up even the first step that would allow
her, even in the far future, to come close to what they meant. They
were talking about things out of doors when they talked about trees
and sunsets. And what was the good of that? You could go out of
doors. The blueness of the sky, the brightness of the sun, the freshness of a tree would greet you, but in the end you would only have
to go back somewhere to sleep. And that would not be beautiful; it
would be where you lived. So beauty seemed a dangerous, foreign,

and irrelevant idea. She turned for solace, not to it, but to the nature of enclosure. Everything in her life strained toward the ideal of separations: how to keep the horror of her parents' life from everything that could be called her life.

She learned what it was she wanted from watching her grade school teachers cutting simple shapes—squares, triangles—and writing numbers in straight columns on the blackboard or on paper with crisp, straight blues lines. The whiteness of pages, the unmuddled black of print, struck her as desirable; the dry rasping of the scissors, the click of a stapler, the riffling of a rubber band around a set of children's test. She understood all these things as prosperity, and knew that her family was not prosperous; they were poor. But she knew as well that their real affliction wasn't poverty but something different—you might, perhaps, say worse—but not connected to money. If she could have pointed to that—a simple lack of money—it would have been more hopeful for her. But she knew it wasn't poverty that was the problem. It was the way her parents were. It was what they did.

They drank. That was what they did. It was, properly speaking, the only thing they did. But no, she always told herself when she began to think that way, it wasn't the only thing. Her father, after all, had gone out to work. He was a gravedigger in a Catholic cemetery. Each morning he woke in the dark house. Massive, nearly toothless, and still in his underwear, he drank black coffee with a shot in it for breakfast, and then put on his dark-olive work pants and shirts, his heavy boots—in winter a fleece-lined coat and cap—and started the reluctant car driving down the dirt road. He came home at night, with a clutch of bottles in a paper bag, to begin drinking. He wasn't violent or abusive; he was interested only in the stupor he could enter and inhabit. This, Beatrice knew early on, was his true home.

Her mother woke late, her hair in pin curls wrapped in a kerchief, which she rarely bothered to undo. She was skeletally thin; her skin was always in a state of dull eruptions; red spidery veins on her legs always seemed to Beatrice to be the tracks of a slow disease. Just out of bed, she poured herself a drink, not bothering to hide it in coffee, and drank it from a glass that had held cheese spread mixed with pimentos, which her parents ate on crackers when they drank, and which was often Beatrice's supper. Beatrice's mother would sit for a while on the plaid couch, watch television, then go back to bed. The house was nearly always silent; there were as few words in the house as there were ornaments. It was another reason Peter liked her. She had a gift, he said, for silence, a gift he respected, that he said too few people had. She wondered if he would have prized this treasure if he'd known its provenance.

Beatrice saw everything her parents did because she slept in the large room. When she was born, her parents had put a crib for her in the corner of the room nearest their bedroom, opposite the wall where the sink, the stove, and the refrigerator were. It didn't occur to them that she might want privacy; when she grew taller, they replaced her crib with a bed, but they never imagined she had any more rights or desires than an infant. The torpor, the disorder of their lives, spread into her quarters. For years, it anguished her to see their slippers, their half-read newspapers, broken bobby pins, half-empty glasses, butt-filled ashtrays traveling like bacilli into the area she thought of as hers. When she was ten, she bought some clothesline and some tacks. She bought an Indian bedspread from a hippie store in town; rose-colored, with a print of tigers; the only vivid thing in the place. She made a barrier between herself and them. Her father said something unkind about it, but she took no notice.

For the six years after that, she came home as little as she could, staying in the school library until it closed, walking home miles in the darkness. She sat on her bed, did what was left of her home-work, and, as early as possible, lay down to sleep. At sunrise, she would leave the house, walking the roads till something opened in the town—the library, the five-and-ten, the luncheonette—then walking for more hours till sun set. She didn't love the woods; she didn't think of them as nature, with all the implications she had read about. But they were someplace she could be until she had no choice but to be *there* again, but not quite *there,* not in the place that was *theirs,* but her place, behind her curtain, where she needn't see the way they lived.

□ □ □ □

She moved out of her parents' house two days after she graduated from high school. She packed her few things and moved to Buffalo, where she got a job in a tool and die factory, took night courses at the community college. She did this for five years, then took all her savings and enrolled in the elementary education program at the University of Buffalo full time. She'd planned it all out carefully, in her tiny room, living on yogurt she made from powdered milk, allowing it to ferment in a series of thermoses she'd bought at garage sales, eating the good parts of half-rotten fruit and vegetables she'd bought for pennies, the fresh middle parts of loaves of day-old bread. Never, in those years, did she buy a new blouse or skirt or pair of jeans. She got her clothes from the Salvation Army; it was only later, after she married, that she learned to sew.

In her second semester, she met Peter in a very large class: European History 1789–1945. He said he'd fallen in love with several things about her almost at once: the look of her notebooks, the brilliant white of the collar of her shirt as it peeked over the top of her pastel-blue Shetland sweater, the sheer pink curves of her fingernails. He said he'd been particularly taken by her thumb. Most women's thumbs were ugly and betrayed the incompleteness of their femininity, the essential coarseness of it. The fineness of her thumb, the way the nail curved and was placed within the flesh, showed there wasn't a trace of coarseness in her: everything connected with her was, and would always be, fine. He didn't find out until they'd dated a few times that she was older, more than three years older than he was. He accepted that she'd had to work those years because her parents had—tragically—died.

Beatrice knew what Peter saw when he looked at her: clarity and simplicity and thrift, an almost holy sign of order, a plain creature without hidden parts or edges, who would sail through life before him making a path through murky seas, leaving to him plain sailing: nothing in the world to obstruct him or the free play of his mind. She knew that he didn't realize that he had picked her in part for the emptiness of her past, imagining a beautiful blankness, blameless, unpopulated, clear. His pity for her increased her value for him: she was an exile in the ordinary world he was born into, lacking the encumbrances that could make for problems in his life. He believed that life could be simple, that he would leave from a cloudless day and drop into the teeming fog of mathematics, which for him was peopled, creatured, a tumultuous society he had to colonize and civilize and rule.

She knew he felt he could leave all the rest to her, turning to her at night with the anomaly of his ardor, another equation she could elegantly solve. His curiosity about the shape of her desire was as tenderly blunted as his curiosity about her past, and she was as glad of the one as of the other. Making love to him, an occurrence she found surprisingly frequent, she could pretend she was sitting through a violent and fascinating storm that certainly would pass. Having got through it, she could be covered over in grateful tenderness for the life that he made possible: a life of clean linen and bright rooms, of matched dishes and a variety of specialized kitchen items: each unique, for one use only, and not, as everything in her mother's house was, interchangeable.

So the children came, three boys, and then the farmhouse, bought as a wreck, transformed by Beatrice Talbot into a treasure, something acquaintances came to see as much (more, she thought, if they were honest) as they did the family itself. Then Peter's tenure, and additions on the house: a sewing room, a greenhouse, then uncovering the old woodwork, searching out antique stores, auctions, flea markets for the right furniture—all this researched in the university library and in the local library—and the children growing and needing care so that by the time Peter came home with the news that was the first breakup of the smooth plane that had been their life together, the children had become, somehow, twelve, ten, and eight.

He had won a really spectacular fellowship at Columbia, three years being paid twice what he made at Cornell and no teaching, and a chance to work beside the man who was tops in his field. Peter asked Beatrice what she thought, but only formally. They both knew. They would be going to New York.

Nights in the house ten miles above Ithaca—it was summer and in her panic she could hear the crickets and, toward dawn, smell the freshness of the wet grass—she lay awake in terror of the packing job ahead of her. Everything, each thing she owned, would have to be wrapped and collected. She lived in dread of losing something, breaking something, for each carefully selected, carefully tended object that she owned was a proof of faith against the dark clutching power of the past. She typed on an index card a brief but wholly accurate description of the house, and the housing office presented her with a couple from Berlin—particle physicists, the both of them, and without children, she was grateful to hear. They seemed clean and thorough; they wanted to live in the country, they were the type who would know enough to act in time if a problem were occurring, who wouldn't let things get too far.

Peter and Beatrice were assured by everyone they talked to in New York that their apartment was a jewel. Sally Rodier, the wife of Peter's collaborator, who also helped Beatrice place the children in private schools, kept telling her how incredibly lucky they were, to have been given an apartment in one of the buildings on Riverside Drive. The view could be better, but they had a glimpse of the river. Really, they were almost disgustingly lucky, she said, laughing. Did they know what people would do to get what they had?

But Beatrice's heart sank at the grayness of the grout between the small octagonal bathroom floor tiles, the uneven job of polyurethaning on the living room floor, the small hole in the floor by the radiator base, the stiff door on one of the kitchen cabinets, the frosted glass on the window near the shower that she couldn't, whatever she did, make look clean.

For nearly a month she worked, making the small repairs herself, unheard-of behavior, Sally Rodier said, in a Columbia tenant. She poured a lake of bleach on the bathroom floor, left it for six hours, then, sopping it up, found she had created a field of dazzling whiteness. She made curtains; she scraped the edges of the window frames. Then she began to venture out. She had been so few places, had done so little, that the city streets, although they frightened her, began to seem a place of quite exciting possibilities. Because she did her errands, for the first time in her life, on foot, she could have human contact with no fear of revelation. She could be among her kind without fear every second that they would find out about her: where and what she'd come from, who she really was. Each day the super left mail on her threshold; they would exchange a pleasant word or two. He was a compact and competent man who had left his family in Peru. She could imagine that he and the Bangladeshi doormen, and the people on the streets, all possessed a dark and complicated past, things they'd prefer to have hidden as she did. In Buffalo, in Ithaca, people had seemed to be expressing everything they were. Even their reserves seemed legible and therefore relatively simple. But, riding on the bus and walking out on Broadway, she felt for the first time part of the web of concealment, of lives constructed like a house with rooms that gave access only to each other, rooms far from the initial entrance, with no source of natural light.

By Thanksgiving, she was able to tell Peter, who feared that she would suffer separation from her beloved house, that she was enjoying herself very much. The boys, whose lives, apart from their aspects of animal survival, never seemed to have much to do with her, were absorbed in the thick worlds of their schools—activities till five or six most nights, homework, and supper and more homework. Weekends, she could leave them to Peter, who was happy to take them to the park for football, or to the university pool, or the indoor track. She would often go to the Metropolitan Museum, to look at the collection of American furniture or, accompanied by a guide book, on an architectural tour.

One Thursday night, Peter was working in the library and the boys were playing basketball in the room the two younger ones shared, throwing a ball made of foam through the hoop Peter had nailed against the door. Beatrice was surprised to hear the bell ring; people rarely came without telephoning first. She opened the door to a stranger, but catching a glimpse of her neighbor across the hall, a history professor, opening her door, she didn't feel afraid.

The man at the doorway was unlike anyone she had spoken to in New York, anyone she'd spoken to since she'd left home. But in an instant she recognized him. She thought he was there to tell her the story of her life, and to tell Peter and everyone she knew. She'd never met him, as himself, before. But he could have lived in the house she'd been born in. He had an unrushed look, as if he had all the time in the world. He took a moment to meet her eyes, but when he did, finally, she understood the scope of everything he knew.

She kept the door mostly closed, leaving only enough space for her body. She would allow him to hurt her, if that was what he came for, but she wouldn't let him in the house.

"I'm your downstairs neighbor," he said.

She opened the door wider. He was wearing a greasy-looking ski jacket which had once been royal blue; a shiny layer of black grime covered the surface like soot on old snow. The laces on his black sneakers had no tips. His pants were olive green; his hands were in his pockets. It was impossible to guess how old he was. He was missing several top teeth, which made him look not young, but his hair fell over his eyes in a way that bestowed youth. She stepped back a pace further into the hall.

"What can I do for you?"

"You've got kids?"

For a moment, she thought he meant to take the children. She could hear them in the back of the apartment, running, laughing, innocent of what she was sure would befall them. A sense of heavy torpor took her up. She felt that whatever this man wanted, she would have to let him take. A half-enjoyable lassitude came over her. She knew she couldn't move.

He was waiting for her answer. "I have three boys," she said.

"Well, what you can do for me is to tell them to stop their racket. All day, all night, night and day, bouncing the ball. The plaster is coming down off the ceiling. It's hitting me in my bed. That's not too much to ask, is it? You can see that's not too much to ask."

"No, of course not. No," she said. "I'll see to it right away."

She closed the door very quickly. Walking to the back part of the apartment, she had to dig her nails into the palms of her hands so that she wouldn't scream the words to her children. "They didn't know, they didn't know," she kept saying to herself. It wasn't their fault. They weren't used to living in an apartment. It wasn't anybody's fault. But she was longing to scream at them, for having made this happen. For doing something so she would have to see that man, would have to think about him. An immense distaste for her children came over her. They seemed loud and gross and spoiled and careless. They knew nothing of the world. They were passing the ball back and forth to one another, their blond hair gleaming in the light that shone down from the fixture overhead.

She forced herself to speak calmly. "I'm afraid you can't play basketball here," she said. "The man downstairs complained."

"What'd you say to him?" asked Jeff, the oldest.

"I said I'd make you stop."

"What'd you say that for? We have just as much right as he does."

She looked at her son coldly. "I'm afraid you don't."

The three of them looked back at her, as if they'd never seen her.

"I'll make supper now," she said. "But I have a terrible headache. After I put dinner on the table, I'm going to lie down."

While she was cooking, the phone rang. It was her neighbor across the hall. "Terribly sorry to intrude," she said. "I hope I'm not being a busybody, but I couldn't help overhear the rather unpleasant exchange you had with our neighbor. I just thought you should understand a few things."

I understand everything, Beatrice wanted to say. There's nothing I don't understand.

"He's a pathetic case. Used to be a big shot in the chemistry department. Boy genius. Then he blew it. Just stopped going to classes, stopped showing up in the department. But some bigwigs in the administration were on his side, and he's been on disability and allowed to keep the apartment. We're all stuck with him. If he ever opens the door and you're near, you get a whiff of the place. Unbelievable. It's unbelievable how people live. What I'm trying to tell you is, don't let him get you bent out of shape. Occasionally he crawls out of his cave and growls something, but he's quite harmless."

"Thank you," said Beatrice. "Thank you for calling. Thank you very much."

She put down the phone, walked into her bedroom, turned out all the lights, and lay down on her bed.

❑ ❑ ❑ ❑

Lying in the dark, she knew it was impossible that he was under-neath her. If his room was below the children's, it was near the other side of the apartment, far from where she was.

But she imagined she could hear his breathing. It matched her own: in-out-in-out. Just like hers.

She breathed with him. In and out, and in and out. Frightened, afraid to leave the bed, she lay under a quilt she'd made herself. She forced herself to think of the silver scissors, her gold thimble, the spools and spools of pale thread. Tried and tried to call them back, a pastel shimmering cloud, a thickness glowing softly in this dark-ness. It would come, then fade, swallowed up in darkness. Soon the darkness was all there was. It was everything. It was everything she wanted and her only terror was that she would have to leave it and go back. Outside the closed door, she could hear the voices of her husband and her sons. She put her fingers in her ears so she couldn't hear them. She prayed, she didn't know to whom, to someone who inhabited the same darkness. This was the only thing about the one she prayed to that she knew. She prayed that her family would forget about her, leave her. She dreaded the door's cracking, the intrusion of the light. If she could just be here, in darkness, breathing in and out, with him as he breathed in and out. Then. Then she didn't know. But it would be something that she feared.

"How about you tone it down and let your mother sleep?"

She closed her eyes as tightly as a child in nightmare. Then she knew that she had been, in fact, asleep because when Peter came in, sank his weight onto the bed, she understood she had to start pre-tending to be sleeping.

After that night, she began staying in bed all day long. She had so rarely been sick, had met the occasional cold or bout of flu with so much stoicism that Peter couldn't help but believe her when she complained of a debilitating headache. And it would have been impossible for him to connect her behavior with the man down-stairs. He hadn't even seen him. No one had seen him except her and the woman across the hall who told her what she didn't need to know, what she already knew, what she couldn't help knowing.

She wondered how long it would be before Peter suggested calling a doctor. That was what worried her as she lay in the darkness: what would happen, what would be the thing she wouldn't be able to resist, the thing that would force her to get up.

She cut herself off fully from the life of the family. She had no idea what kind of life was going on outside her door. Peter was coping very well, without a question or murmur of complaint. Cynically, she thought it was easier for him not to question: he might learn something he didn't want to know. He had joined up with her so they could create a world free from disturbance, from disturbances. Now the disturbance rumbled beneath them, and it only stood to reason that he wouldn't know of it and wouldn't want to know.

Each morning, she heard the door close as Peter left with the children for school. Then she got up, bathed, fixed herself a breakfast, and, exhausted, fell back into a heavy sleep. She would sleep through the afternoon. In the evening, Peter brought her supper on a tray. The weak light from the lamp on the bed table hurt her eyes; the taste and textures of the food hurt her palate, grown fragile from so much silence, so much sleep.

She didn't ask what the children were doing and they didn't come in to see her. Peter assumed she was in excruciating pain. She said nothing to give him that idea, and nothing to relieve him of it.

After her fourth day in the dark, she heard the doorbell ring. It was early evening, the beginning of December. Night had completely fallen and the radiators hissed and cooed. She tried not to hear what was going on outside, so at first she only heard isolated words that Peter was shouting. "Children." "Natural." "Ordinary." "Play." "Rights." "No right."

Alarm, a spot of electric blue spreading beneath one of her ribs, made her understand that Peter was shouting at the man downstairs. She jumped out of bed and stood at the door of the bedroom. She could see Peter's back, tensed as she had, in fourteen years of marriage, never seen it. His fists were clenched at his side.

"You come here, bothering my wife, disturbing my family. I don't know where the hell . . . what makes you think . . . but you've got the wrong number, mister. My sons are going to play ball occasionally at a reasonable hour. It's five-ten in the afternoon. Don't tell me you're trying to sleep."

"All right, buddy. All right. We'll just see about sleeping. Some night come midnight when everyone in your house is fast asleep, you want to hear about disturbing. Believe me, buddy, I know how to make a disturbance."

Peter shut the door in the man's face. He turned around, pale, his fists not yet unclenched.

"Why didn't you tell me about that guy?" he said, standing so close to her that his voice hurt her ears, which had heard very little in the last four days.

"I wasn't feeling well," she said.

He nodded. She knew he hadn't heard her.

"Better get back into bed."

The doorbell rang again. Peter ran to it, his fists clenched once again. But it wasn't the man downstairs, it was the woman across the hall. Beatrice could hear her telling Peter the same story she'd told her, but with more details. "The house is full of broken machines, he takes them apart for some experiment he says he's doing. He says he's going to be able to create enough energy to power the whole world. He brags that he can live on five dollars a week."

"Low overhead," said Peter, and the two of them laughed.

She was back in the darkness. Her heart was a swollen muscle; she spread her hands over her chest to slow it down. She heard Peter calling Al Rodier.

"Do you believe it . . . university building . . . speak to someone in real estate first thing . . . right to the top if necessary . . . will not put up with it . . . hard to evict, but not impossible. Despoiling the environment . . . polluting the air we breathe."

The word "pollution" spun in her brain like one of those headlines in old movies: one word finally comprehensible after the turning blur: Strike. War.

Pollution. It suggested a defilement so complete, so permanent, that nothing could reverse it. Clear streams turned black and tar-like, verdant forests transformed to soot-covered stumps, the air full of black flakes that settled on the skin and couldn't be washed off.

Was that what the man downstairs was doing? He was living the way he wanted to, perhaps the only way he could. Before this incident, he hadn't disturbed them. They were the first to disturb him. People had a right not to hear thumping over their heads. Supposing he was trying to read, listening to music, working out a scientific formula. Suppose, when the children were making that noise, he was on the phone making an important call, the call that could change his life.

It wasn't likely. What was more likely was that he was lying in the dark, as she was. But not as she was. He wasn't lying in an empty bed. He bedded down in garbage. And the sound of thumping over his head was the sound of all his fear: that he would be named the names that he knew fit him, but could bear if they weren't said. "Disreputable." "Illegitimate."

They would send him out into the world. If only he could be left alone. If only he could be left to himself. And her children with their loud feet, the shouts of their unknowingness told him what he most feared, what he was right to fear, but what he only wanted to forget. At any minute they would tell him he was nothing, he was worse than nothing. Everything was theirs and they could take it rightfully, at any moment. Not because they were unjust or cruel. They were not unjust. Justice was entirely on their side. He couldn't possibly, in justice, speak a word in his own defense. Stone-faced, empty-handed, he would have to follow them into the open air.

She heard Peter on the phone calling the people they knew in the building who'd invited them for coffee or for brunch. She kept hearing him say his name—Peter Talbot—and his department—Mathematics, and the number of their apartment—4A. He was urging them to band together in his living room, the next night, to come up with a plan of action before, he kept saying, over and over, "things get more out of hand. And when you think," he kept saying, "of the qualified people who'd give their eyeteeth for what he's got, what he's destroying for everyone who comes after him.

I'll bet every one of you knows someone who deserves that apartment more than him."

She saw them filing into her house, their crisp short hair, their well-tended shoes, the smiles cutting across their faces like a rifle shot. They would march in, certain of their right to be there, their duty to keep order. Not questioning the essential rightness of clearing out the swamp, the place where disease bred, and necessarily, of course, removing the breeders and the spreaders who, if left to themselves, would contaminate the world.

And Beatrice knew that they were right, that was the terrible thing about them, their unquestionable rightness. Right to clear out, break in, burn, tear, demolish, so that the health of the world might be preserved.

She sank down deeper. She was there with those who wallowed, burrowed, hoarded, their weak eyes half-closed, their sour voices, not really sour but hopeless at the prospect of trying to raise some objection, of offering some resistance. They knew there could be no negotiation, since they had no rights. So their petition turned into a growl, a growl that only stiffened the righteousness of their purpose. "Leave me alone," is all the ones who hid were saying. They would have liked to beseech but they were afraid to. Also full of hate. "Leave me alone."

Of course they wouldn't be left alone. They couldn't be. Beatrice understood that.

The skin around her eyes felt flayed, her limbs were heavy, her spine too weak to hold her up. "Leave me alone." The sweetness of the warm darkness, like a poultice, was all that could protect her from the brutality of open air on her raw skin.

She and the man downstairs breathed. In and out. She heard their joined breath and, underneath that sound, the opening of doors, the rush of violent armies, of flame, of tidal wave, lightning cleaving a moss-covered tree in two. And then something else below that: "Cannot. Cannot. Leave me alone." Unheeded.

She turned the light on in the bedroom. She put on a pair of light blue sweatpants and a matching sweatshirt. On her feet she wore immaculate white socks and the white sneakers she'd varnished to brilliance with a product called Sneaker White she'd bought especially. She put on earrings, perfume, but no lipstick and no blush. She walked out of the apartment. She knew that Peter, in the back with the children, wouldn't hear the door close.

She walked down the dank, faintly ill-smelling stairs to the apartment situated exactly as hers was—3A—and rang the bell.

He opened the door a crack. The stench of rotting food and unwashed clothes ought to have made her sick, but she knew she was beyond that sort of thing.

She looked him in the eye. "I need to talk to you," she said.

He shrugged then smiled. Most of his top teeth were gone and the ones that were left were yellowed and streaked. He pushed the lock of his blondish hair that fell into his forehead back, away from his eyes. Then he took a comb out of his pocket and pulled it through his hair.

"Make yourself at home," he said, laughing morosely.

There was hardly a place to stand. The floor space was taken up by broken radios, blenders, ancient portable TVs revealing blown tubes, disconnected wires, a double-size mattress. Beside the mattress were paper plates with hardened sandwiches, glimpses of pink ham, tomatoes turned to felt between stone-colored slices of bread, magazines with wrinkled pages, unopened envelopes (yellow, white, mustard-colored), sloping hills of clean underwear mixed up with balled socks, and opened cans of Coke. There were no sheets on the mattress; sheets, she could tell, had been given up long ago. Loosely spread over the blue ticking was a pinkish blanket, its trim a trap, a bracelet for the foot to catch itself in during the uneasy night.

A few feet from the mattress was a Barcalounger whose upholstery must once have been mustard-colored. The headrest was a darker shade, almost brown; she understood that the discoloration was from the grease of his hair when he leaned back. She moved some copies of *Popular Mechanics* and some Styrofoam containers, hamburger-sized, to make room for herself to sit. She tried to imagine what she looked like, in her turquoise sweatsuit, sitting in this chair.

"I came to warn you," she said. "They're having a meeting. Right now in my apartment. They want to have you evicted."

He laughed, and she could see that his top teeth looked striated, lines of brownish yellow striping the enamel in a way she didn't remember seeing on anyone else.

"Relax," he said. "It'll never happen. They keep trying, but it'll never happen. This is New York. I'm a disabled person. I'm on disability. You understand what that means? Nobody like me gets evicted in New York. Don't worry about it. I'll be here forever."

She looked at her neighbor and gave him a smile so radiant that it seemed to partake of prayer. And then a torpor that was not somnolent, but full of joy, took hold of her. Her eyes were closing themselves with happiness. She needed rest. Why hadn't she ever known before that rest was the one thing she had always needed?

She saw her white bathroom floor, gleaming from the lake of bleach she had poured on it. Just thinking of it hurt her eyes. Here, there was nothing that would hurt her. She wanted to tell him it was beautiful here, it was wonderful, it was just like home. But she was too tired to speak. And that was fine, she knew he understood. Here, where they both were, there was no need to say a word.

But he was saying something. She could hear it through her sleep, and she had to swim up to get it, like a fish surfacing for crumbs. She couldn't seem, quite, to open her eyes and she fell back down to the dark water. Then she felt him shaking her by the shoulders.

"What are you doing? What are you doing? You can't do that here."

She looked at his eyes. They weren't looking at her kindly. She had thought he would be kind. She blinked several times, then closed her eyes again. When she opened them, he was still standing above her, his hands on her shoulders, shaking them, his eyes unkind.

"You can't do that here. You can't just come down here and go to sleep like that. This is my place. Now get out."

He was telling her she had to leave. She supposed she understood that. She couldn't stay here if he didn't want her. She had thought he'd understand that what she needed was a place to rest, just that, she wouldn't be taking anything from him. But he was treating her like a thief. He was making her leave as if she were a criminal. There was no choice now but to leave, shamefully, like a criminal.

He closed the door behind her. Although her back was to the door, she felt he was closing it in her face and she felt the force of it exactly on her face as if his hand had struck it. She stood completely still, her back nearly touching the brown door.

She couldn't move. She couldn't move because she could think of no direction that seemed sensible. But the shame of his having thrown her out propelled her toward the stairs. She wondered if she could simply walk out of the building as she was. With no coat, no money, nothing to identify her. But she knew that wasn't possible. It was winter, and it was New York.

She walked up the stairs. She stood on the straw mat in front of her own door. She'd have to ring the bell; she hadn't brought her keys. Peter would wonder where she had gone. She didn't know what she'd tell him. There was nothing to say.

She didn't know what would happen now. She knew only that she must ring the bell and see her husband's face and then walk into the apartment. It was the place she lived and she had nowhere else to go.

George Saunders

The Falls

From *The New Yorker*

MORSE FOUND IT nerve-racking to cross the St. Jude grounds just as the school was being dismissed, because he felt that if he smiled at the uniformed Catholic children they might think he was a wacko or pervert and if he didn't smile they might think he was an old grouch made bitter by the world, which surely, he felt, by certain yardsticks, he was. Sometimes he wasn't entirely sure that he wasn't even a wacko of sorts, although certainly he wasn't a pervert. Of that he was certain. Or relatively certain. Being overly certain, he was relatively sure, was what eventually made one a wacko. So humility was the thing, he thought, arranging his face into what he thought would pass for the expression of a man thinking fondly of his own youth, a face devoid of wackiness or perversion, humility was the thing.

The school sat among maples on a hillside that sloped down to the wide Taganac River, which narrowed and picked up speed and crashed over Bryce Falls a mile downstream near Morse's small rental house, his embarrassingly small rental house, actually, which nevertheless was the best he could do and for which he knew he should be grateful, although at times he wasn't a bit grateful and wondered where he'd gone wrong, although at other times he was quite pleased with the crooked little blue shack covered with peel-ing lead paint and felt great pity for the poor stiffs renting hazardous shitholes even smaller than his hazardous shithole, which was how he felt now as he came down into the bright sunlight and continued his pleasant walk home along the green river lined with expensive mansions whose owners he deeply resented.

Morse was tall and thin and as gray and sepulchral as a church about to be condemned. His pants were too short, and his face periodically broke into a tense, involuntary grin that quickly receded, as if he had just suffered a sharp pain. At work he was known to punctuate his conversations with brief wild laughs and gusts of inchoate enthusiasm and subsequent embarrassment, expressed by a sudden plunging of his hands into his pockets, after which he would yank his hands out of his pockets, too ashamed of his own shame to stand there merely grimacing for even an instant longer.

From behind him on the path came a series of arrhythmic whacking steps. He glanced back to find Aldo Cummings, an odd duck who, though nearly forty, still lived with his mother. Cummings didn't work and had his bangs cut straight across and wore gym shorts even in the dead of winter. Morse hoped Cummings wouldn't collar him. When Cummings didn't collar him, and in fact passed by without even returning his nervous, self-effacing grin, Morse felt guilty for having suspected Cummings of wanting to collar him, then miffed that Cummings, who collared even the city-hall cleaning staff, hadn't tried to collar him. Had he done something to offend Cummings? It worried him that Cummings might not like him, and it worried him that he was worried about whether a nut like Cummings liked him. Was he some kind of worrywart? It worried him. Why should he be worried when all he was doing was going home to enjoy his beautiful children without a care in the world, although on the other hand there was Robert's piano recital, which was sure to be a disaster, since Robert never practiced and they had no piano and weren't even sure where or when the recital was and Annie, God bless her, had eaten the cardboard keyboard he'd made for Robert to practice on. When he got home he would make Robert a new cardboard keyboard and beg him to practice. He might even order him to practice. He might even order him to make his own cardboard keyboard, then practice, although this was unlikely, because when he became forceful with Robert, Robert blubbered, and Morse loved Robert so much he couldn't stand to see him blubbering, although if he didn't become forceful with Robert, Robert tended to lie on his bed with his baseball glove over his face.

Good God, but life could be less than easy, not that he was unaware that it could certainly be a lot worse, but to go about in such a state, pulse high, face red, worried sick that someone would notice how nervous one was, was certainly less than ideal, and he felt sure that his body was secreting all kinds of harmful chemicals and that the more he worried about the harmful chemicals the faster they were pouring out of wherever it was they came from.

When he got home, he would sit on the steps and enjoy a few minutes of centered breathing while reciting his mantra, which was "calm down calm down," before the kids came running out and grabbed his legs and sometimes even bit him quiet hard in their excitement and Ruth came out to remind him in an angry tone that he wasn't the only one who'd worked all day, and as he walked he gazed out at the beautiful Taganac in an effort to absorb something of her serenity but instead found himself obsessing about the faulty latch on the gate, which theoretically could allow Annie to toddle out of the yard and into the river, and he pictured himself weeping on the shore, and to eradicate this thought started manically whistling "The Stars and Stripes Forever," while slapping his hands against his sides.

Cummings bobbed past the restored gristmill, pleased at having so decisively snubbed Morse, a smug member of the power élite in this conspiratorial Village, one of the league of oppressive oppressors who wouldn't know the lot of the struggling artist if the lot of the struggling artist came up with great and beleaguered dignity and bit him on the polyester ass. Over the Pine Street bridge was a fat cloud. To an interviewer in his head, Cummings said he felt the possible rain made the fine bright day even finer and brighter because of the possibility of its loss. The possibility of its ephemeral loss. The ephemeral loss of the day to the fleeting passages of time. Preening time. Preening nascent time, the blackguard. Time made wastrels of us all, did it not, with its gaunt cheeks and its tombly reverberations and its admonishing glances with bony fingers. Bony fingers pointed as if in admonishment, as if to say, "I admonish you to recall your own eventual nascent death, which being on its way is forthcoming. Forthcoming, mortal coil, and don't think its ghastly pall won't settle on your furrowed brow, *pronto,* once I select your fated number from my very dusty book with this selfsame bony finger with which I'm pointing at you now, you vanity of vanities, you luster, you shirker of duties as you shuffle after your worldly pleasure centers."

That was some good stuff, if only he could remember it through the rest of his stroll and the coming storm, to scrawl in a passionate hand in his yellow pad. He thought with longing ardor of his blank yellow pad, he thought. He thought with longing ardor of his blank yellow pad on which, this selfsame day, his fame would be wrought, no, on which, this selfsame day, the first meagre scrawl-ings which would presage his nascent burgeoning fame would be wrought, or rather writ, and someday someone would dig up his yellow pad and virtually cry eureka when they realized what a teeming fragment of minutiae, and yet crucial minutiae, had been found, and wouldn't all kinds of literary women in short black jackets want to meet him then!

In the future he must always remember to bring his pad every-where.

The town had spent a mint on the riverfront, and now the bur-bling, smashing Taganac ran past a nail salon in a restored gristmill and a café in a former coal tower and a quaint public square where some high-school boys with odd haircuts were trying to kick a soccer ball into the partly open window of a parked Colt with a joy so belligerent and obnoxious that it seemed they believed them-selves the first boys ever to walk the face of the earth, which Morse found worrisome. What if Annie grew up and brought one of these freaks home? Not one of these exact freaks, of course, since they were approximately fifteen years her senior, although it was possi-ble that at twenty she could bring home one of these exact freaks, who would then be approximately thirty-five, albeit over Morse's dead body, although in his heart he knew he wouldn't make a stink about it even if she did bring home one of the freaky snots who had just succeeded in kicking the ball into the Colt and were now jumping around joyfully bumping their bare chests together while grunting like walruses, and in fact he knew perfectly well that, rather than expel the thirty-five-year-old freak from his home, he would likely offer him coffee or a soft drink in an attempt to dissuade him from corrupting Annie, who for God's sake was just a baby, because Morse knew very well the kind of man he was at heart, timid of conflict, conciliatory to a fault, pathetically gullible, and with a pang he remembered Len Beck, who senior year had tricked him into painting his ass blue. If there had actually been a secret Blue-Asser's Club, if the ass-painting had in fact been re-quired for membership, it would have been bad enough, but to find out on the eve of one's prom that one had painted one's ass blue simply for the amusement of a clique of unfeeling swimmers who subsequently supplied certain photographs to one's prom date, that was too much, and he had been glad, quite glad actually, at least at first, when Beck, drunk, had tried and failed to swim to Foley's Snag and been swept over the Falls in the dark of night, the great tragedy of their senior year, a tragedy that had mercifully eclipsed Morse's blue ass in the class's collective memory.

Two red-headed girls sailed by in a green canoe, drifting with the current. They yelled something to him, and he waved. Had they yelled something insulting? Certainly it was possible. Certainly today's children had no respect for authority, although one had to admit there was always Ben Akbar, their neighbor, a little Paki-stani genius who sometimes made Morse look askance at Robert. Ben was an all-state cellist, on the wrestling team, who was unfail-ingly sweet to smaller kids and tole-painted and could do a one-handed pushup. Ah, Ben Shmen, Morse thought, ten Bens weren't worth a single Robert, although he couldn't think of one area in which Robert was superior or even equal to Ben, the little smarty-pants, although certainly he had nothing against Ben, Ben being a mere boy, but if Ben thought for a minute that his being more accomplished and friendly and talented than Robert somehow enti-tled him to lord it over Robert, Ben had another think coming, not that Ben had ever actually lorded it over Robert. On the contrary, Robert often lorded it over Ben, or tried to, although he always failed, because Ben was too sharp to be taken in by a little con man like Robert, and Morse's face reddened at the realization that he had just characterized his own son as a con man.

Boy, oh boy, could life be a torture. Could life ever force a fellow into a strange, dark place from which he found himself doing graceless, unforgivable things like casting aspersions on his beloved firstborn. If only he could escape BlasCorp and do something significant, such as discovering a critical vaccine. But it was too late, and he had never been good at biology and in fact had flunked it twice. But some kind of moment in the sun would certainly not be unwelcome. If only he could be a tortured prisoner of war who not only refused to talk but led the other prisoners in rousing hymns at great personal risk. If only he could witness an actual miracle or save the President from an assassin or win the Lotto and give it all to charity. If only he could be part of some great historical event like the codgers he saw on PBS who had been slugged in the Haymarket Riot or known Medgar Evers or lost beatific mothers on the Titanic. His childhood dreams had been so bright, he had hoped for so much, it couldn't be true that he was a nobody, although, on the other hand, what kind of somebody spends the best years of his life swearing at a photocopier? Not that he was complaining. Not that he was unaware he had plenty to be thankful for. He loved his children. He loved the way Ruth looked in bed by candlelight when he had wedged the laundry basket against the door that wouldn't shut because the house was settling alarmingly, loved the face she made when he entered her, loved the way she made light of the blue-ass story, although he didn't particularly love the way she sometimes trotted it out when they were fighting—for example, on the dreadful night when the piano had been repossessed—or the way she blamed his passivity for their poverty within earshot of the kids or the fact that at the height of her infatuation with Robert's karate instructor, Master Li, she had been dragging Robert to class as often as six times a week, the poor little exhausted guy, but the point was, in spite of certain difficulties he truly loved Ruth. So what if their bodies were failing and fattening and they undressed in the dark and Robert admired strapping athletes on television while looking askance at Morse's rounded, pimpled back? It didn't matter, because someday, when Robert had a rounded, pimpled back of his own, he would appreciate his father, who had subjugated his petty personal desires for the good of his family, although, God willing, Robert would have a decent career by then and could afford to join a gym and see a dermatologist.

And Morse stopped in his tracks, wondering what in the world two little girls were doing alone in a canoe speeding toward the Falls, apparently oarless.

Cummings walked along, gazing into a mythic dusky arboreal Wood that put him in mind of the archetypal vision he had numbered 114 in his "Book of Archetypal Visions," on which Mom that nitwit had recently spilled grape pop. Vision 114 concerned standing on the edge of an ancient dense Wood at twilight, with the safe harbor of one's abode behind and the deep Wild ahead, replete with dark fearsome bears looming from albeit dingy covens. What would that twitching nervous wage slave Morse think if he were to dip his dim brow into the heady brew that was the "Archetypal Visions"? Morse, ha, Cummings thought, I'm glad I'm not Morse, a dullard in corporate pants trudging home to his threadbare brats in the gathering loam, born, like the rest of his ilk with their feet of clay thrust down the maw of conventionality, content to cheerfully work lemminglike in moribund cubicles while comparing their stocks and bonds between bouts of tedious lawnmowing, then chortling while holding their suckling brats to the Nintendo breast. That was a powerful image, Cummings thought, one that he might develop some brooding night into a herculean prome that some Hollywood smoothie would eat like a hotcake, so he could buy Mom a Lexus and go with someone leggy and blowsy to Paris after taking some time to build up his body with arm curls so as to captivate her physically as well as mentally, and in Paris the leggy girl, in perhaps tight leather pants, would sit on an old-time bed with a beautiful shawl or blanket around her shoulders and gaze at him with doe eyes as he stood on the balcony brooding about the

Parisian rain and so forth, and wouldn't Morse and his ilk stew in considerable juice when he sent home a postcard just to be nice!

And wouldn't the Village fall before him on repentant knees when T-shirts imprinted with his hard-won visage, his heraldic leonine visage, one might say, were available to all at the five-and-dime and he held court on the porch in a white Whitmanesque suit while Mom hovered behind him getting everything wrong about his work and proffering inane snacks to his manifold admirers, and wouldn't revenge be sweet when such former football players as Ned Wentz began begging him for lessons in the sonnet? And all that was required for these things to come to pass was some paper and pens and a quixotic blathering talent the likes of which would not be seen again soon, the critics would write, all of which he had in spades, and he rounded the last bend before the Falls, euphoric with his own possibilities, and saw a canoe the color of summer leaves ram the steep upstream wall of the Snag. The girls inside were thrown forward and shrieked with open mouths over frothing waves that would not let them be heard as the boat split open along some kind of seam and began taking on water in doomful fast quantities. Cummings stood stunned, his body electrified, hairs standing up on the back of his craning neck, thinking, I must do something, their faces are bloody, but what, such fast cold water, still I must do something, and he stumbled over the berm uncertainly, looking for help but finding only a farm field of tall dry corn.

Morse began to run. In all probability this was silly. In all probability the girls were safe onshore, or, if not, help was already on its way, although certainly it was possible that the girls were not safe onshore and help was not on its way, and in fact it was even possible that the help that was on its way was him, which was worrisome, because he had never been good under pressure and in a crisis often stood mentally debating possible options with his mouth hanging open. Come to think of it, it was possible, even probable, that the boat had already gone over the Falls or hit the Snag. He remembered the crew of the barge Fat Chance, rescued via rope bridge in the early Carter years. He hoped several sweaty, decisive men were already on the scene and that one of them would send him off to make a phone call, although what if on the way he forgot the phone number and had to go back and ask the sweaty decisive man to repeat it? And what if this failure got back to Ruth and she was filled with shame and divorced him and forbade him to see the kids, who didn't want to see him anyway because he was such a panicky screwup? This was certainly not positive thinking. This was certainly an example of predestining failure via negativity. Because, who could tell, maybe he would stand in line assisting the decisive men and incur a nasty rope burn and go home a hero wearing a bandage, which might cause Ruth to regard him in a more favorable sexual light, and they would stay up all night celebrating his new manhood and exchanging sweet words between bouts of energetic lovemaking, although what kind of thing was that to be thinking at a time like this, with children's lives at stake? He was bad, that was for sure. There wasn't an earnest bone in his body. Other people were simpler and looked at the world with clearer eyes, but he was self-absorbed and insincere and mucked everything up, and he hoped this wasn't one more thing he was destined to muck up, because mucking up a rescue was altogether different from forgetting to mail out the invitations to your son's birthday party, which he had recently done, although certainly they had spent a small fortune rectifying the situation, stopping just short of putting an actual pony on Visa, but the point was, this was serious and he had to bear down. And throwing his thin legs out ahead of him, awkwardly bent at the waist, shirttails trailing behind and bum knee hurting, he remonstrated with himself to put aside all self-doubt and negativity and prepare to assist the decisive men in whatever way he could once he had rounded the bend and assessed the situation.

But when he rounded the bend and assessed the situation, he found no rope bridge or decisive men, only a canoe coming apart at the base of the Snag and two small girls in matching sweaters trying to bail with a bait bucket. What to do? This was a shocker. Go for help? Sprint to the Outlet Mall and call 911 from Knife World? There was no time. The canoe was sinking before his eyes. The girls would be drowned before he reached Route 8. Could one swim to the Snag? Certainly one could not. No one ever had. Was he a good swimmer? He was mediocre at best. Therefore he would have to run for help. But running was futile. Because there was not time. He had just decided that. And swimming was out of the question. Therefore the girls would die. They were basically dead. Although that couldn't be. That was too sad. What would become of the mother who this morning had dressed them in matching sweaters? How would she cope? Soon her girls would be nude and bruised and dead on a table. It was unthinkable. He thought of Robert nude and bruised and dead on a table. What to do? He fiercely wished himself elsewhere. The girls saw him now and with their hands appeared to be trying to explain that they would be dead soon. My God, did they think he was blind? Did they think he was stupid? Was he their father? Did they think he was Christ? They were dead. They were frantic, calling out to him, but they were dead, as dead as the ancient dead, and he was alive, he was needed at home, it was a no-brainer, no one could possibly blame him for this one, and making a low sound of despair in his throat he kicked off his loafers and threw his long ugly body out across the water.

Lee K. Abbott

The Talk Talked Between Worms

From *The Georgia Review*

I

ACCORDING to the tapes, my father, then about as run-of-the-mill a man as Joe Blow himself, didn't want to see the thing. *Not a damn bit,* he says. But there it came anyhow, roaring in hard and cockeyed from the west with a comet's fiery tail, and then ka-BOOM—enough bang to rock Chaves County left and right like a quake.

This was summer 1947, almost nothing between points A and B but weeds and hummocks and desert all the way east to the red clay of Texas, and my father, Totenham Gregory Hamsey, gentleman cowboy, was out there. Riding his pickup bouncylike on the fence line, he was hunting for the gaps in the barbed wire that several yearlings had escaped through, when it—the UFO—went *whump* to the east of him. Maybe like your own self—certainly like me in a similarly serious moment—he was dumbstruck. His blood ran rank and grainy in his chest, his mouth opening and closing on thinnest air. Something from the clouds had tumbled earthward, and nobody had seen it but a twenty-nine-year-old red-haired rancher with thirty dollars in his pocket and the current issue of the *Saturday Evening Post* on the seat beside him.

His truck had stalled on him, another mystery he lived to tell about, so presently he gave up on it and hopped onto the hood to study the scattered fires and the long, raggedy trench the Martians—or whatever the hell they were—had made when they quit their element for ours. First he thought it was a plane, a top secret jet out of Roswell Army Air Field, or a V-2 rocket gone haywire from White Sands, which gave him, naturally, to expect company—more planes maybe, or soldiers with rifles to shoo him out of there. These were the days of Communists, he says on the tapes: sour-minded hordes from Korea and the Soviet Union that even Governor Whitman had warned you to expect on the doorstep of city hall itself. One hour went by that way—Tot Hamsey, rich man's youngest son, saying to himself what he'd say to others if they, in pairs or in a mob, were to rumble over that hill yonder and want their busted contraption back. But none did. Not for that hour anyway. Nor for the several that followed. Nothing arrived but a turkey buzzard, wings glossy and black as crude oil, which gave everything a look-see—the smoking debris, the perplexed human being, the hostile flora all about—before, screeching in disappointment, it wheeled west for better pickings.

That's when Tot Hamsey, my father, gave his Ford a second chance. Climbed back in the cab, spoke an angry sentence in the direction of the starter button, and breathed deeply with relief when its six cylinders clattered to life—as welcome a noise to hear under those circumstances as conversation from the lady you love. He could go back to town, he figured. Thirty-five miles. Find Sheriff Johnny Freel. Maybe Cheek Watson, the dumbbell deputy. Tell them the whole story—the sky a menace of streaky orange and yellow, the howl coming at him over his shoulder, the boom, and afterward soil and rock pitched up everywhere. Be done with it then. Bring the bigwigs back here, sure. Possibly hang around to gab with whatever colonel or general showed up to get his property back. Still get home in time for supper.

But Tot Hamsey was a curious man—a habit of character, my mother once said, you like to see in those you're to spend a lifetime with—and he was curious now, more curious than hungry or tired or wary-witted, and so he put himself in gear to drive slowly down a sandy draw and up an easy rise until he had nowhere to turn but into the raw and burned-up acreage this part of New Mexico would ever after be famous for.

Everywhere was space-age junk, various foils and joints and milled metals as peculiar to him as maybe we are to critters. All the way to more sizable hills a half-mile east, the landscape had been split and gouged—the handiwork, it appeared, of a giant from Homer or the Holy Bible racing toward sunrise and dragging a plow behind. Fires flickered near and far, and Tot Hamsey, father of one, could imagine that these were the cooking fires of an army heedless enough to make war against God. The sky had gone mostly dark, several stars twinkling, but no moon to make out specifics by. Just dark upon dark, and sky upon sky, and one, quote, innocent bystander in a hat from the El Paso Hat Company tying a bandanna over his mouth and nose to keep from breathing so much vile smoke.

The silence was likewise odd, somehow cold and leaden, another thing to spook you in the night. He thought he'd hear wildlife, certainly. Coyotes in a pack. The sheep from Albert Tulk's place. But nothing, not even a dry wind to sweep noises here from civilization, which gave him suddenly to believe that all he'd known had vanished from the empire of man. His daddy's banks. His mother Rilla and his two brothers. Mac Brazeall, his own hired hand. His wife, who was my mother Corrine, and me as well, only a toddler. Even the town of Roswell and all others he'd suffered the bother to visit.

He turned himself on his heels, eyes fixed on the collapsed horizon, a full circle. Panic had begun to rise in Mister Hamsey, him a man reared to believe in peril and the calamitous end of everything. It did seem possible, he thought. All of modern life, now gone. Streets he knew. The Liberty Bar, Brother Bill Toomey's radio station, his grammar school on Hardesty Road and the crotchety marms that taught there. Every bit of it, great and small. The president of the United States, not to mention those muckety-mucks who ruled the world beyond. Maybe even the vast world itself. Which was probably all rubble and flame and smoke and which, as he thought about it, meant, Lord Almighty, that maybe Tot Hamsey was the last of whatever was—the last man in the last place on the last day with the last mind to think of last things on Planet Earth.

You can go out there your own self, if you wish. Just visit the UFO Museum. Not the classy outfit across from the courthouse near Denny's, but the low-rent enterprise way south on Main Street, past the Levi's plant and Mrs. Blake's House of Christmas. The man there is Boyd Pickett, to matters of heaven and earth what, say, the Devil is to truth and fruit from a tree. For ten dollars a head, he'll drive you out there in his Crown Victoria—it's private property, he'll tell you, him with a sweetheart-lease arrangement—and show you the sights such as they currently are. For five more dollars, he'll dangle a Tyco model flying saucer on #10 fishing filament behind you and snap you a full-color Polaroid suitable for framing, which means—ha-ha-ha—you with a dimwit's grin and hovering over your shoulder physical evidence of a superior intelligence, which you are encouraged to show to your faithless friends and neighbors in, oh, Timbuktu or wherever it is you tote your own heavy bale.

For $8.50, you can have the as-told-to story between covers: how in July of 1947, one Mac Brazeall, ramrod for the Bar H spread out of Corona, heard a boom bigger than thunder and, as dutiful a Democrat as Harry Truman himself, went out to investigate; how he found what he found, which was wreckage and scalded rock and scorched grama grass, and how he took a piece of the former to Sheriff Johnny Freel who viewed the affair with skepticism until Mac Brazeall, patriot and full-time redneck, crumpled a square of metal in his hands and put it on the table, whereupon, like an instance of infernal hocus-pocus, it sprung back into its original shape; and how Sheriff Freel, heart pounding in his throat, got on the phone to his Army counterpart at the air base; and how, in the hours that passed, much ordnance was mobilized and dispatched, and heads were scratched and oaths sworn; and how by, quote, dawn's early light, you could look at the front page of *The Daily Record* and see there a picture of jug-eared Mac Brazeall, smug as a gambler atop a pyramid of loot, taking credit for a historical fact that had begun when my father, Tot Hamsey, heard the air whip and crack and, as if in a nightmare, witnessed his paid-for real estate turn to fire and ruin in front of him.

I've been out there a few times, the first with Cece Phillips (now my ex-wife) when we were hot for each other and stupid with youth. This was summer 1964, me only fresh out of high school and not yet in possession of the tapes my father, once a doctor-certified crazy man, would one day oblige me to listen to. Ignorant is what I'm trying to say, just a boy, like his long-gone daddy, unaware that what lay before him was a land of miracles terrifying but necessary to behold; just a boy fumbling at his girlfriend's underclothes while everywhere, invisible above, eyes might have been looking down.

That night the moon was up, golden as a supper plate from the table of King Midas himself. In the back seat of my mother's Chevrolet we had gone round and round for a time, Cece Phillips and me, breathless and eager-beaver, nothing there or there or there outdoors but sagebrush and the shapely shadows hills make. We must've seemed like wrestlers, I'm thinking now. Clinch, paw, and part. Look this way and that, not much coming out of our mouths but breath and syllables a whole lot like "eeeff" and "ooohh." Cece said she couldn't—not now anyways, not in this creepy place. And I, an hour of lukewarm Coors beer my motivation, said she could. Which gave us, for a little while, something else to talk about before it became clear she would.

Not much to report here. Nothing oooeey-gooey, anyway, from storybooks or love songs. Just how time seemed to me to pass. One second and then another, like links on a chain that one day has to end. This is who we were: Reilly Hamsey, beefy enough to be of some use to the Coyotes' coach for football; and Cece Phillips, hair in the suave beehive style of the stewardess she intended to be. We had music from KOMA out of Oklahoma City, and no school tomorrow or anytime until fall when we were to take up college life at New Mexico State University in Las Cruces. This was us: bone and heat and movement, as we had been at the drive-in or in my mother's rec room when she was away at work. Just us, youngsters who knew how to say "sir" and "ma'am" and "thank you" and be the seen-not-heard types adults are tickled silly to brag about.

Then this was over, and I was out of doors.

Was anything wrong, Cece wanted to know, and for a second I believed there wasn't.

"I'm gonna take a leak," I told her and moseyed away to find a bush to stand behind.

A pall had fallen over me, I think now. A curtain had come down, or a wall gone up. Something that, as I stood with my back to the car and Cece, I could feel as plainly as I now feel this keyboard upon which I am typing this true tale.

Behind me, Cece was singing with the Rolling Stones, hers a voice vigorous enough to be admired by Baptists, and I, maybe for the first time, was doing some serious thinking about her. About the muscles she had, and the dances she was unashamed to do at the Pit Stop or in the gym. She could stick-shift fast as I and knew as much as many about engines, those farm-related and not. She was tall, which appealed, and loose in the legs, swift as a sprinter.

"Don't go too far," she was saying. "We got to go pretty soon."

Thinking about her. Then me. Then, oddly, my dog Red and how the fur bristled on his rump when the unexpected rapped at our front door on Missouri Street. Then my still pretty mother and the colonel from the Institute she was dating, him with a posture rigid as plank flooring. Then, inevitably, my father, Tot Hamsey.

"Darn you, Reilly Jay," she hollered out. "You tore my skirt."

I imagined my father exactly as my mother had once described him: in front of the TV in the dayroom of his ward, his long face empty of everything but shock and sadness, his eyes glassy as marbles, the sense that in his head were only sparks and such thoughts as are thought by birds.

"You all right?" Cece called. "Reilly, you hear me?"

I was done with thinking then. I had reached a conclusion about Cece and me, one I was surer and surer of the closer I came to the car.

"Reilly," she said, "what's wrong with your face?"

We were doomed, I was thinking, the fact of it suddenly no more surprising than is the news that it's hot in hell. We would go to college, that was clear. Cece, I guessed, would become pregnant. Yours truly would graduate and work for, say, Sinclair Oil in Midland and Odessa or thereabouts. More years would then roll over us, a tidal wave washing through our lives as one had smashed through my parents' own. Eventually, I would find myself back here in Roswell—exactly, friends, as it has come to pass—and very likely I would be alone. As alone, according to the story, as my father had been the night he, years and years before, learned what he learned when the sun was down in this weird place and there was nothing else to do but heave himself into madness.

"I'm fine," I told her. "Put your clothes on."

Tot Hamsey finds the body in this part. The extraterrestrial. Finds it, listens to it, watches it expire. Then, having wandered a considerable distance away, he leans himself against the crumbling bank of an arroyo and, hasp by hook by hinge, feels his own simple self come plumb apart. The very *him* of him disassembled, which are his own words on one cassette. His boyhood, which was largely carefree and conducted out of doors. His school years, which go as they came, autumn by autumn. His playing basketball. He had popped an eardrum by diving in the wrong place at the Bottomless Lakes, and that went, as did the courtship of several town girls, including Corrine Rains, who became his wife and my mother, as well as his years at the Nazarene college in Idaho. He put aside— *"Very carefully,"* he says on the tapes, likening himself to a gizmo of cogs and levers and wheels—all he'd done and thought about doing. About being for two whole days the property of Uncle Sam, and the skinny doctor who discovered that Tot Hamsey was one inch shorter on the left side. About working carpentry with his brother Ben at the German POW camp south of town. About being another man's boss, and knowledge to have through the hands. About me even, the tiny look-alike of him. For almost an hour, until he heard the sputter of Mac Brazeall's flatbed well east of him, he sat there. He was only mass and weight, one more creature to take up space in the world, more or less the man I visited in 1981, the year after I came back to this corner of America—a man who regarded you as though he expected you to reach behind your head to yank off your face and thus reveal yourself as a monster, too.

For a time, so he says on one tape, he didn't do much of anything that July night in 1947. Sound had returned to the world, it seemed. He could hear the cows he'd been searching for bawling in the hard darkness south of him. He was in and out of the debris field now— back and forth, back and forth—the smell of char and ravaged earth sometimes strong enough to gag him, so he kept the Ford moving. Every now and then, slowing to roll down the window, he hollered into the blackness. If it was a plane from the Army base, then, shoot, maybe somebody had bailed out before or otherwise survived the crash. He might even know the pilot or those the pilot knew. But no answer ever came back. Not at point X or the other points, to and fro, he found interesting. So for a while he didn't stop at all, fearing that if he did leave his truck he might find only a torn-off part of somebody—a leg, maybe, or a familiar head rolled up into some creosote bush—and that was nothing at all Tot Hamsey cared to find by himself. You could be scared, yes. But you didn't have to be foolish. Instead, you would just stay in the cab of your nearly new Ford pickup and if, courtesy of your headlights, something should appear, well, you would just have to see that, wouldn't you, and thereafter make up your own mind about what smart thing to do next.

He's hearing the voice now, he says on the cassette. He's been hearing it for a while, he thinks. Not a voice exactly, but chatter akin to static—like communication you might imagine from Shangri-la or a risen and busy Atlantis. Bursts of it. Ancient as Eden or new as tomorrow. The language of fish, maybe. Or what the trees confide in each other.

"Trees," he says, his own voice a whisper you would not want to hear more than once after sundown. *"Vipers. And bugs. And rocks. The talk talked between worms."*

He's stopped the truck now. But he's not jumpy anymore—not at all. This could be a dream, he thinks, him still at home with Corrine and nothing but work in the sunshine to look forward to. He thinks about his friends, Straightleg Harry Peterson and Sonny Fitzpatrick, and the pheasant they'll hunt come winter. He thinks about his daddy's deacon, Martin Willis, whose porch he's promised to fix on Saturday.

It's a dream, he tells himself, feeling himself move left and right in it, nothing to keep him from falling over the edge. It's a dream, water a medium to stand upon and wings everywhere to wear. It's a dream, yes, time a rope to hang from and you on a root in the clouds.

It's a dream, Tot Hamsey says on the tape, but then it is not— never has been—and there he is at last, staring into the face of one sign and terrible wonder.

The books describe it as tiny, like a fourth-grader, with a head like a bowling ball on a stick. *The Roswell Incident* by Charles Berlitz and Bill Moore. *UFO Crash at Roswell* by those smart alecks from England. They all say that it—the spaceman my father found—was hairless, skin gray as ash, its eyes big as a prize fighter's fists. Something you could lug for a mile or two, easy. They're wrong. The thing had skin pink as a newborn's with hands like claws. You could see into it, my father says on the tapes. See its fluids pumping, an ooze that could be blood or sparkly liquids or goo there aren't yet names for. And probably it could see into you. At least that's the way it seemed to him—it with a Chinaman's eyes that didn't close and no ears and nothing but sloppy, wet holes the size of peach pits to breathe through.

"Touch," the thing said. The static was gone, English in its place—more phenomena we're told that Uncle Sam has an interest in keeping hush-hush. "Don't be afraid."

My father looked around, no help on the horizon. He'd been given an order, it seemed, and there appeared to be no good reason not to obey it. So his hand went out, as if they knew each other and had been summoned hereabouts to do common business.

It was like touching a snake, he says. *Or the deepest thing from the deepest blue sea.*

"Help them," the thing said—another sentence you probably find silly to believe—and only a moment passed before my father noticed the three others nearby.

They were dead. That was easy to tell. Like oversize dolls that have lost their air—a sight downright sad to see but one Tot Hamsey told himself he could forget provided he now had nothing else awful to know and thereafter nothing more to remember.

"Wait," the thing told him. "Sit."

Ten paces away the pickup was still running at idle, headlights on but aimed elsewhere, and my father imagined himself able enough to walk toward it.

In an hour he could be home. He would eat supper, play with his boy, listen to the radio. Corrine was making apricot jam, so he would sample it. He would take a bath, hot as he could tolerate. And then shave, using the razor his father had given him for Christmas. He could shine his lace-up shoes, read a true story in the *Reader's Digest,* or tell Reilly more about Huck and Tom and Nigger Jim.

Sonny Fitzpatrick wanted him to help put the plumbing in a bungalow being built by the road to Artesia, so he could puzzle over that—the supplies he'd need and what to charge Sonny's father for the hours involved. He'd been good at math. At geometry and angles to draw. He'd been better at literature, the go-getters and backsliders that books told about. He was only twenty-nine. A husband and a father. Much remained to be done in life.

But this, he thought. This was like dying. Like watching an evil storm bear down on you from heaven. Nowhere at all to hide from the ordained end of you.

"Listen," the thing said, and Tot Hamsey was powerless not to.

My mother has told me that he came home around sunrise. He'd been gone overnight before, so that hadn't worried her. Sometimes he had a two-man project to do—a new windmill to get up or a stock tank that needed to be mucked out—so she had slept that night, me in my crib in the other bedroom, imagining him holed up in a rickety outbuilding in the badlands, eating biscuits hard as stones and listening to that blowhard Mac Brazeall say how it was in moldy-oldy times. She was not surprised when she heard the truck, nor when she looked out the window to see him standing at the gate to the yard. He would do that on occasion, she thought. Collect himself for a minute. Slap the dust from his jeans or shake out his slicker and scrape his boots clean if it had rained. Then he'd come in, say howdy to Reilly, maybe swing him around a time or two, and over breakfast thereafter tell what could be told about doings in the hardscrabble way west of them.

But for a long time, too long to be unimportant, he didn't move. He had a finger on the gatepost and it seemed he was taking its pulse. Behind the curtain, my mother watched, her own self as still as he. He'd lost his hat, evidently, and half of his face, like a clown's, seemed red as warpaint. She wasn't scared, she said to me more than once. Not yet. This was her husband, a decent man top to bottom, and she had known him since the third grade. She'd seen him dance and, drunk on whiskey, play the piano with his elbows. He could sit a horse well and had a concern for the small gestures of courtesy that are now and then necessary to use between folks. So there was nothing to be frightened of, not even when he came in the front door and she could see that his eyes had turned small and hard, like gravel.

Whatever wound in him was wound too tight, she thought. Whatever spun, now spinning too fast.

After that, she says, events happened very quickly. He gathered up several tablets and disappeared into his workshop, a pole barn he'd built himself back behind the clothesline. She put his breakfast out—bacon from Milt Morris' slaughterhouse and eggs she'd put a little Tabasco in—but in an hour it was still outside the door. She could hear him in there, a man with a hammer and saw, something being built. Or something coming apart. She took me to Hawkins' house so I could play with their boy Michael. At noon he was still in the shop, the door shut.

"Tot," she said. "You hungry for lunch?"

She could hear him, she thought. Like the fevered scraping and scratching of a rodent in a wall.

Later, the afternoon worn white with sunlight, she told him Sonny Fitzpatrick was on the phone.

"He wants you there first thing in the morning, okay?"

She tried the door then, but something was blocking it, and she could only see a little through the space: Tot Hamsey's back bent to a task on the table in front of him.

"Tot?" she said.

He turned then, eyes hooded, nothing in his expression to suggest that he knew her from anybody else who'd once upon a time crossed his narrow path—a look, she said later, that froze the innermost part of her. A tissue or the nerve that was like wire at her very center.

"I'll tell him you'll be there," she said.

After she picked me up at the Hawkins' house, she tried the door again. This time it didn't move, so she went to the window. He was still at the bench, a leather apron on, passing a piece of metal back and forth in his big hands. She could see now that the door had been blocked by his table saw, a machine that had taken both him and her to move four months before. Exasperated, she rapped on the window.

"Supper in an hour," she said.

But he didn't come out for that. Nor for the serial on the radio. Nor for my bath, or for the storytime that was supposed to follow. At the back door, she stood to watch the workshop. The lights were on, but he'd put a cover over the window. A sheet possibly.

This time she knocked harder. His supper dishes were still on the step. Untouched. "You've got to eat something," she called. "Tot Hamsey?"

A moment later, she'd said his name again. And again. She thought he was just on the other side of the door, maybe his face, like her own, against the wood, the two of them—except for the pine boards—cheek to cheek. He was huffing, she thought. As if he'd raced a mile to be there. As if he had more miles to go.

"Oh, honey," she sighed.

It was the same the next day, she has said. And the day after that. No evidence that he'd come out of the workshop. Only the slightest sign that he'd eaten. Once she thought to call his father, Milt Hamsey, but he was the meddlesome type, quick to condemn, slow to forgive. A holier-than-thou sort with a walleye and hair in his ears and no patience whatsoever with the ordinary back and forth of lived life. Too much anger in him. Like a spike in the heart.

No, she thought. Tot was only fretful about something. Or working an idea to a point. Besides, it was nobody's business what went on in Tot and Corrine Hamsey's house.

On the fourth day, she got the newspaper from the box by the fence line near the road. Whiskered Mac Brazeall was in it, a picture of his idiotic self on the front page, with his cockamamie story about the flying saucer parts he'd found off the Elko trail leading into the Jornada. Other articles about bogeymen in the skies above Canada and Kansas and all over the West. The base was involved, she read. Soldiers and officials from the government everywhere. Maybe spies. Just about the most far-fetched thing she'd ever heard of.

At the step to the workshop, she asked Tot if he knew anything about this. "You were out there," she said. "That's where you were, right?"

Tot Hamsey came to the door then. She heard the table saw being shoved aside. He would look like a hermit, she believed. Ravaged and blighted. Then he was in front of her, not a giant step away, and she thought briefly that he'd been turned inside out.

"What's it say?" he asked, his first words in nearly two hundred hours.

"You coming out?" she wondered.

He had that look still. Murder in him maybe. Or fear. "Give it here," he said.

Now she was scared, a part of her already edging back toward the house. The room behind him, though ordered as her own kitchen, was cold as an icebox, the smell of it stale, like what you might find if you opened a crate from another century. She told herself not to gasp.

"This has to stop," she said.

"It will," he told her. He was reading the paper now, his lips moving as if he were chewing up the words.

"When?" she said, but the door was already closing.

They had reached an understanding, she decided. She was not to trouble him anymore. She had her own self and me to tend to. If anybody called—Sonny again, for example, or nosy Norris Proctor or Tommy Tyree from the Elks Club, anybody wanting anything from citizen Hamsey—she was to make up an excuse. A broken leg, maybe. The summer flu. A lie, anyway, he and she could one day laugh about. In turn, she was to get about her own business.

She would have to call her dad for money, but that was okay. He owned two hardware stores and was rich enough for three families.

She was to wait, she thought. A hole had opened in her life, hers now the job to see what creature crawled free from it.

He possessed treasure, he says on the tapes. Not the pirate kind. Not wealth, but secrets. "My name is Totenham Gregory Hamsey," he scribbled on the first page of the tablet I would one day find. "I was born in 1918, on March the 13th. My mother says I was a sweet child." For page after page, he goes on that way, his handwriting like a million spiders seen from above. He'd seen a human die, he wrote, and had watched another, me, being birthed. He knew a US senator and had shaken the hand of Roy Rogers. In Espanola, he'd ridden a Brahman bull and had taken a trolley in Juarez, Mexico. "I look good in swim trunks," he says on one page, "and have a membership at the Roswell Country Club. I am no golfer, though." He knows bridge and canasta and can juggle five apples. Jazz music he doesn't like, but he'll listen once to whatever you put on the record player.

"I have knowledge," he writes, and by page 26 he has started to give it. Pictures of how it is where they live. Their tribe name and what they do in space. The beliefs of them, their many conquests. They are us, he says, but for the accidents of where and when we are.

On the fifth day, according to the tapes in his file cabinets, he goes into the house. He doesn't know where his wife and child are. Nor does he much care. They could be strangers, people at a wayside: they're going one way, he another.

Beside the couch in the living room, he finds the stack of newspapers—the Army everywhere and Sheriff Johnny Freel looking boneheaded. It's a weather balloon, my father reads. A rawinsonde, a new design, a balloon big as a building in New York City. A colonel from Ft. Worth has confirmed this to all who thought the opposite. The intelligence officer from the base, Jesse Marcel himself, has put minds at rest. Mac Brazeall, cowpuncher, was mistaken, wrong as wrong could be. Not spacemen after all. Not Communists either. Just Uncle Sam measuring winds aloft. All is well again.

He feels sorry for them, my father says. They have small minds. They are insects.

For the next hour, he busies himself with practical matters. He gets out his good suit. For the journey. He showers, shaves, brushes his teeth. He eats, for fuel only. He settles his affairs. "I am not coming back," he writes to my mother in a note he'll put on the dining room table. "You are young. You can be good to someone else."

Outside, the landscape fascinates. Dry and cracked and endless. Storm clouds boiling up in the distance. They are there. His friends.

"Reilly," he writes to me in the same note, "study. Know your sentences and your sums. Do not give offense to your elders. Keep yourself clean. We move. We ascend. We vanish.

Carefully, he dresses. It is important, he thinks, that he look presentable. He wears cuff links, stuffs a handkerchief in his coat pocket. In the mirror, he sees a man of virtuous aspect—hair nicely combed, shoulders squared, tie in a handsome Windsor knot. He hears himself breathing, amused that he still needs our air.

On the phone, he asks for Charlie Spiller personally. "I need a taxi," he says. "In one hour." He imagines Charlie Spiller on the other end of the line. A man with a fake leg. A lodge brother. Another creepy-crawly thing from a vulgar kingdom.

"One hour," he says. "Exactly."

He's at the end of something, clearly. All that can be done has been done. He is not here. Not really. The past has closed behind him. He's gone through a door, a seam. There is no point in looking back.

On the dresser in the bedroom, he leaves his wallet and his Longines wristwatch. For a little while, sadly, he will need money. To pay Charlie. To pay for the Greyhound bus. To eat a sandwich along the way. He will not need his driver's license. Nor other papers. He is not anybody to know. *None of us is. We are wind and dirt and ash. We are weight that falls, flesh that burns. We are oil and mud. We are slow and cannot run. We are blind and do not see. We are echo and shadow and mist.*

At the workshop, he checks the padlock. Inside, beneath the floorboards in a pit he has dug, are his secrets. His papers wrapped in oilcloth. In the box are the metals. The meshlike panels. The tiny I-beams. Dials and switches and wires. His keepsakes from the future.

He turns once to look at the house. He imagines his thoughts like laundry on a line. All is well.

"This is not lunacy," he says on the tapes I would find. *"I'm a man who's died and come back, is all."*

At the dirt road by the fence line is the place he needs to be in a minute. Charlie Spiller drives a Dodge, a big car to go places in. Charlie Spiller cackles like a crone and can take direction. He can tell a joke and crack his knuckles, tricks to perform in the places he goes. Charlie Spiller: another human to forget about.

From his pocket, my father takes his keys and throws them as far as he can into the desert. He straightens his tie, shoots his cuffs, buttons his suit coat.

If it is sunny, he does not know. If raining, he cannot feel it. Instead, he has a place to be and a passel of desire to be there. He speaks to his feet, to his legs and hips, to the obedient muscles in each.

The voices. They've returned. The stones have messages for him. The cactus. The furniture he's leaving behind. Much is being revealed. Of spirits and haints. Of sand and of rocks. Listen. You can hear them. Like water. Like lava a mile beneath your feet.

"I had knowledge," he says. *"My name was Tot Hamsey. All was well."*

2

In 1980, for all the reasons unique to modern times (boredom, mainly, plus anger and some sickness at the pickiness of us), Cece Phillips and I went bust. She got the house in Odessa, not to mention custody of Nora Jane (like her mother, a specimen of womanhood sharp-tougued and fast to laugh at dimwittedness), and I came back here, to Roswell. The city liked well enough what it read on paper and so put me to work in the engineering department where I compute the numbers relevant to curbs and gutters and how you get streets to drain. Besides the physical, much had changed about me, you have to know. I'd sworn off anything stronger than Pepsi and did not use a credit card and had learned to play handball at the YMCA on Washington Avenue. In the mayor's office next door, I met a Clerical II, Sharon Sweeny, and spent enough agreeable hours with her at the movies and the like to think, in matters of romance at least, that two and two equaled more than the four you'd expect. I ate square meals, cleaned up my apartment regularly, and kept my p's and q's in the order they're notorious for.

Then, in 1981, the curious son of a curious man, I went to visit my father.

"You're Reilly," he said, his first words to me in decades.

"I am," I said, mine to him.

He was living in, quote, a residential facility, meaning that if you've got enough money, you can break bread in what looks like a combination hospital and resort motel with a bunch of harmless drunks and narcotics addicts and taxpayers who need to scrub their hands thirty times before they can dress in the morning. He'd been there since early in 1954, after my grandfather—who is himself dead now—found him up at the New Mexico State Hospital in Las Vegas and drew up papers that said, as papers from rich men can, that T. G. Hamsey could live at the Sunset Manor here until the day arrived to put him in the family plot in the cemetery on Pennsylvania Street.

I didn't recognize him. Umpteen-umpteens had gone by, and I was looking for the stringbean adult in the snapshots my mother had given me. He was collapsed, if you must know. Time had come down cruel on him, the way it will on all of us. Plus he was over sixty years old.

"Do you have a cigarette?" he said.

We were standing in a lobbylike affair, couches and end tables with lamps on them, the windows beyond us giving onto a view of

Kmart and Dairy Queen and all else crummy the block had become.

I'd quit, I told him.

"Perhaps next time," he said.

He was a stranger, as unknown to me as I am to the queen of England. He was just a man, I was telling myself, one I shared no more than cell matter with.

"Are you scared, Reilly?"

That wasn't the word, I told him. Not scared.

"What is the word then, Son?"

I didn't know. Honest.

"I'm something you've heard of, right? I'm a river to visit. A monument somebody wrote about. Maybe a city to go to."

We had sat, him in an armchair that seemed too small, me catty-corner on a leather couch so slick you could slide off. I wanted to leave, I'll admit. It was my lunch hour, and I thought of myself at El Popo's, eating Mexican food with my friends, little more to fret about than what paper needed to be pushed in the afternoon and which shoot-'em-up Sharon Sweeny and I could munch popcorn in front of that night at the Fiesta.

"I knew you'd come," he said.

It was hot outside, the heat shimmering up in waves from the asphalt parking lot, but I yearned to be out there in it, striding toward my car.

"Just didn't know when," he said. "You're a Hamsey."

True enough, I thought. Cece Phillips had once told me that I was about as predictable as time itself.

"How is she?" he asked. "Your mother."

She was in Albuquerque now, I said. She'd married again—not the colonel from NMMI when I was in high school, but the man after the man after the man after him.

"That's good," he said. "She used to come by, you know."

"A long time ago," I said.

That was right, he said. A long time ago, she used to visit with him, in this very room, tell him how it was with his parents and his brothers. With herself. With even their growing-up son.

"You didn't say much," I told him. "That's what Mother told me."

He cast me a look then—equal parts disappointment and confusion. "That's not how I remember it."

He seemd fragile and delicate, not a man who once upon a time could heft a hay bale or hogtie a calf. He was neither the snapshots I'd seen nor the stories I'd heard. He was just a human being the government counts every ten years.

"I'm tired," he said.

He was dismissing me, so I stood.

"Shall we shake hands?" he asked.

I had no reason not to, so we did, his the full and firm squeeze of a candidate for Congress.

"You'll come back?" he said.

I had been raised to be polite, I was thinking. Plus this had only cost me minutes, of which I had a zillion.

"Next Friday," I said.

Nodding, he let my hand go then, and I turned. This was my father, crackpot. Loony-bird. This was Totenham Gregory Hamsey. And I, suddenly thick-jointed and lightheaded and not breathing very well, was his son.

"Reilly," he called.

I had reached the door, only a few feet between his life and my own.

"Don't forget those smokes, okay?"

He was a man who'd survived a disaster, I thought. A fall from a ship or a tumble down the side of a mountain. He'd walked through a jungle or maybe had himself washed miles and miles away by a flash flood. Buried alive or lost on Antarctica, sucked up in a tornado or raised by wolves—he was as much a character out of a fairy tale as he was a man whose scribblings on the subjects of time and space and visitors I would eventually read often enough to memorize whole sections. Yes, he had horror in his head, events and visions and dreams like layers of sediment, but that day he only wanted cigarettes. So, the next week, I brought them.

"Luckies," he said, smelling the carton. "A good choice."

"A guess," I said, "I didn't know you smoked."

"I have seniority," he told me. "I do what I like."

This time we didn't sit in the lobby. We went to his room, and walking down the corridor he pointed at various doors. "Estelle Barnes," he said at one. "A dingbat. Nice woman, but thinks she's a ballet dancer. Sad." At another, he said, "Marcus Stillwell. Barks a lot. Sounds like a fox terrier." It was like that all the way: people said to weep or babble or to seek instruction and insight from their house pets—our own selves, I told Sharon Sweeny that night, except for chance and dread and bubbles in the brain.

At his own door, he jiggled the knob. "Locks," he said, "I'm the king of the hill here."

It was like an apartment—a class-A kitchen, a sitting room, a sizable bath, a bedroom—the fussed over living quarters of a tenant whose only bad habit is watching the clock.

"You like?" he asked.

I'd thought it would be different, I told him. Smaller.

He looked around then, as if this were the first time that he himself had seen the place. "Yeah," he said. "Me too."

I almost asked him then—I really did. I almost asked what you would, which is *Why* and *What* and *Why* again. But, owing to what I guess is the *me* of me—which has nothing to do with the pounds and inches of you nor the face you're born with—I didn't. I was only a visitor; he, just an old fellow with a dozen file cabinets and maybe a thousand books to call his pals.

"You turned out okay," he said.

I had, I thought. I really had.

"You know," he began, "I've seen you a couple of times before." He was sitting across from me, his head tilted, a cigarette held to his lips. "Come here," he said, rising and beckoning me to his window. "Over there."

Outside, nearly a hundred yards away, stood the back of a Seven-Eleven. Beyond that ran the highway to Clovis—the Cactus Motel and the Wilson Brothers' Feed and Seed. The sight wasn't much to whoop over, just buildings and dirt and three roads I had once calculated the code-meeting dimensions of.

"You had a city car," he said, gazing yonder as though I were out there now. "You wore a tie. And cowboy boots."

He was right. Eight months earlier I'd been with a survey crew—storm drains and new concrete guttering—and now I was standing here, seeing what he'd seen.

"You have your mother's walk," he said.

Cars were going up that street, and I remembered being out there, once or twice turning to look at where I stood now, once or twice one wet winter day thinking I knew somebody in that building. My father.

"You're a boss, I take it."

Sort of, I told him. There was a wisenheimer, Phelps Boykin, I reported to.

He was still staring straight ahead, and as if by magic I imagined I was inside his head, feeling time snag and back up, the present overwhelmed by the past. He was at my shoulder, me close enough to smell him, and he was leaning forward, nose almost to the glass. His hand had come up, small and speckled with liver spots, my own hand in twenty or thirty more years, and it seemed, having recognized something out there, he was going to wave hello.

"You know what I'd like?" he said.

That hand, unmoving and open and pale, was still up, while my own hand was twitching at my side. I had no idea what he'd like.

"An ice cream," he said. "I'd like a dish of vanilla ice cream."

The tapes don't say a lot about the State Hospital in Las Vegas, a ragtag collection of brick buildings—one of them, maximum security, surrounded by concertina wire atop chain-link high enough to fence out giraffes, and each with a view of the boring flatlands you have to traipse across to get out of The Land of Enchantment. All I am to know is that Charlie Spiller drove Totenham G. Hamsey to the Greyhound bus station, where the latter bought his ticket and got aboard with nothing in his hands but air and heat, him in a seat all to himself. He says he stood at the State's door until they took him in. Says he marched up to the receptionist's desk and told that wig-wearing woman that he knew exactly where he belonged, that he could see into the knobs and fissures of her soul, that she was like we all are, which is puny and whiny and weak—just spines with blabbing meat at the top.

She was goggle-eyed, he says, and looked up and down for the joke. Says he stripped to his undershorts and shoes then, to show her that he meant business, and uttered not another peep until a director, a fussbudget with an eyebrow like a caterpillar and hair like a thatched roof, escorted him into an office for a man-to-man chat, whereupon time—"Of which," he says, "there is too goddam much"—went zoom, zoom, zoom, and the past snapped away from him like a kite in a hurricane.

I'm not sure I believe any of this, though I like the idea of a Hamsey seminaked in a public place. Still, given what I know— from the tapes, from the papers in the boxes and files in his apartment, from two visits to his hidey-hole at the farm—all he said seems as straightforward as breakfast. Given the givens, especially how I turn out in this story, I sometimes see him chalk-faced, his teeth gritted, outerwear at his feet, no light or noise in his world except that rising up in him from memory, nothing but gravity to keep him earthbound, only ordinary years between him and eternity.

When he was alive—when I was visiting on Fridays and taking him to the Sonic for a chili-cheeseburger or out with Sharon Sweeny and me to the Bottomless Lakes for a cookout—he didn't talk much about such matters. Talked instead about the Texas Rangers, whose games he listened to on KBIM, and about the mayor's father, Hob Lucero, a man he'd busted broncos with, and what it's like to cha-cha-cha with someone named Flo, and how to tell if your cantaloupe is ripe or which nail to use when you're pounding up wallboard.

He was a Republican, he said one week. Which meant to him gold bullion and gushing smokestacks and cars you hired a wetback to polish twice a month.

Then, a week later, he asked me about NORAD—what I knew of it.

"What?" I said. I was preoccupied by a loud difference of opinions I'd had with Phelps Boykin earlier that morning.

"The Marine Corps has a metallurgy lab in Hagerstown, Maryland," he said.

He was mainly talking to himself, I thought. Didn't make a whit of difference who sat in the seat beside him.

They were liars, he said. Lowdown pencil pushers who wouldn't know the truth if it bit them on the hindmost.

Here it was I left off thinking about crabby Phelps Boykin, supervisor, and took up the subject of cracked Totenham Hamsey, father. It was a moment, I think now, as dramatic in its circumstances as maybe gunfire is to you in yours.

"Del Rio, Texas," he announced. "December 1950. A colonel—one Robert Willingham—reports an object flying at high speed. Crashes. He finds a piece of metal, honeycombed. Had a lot of carbon in it. Cutting torch wouldn't melt the damn thing."

He put a Lucky to his lips, took a puff, held it for seven beats of my crosswise heart. "There's more," he said. "A whole lot more."

We were parked off McGaffey Road, southwest of town, the two of us eating burritos in a city car. Across the prairie the humps of the Capitan Mountains were the nearest geography between us and another time zone. We'd been doing this for nearly two years, going to Cahoon Park or down to Dexter or up to Six-Mile Hill. Father and son—an hour or two of this or that.

"There's hoaxes," he said, still gazing afar. "Spitsbergen Island off Norway, September 1952. Aztec, New Mexico, March 1948. A yahoo named Silas Newton says there were 1,700 scientists out there. You can't imagine some of the goofballs running around."

I was looking at the ground, specifically a slumped area a few yards ahead of us. For a moment it seemed that something monstrous might charge out of it, and me with only a greasy paper bag and a new driver's license to defend myself.

"You don't believe this, do you?"

I could see clouds in this distance, shapes that ought to be meaningful to someone like me. "Not really," I said.

"It's like God, isn't it?" he said. "Maybe necromancy. Or fortune-telling."

Sharon Sweeny believed in God, I told him. Which was all right. And Cece Phillips had recently said that our daughter, Nora Jane, believed in ghosts and astrology. But me, I didn't blow much one way or the other.

"That's too bad," he said.

It was about as useful, I told him, as pretending you could fly or see through walls.

"There's a lot like you," he said.

I had started the car, the air conditioning throwing a fine cold blast on my hot face. "I gotta get back," I said. "There's a man I gotta see."

He was sitting up straight now, his the expression teachers get when you mess up, and I realized that two conversations had been taking place, but me with only ears enough for one.

"I could tell you everything," he said at last.

I revved the engine—more cold air, more words in it to worry about.

"I could do that right now, Reilly. All you have to do is give me the go-ahead."

I was thinking furiously. Me with a brain like a cartoon engine, all its clever gears whirling and spitting off sparks. He could tell me. About the 3rd of July in 1947 and all since. About his leaving. About my mother and me, left behind.

"What do you say, Son?"

We stood at a crossroads, I believed. In one direction lay the past; in the other, tomorrow and the tomorrows after that. One was mystery and sore hearts and done deeds you couldn't undo; the other, me and a girlfriend and a GMC truck to make payments on.

"No, sir," I told him. "I don't need to know any of that."

Which is how we left it for that month, August, and the next, and those others that passed before he showed up at my office late in May, him in a suitcoat and white shirt and handsome string tie. As stylish as a State Farm agent.

"I walked," he said. He looked flushed, maybe thirsty for an ocean of water, so I asked him if he wanted a fruit juice or an RC from the machine in Drafting.

"You're a messy one, aren't you?" he said, waving at my desk and my table and my cabinets, charts and state-issue reference works piled haphazardly atop each. "Hamseys, so far as I can tell, are not a cluttering people."

"Yes, sir," I said. Clearly, he had something in mind. A surprise to spring on his only child.

"Your mother kept a clean house."

He was right about that, too. So spotless and tidied that one Friday near Easter I'd come home from school after track practice (I threw the shot) and, my house as still as a tomb, I'd thought that my mother, like her husband before her, had also vanished.

"Tell me about her," he said. "The man she married." He was smoking now, flicking his ashes in his cuff, his movements deliberate and precise, as if he had to explain to his shoulder and his elbow and his fingers what to do.

"His name is Barnett," I said. "Mother calls him Hub. He's something at Sandia Labs. Management of some sort."

He took another drag—not much air in here to push the smoke around. "Military?" he asked.

I didn't think so, I said. He was about to retire.

"A big man, I'm guessing. Your mother liked big men."

I hadn't thought about it, I admitted. Hub was about average size, maybe a bit overweight. Had a big laugh, though. Like Santa Claus.

"A man of substance, I take it."

Tot Hamsey was like an adding machine, I thought. This information, then more, eventually the sum he was adding for.

"Is he kind?" my father said.

I guessed so, I told him. Didn't exactly know.

"Corrine never went for coarse types," he said. "Ask Norris Proctor."

It was a name, like many others, I could not attach to a face. Tommy Murphy, Pug Thigpen, Mutt Mantle, Judge Willy Freedlander—these were people I'd only heard of, names no more than jibber-jabber to go in one ear and out the other. Folks either old or gone or dead.

"I don't have any regrets, Reilly. Not a one."

He was gazing at the most impressive of my wall maps, the city's zoning laid out in a patchwork of pink and blue and red and yellow, section after section after section of *do*'s and *don't*'s—where you could manufacture and peddle, where you could only sleep and mow your lawn—a world I probably took too much satisfaction in being semiresponsible for.

"Project Mogul, they called it," he was saying. "Radar targets— foil, so the story goes—being strung from a balloon."

"Yes, sir," I said. This was his surprise: the there and then that had become the here and now.

"The 509th," he said, "right here in Roswell. Only air group trained to handle and drop atomic bombs."

I felt as I had that Friday afternoon near Easter. With my heart like a plug in my throat, I started to tell him again that I didn't want to hear any more of that talk.

"Sit down, Reilly," he said. He was speaking to me as he'd once himself been spoken to; so, maybe looking at him as I guess he'd looked at it, I did. "Pay attention, boy. I don't have all day."

I was to wait. To sit here as I had there. I was to be quiet. Above all, I was to concentrate on something—that color photograph, say—and not look away from it until the floor was the floor again, and I would not be falling toward it.

"Project Sign," he was saying, "ATIC in Dayton. Hell, Barry Goldwater's in this. You still with me?"

I was. Me. And the photo. And the floor. And one man of substance.

CUFOS, Erv Dill, Ubatuba in Brazil, 1957, 1968, Nellis Air Force base in Nevada, magnesium, strontium, the Dew Line, *True* magazine, radio intercepts, MUFON, the sky, the Vega Galaxy, the suits they wear, the vapors we are helpless without, the bodies in the desert, the no-account home our rock is, the swoop and swell, the various holes in heaven—all this and more he said, me and the walls his respectful audience. And then, loopy as time to a toad, a half-hour had gone by, and he was through looking at the map.

"I'm not crazy, Reilly."

I told Sharon Sweeny later that I was playing a game in my head—*A* is for apple, *B* for ball—me not capable of offering aloud anything neutral yet. I was at *F*—for fog—when he spoke again.

"There's no power, Son, no glory. There's nothing—just them and us and the things we walk on. I have proof." Wiping his forehead with a tissue he'd drawn from his trousers, he seemed finished, the back a little straighter, no spit at the corners of the mouth. "Here," he said, another item from his pocket.

I took it. A key ring. Maybe ten keys attached.

"My files," he said.

G, I was thinking. What was *G* for?

Sharon Sweeny—my sweetie then, my Mrs. now—says the call Thursday came at about the exact minute Dan Rather was demonstrating how soggy it was in rain-soaked West Table, Missouri. I have no memory of this; nor have I any recollection of going to the phone and barking "hello" in a manner meant to mean "no" to those interrupting my dinner to sell me something.

Sharon Sweeny—as right a wife for me as white is right for rice—reports I said "yes" two times, the latter less loud and certainly with too much "s" in it.

Next, I've heard, I sat. In the chair by the table I usually pay my bills from. I eased the phone away from my ear, I am told, and regarded it as naked primitives are said to stare at mirrors. I appeared frazzled, my foot tapping as it will when I have eight somethings to say but only one something to say it with. I am told—by Sharon Sweeny, who was between bites and only five giant steps away—that I mumbled only one sentence before I hung up, which was "I see," words she thinks must've taken all I had of strength and will to get loose. When I stood, she tells me, it seemed likewise an act with maximum effort in it.

"Where're you going?" she says she said.

On a hook by the front door hung my jacket, and Sharon Sweeny claims I approached it as though I expected the sleeves to choke me.

"Quik-Mart," I evidently told her. "I'd like a cigarette."

She was frightened, hers truly on the verge of teetering or breaking into a full run. "Who was on the phone?" she asked.

"I haven't smoked in years," it's said I said. "But tonight, just now, I'd like a pack. It's a foul habit, you know. Hard as the dickens to break. I wouldn't wish it on anyone. Not a blessed soul. You believe me, right?"

She had come toward me, I understand, a woman now close

enough to see the focus flashing in an out of her man's eyes, him with his head cocked as though listening for a sound not to be heard twice in a lifetime.

"Reilly?"

So, his own strange news to deliver, the son told her: Totenham Hamsey, middle initial G., was dead.

Congestive heart failure, it was, that old man going down at the feet of his dance partner Estelle Barnes, would-be ballerina, still eight or nine bars left of "Woodchoppers' Ball." But, as I say, I remember not an iota of how I came to share this knowledge with my beloved big-boned Clerical II. I do not remember the next day either, nor the day that replaced it. About the funeral, at the gravesite his father had paid for years and years earlier, I recall only a single incident—me and my mother and her husband Hub and a preacher named Wyatt who looked like he was trying out for a community-theater musical, plus seven residents from the Sunset Manor, accompanied by a nurse who stood as though she had wood screws in her heels, and sunlight pouring down on us like molten metal but me not melted in the middle, and then Sharon Sweeny, my hand held in hers, leaning to my ear to whisper, "Stop humming, sweetheart. I can't hear what the man's saying."

The day after that, I came to—in my father's apartment, me appointed to move his stuff out to somewhere else. His colognes, I think, hastened me back. Frenchy fragrances of vanilla and briar and oily smoke—odd for a fellow never known, so my mother has since said, for other than Vicks or Old Spice. "Sweet smellies," he'd called them that first day he'd showed me around. So there I was, with several packing boxes from city hall, me too big in a bathroom too brightly lit to flatter, feeling myself return, as if to earth itself, inch by inch by inch, until I had no one to lead me about except the familiar fool in the mirror and him in need of both a haircut and a professional shave. Mother wanted none of this—not out of meanness, I hold—so Sharon Sweeny had made arrangements with the Salvation Army to take all it had a use for; I was the help, a job I'd apparently said "Yes" to when, after the casket was lowered, that nurse with the sore feet waddled over to remind me of the workaday consequences of death.

I packed his clothes next, only two sacks of mostly white dress shirts and slacks you apparently are urged to buy in lots of ten, plus lace-up shoes—all black—you could actually see your shiny self in. For reasons owing to sentimentality and the like, or so Sharon Sweeny later insisted, I kept the string tie for myself, it being his neckwear the last time we'd visited. Then, the kitchen having only food and drink to throw away and not much of either, I went to the living room and, my innards clotted and pebbly and heaped up hard beneath my ribs, stood in front of the steel cabinets I had the keys for.

"My treasure," he'd said four days earlier. "Yours now."

Out the window I noticed the spot where, years before, he'd seen me at work in boots and my own starched white shirt. I imagined him watching me then, as abstract and fixed as my mother had been the morning, years and years before that, when she stood behind her curtains to study him at their gate, nothing in him—I would later learn—but ice and wind and heavy silence.

"You take care, Reilly," he had said in my office, and now, no other chore to distract me, I would.

For company, I had turned the TV on—*General Hospital,* I think, in which attractive inhabitants from a made-up metropolis were falling in love or scheming mightily against one another. They were named Scorpio and Monica and Laura and Bobbi, and for a moment—it as long as one in war—I desired to be at the center of them: Reilly Jay Hamsey in a fancy Italian suit, his teeth as white as Chiclets, him with lines to orate and a well-groomed crowd happy to hear them.

"In the shop," he had said. "At the farm. That's where."

I was fingering the keys, each no bigger than my thumb. One fit one cabinet, another another, and all I had to do was turn locks clockwise, no real work whatsoever for the hand and wrist of me.

"Under the floorboards, Son."

T. G. Hamsey, I was thinking. Son of Milton Hamsey, banker, and Virginia Fountain Hamsey, homemaker. Brother of Winston Lee, oil man, and Benjamin Wright, bankrupt cattle baron. All deceased. Nothing now but these cabinets and me. In one, only papers and tape recordings; in the other, bone and flesh and blood.

Music had come up from next door, a singsongy thing that for a minute I endeavored to keep the steady beat of.

In the desert that night years ago, Cece Phillips had declared that we—you, me, all the king's men—had been put here on earth for a purpose: "We're meant to be the things we are," she said. It was an idea fine to have, I told her, if you're sitting atop a pile of us and have nothing at all but more whoop-de-do to look forward to. "Fine to have," I'd said, "if you don't have to get up when the alarm says to."

That's what I was thinking when I slipped the key in the lock of the leftmost cabinet. What if you're one Reilly Hamsey, a middle-aged municipal employee with only a remote control to boss around and tomorrow already coming up over England? What if, no matter the wishes you've wished, you've nothing above your shoulders but pulp and nothing in your wallet but five dollars and nothing in your pants pockets but Juicy Fruit gum? What if, when your hand turns and the lock clicks open and that first drawer slides out, you're always going to be the you you are, and this will always be the air you breathe, and that will always be the ragged rim of the world you see?

"I hate them," my father had said, teary eyed. "Look what they've done to me."

On the TV a wedding was taking place, Lance to Marissa, their friends and relations nearabout and beaming, squabbles and woes set for the occasion aside. They were gowned and sequined and fit, no illnesses to afflict, no worries that wouldn't—in one episode or another—disappear, theirs the tragedies you only need a wand to wave away.

"Hey," I said, addressing those creatures from the American Broadcasting Company. "Look what I'm doing here."

3

They had crammed it all in his head, he'd said on the tapes. What conveyances to take hither and yon, the packs of them, their minerals and gases, the councils they sit at, their vigilance in matters moral, their currencies, their contempt for us. They have prisons for their villains, schools for their youngsters. They have nationalities, races, blood allegiances to fight for. Leaders have risen up among them. They are disappointed, spite filled. "They have been to the end of it," he'd said. "Where the days run out. The minutes. Where the fires are."

The fires—one image to have between the ears the day Sharon Sweeny and I parked at the road leading to the farm. The place wasn't much to look at, the city having crept up to the nearby cotton fields, the irrigation canals mostly intact but the fence line in need of expensive repair.

"You still own it?" Sharon asked.

My grandfather had sold it, I told her, maybe five years after. Part of the proceeds had put me through college. The rest my mother had given me for the house in Odessa.

We'd stopped for a Coke on the way out, and she was drinking the last of it now, looking at the tumbledown buildings, while I, like a clerk, was scrambling to sort out my thoughts big to little. "Seems tiny, doesn't it?" I said at last.

"When I visit my parents in Socorro," she began, "I can't believe I ever lived there. I mean, it's like a doll house."

The day was bright, the sun as fierce this morning as it would be this afternoon, nothing between it and us but seconds, and I was glad I'd brought a hat.

"You ready?" she asked.

Briefly, before the roof of my stomach caved in, I thought I was. "Give me a moment, okay?"

I'd dreamed about this last night. I'd read his documents, page after page that seemed less scribbled on than shouted at. I'd listened to his tapes, hours and hours of them, and then, Saturday already faint in the east, I'd dreamed. Me. And treasure to find. And strong Sharon Sweeny to help.

"You think she'll like me?" she was saying.

My eye was focused on a tumbleweed snagged on the barbed wire at the gate, my mind on the single reason for not backing out of there. "Who?"

Nora, she said. Nora Jane.

I had forgotten. My daughter, a sophomore at Sul Ross, was

coming over for summer break—a chance to meet Sharon Sweeny and maybe later tell her mother, Cece Phillips Hamsey, what good fortune her old man had stumbled into—and, Christ, I had forgotten.

"Cece says she likes golf," I said. "Maybe you can take her over to Spring River for a round."

I felt tottery, I tell you, as different from myself as tea is from tin. And before I gave in to the coward in me, I imagined myself standing down the way a bit toward town, me a shitkicker with nothing to do but stroll past that unremarkable couple sitting in the city car at the end of a rutted road leading to one ramshackle house.

"We could leave," I told Sharon Sweeny, which prompted her to lift her eyebrows and take my closest hand.

"No, we couldn't, Reilly."

She was right, but I would require several more moments, thoughts surfacing twelve at a time, to realize that.

"There's money," I said. "Seems he had a lot of it. I found a Norwest bankbook."

That was dandy, she said. And I believed she meant it.

"We could get a house," I told her. "I always wanted a swimming pool."

That was also dandy, vocabulary I now couldn't hear too much of.

"Nora could have her own room. Maybe spend more time with us. A real family."

Her hand tightened on mine, and something sharp and whole and nearly perfect passed between us. "Reilly," she said. "Start the car."

Like my father, I guess now, I too am excellent at following orders, so I did as told, pleased both by how I kept my hands on the wheel as we rolled up closer and closer and closer, and by the fact that I could look left and right if I wanted to.

"How long's it been abandoned?" she asked.

Didn't know, I told her. Tax records described it as a lease farm, the land owned by a conglomerate out of Lubbock. Mostly silage was being grown. Cotton every now and then.

"It was pretty, I bet."

The night before, I say, I had dreamed about this. One tape, then another. Tot Hamsey's voice raspy and thick and slow, as though it was oozing up through his legs out of the ground itself. Then, my bed ten sizes too small and ten times too lumpy, dreams. Of spacemen. Of smoke. Of one sky rent clean in half.

"It won't be there," she was saying. "The box."

I had braked to a stop beneath a Chinese elm more dead than alive, the uprights for the adjacent wood fence windbent in a way not comforting to contemplate.

"You'll see," she said. "It's a delusion. A fantasy."

Half of me wanted her to be right, and it said so.

"He was a nice man," she said. "Just—well, you know."

I did, and said as much—not the worst sentiment, even if wrong, that can go back and forth between beings.

"Let's eat afterwards," she said. "I'm starved." She had her sunglasses on now, her feet on the dash, a paperback mystery in her lap. Her toenails were painted and, time creaking backwards inside of me, I believed pink the finest, smartest color ever invented by the finest and smartest of our kind.

"Sweetheart," she said. "Put your hat on."

Which I did. And soon I was out and the trunk was open and shut, and there I was, Sharon Sweeny's garden shovel in hand, already halfway to the square building on the right, nothing but dust to raise with every step, nothing to hear but a fistlike muscle in me going thump-thump-thump.

The padlock was gone, as he'd figured it would be, so I had little trouble tugging that door open, its hinges flaky with rust. This was five months ago now—before I went back a second time for the box—but I still see myself plainly, me smelling the musty smell of it and going in, the darkness striped by sunlight slicing through many seams in the wall, and the scratching of mice or lizards finding holes to hide in. The room was not as he recalled. No jig or bandsaw. No hammers or clamps or drills hanging in their places on the walls. No work apron on a peg. Just dirt and cobwebs and broken lengths of wood, plus a bench toppled on its side and a huge spool of baling wire and a short-block V-6 engine and a far corner stacked with cardboard high as the ceiling.

I felt juvenile, I tell you, this too much like a scavenger hunt for an adult to be doing, and for an instant it seemed likey that I would leave, me suddenly with an appetite, too. In ten minutes, Sharon and I could be at the Kountry Kitchen, only a table and two cups of coffee between us. But then something hooked and serious seemed to twist in me—a gland perhaps, or a not-much-talked-about organ, or whatever in us an obligation looks like—and, the air in that room dense and hot as bath water, I found myself knocking on the floorboards with the shovel—whack, whack, whack—listening for one hollow whump, me the next Hamsey man to hunt for something in the dark.

Three times I traveled the length of that room—shoving junk out of my path, twice banging my shins, once almost smacking myself in the forehead on a two-by-four hanging from a rafter—before I heard it, and heard it again. Which means you are free to imagine me as I was: unmoving for two and twenty heartbeats, in me not much from the neck up—exactly, years and years before, as my father must've felt in the desert when he rode over that hill and saw what he saw. Then sense began coming back, thread by thread, and I crouched, knees cracking. Sound was again plain from the outside world—a tractor's diesel motor and the corrugated metal roof squeaking and groaning in the wind—but that shovel now weighed at least one thousand ugly pounds, and cold upon cold upon cold was falling through the core of me, light raining down like needles, with darkness there and there in spouts and columns, and no terrors to know but those you can't yet see.

"Oh," I think I said. Thereafter, nothing more to exclaim, I was on my fanny, prying up the first of four boards.

I was thirty-seven years old and thinking of those years placed end to end, which gave me to wonder where they had led and how many more I had, and finally those floorboards were loose and flung aside and at least the easiest of those questions had been answered.

It was like a root cellar, roomy enough for you to lie at the bottom of and throw open your arms.

"Okay," I said, my last sensible remark that hour.

❑ ❑ ❑ ❑

I'd had a vision years before—me and Cece Phillips and the desert at night and how the future would turn out between me and her. This time, empty-handed on the way to a different car and a different woman, I had none. I had lifted the box, skimmed the bundle of papers wrapped in oil cloth, put it back, and now—well, I didn't know. Thousands and thousands of days ago, a terrible thing had crashed in my father's life. Today, something equally impossible had landed in mine.

"It wasn't there, was it?" Sharon Sweeny said.

I put the shovel in the trunk and, brushing the dust off my pants next to her door, I thought of worms. Their wriggly, soft bodies. The talk they talk. "Just a lot of trash," I said.

She was relieved, I could tell, me once again as simple a character as any between the covers of the book in her lap. "What took you so long?"

My father had died, so Estelle Barnes had said, with his face composed, maybe even peaceful, and to my mind came a picture of him curled on the floor at her feet—his eyes blank, his thin lips parted, his hair flyaway and wild. The end of him, the beginning of me.

"What do you think I'd look like with a moustache?" I asked Sharon Sweeny.

"I don't like them droopy," she said. "Makes a fellow appear sinister."

I needed another minute here, I was thinking—time that had to pass before anything else could commence.

"You still hungry?" I asked.

She nodded, a gesture as good to see as are presents under the tree at Christmas, so I started around the car to the driver's seat. I was counting the parts of me—the head I had, the heart—and for the next few steps I had nothing at all to be scared of.

pens, she and Howard romantically "ran off" to, honeymooned in, and vacationed at, in turn, back in the palmy years before their children came along; before Howard's "mid-career course correction" failed to correct it; before her own work history mainly spun its wheels, and their marriage, to both parties' dismay, went belly-up. No Island Paradises in Alice's foreseeable future: for the past half-dozen years at least, her idea of a quality vacation has been a weekend's state-park camping with the kids (but they're in junior high and high school now, ever less interested in roughing it *en famille,* especially just with Mom) or a week at her parents' summer place on Cape Cod. It's from one of those latter that she's just now returning, leaving Jessica and Sam for an additional fortnight with their maternal grandparents. To Alice's embarrassment, all hands' airfares have had to be on the old folks' tab; she and Howard simply haven't the resources to finance cross-country family visits. They haven't even a savings fund for the kids' rapidly upcoming college expenses, for pity's sake, typically the middle-class American family's single largest capital outlay. After eighteen years of marriage, this decoupling couple's only real nest egg is a few thousand dollars gained not by programmatic saving but by refinancing the nest when home-mortgage rates dropped a few years ago—and now Howard's insisting that that egg be split fifty-fifty. Likewise their equity in the house itself, which he wants sold; likewise further their children's custody, although his proposals for the logistical management of that last item strike Alice as risible if not disingenuous—possibly a ploy to reduce his child-support payments.

How in the world, she has wondered in mid-photo-spread ("The *Other* British Virgins"), did her parents' generation—the generation that generated the postwar Baby Boom whereof she and Howard are dues-paying members—manage? Typically on one income, or one and a fraction, American middle-class couples like Alice's folks and Howard's contrived to send two, three, even four offspring through college—sometimes even through private colleges, not the local state diploma-mills that Sam and Jessica will have to make do with—and in Alice's case to private high school before that, not to mention affording them piano lessons, dance and horseback-riding lessons, art lessons, a house to grow up in considerably more spacious than Sam and Jessica's (in a better neighborhood, too), and in later years even a vacation home as well? Howard's father, moreover, managed all this while himself divorcing and remarrying at his son's present age; gave his first wife their commodious house free and clear for the children to finish their high-school years in, plus enough alimony to maintain her and them therein till they were off to college at his expense and she remarried—and on top of that paid all of her divorce-lawyer's fees as well as his own, with the result that Howard's mother (how Alice now envies her in this!) had had the luxury of protracting the negotiations at her leisure and at her estranged husband's cost. All this, mind, in a divorce action that, like Alice and Howard's, was no-fault, by pained mutual consent—not one party dumping the other and therefore becoming willy-nilly the "buyer" of the divorce, the aggrieved other party the "seller." Alice's dad (still contentedly married to her mom) is a retired history professor of modest repute with a couple of royalty-producing textbooks as well as scholarly articles in his bibliography; her mother was for decades a part-time special ed teacher in the public schools. Howard's father and mother, a bit more affluent but scarcely rich, are or were respectively a research chemist with a few process-patents on the side and a classic 1950s *homemaker* who did volunteer charity work at her church and the county hospice. In those Kennedy/Johnson, *Leave It to Beaver* years, where on earth had the money come from?

Alice exhaled audibly, shook her head, and turned to the final page of "Island Paradises": Norman Island in the BVI, now about to be "developed" with resort hotels, but almost pristine fifteen years ago when Howard and she, already a few months pregnant with Sam, had anchored a chartered sailboat in its splendid Bight on the third Thanksgiving of their marriage.

"Beats Boston, right?" the fellow in the aisle seat beside her commented at this point. He, too, she'd noticed, had been leafing through the airline's in-flight mag and, evidently, eyeing Alice's progress therethrough. Whether by coincidence or as a conversation-starting gambit on his part, they reached Norman Island separately together.

"Careful, there," Alice replied—cordially but coolly, in her judgment, as she was not much up for conversation: "You're talking to an old Bostonian."

"Am I, now?" To Alice (who wasn't looking closely) the man looked to be maybe twenty years older than herself, same general ethnicity and class, standard navy blazer, khaki slacks, open sport shirt, lanky build, graying hair, nice tan, easy smile. "So are you, as it happens. But I don't object to an island paradise from time to time."

"Likewise, I'm sure."

His accent wasn't Boston—but then neither is Alice's, and "old Bostonian" scarcely describes her. Child of academic parents, she and her brothers were born in Bloomington, Indiana, spent their elementary-school years in Santa Barbara, California, and only their high-school years in suburban Boston, as their father moved from campus to campus up the professional ladder. If Alice thinks of any place as her childhood home, it's that cottage on the Cape, where the family spent more summers together than school years anywhere.

Her tone and manner did the job, if there was any to be done. Both passengers returned to their magazines, wherein "Island Paradises" turns out to be followed—unusual for an in-flight publication—by a bit of fiction: a short story called "Freeze Frame," its author's name unfamiliar to our protagonist. Alice is not, these days at least, much of a reader, of fiction or anything else beyond the lease- and sale-contracts that come across her part-time office desk and the textbooks on real-estate law, of all things, that she's been cramming lately in half-hearted preparation for her Oregon licensing exam. As a girl (whose parents strictly rationed their children's diet of television) she consumed novels the way Sam and Jessica consume Nintendo and junk food—and not just kiddie-novels. In her first-rate private high school (she wished Sam's public one were half as good!), Fitzgerald's *Great Gatsby* and Turgenev's *Fathers and Sons* joyously broke her heart and enlarged her spirit. At Reed College in Portland (where she'd met pre-law Howard), she'd been a sociology major with a serious minor in her favorite subject, literature; she read rapturously through the big Victorians and the early Modernists, and in her senior year considered with her dad and with Howard (by then her virtual fiancé) the merits of sundry graduate departments of literature as well as sociology, with an eye toward advanced degrees in one or the other and an academic career.

All that seems another world to her now. She and Howard "ran off" to Barbados on holiday after graduation and presently thereafter married. She followed him to law school in New York, where she did pick-up copyediting to help pay the rent, and then—when he dropped out for reasons that they still argue over—to Chicago on an initially successful business venture with one of his father's chemical-patent partners (their Virgin Islands cruise and her happy first pregnancy date from this period). When the Chicago venture fizzled, she and young Sam and Jessica-in-the-works followed him back out to Portland and his present restless employ as a "product developer" for a pharmaceutical concern—while Alice herself, *faute de mieux,* "helps out" half-time these days in a downtown real-estate office. She has thus far resisted the mild advances of her more-or-less mentor there, although he's a civilized-seeming divorcé himself and she's lonesome for adult male company now that she and Howard have split; but she guesses unenthusiastically that she'll take his advice and go for her broker's license. In the interstices of her frazzled life: videos with the kids, when she can get them peaceably assembled; regular jogging, to keep her spirits up and her body in shape for whatever next episode in her life-story; telephonic set-tos with Howard about economic and parental matters; the aforementioned odd camping weekend; maybe half an hour's thumbing through some glossy magazine like *Elle* or *Vanity Fair:* snapshots from yet another world. She scarcely manages to read the daily *Oregonian* these days beyond its real-estate section, much less *literature;* indeed, she probably ought to be re-reviewing the R.E. Board-exam stuff right now, as she has spent most of her "vacation" week doing. But she's supersaturated in that line; also depressed by her parents' loving, unspoken, but obvious disappointment in their only daughter's life-trajectory thus far and even with her upbringing of their grandchildren (*"Mortal Kombat!"* her dad had groaned in disbelief when young Sam fished out that video game—popular, portable, stupefying, and relentlessly violent—from his backpack the minute they arrived at the Cape Cod cottage, like a junkie in need of a fix).

Alice is, in fact, for perhaps the first time in her forty years, truly fearful of the future, whereof that real-estate-law manual is a token and wherefrom this in-flight magazine—like the round-trip flight itself and the less-than-refreshing vacation that it has bracketed—is an all-too-brief reprieve.

Literature, hah: Those were the days!

Thus the odd opening of that "Freeze Frame" story catches her attention. As she reads on, moreover, she finds herself involved in (and she'll presently be stopped still by) one of those vertiginous coincidences that happen now and then to readers of stories, attenders of movies, even swappers of anecdotes with one's fellow passengers through life: a correspondence stranger than fiction (even when one of the corresponding items *is* fiction) between the situation one is reading or hearing about and one's own. "Freeze Frame"—its first half, anyhow—turns out to involve a forty-year-old White-Anglo-Saxon-(lapsed)-Protestant middle-class American woman (name not given) who, like Alice, acutely knows herself to have passed the classical *mezzo del cammin de nostra vita,* as the author puts it, quoting the opening lines of Dante's *Divine Comedy:* a little past the halfway point of the Biblically allotted three-score-and-ten. Like Alice, "she" is a healthy human animal, though under sustained stress lately, and the daughter of still-living parents who themselves are in good health for their age. She knows therefore her expectable remaining life span, barring accident, to be slightly longer than the span behind her—more trying, too, she expects, although her story thus far, while relatively privileged, has by no means been carefree. The story's narrator calls its lead character's malaise "the Boomer Syndrome": Just as her middle-class-American generation is, by and large, the first of the century not to surpass its forebears in physical height and general health, so with many exceptions are its members likewise falling short, or feel themselves to be, in material, perhaps even spiritual, well-being. "Her" father and mother respectively GI-Billed through state university and worked through secretarial school, the first in their families' history to "go past high school"; they flourished as a one-and-a-half-income family in the booming postwar U.S. economy and provided their children (four!) with a suburban upbringing at least as favored as Alice's and her brothers', substantially more favored than their own had been, and downright sybaritic compared to that of "her" grandparents. The paternal generation managed the class-climb from small-shopkeeper to professional ("her" father was an estate-and-trust lawyer) and confidently supposed that their sons—maybe even their daughters—would likewise enter the professions on the strength of their excellent educations. But something—"Call it the countercultural Sixties," the author suggests in the story, "the oil-embargoed, 'stagflated' Seventies, the TV-narcotized beginning of the end of the American Century"—something had gone quietly but profoundly wrong.

And then less quietly. Of "her" two brothers, one has drifted from commune to hippie commune right up into the Reagan Eighties, his circuits blown on sixties methedrine; in his late thirties he half-supports himself as a longhaired mower of suburban lawns who converses with spirits as he maneuvers his Kubota wide-blade rig through the greenswards of Newton, Massachusetts. The other, after dropping out of two colleges plus law school (shades of Alice's Howard), is doing modestly in rural Maryland as a remodeler of small-town kitchens and bathrooms; he likes to work with his hands. Of the two girls, one has broken her parents' officially liberal hearts by "coming out" as a lesbian and—after a creditable West African tour of duty in the Peace Corps, a halfhearted suicide attempt, and a parentally subsidized stay in a Pittsburgh psychiatric hospital—settling down with her same-sex Significant Other to run a marginally successful New Age gift shop in San Diego. Not all that different a resume, changes changed, from Alice's gay brother's in his Key West cappuccino bar, which her parents gamely visit every second or third winter, not to lose touch altogether.

As for Her herself, whom let's capitalize henceforth for clarity and convenience: After "Freeze Frame"'s opening address to the dear present reader, said reader finds Her gridlocked in downtown

St. Louis traffic, not at morning or evening rush-time but, curiously, just a bit past noon—owing perhaps to a routine lunchtime-traffic congestion that She didn't know to allow for, perhaps to some out-of-view accident or other bottleneck. In any case, en route to the riverside expressway in her ailing, high-mileage Subaru wagon after an upsetting legal confrontation with her estranged husband—a confrontation between their respective divorce lawyers, actually, through which the parties to the action sat in stony silence—and running late already for a job-interview appointment in University City (She'll be needing a better job than her current office-temping, all right, given the likely outcome of those settlement negotiations, but she's not at all sure that her indifferent work history qualifies her for anything remotely approaching her vague expectations back when she took her M.A. in Art History fifteen years ago), She's stopped dead in this humongous traffic jam and verging on tears as her aged station wagon verges on overheating. How could "her" Bill have sat there so damned impassively—her longtime, once-so-loving spouse, father of their twins, her graduate-school lover and best of friends—in those hateful new wire-rimmed, double-bridged eyeglasses that She supposes are an aspect of this new, intransigently hostile William Alfred Barnes, and that she suspects are meant to please some other her than Her?

The cold-hearted bastard, Alice remarks to herself. The DC10's captain announces at this point that owing to turbulent weather over Chicago, the plane's course has been diverted south; they are crossing the Mississippi just below Hannibal, Missouri—Mark Twain's birthplace.

She (I mean our distraught "Freeze Frame" protagonist) happens to be gridlocked in actual sight of that river: There's the symbolic catenary arch of the "Gateway to the West," and beyond it are the sightseeing boats along the parkfront and out among the freight-barge strings. As She tries to divert and calm herself by regarding the nearest of those tourist boats—an ornate replica of a Mark-Twain-vintage sternwheeler, just leaving its pier to nose upstream—her attention is caught by an odd phenomenon that, come to think of it, has fascinated her since small-girlhood (happier days!) whenever she has happened to see it: The river is, as ever, flowing south, New Orleansward; the paddle steamer is headed north, gaining slow upstream momentum (standard procedure for sightseeing boats, in order to abbreviate the anticlimactic return leg of their tour), and as it begins to make headway, a deckhand ambles aft in process of casting off the vessel's docklines, with the effect that he appears to be walking in place, with respect to the shore and Her angle of view, while the boat moves under him. It is the same disconcerting illusion, She guesses, as that sometimes experienced when two trains stand side by side in the station and a passenger on one thinks momentarily that the other has begun to move, when in fact the movement is his own—an illusion compoundable if the observer on Train A (this has happened to Her at least once) happens to be strolling down the car's aisle like that crewman on the sternwheeler's deck, at approximately equal speed in the opposite direction as the train pulls out. Dear-present-reader Alice here suddenly remembers one such occasion, somewhere or other, when for a giddy moment it appeared to her that she herself, aisle-walking, was standing still, while Train A, Train B, and Boston's South Street Station platform (it now comes back to her) all seemed in various motion.

As in fact they were, the "Freeze Frame" narrator declares in italics at this point, his end-of-paragraph language having echoed mine above, or vice versa—and here the narrative, after a space-break, takes a curious turn. Instead of proceeding with the story of Her several concentric plights—how she extricates or fails to extricate herself from the traffic jam; whether she misses the interview appointment or, making it despite all, nevertheless fails to get the university job; whether or not in either case She and the twins slip even farther down the middle-class scale (right now, alarmingly, if Bill really "cuts her off" as threatened, she's literally about two months away from the public-assistance rolls, unless her aging parents bail her out—she who once seriously considered Ph.D.hood and professorship); and whether in either of *those* cases anything really satisfying, not to say fulfilling, lies ahead for her in the second half of her life, comparable to the early joys of her marriage and motherhood—instead of going on with these nested stories, in which our Alice understandably takes a more than literary interest, the author here suspends the action and launches into an elaborate digression upon, of all things, the physics of relative motion in the universe as currently understood, together with the spatiotemporal nature of written narrative and—Ready?—Zeno's Seventh Paradox, which three phenomena he attempts to interconnect more or less as follows:

Seat-belted in her gridlocked and overheating Subaru, the protagonist of "Freeze Frame" is moving from St. Louis's Gateway Arch toward University City at a velocity, alas, of zero miles per hour. Likewise (although her nerves are twinging, her hazel eyes brimming, her pulse and respiration pulsing and respiring, and her thoughts returning already from tourist boats to the life problems that have her by the throat) from the recentest event in her troubled story to whatever next: zero narrative mph, so to speak, as the station wagon idles and the author digresses.

Even as the clock of her life is running, however, so are time in general and the physical universe. The city of St. Louis and its temporarily stalled downtown traffic, together with our now-sobbing protagonist, the state of Missouri, and variously troubled America, all spin eastward on Earth's axis at roughly a thousand miles per hour. The rotating planet itself careens through its solar orbit at a dizzying 66,662 miles per hour (with the incidental effect that even "stationary" objects on its surface, like Her Subaru, for half of every daily rotation are "strolling aft" with respect to orbital direction, though at nothing approaching orbital velocity). Our entire whirling solar system, meanwhile, is rushing in its own orbit through our Milky Way Galaxy at the stupendous rate of nearly half a million miles per hour: lots of compounded South Street Station effects going on within that overall motion! What's more, although our galaxy appears to have no relative motion within its Local Group of celestial companions, that whole Local group—plus the great Virgo Cluster of which it's a member, plus other, neighboring multigalactic clusters—is apparently rushing *en bloc* at a staggering near-million miles per hour (950,724) toward some point in interclusteral space known as the Great Attractor. And moreover yet—but who's to say *finally?*—that Attractor and everything thereto so ardently attracted would seem to be speeding at an only slightly less staggering 805,319 mph toward another supercluster, as yet ill-mapped, called the Shapley Concentration, or, to put it mildly, the Even Greater Attractor. All these several motions-within-motions, mind, over and above the grand general expansion of the universe, wherein even as the present reader reads this present sentence, the galaxies all flee one another's company at speeds proportional to their respective distances (specifically, in scientific metrics, at the rate of fifty to eighty kilometers per second—let's say 150,000 miles per hour—per "megaparsec" from the observer, a megaparsec being one thousand parsecs and each parsec 3.26 light-years).

Don't think about this last too closely, advises the author of "Freeze Frame," but in fact our Alice—who has always had a head for figures, and who once upon a time maintained a lively curiosity about such impersonal matters as the constellations, at least, if not the overall structure of the universe—is at this point stopped quite as still by vertiginous reflection as is the unnamed Mrs. William Alfred Barnes by traffic down there in her gridlocked Subaru, and this for several reasons. Apart from the similarities between Her situation vis-à-vis "Bill" and Alice's vis-à-vis Howard—unsettling, but not extraordinary in a time and place where half of all marriages end in separation or divorce—is the coincidence of her happening upon "Freeze Frame" during a caesura in her own life-story and reading through the narrative of Her nonplusment up to the author's digression-in-progress just as, lap-belted in a DC10 at thirty-two thousand feet, she's crossing the Mississippi River in virtual sight of St. Louis not long past midday (Central Daylight Savings Time), flying westward at an airspeed of six hundred eight miles per hour (so the captain has announced), against a contrary prevailing jet stream of maybe a hundred mph, for a net speed-over-ground of let's say five hundred, while Earth and its atmosphere spin eastward under her, carrying the DC10 backward (though not relatively) at maybe double its forward air speed, while simultaneously the planet, the solar system, the galaxy, and so forth all tear along in their various directions at their various clips—and just now two flight attendants emerge from the forward galley and stroll aft down the parallel aisles like that deckhand on the tourist sternwheeler, taking the passengers' drink orders before the meal service. Alice stares awhile, transfixed, almost literally dizzied, remembering from her happier schooldays (and from trying to explain relative motion to Sam and Jessica one evening as the family camped out under the stars) that any point or object in the universe can be considered to be at rest, the unmoving center of it all, while everything else is in complex motion with respect to it. The arrow, released, may be said to stand still while the earth rushes under, the target toward, the archer away from it, et cetera.

Her seatmate-on-the-aisle, fortunately, is too preoccupied with punching a pocket calculator and scribbling on a notepad (atop his in-flight mag atop his tray-table) to notice her looking up from her reading. Alice decides she'll order white wine and club soda when her turn comes, and goes back to the suspended non-action of "Freeze Frame" lest he disturb her reflections with another attempt at conversation.

Back, rather, she goes, to that extended digression, wherein by one more coincidence (she having just imaged the arrow in "stationary" flight—but not impossibly she glanced ahead in "Freeze Frame" before those flight attendants caught her eye) the author now invokes two other arrows: the celebrated Arrow of Time, along whose irreversible trajectory the universe has expanded ever since the Big Bang, generating and carrying with it not only all those internal relative celestial motions but also the story of Mr. and Mrs. W.A. Barnes from wedlock through deadlock to gridlock (and of Alice and Howard likewise, up to her reading of these sentences); and the arrow in Zeno's Seventh Paradox, which Alice may long ago have heard of but can't recollect until the author now reminds her. If an arrow in flight can be said to traverse every point in its path from bow to target, Zeno teases, and if at any given moment it can be said to be at and only at some one of those points, then it must be at rest for the moment it's there (otherwise it's not "there"); therefore it's at rest at every moment of its flight, and its apparent motion is illusory. To the author's way of thinking, Zeno's Seventh Paradox oddly anticipates not only motion pictures (whose motion truly *is* illusory in a different sense, our brain's reconstruction of the serial "freeze-frames" on the film) but also Werner Heisenberg's celebrated Uncertainty Principle, which maintains in effect that the more we can say about a particle's position, the less we can say about its momentum, and vice versa—although how that principle relates to Mrs. Barnes's sore predicament, Alice herself is uncertain. In her own mind, the paradox recalls that arrow "at rest" in mid-flight aforeposited as the center of the exploding universe . . . like Her herself down there at this moment of Her story; like Alice herself at this moment of hers, reading about Hers and from time to time pausing to reflect as she reads; like every one of us—fired from the bow of our mother's loins and arcing toward the bull's-eye of our grave—at any and every moment of our interim life-stories.

"White wine, please," she hears her row-mate say affably in his non-Boston accent. "With a glass of ice and club soda on the side."

"The same," Alice says in hers. He has already fished out his three dollars; for a moment Alice worries that he'll offer to pay for her drink, too, amiably obliging her to conversation. Peter, at work, is forever offering lunch that way, and sometimes, strapped for money and male social conversation, Alice agrees, but she inevitably feels thereby compromised, *transacted,* quid-pro-quo'd and unready to quo. This fellow does not, however, so offer; he goes back to his figuring while Alice scrabbles in her purse, pays, pours, sips (he does glance her way now, smiles slightly, and lifts his plastic tumbler in the merest of toasts to the wine-order coincidence, a toast that it would be gratuitously incordial of her not to respond to in kind), and then returns, glass in hand, to the freeze-framed "Freeze Frame," whose point she thinks she's beginning to see, out of practice though she is in reading "serious" fiction.

To the extent that anything is where it is [the author therein now declares], *it has no momentum. To the extent that it moves, it isn't "where it is." Likewise made-up characters in made-up stories; likewise ourselves in the more-or-less made-up stories of our lives. All freeze-frames* [he concludes (concludes this elaborate digression, that is, with another space-break, after which the text, perhaps even the story, resumes)], *are blurred at the edges.*

❑ ❑ ❑ ❑

An arresting passage, Alice acknowledges to herself. Her reflective circuits stirred by the story-thus-far as they haven't been in too long, she smiles at the contradiction in that phrase. *An arresting passage:* Alice's First Paradox.

"Hmp," she hears herself say aloud, amused at that. Amused at *that,* she stifles a chuckle and helps herself to another dollop of wine.

"Fuff," the fellow on the aisle replies, anyhow says, as if to his notepad—and Alice remarks for the first time that he's been annotating not only that pad but the margins of the "Freeze Frame" story in his copy of the in-flight magazine: "Forgot continental drift."

"Excuse me?" She's still smiling, partly at her little witticism, partly at the pleasure, unfamiliar lately, of smiling spontaneously from pure innocent amusement rather than grimly, to keep her spirits up. Another brace of flight attendants—a brace of braces, actually, she supposes in her lingering amusement—is beginning the meal service in the DC10's twin aisles. Bemused, Alice decides to take time out from "Freeze Frame" (whose author has been taking a prolonged time-out from telling the story) and give sociability a try through lunch.

"I'm rechecking the numbers in this crazy story," the fellow says wryly, "and it just occurred to me that continental drift wasn't factored in." He smiles: a friendly smile, confident but unassuming. "You're reading the thing, too, I see. Did you get to the numbers part yet?"

"That's where I am now, and the arrow business. Pretty dizzy-making." She sips her wine.

He taps the text with his ballpoint. "Shouldn't the Earth's rotational speed be corrected for the latitude of St. Louis, the way an LP record moves faster at its edge than halfway in toward its hole? And then there's the wobbling of the earth's axis, right?—that causes the precession of the equinoxes. Plus or minus the couple of millimeters a year that the crustal plates grind along." He grins and shrugs his eyebrows. "Too late now. May I have another white wine, please, to go with lunch," he asks the stewardess who here hands them their meal trays.

"Another white wine. And you, ma'am?"

"I'm fine," Alice says, who isn't; who would quite enjoy a second drink, to enhance this recess from her troubles and lubricate the conversation a bit, but who feels she can't afford another three dollars. "Maybe just a refill on the club soda. How's it too late?" she asks the aisle-chap. "You mean too late for the author to throw in plate tectonics?" She's pleased with herself for remembering that term—Jee-sus, is she ever rusty in the areas of knowledge for its own sake and disinterested reflection!—and the guy responds to it with a clearly appreciative glance. She wonders, whether he's some sort of academic like her dad, or, more admirably (what Howard used to be before he autodestructed, and she before the burdens of parenthood and downward mobility in a souring marriage numbed her mind to everything except economic and psychological survival), a *non*-academic who maintains a lively intellectual curiosity beyond his professional concerns.

"Right." He opens his second pony of California Chablis, pours some of it over the wine/ice/soda mix already in his glass, and with a gesture of his bottle-hand offers to top up Alice's as well. Caught off-balance, she shrugs acceptance and holds her glass himward. It is to prevent spillage that he rests the bottleneck on her glass-rim as he pours, but that light brief steady contact has a tiny voltage on it, as if their hands were touching.

"Much obliged, kind sir."

He lifts his glass to her again; Alice simply makes a pleasant smile and nods. He's not being pushy, she decides, sipping; just normally sociable.

"So what do you think of the story so far?" he asks her: a nondirective question if she ever heard one.

"Well . . ." Why not say it? With a smile, of course: "I happen to identify completely with the woman in the car, so it's not easy for me to be objective."

"Mm." His glance is sympathetic, but instead of inviting details, as she rather expected he would (there was no question mark after that "Mm"), he asks whether she happens to know what *Subaru* means in Japanese. Alice doesn't; he surprises her again by neither supplying that datum, nor acknowledging that *he* doesn't know either, nor explaining why he asked in the first place: what that question has to do with the story. He registers her amused negative headshake with a minimal nod and asks "What about this gimmick of hitting the narrative Pause button and smarting off about relative motion and Zeno's paradoxes? Is that any way to tell a story?"

He has begun his lunch. Alice turns to hers: a grilled-chicken-breast salad, not bad at all and appropriate with the white wine, or vice versa. His question sounds to her more testing than testy (she likes that unspoken little wordplay: her second in five minutes, and maybe five years). "Well," she ventures, testing the idea herself: "The piece is called 'Freeze Frame,' right? The woman's stuck in traffic the way she's stuck in her life-story, and the author dollies back to give us the Big Picture. . . ."

"Nicely said."

Encouraged, Alice adds "It's motions within motions, but it's also pauses within pauses. It's freeze-frames framing freeze-frames."

When was the last time she ever talked like this?

"Brava," her neighbor applauds: "The point being that all of those freeze-frames are in motion—spacewise, timewise—just as we are, sitting here. So why is the time of day a bit past noon, instead of morning or evening rush hour?"

"Is this a quiz, or what?" For his tone, good-humored but serious, is clearly not that of puzzlement.

"More like a map-check, I guess," he allows between forkfuls. "Or a reader-poll. I'm out of practice in the short-story way."

That makes two of them, Alice assures him. And she was so crazy about literature in college; couldn't get enough. But then, you know, the hassles of real life: scrabbling for a living, raising kids—plus television, and everybody's attention span getting shorter. God knows *hers* isn't what it used to be; it's only at times like this that she can settle in to really read: long plane-rides and such, and unfortunately her life these days doesn't include very many of those. Sometimes, she declares, she really thinks—well, he's older, halfway between her parents' generation and her own, she'd guess, so maybe he'll say this is just Baby-Boomer self-pity, but it really does seem to her sometimes that her whole American generation is

. . . not *lost,* like Hemingway's Lost Generation, but there's been a real slippage: economic slippage, obviously, but *gumptional* slippage, too, if he knows what she means. Is that a word, gumptional?

He smiles. "It is now."

She's an attractive woman (I shift this story's narrative point of view to have our man-on-the-aisle affirm to himself); rather more so, actually, in her present agitation. Bright, articulate, well put together, well turned out in her light summer linens, and obviously as stressed for whatever reasons as is his nameless lady-in-the-Subaru. Not to play games or seem importunate, he was about to own up to her that the "Freeze Frame" story is his: a bit of a time out from his usual occupation. By temperament and profession he's a novelist, more accustomed to the narrative long haul than to the sprint. It has been twenty-plus years since he last wrote short stories. Back in the sixties, when his first and only collection of them was published, the woman beside him—laughing now at her sudden effusiveness and at the same time knuckling tears until he offers her a dry cocktail napkin to dab with—will have been a high-schooler. But as it happens he's between larger projects just now, and at his age and stage one never knows but what the pause-in-progress, so to speak, might be one's artistic menopause. That possibility, while certainly not cheering, doesn't greatly alarm him, any more than does the regrettable prospect of losing sexual desire and potency, say, somewhere down the road (in that order, he hopes). He has had a gratifying if less than epical career in both areas, and in others as well; he is in fact on tour just now to help promote his latest midlist novel, and missing his wife, and feeling rather too far along for this sort of thing—while at the same time mildly enjoying the break in his unglamorous but still deeply satisfying daily routine of dreaming up people and situations, putting thoughts and feelings and actions into English sentences, and in the process discovering what's on his imagination's mind, as it were: what his muse has up her sleeve; what she'll do for an encore this late in the day.

It was in this spirit, he's telling Alice now (Yeah, he 'fessed up. Why not? Strangers in transit, never see each other again, et cetera), that he wrote the "Freeze Frame" story a few months back—all those motions-within-motions and pauses-within-pauses, as she accurately put it—and even urged his agent, half as a lark, half seriously, to try placing it in some in-flight mag, of all odd places, instead of in one of the few large-circulation American magazines that still publish "literary" fiction. But of course he hadn't anticpated the happy coincidence that he would first see it in print while flying virtually over the scene of its stalled action. Truth stranger than fiction, et cet.

"Not to mention the *un*happy coincidence that you'd get stuck with old capital-H Her," Alice says, "in the flesh." Her sniffles are O.K. now; not stopped, but under adequate control and anyhow O.K.

She's impressed, mildly; has never met a writer in person before (she thinks now she remembers his name from some classroom anthology, light-years ago); is amused to hear him say "et cet" in his ordinary speech just the way it comes up in his story, almost a stylistic tic; recalls now that in fact he said he was *re*checking those numbers, not checking them. He doesn't seem boastful or otherwise pretentious or affected: a regular fellow, self-ironic but serious; *likable,* she decides, and O.K.-looking for his presumable age, but who cares about that? Who cares, for that matter, whether he's thinking Get this dip out of here! He seems nice: not pressing, not turning her off; letting her babble, but companionably running on a bit himself. She finds herself doing a self-surprising thing: actually catching his hand in hers for a moment—Thanks for the Kleenex—giving it a comradely squeeze (same small voltage as that wine-bottle/glass-rim contact), and declaring she can't spare a damn dime in her present pass but would certainly enjoy another glass of wine with him if he'll be kind enough to stand her one. She'll return the favor in some other life.

"There is no other life," he declares pleasantly. "That's why some of us make up stories." As for the wine, no problem: He'll put it on his publisher's tab; she'll buy a copy of his current novel as soon as she can afford one, but no sooner, and if she enjoys it she'll tell her friends to do likewise. All debts squared.

"Done."

❑ ❑ ❑ ❑

And so at 608 mph et cetera et cetera et cetera this pair relax as if suspended in space and time. Never mind the in-flight movie now framing along on the video screens: In the cozily darkened cabin, all its window shades drawn for viewing purposes, they sip white wine and exchange information about their lives. Alice, forgivably, speaks mainly of her marital problems and her anxieties with regard to the future. He counsels courage, patience, and goodwill; he went through that wringer himself a couple decades back and can attest that, with luck, there's life after the midlife crisis. He can't argue, however, with her envious observation that a man out in the world, like Howard, is better positioned to meet significant new others than is a full-time mother with a ratsy part-time job. How she wishes, now, that she'd taken her doctorate in whatever and made her own career moves instead of doing the fifties-housewife trip like Howard's mother! Though she wishes even more that her husband's career had really flown, and that they'd aged and grown in synch, still loving each other and their life together. . . .

Out come the Kleenex: Excuse her.

With fair candor he responds to her questions, when she thinks to ask them, about how it was with him twenty-some years ago. "I wrote a lot of short stories, for one thing," he reminds her. "Too scattered for anything longer."

She gestures toward the text of "Freeze Frame," tucked into the seat-back pocket before her, and raises her eyebrows at him. "Does this mean there's trouble again at home?"

He smiles at that, shakes his head, raps on the plastic tray-table in lieu of wood.

Does Alice really mock-sigh then and say "Too bad for *our* story!" Or, perhaps, "In that case, how do we get me and Miz Whatsername out of gridlock?" Do they chuckle at her plainly experimental flirtsomeness and raise the intimacy-level of their dialogue a notch or two, so that by final approach their hands are touching freely? And when at the airport baggage-claim he offers her a lift downtown in his cab—even dinner at his hotel, if she's up for it (Portland's splendidly refurbished old Heathman), before his scheduled appearance that evening at Powell's Bookstore—does she say, in a spirit clearly ready for adventure, "I'll say I missed my connection," and then, as the circumstance dawns on her, snatch up his hand in both of hers and declare "No, damn it: I don't have to say anything! *There's nobody home to say it to!"*?

More reasonably, their mid-flight tête-à-tête having run its transitory course along with that sufficiency of wine, do they presently unbuckle to visit the lavatories aft and then return separately to their seats: she to go on with the "Freeze Frame" story, more curious even than before to find out what its author has in store for Her; he to go back to his notepad, in which for all Alice knows he's now jotting notes for some story about *her* as they rush motionlessly together through the time of their lives, their life-stories meanwhile suspeneded? . . .

Given the age and stage of the woman in the gridlocked car, that "just past noon" business in "Freeze Frame" strikes me as obvious to the point of heavyhandedness. I apologize on behalf of the author, who has also not gotten it said to our Alice that *Subaru* is Japanese for the Pleiades cluster (see the automaker's logo) in the constellation Taurus—much farther now from the dear present reader than it was even a sentence ago. On the other hand, *I* haven't yet managed to get it said (what the "Freeze Frame" story declares somewhere in that digressive pause before the space-break beyond which Alice is currently reading) that all stories are essentially constructs in time, and only incidentally in the linear space of written words. Written or spoken, however, these words are *like* points in space, through which the story-arrow travels in time. Just now it rests at *this* point, this word, this—yet of course never resting there, but ever en route through it to the next, the next, from Beginning through Middle et cetera. Even if and when we linger over an "arresting passage," we're only apparently at rest in the story's suspended but incessant motion; likewise in our manifold own.

There. Said.

"On with the story?"

Alice Munro

The Love of a Good Woman

From *The New Yorker*

FOR THE LAST couple of decades, there has been a museum in Walley, dedicated to preserving photos and butter churns and horse harnesses and an old dentist's chair and a cumbersome apple peeler and such curiosities as the pretty little porcelain-and-glass insulators that were used on telegraph poles.

Also there is a red box, which has the letters "D. M. Willens, Optometrist," printed on it, and a note beside it, saying, "This box of optometrist's instruments though not very old has considerable local significance, since it belonged to Mr. D. M. Willens, who drowned in the Peregrine River, 1951. It escaped the catastrophe and was found, presumably by the anonymous donor, who dispatched it to be a feature of our collection."

The ophthalmoscope could make you think of a snowman. The top part, that is—the part that's fastened onto the hollow handle. A large disk, with a smaller disk on top. In the large disk a hole to look through, as the various lenses are moved. The handle is heavy because the batteries are still inside. If you took the batteries out and put in the rod that is provided, with a disk on either end, you could plug in an electric cord. But it might have been necessary to use the instrument in places where there wasn't any electricity.

The retinoscope looks more complicated. Underneath the round forehead clamp is something like an elf's head, with a round flat face and a pointed metal cap. This is tilted at a forty-five-degree angle to a slim column, and out of the top of the column a tiny light is supposed to shine. The flat face is made of glass and is a dark sort of mirror.

Everything is black, but that is only paint. In some places where the optometrist's hand must have rubbed most often, the paint has disappeared and you can see a patch of shiny silver metal.

I. Jutland

This place was called Jutland. There had been a mill once, and some kind of small settlement, but that had all gone by the end of the last century, and the place had never amounted to much at any time. Many people believed that it had been named in honor of the famous sea battle fought during the First World War, but actually everything had been in ruins years before that battle ever took place.

The three boys who came out here on a Saturday morning early in the spring of 1951 believed, as most children did, that the name came from the old wooden planks that jutted out of the earth of the riverbank and from the other straight thick boards that stood up in the nearby water, making an uneven palisade. (These were in fact the remains of a dam, built before the days of cement.) The planks and a heap of foundation stones and a lilac bush and some huge apple trees deformed by black knot and the shallow ditch of the millrace that filled up with nettles every summer were the only other signs of what had been here before.

There was a road, or a track, coming back from the township road, but it had never been gravelled, and appeared on the maps only as a dotted line, a road allowance. It was used quite a bit in the summer by people driving to the river to swim or at night by couples looking for a place to park. The turnaround spot came before you got to the ditch, but the whole area was so overrun by nettles, and cow parsnip, and woody wild hemlock in a wet year, that cars would sometimes have to back out all the way to the proper road.

The car tracks to the water's edge on that spring morning were easy to spot but were not taken notice of by these boys, who were thinking only about swimming. At least, they would call it swimming; they would go back to town and say that they had been swimming at Jutland before the snow was off the ground.

It was colder here upstream than on the river flats close to the town. There was not a leaf out yet on the riverbank trees—the only green you saw was from patches of leeks on the ground and marsh marigolds fresh as spinach, spread along any little stream that gullied its way down to the river. And on the opposite bank under some cedars they saw what they were especially looking for—a long, low, stubborn snowbank, gray as stones.

Not off the ground.

So they would jump into the water and feel the cold hit them like ice daggers. Ice daggers shooting up behind their eyes and jabbing the tops of their skulls from the inside. Then they would move their arms and legs a few times and haul themselves out, quaking and letting their teeth rattle; they would push their numb limbs into their clothes and feel the painful recapture of their bodies by their startled blood and the relief of making their brag true.

The tracks that they didn't notice came right through the ditch—in which there was nothing growing now, there was only the flat dead straw-colored grass of the year before. Through the ditch and into the river without trying to turn around. The boys tramped over them. But by this time they were close enough to the water to have had their attention caught by something more extraordinary than car tracks.

There was a pale-blue shine to the water that was not a reflection of sky. It was a whole car, down in the pond on a slant, the front wheels and the nose of it poking into the mud on the bottom, and the bump of the trunk nearly breaking the surface. Light blue was in those days an unusual color for a car, and its bulgy shape was unusual, too. They knew it right away. The little English car, the Austin, the only one of its kind surely in the whole county. It belonged to Mr. Willens, the optometrist. He looked like a cartoon character when he drove it, because he was a short but thick man, with heavy shoulders and a large head. He always seemed to be crammed into his little car as if it were a bursting suit of clothes.

The car had a panel in its roof, which Mr. Willens opened in warm weather. It was open now. They could not see very well what was inside. The color of the car made its shape plain in the water, but the water was really not very clear, and it obscured what was not so bright. The boys squatted down on the bank, then lay on their stomachs and pushed their heads out like turtles, trying to see. There was something dark and furry, something like a big animal tail, pushed up through the hole in the roof and moving idly in the water. This was shortly seen to be an arm, covered by the sleeve of a dark jacket of some heavy and hairy material. It seemed that inside the car a man's body—it had to be the body of Mr. Willens—had got into a peculiar position. The force of the water—for even in the millpond there was a good deal of force in the water at this time of year—must have somehow lifted him from the seat and pushed him about, so that one shoulder was up near the car roof and one arm had got free. His head must have been shoved down against the driver's door and window. One front wheel was stuck deeper in the river bottom than the other, which meant that the car was on a slant from side to side as well as back to front. The window in fact must be open and the head sticking out for the body to be lodged in that position. But they could not get to see that. They could picture Mr. Willens's face as they knew it—a big square face, which often wore a theatrical sort of frown but was never seriously intimidating. His thin crinkly hair was reddish or brassy on top, and combed diagonally over his forehead. His eyebrows were darker than his hair, thick and fuzzy like caterpillars stuck above his eyes. This was a face already grotesque to them, in the way that many adult faces were, and they were not afraid to see it drowned. But all they got to see was that arm and his pale hand. They could see the hand quite plain once they got used to looking through the water. It rode there tremulously and irresolutely, like a feather, though it looked as solid as dough. And as ordinary, once you got used to its being there at all. The fingernails were all like neat little faces, with their intelligent everyday look of greeting, their sensible disowning of their circumstances.

"Son of a gun," these boys said. With gathering energy and a tone of deepening respect, even of gratitude. *"Son of a gun."*

❑ ❑ ❑ ❑

It was their first time out this year. First, they had come across the bridge over the Peregrine River, the single-lane double-span bridge known locally as Hell's Gate or the Death Trap—though the danger had really more to do with the sharp turn the road took at the south end of it than with the bridge itself.

There was a regular walkway for pedestrians, but they didn't use it. They never remembered using it. Perhaps years ago, when they were so young as to be held by the hand. But that time had vanished for them; they refused to recognize it even if they were shown the evidence in snapshots or forced to listen to it in family conversation.

They walked now along the iron shelf that ran on the opposite side of the bridge from the walkway. It was about eight inches wide and a foot or so above the bridge floor. The Peregrine River was rushing the winter load of ice and snow, now melted, out into Lake Huron. It was barely back within its banks after the yearly flood that turned the flats into a lake and tore out the young trees and bashed any boat or hut within its reach. With the runoff from the fields muddying the water and the pale sunlight on its surface, the water looked like butterscotch pudding on the boil. But if you fell into it it would freeze your blood and fling you out into the lake, if it didn't brain you against the buttresses first.

Cars honked at them—a warning or a reproof—but they paid no attention. They proceeded single file, as self-possessed as sleepwalkers. Then, at the north end of the bridge, they cut down to the flats, locating the paths they remembered from the year before. The flood had been so recent that these paths were not easy to follow. You had to kick your way through beaten-down brush and jump from one hummock of mud-plastered grass to another. Sometimes they jumped carelessly and landed in mud or pools of leftover floodwater, and once their feet were wet they gave up caring where they landed. They squelched through the mud and splashed in the pools so that the water came in over the tops of their rubber boots. The wind was warm; it was pulling the clouds apart into threads of old wool, and the gulls and crows were quarrelling and diving over the river. Buzzards were circling over them, on the high lookout;

the robins had just returned, and the red-winged blackbirds were darting in pairs, striking bright on your eyes as if they had been dipped in paint.

"Should've brought a twenty-two."

"Should've brought a twelve-gauge."

They were too old to raise sticks and make shooting noises. They spoke with casual regret, as if guns were readily available to them.

They climbed up the north banks to a place where there was bare sand. Turtles were supposed to lay their eggs in this sand. It was too early yet for that to happen, and in fact the story of turtle eggs dated from years back—none of these boys had ever seen any. But they kicked and stomped the sand, just in case. Then they looked around for the place where last year one of them, in company with another boy, had found a cow's hipbone, carried off by the flood from some slaughter pile. The river could be counted on every year to sweep off and deposit elsewhere a good number of surprising or cumbersome or bizarre or homely objects. Rolls of wire, an intact set of steps, a bent shovel, a corn kettle. The hipbone had been found caught on the branch of a sumac—which seemed proper, because all those smooth branches were like cow horns or deer antlers, some with rusty cone tips. They crashed around for some time—Cece Ferns showed them the exact branch—but they found nothing.

It was Cece Ferns and Ralph Diller who had made that find, and when asked where it was at present Cece Ferns said, "Ralph took it." The two boys who were with him now—Jimmy Box and Bud Salter—knew why that would have to be. Cece could never take anything home unless it was of a size to be easily concealed from his father.

They talked of more useful finds that might be made or had been made in past years. Fence rails could be used to build a raft, pieces of stray lumber could be collected for a planned shack or boat. Real luck would be to get hold of some loose muskrat traps. Then you could go into business. You could pick up enough lumber for stretching boards and steal the knives for skinning. They spoke of taking over an empty shed they knew of, in the blind alley behind what used to be the livery barn. There was a padlock on it, but you could probably get in through the window, taking the boards off it at night and replacing them at daybreak. You could take a flashlight to work by. No—a lantern. You could skin the muskrats and stretch the pelts and sell them for a lot of money.

This project became so real to them that they started to worry about leaving valuable pelts in the shed all day. One of them would have to stand watch while the others went out on the traplines. (Nobody mentioned school.)

This was the way they talked when they got clear of town. They talked as if they were free—or almost free—agents, as if they didn't go to school or live with families or suffer any of the indignities put on them because of their age. Also as if the countryside and other people's establishments would provide them with all they needed for their undertakings and adventures, with only the smallest risk and effort on their part.

Another change in their conversation out here was that they practically gave up using names. They didn't use each other's real names much anyway—not even family nicknames such as Bud. But at school nearly everyone had another name, some of these having to do with the way people looked or talked, like Goggle or Jabber, and some, like Sorearse and Chickenfucker, having to do with incidents real or fabulous in the lives of those named, or in the lives—such names were handed down for decades—of their brothers, fathers, or uncles. These were the names they let go of when they were out in the bush or on the river flats. If they had to get one another's attention, all they said was "Hey." Even the use of names that were outrageous and obscene and that grownups supposedly never heard would have spoiled a sense they had at these times, of taking each other's looks, habits, family, and personal history entirely for granted.

And yet they hardly thought of each other as friends. They would never have designated someone as a best friend or a next-best friend, or joggled people around in these positions, the way girls did. Any one of at least a dozen boys could have been substituted for any one of these three, and accepted by the others in exactly the same way. Most members of that company were between nine and twelve years old, too old to be bound by yards and neighborhoods but too young to have jobs—even jobs sweeping the sidewalk in front of stores or delivering groceries by bicycle. Most of them lived in the north end of town, which meant that they would be expected to get a job of that sort as soon as they were old enough, and that none of them would ever be sent away to Appleby or to Upper Canada College. And none of them lived in a shack or had a relative in jail. Just the same, there were notable differences as to how they lived at home and what was expected of them in life. But these differences dropped away as soon as they were out of sight of the county jail and the grain elevator and the church steeples and out of range of the chimes of the courthouse clock.

On their way back they walked fast. Sometimes they trotted but did not run. Jumping, dallying, splashing were all abandoned, and the noises they'd made on their way out, the hoots and howls, were put aside as well. Any windfall of the flood was taken note of but passed by. In fact they made their way as adults would do, at a fairly steady speed and by the most reasonable route, with the weight on them of where they had to go and what had to be done next. They had something close in front of them, a picture in front of their eyes that came between them and the world, which was exactly the thing most adults seemed to have. The pond, the car, the arm, the hand. They had some idea that when they got to a certain spot they would start to shout. They would come into town yelling and waving their news around them and everybody would be stock still, taking it in.

They crossed the bridge the same way as always, on the shelf. But they had no sense of risk or courage or nonchalance. They might as well have taken the walkway.

Instead of following the sharp-turning road from which you could reach both the harbor and the square, they climbed straight up the bank on a path that came out near the railway sheds. The clock played its quarter-after chimes. A quarter after twelve.

This was the time when people were walking home for dinner. People from offices had the afternoon off. But people who worked in stores were getting only their customary hour—the stores stayed open till ten or eleven o'clock on Saturday night.

Most people were going home to a hot, filling meal. Pork chops, or sausages, or boiled beef, or cottage roll. Potatoes for certain, mashed or fried; winter-stored root vegetables or cabbage or creamed onions. (A few housewives, richer or more feckless, might have opened a tin of peas or butter beans.) Bread, muffins, preserves, pie. Even those people who didn't have a home to go to, or who for some reason didn't want to go there, would be sitting down to much the same sort of food at the Duke of Cumberland, or the Merchants' Hotel, or for less money behind the foggy windows of Shervill's Dairy Bar.

Those walking home were mostly men. The women were already there—they were there all the time. But some women of middle age who worked in stores or offices for a reason that was not their fault—dead husbands or sick husbands or never any husband at all—were friends of the boys' mothers, and they called out greetings even across the street (it was worst for Bud Salter, whom they called Buddy) in a certain amused or sprightly way that brought to mind all they knew of family matters, of distant infancies.

Men didn't bother greeting boys by name, even if they knew them well. They called them "boys" or "young fellows" or, occasionally, "sirs."

"Good day to you, sirs."

"You boys going straight home now?"

"What monkey business you young fellows been up to this morning?"

All these greetings had a degree of jocularity, but there were differences. The men who said "young fellows" were better disposed—or wished to seem better disposed—than the ones who said "boys." "Boys" could be the signal that a telling off was to follow, for offenses that could be either vague or specific. "Young fellows" indicated that the speaker had once been young himself. "Sirs" was outright mockery and disparagement but didn't open the way to any scolding, because the person who said that could not be bothered.

When answering, the boys didn't look up past any lady's purse or any man's Adam's apple. They said "Hullo" clearly because there might be some kind of trouble if you didn't, and in answer to queries they said "Yessir" and "Nosir" and "Nothing much." Even on this day, such voices speaking to them caused some alarm and confusion, and they replied with the usual reticence.

At a certain corner they had to separate. Cece Ferns, always the most anxious about getting home, pulled away first. He said, "See you after dinner."

Bud Salter said, "Yeah. We got to go downtown then."

This meant, as they all understood, "downtown to the Police Office." It seemed that without needing to consult each other they had taken up a new plan of operation, a soberer way of telling their news. But it wasn't clearly said that they wouldn't be telling anything at home. There wasn't any good reason why Bud Salter or Jimmy Box couldn't have done that.

Cece Ferns never told anything at home.

Cece Ferns was an only child. His parents were older than most boys' parents, or perhaps they only seemed older, because of the disabling life they lived together. When he got away from the other boys, Cece started to trot, as he usually did for the last block home. This was not because he was eager to get there or because he thought he could make anything better when he did. It may have been to make the time pass quickly, because the last block had to be full of apprehension.

His mother was in the kitchen. Good. She was out of bed though still in her wrapper. His father wasn't there, and that was good, too. His father worked at the grain elevator and got Saturday afternoon off, and if he wasn't home by now it was likely that he had gone straight to the Cumberland. That meant it would be late in the day before they had to deal with him.

Cece's father's name was Cece Ferns, too. It was a well-known and generally an affectionately known name in Walley, and some-body telling a story even thirty or forty years later would take it for granted that everybody would know it was the father who was being talked about, not the son. If a person relatively new in town said, "That doesn't sound like Cece," he would be told that nobody meant *that* Cece.

"Not him, we're talking about his old man."

They talked about the time Cece Ferns went to the hospital—or was taken there—with pneumonia, or some other desperate thing, and the nurses wrapped him in wet towels or sheets to get the fever down. The fever sweated out of him, and all the towels and sheets turned brown. It was the nicotine in him. The nurses had never seen anything like it. Cece was delighted. He claimed to have been smoking tobacco and drinking alcohol since he was ten years old.

And the time he went to church. It was hard to imagine why, but it was the Baptist church, and his wife was a Baptist, so perhaps he went to please her, though that was even harder to imagine. They were serving Communion the Sunday he went, and in the Baptist Church the bread is bread but the wine is grape juice. "What's this?" cried Cece Ferns aloud. "If this is the blood of the Lamb then He must've been pretty damn anemic."

Preparations for the noon meal were under way in the Fernses' kitchen. A loaf of sliced bread was sitting on the table and a can of diced beets had been opened. A few slices of bologna had been fried—before the eggs, though they should have been done after—and were being kept slightly warm on top of the stove. And now Cece's mother had started the eggs. She was bending over the stove with the egg lifter in one hand and the other hand pressed to her stomach, cradling a pain.

Cece took the egg lifter out of her hand and turned down the electric heat, which was way too high. He had to hold the pan off the burner while the burner cooled down, in order to keep the egg whites from getting too tough or burning at the edges. He hadn't been in time to wipe out the old grease and plop a bit of fresh lard in the pan. His mother never wiped out the old grease, just let it sit from one meal to the next and put in a bit of lard when she had to.

When the heat was more to his liking, he put the pan down and coaxed the lacy edges of the eggs into tidy circles. He found a clean spoon and dribbled a little hot fat over the yokes to set them. He and his mother liked their eggs cooked this way, but his mother often couldn't manage it right. His father liked his eggs turned over and flattened out like pancakes, cooked hard as shoe leather and blackened with pepper. Cece could cook them the way he wanted, too.

None of the other boys knew how practiced he was in the kitchen—just as none of them knew about the hiding place he had made outside the house in the blind corner past the dining-room window, behind the Japanese barberry.

His mother sat in the chair by the window while he was finishing up the eggs. She kept an eye on the street. There was still a chance that his father would come home for something to eat. He might not be drunk yet. But the way he behaved didn't always depend on how drunk he was. If he came into the kitchen now he might tell Cece to make him some eggs, too. Then he might ask him where his apron was and say that he would make some fellow a dandy wife. That would be how he'd behave if he was in a good mood. In another sort of mood he would start off by staring at Cece in a certain way—that is, with an exaggerated, absurdly threatening expression—and telling him he better watch out.

"Smart bugger, aren't you? Well, all I got to say to you is, better watch out."

Then if Cece looked back at him, or maybe if he didn't look back, or if he dropped the egg lifter or set it down with a clatter—or even if he was sliding around being extra cautious about not dropping anything and not making a noise—his father was apt to start showing his teeth and snarling like a dog. It would have been ridiculous—it was ridiculous—except that he meant business. A minute later the food and the dishes might be on the floor and the chairs or the table overturned and he might be chasing Cece around the room yelling how he was going to get him this time, flatten his face on the hot burner, how would he like that? You would be certain he'd gone crazy. But if at this moment a knock came at the door—if a friend of his arrived, say, to pick him up—his face would reassemble itself in no time and he would open the door and call out the friend's name in a loud bantering voice.

"I'll be with you in two shakes. I'd ask you in, but the wife's been pitching the dishes around again."

He didn't intend this to be believed. He said such things in order to turn whatever happened in his house into a joke.

Cece's mother asked him if the weather was warming up and where he had been that morning.

"Yeah," he said, and, "Out on the flats."

She said that she'd thought she could smell the wind on him.

"You know what I'm going to do right after we eat?" she said. "I'm going to take a hot-water bottle and go right back to bed and maybe I'll get my strength back and feel like doing something."

That was what she nearly always said she was going to do, but she always announced it as if it were an idea that had just occurred to her, a hopeful decision.

Bud Salter had two older sisters who never did anything useful unless his mother made them. And they never confined their hair arranging, nail polishing, shoe cleaning, making up, or even dressing activities to their bedrooms or the bathroom. They spread their combs and curlers and face powder and nail polish and shoe polish all over the house. Also they loaded every chair back with their newly ironed dresses and blouses and spread out their drying sweaters on towels on every clear space of floor. (Then they screamed at you if you walked near them.) They stationed themselves in front of various mirrors—the mirror in the hall coat stand, the mirror in the dining-room buffet, and the mirror beside the kitchen door with the shelf underneath always loaded with safety pins, bobby pins, pennies, buttons, bits of pencils. Sometimes one of them would stand in front of a mirror for twenty minutes or so, checking herself from various angles, inspecting her teeth and pulling her hair back then shaking it forward. Then she would walk away apparently satisfied or at least finished—but only as far as the next room, the next mirror, where she would begin all over again just as if she had been delivered a new head.

Right now his older sister, the one who was supposed to be good-looking, was taking the pins out of her hair in front of the kitchen mirror. Her head was covered with shiny curls like snails. His other sister, on orders from his mother, was mashing the potatoes. His five-year-old brother was sitting in place at the table, banging his knife and fork up and down and yelling, "Want some service. Want some service."

He got that from their father, who did it for a joke.

Bud passed by his brother's chair and said quietly, "Look. She's putting lumps in the mashed potatoes again."

He had his brother convinced that lumps were something you added, like raisins to rice pudding, from a supply in the cupboard.

His brother stopped chanting and began complaining.

"I won't eat none if she puts in lumps. Mama, I won't eat none if she puts in lumps."

"Oh, don't be silly," Bud's mother said. She was frying apple slices and onion rings with the pork chops. "Quit whining like a baby."

"It was Bud got him started," the older sister said. "Bud went and told him she was putting lumps in. Bud always tells him that and he doesn't know any better."

"Bud ought to get his face smashed," said Doris, the sister who was mashing the potatoes. She didn't always say such things idly— she had once left a claw scar down the side of Bud's cheek.

Bud went over to the dresser, where there was a rhubarb pie cooling. He took a fork and began carefully, secretly prying at it, letting out delicious steam, a delicate smell of cinnamon. He was trying to open one of the vents in the top of it so that he could get a taste of the filling. His brother saw what he was doing but was too scared to say anything. His brother was spoiled and was defended by his sisters all the time—Bud was the only person in the house he respected.

"Want some service," he repeated, speaking now in a thoughtful undertone.

Doris came over to the dresser to get the bowl for the mashed potatoes. Bud made an incautious movement, and part of the top crust caved in.

"So now he's wrecking the pie," Doris said. "Mama—he's wrecking your pie."

"Shut your damn mouth," Bud said.

"Leave that pie alone," said Bud's mother with a practiced, al- most serene severity. "Stop swearing. Stop tattle-telling. Grow up."

□ □ □ □

Jimmy Box sat down to dinner at a crowded table. He and his father and his mother and his four-year-old and six-year-old sisters lived in his grandmother's house with his grandmother and his great-aunt Mary and his bachelor uncle. His father had a bicycle-repair shop in the shed behind the house, and his mother worked in Honeker's Department Store.

Jimmy's father was crippled—the result of a polio attack when he was twenty-two years old. He walked bent forward from the hips, using a cane. This didn't show so much when he was working in the shop, because such work often means being bent over anyway. When he walked along the street he did look very strange, but nobody called him names or did an imitation of him. He had once been a notable hockey player and baseball player for the town, and some of the grace and valor of the past still hung around him, putting his present state into perspective, so that it could be seen as a phase (though a final one). He helped this perception along by cracking silly jokes and taking an optimistic tone, denying the pain that showed in his sunken eyes and kept him awake many nights. And, unlike Cece Fern's father, he didn't change his tune when he came into his own house.

But, of course, it wasn't his own house. His wife had married him after he was crippled, though she had got engaged to him before, and it seemed the natural thing to do to move in with her mother, so that the mother could look after any children who came along while the wife went on working at her job. It seemed the natural thing to the wife's mother as well, to take on another family—just as it seemed natural that her sister Mary should move in with the rest of them when her eyesight failed, and that her son Fred, who was extraordinarily shy, should continue to live at home unless he found some place he liked better. This was a family who accepted burdens of one kind or another with even less fuss than they accepted the weather. In fact, nobody in that house would have spoken of Jimmy's father's condition or Aunt Mary's eyesight as burdens or problems, any more than they would of Fred's shyness. Drawbacks and adversity were not to be noticed, not to be distinguished from their opposites.

There was a traditional belief in the family that Jimmy's grandmother was an excellent cook, and this might have been true at one time, but in recent years there had been a falling off. Economies were practiced beyond what there was any need for now. Jimmy's mother and his uncle made decent wages and his Aunt Mary got a pension and the bicycle shop was fairly busy, but one egg was used instead of three and the meat loaf got an extra cup of oatmeal. There was an attempt to compensate by overdoing the Worcestershire sauce or sprinkling too much nutmeg on the custard. But nobody complained. Everybody praised. Complaints were as rare as lightning balls in that house. And everybody said "Excuse me," even the little girls said "Excuse me," when they bumped into each other. Everybody passed and pleased and thank-you'd at the table as if there were company every day. This was the way they managed, all of them crammed so tight in the house, with clothes piled on every hook, coats hung over the bannister, and cots set up permanently in the dining room for Jimmy and his Uncle Fred, and the buffet hidden under a load of clothing waiting to be ironed or mended. Nobody pounded on the stairsteps or shut doors hard or turned the radio up loud or said anything disagreeable.

Did this explain why Jimmy kept his mouth shut that Saturday at dinnertime? They all kept their mouths shut, all three of them. In Cece's case it was easy to understand. His father would never have stood for Cece's claiming so important a discovery. He would have called him a liar as a matter of course. And Cece's mother, judging everything by the effect it would have on his father, would have understood—correctly—that even his going to the Police Office with his story would cause disruption at home, so she would have told him to please just keep quiet. But the two other boys lived in quite reasonable homes and they could have spoken. In Jimmy's house there would have been consternation and some disapproval, but soon enough they would have admitted that it was not Jimmy's fault.

Bud's sisters would have asked if he was crazy. They might even have twisted things around to imply that it was just like him, with his unpleasant habits, to come upon a dead body. His father, however, was a sensible, patient man, used to listening to many strange rigmaroles in his job, as a freight agent at the railway station. He would have made Bud's sisters shut up, and after some serious talk to make sure Bud was telling the truth and not exaggerating he would have phoned the Police Office.

It was just that their houses seemed too full. Too much was going on already. This was true in Cece's house just as much as in the others, because even in his father's absence there was the threat and memory all the time of his haywire presence.

"Did you tell?"

"Did you?"

"Me neither."

They walked downtown, not thinking about the way they were going. They turned on to Shipka Street and found themselves going past the stucco bungalow where Mr. and Mrs. Willens lived. They were right in front of it before they recognized it. It had a small bay window on either side of the front door and a top step wide enough for two chairs, not there at present but occupied on summer evenings by Mr. Willens and his wife. There was a flat-roofed addition to one side of the house, with another door opening toward the street and a separate walk leading up to it. A sign beside that door said "D. M. Willens, Optometrist." None of the boys themselves had visited that office, but Jimmy's Aunt Mary went there regularly for her eyedrops, and his grandmother got her glasses there. So did Bud Salter's mother.

The stucco was a muddy pink color and the doors and window frames were painted brown. The storm windows had not been taken off yet, as they hadn't from most of the houses in town. There was nothing special at all about the house, but the front yard was famous for its flowers. Mrs. Willens was a renowned gardener who didn't grow her flowers in long rows beside the vegetable garden, as Jimmy's grandmother and Bud's mother grew theirs. She had them in round beds and crescent beds and all over, and in circles under the trees. In a couple of weeks daffodils would fill this lawn. But at present the only thing in bloom was a forsythia bush at the corner of the house. It was nearly as high as the eaves and it sprayed yellow into the air the way a fountain shoots water.

The forsythia shook, not with the wind, and out came a stooped brown figure. It was Mrs. Willens in her old gardening clothes, a lumpy little woman in baggy slacks and a ripped jacket and a peaked cap that might have been her husband's—it slipped down too low and almost hid her eyes. She was carrying a pair of shears.

They slowed right down—it was either that or run. Maybe they thought that she wouldn't notice them, that they could turn themselves into posts. But she had seen them already; that was why she came hastening through.

"I see you're gawking at my forsythia," said Mrs. Willens. "Would you like some to take home?"

What they had been gawking at was not the forsythia but the whole scene—the house looking just as usual, the sign by the office door, the curtains letting light in. Nothing hollow or ominous, nothing that said that Mr. Willens was not inside and that his car was not in the garage behind his office but in Jutland Pond. And Mrs. Willens out working in her yard, where anybody would expect her to be—everybody in town said so—the minute the snow was melted. And calling out in her familiar tobacco-roughened voice, abrupt and challenging but not unfriendly—a voice indentifiable half a block away or coming from the back of any store.

"Wait," she said. "Wait, now, I'll get you some."

She began smartly, selectively snapping off the bright-yellow branches, and when she had all she wanted she came toward them behind a screen of flowers.

"Here you are," she said. "Take these home to your mothers. It's always good to see the forsythia, it's the very first thing in the spring." She was dividing the branches among them. "Like all Gaul," she said. "All Gaul is divided into three parts. You must know about that if you take Latin."

"We aren't in high school yet," said Jimmy, whose life at home had readied him, better than the others, for talking to ladies.

"Aren't you?" she said. "Well, you've got all sorts of things to look forward to. Tell your mothers to put them in lukewarm water. Oh, I'm sure they already know that. I've given you branches that aren't all the way out yet, so they should last and last."

They said thank you—Jimmy first and the others picking it up from him. They walked toward downtown with their arms loaded. They had no intention of turning back and taking the flowers home, and they counted on her not having any good idea of where their homes were. Half a block on, they sneaked looks back to see if she was watching.

She wasn't. The big house near the sidewalk blocked the view in any case.

The forsythia gave them something to think about. The embarrassment of carrying it, the problem of getting rid of it. Otherwise, they would have to think about Mr. Willens and Mrs. Willens. How she could be busy in her yard and he could be drowned in his car. Did she know where he was or did she not? It seemed that she couldn't. Did she even know that he was gone? She had acted as if there was nothing wrong, nothing at all, and when they were standing in front of her this had seemed to be the truth. What they knew, what they had seen, seemed actually to be pushed back, to be defeated, by her not knowing it.

Two girls on bicycles came wheeling around the corner. One was Bud's sister Doris. At once these girls began to hoot and yell.

"Oh, look at the flowers," they shouted. "Where's the wedding? Look at the beautiful bridesmaids."

Bud yelled back the worst thing he could think of.

"You got blood all over your arse."

Of course she didn't, but there had been an occasion when this had really been so—she had come home from school with blood on her skirt. Everybody had seen it and it would never be forgotten.

He was sure she would tell on him at home, but she never did. Her shame about that other time was so great that she could not refer to it even to get him in trouble.

They realized then that they had to dump the flowers at once, so they simply threw the branches under a parked car. They brushed a few stray petals off their clothes as they turned on to the square.

Saturdays were still important then; they brought the country people into town. Cars were already parked around the square and on the side streets. Big country boys and girls and smaller children from the town and the country were heading for the movie mati-née.

It was necessary to pass Honeker's in the first block. And there, in full view in one of the windows, Jimmy saw his mother. Back at work already, she was putting the hat straight on a female dummy, adjusting the veil, then fiddling with the shoulders of the dress. She was a short woman and she had to stand on tiptoe to do this properly. She had taken off her shoes to walk on the window carpet. You could see the rosy plump cushions of her heels through her stockings, and when she stretched you saw the back of her knee through the slit in her skirt. Above that was a wide but shapely behind and the line of her panties or girdle. Jimmy could hear in his mind the little grunts she would be making; also he could smell the stockings that she sometimes took off as soon as she got home, to save them from runs. Stockings and underwear, even clean fe-male underwear, had a faint, private smell that was both appealing and disgusting.

He hoped two things. That the others hadn't noticed her (they had, but the idea of a mother dressed up every day and out in the public world of town was so strange to them that they couldn't comment, could only dismiss it) and that she would not, please not, turn around and spot him. She was capable, if she did that, of rapping on the glass and mouthing hello. At work she lost the hushed discretion, the studied gentleness, of home. Her obliging-ness turned from meek to pert. He used to be delighted by this other side of her, this friskiness, just as he was by Honeker's, with its extensive counters of glass and varnished wood, its big mirrors at the top of the staircase, in which he could see himself climbing up to Ladies' Wear, on the second floor.

"Here's my young mischief," his mother would say, and some-times slip him a dime. He could never stay more than a minute; Mr. or Mrs. Honeker might be watching.

Young mischief.

Words that were once as pleasant to hear as the tinkle of dimes and nickels had now turned slyly shaming.

They were safely past.

In the next block they had to pass the Duke of Cumberland, but

Cece had no worries. If his father had not come home at dinner-time, it meant he would be in there for hours yet. But the word "Cumberland" always fell across his mind heavily. From the days when he hadn't even known what it meant, he got a sense of sorrowful plummeting. A weight hitting dark water, far down.

Between the Cumberland and the Town Hall was an unpaved alley, and at the back of the Town Hall was the Police Office. They turned into this alley and soon a lot of new noise reached them, opposing the street noise. It was not from the Cumberland—the noise in there was all muffled up, the beer parlor having only small, high windows like a public toilet. It was coming from the Police Office. The door to that office was open on account of the mild weather, and even out in the alley you could smell the pipe tobacco and cigars. It wasn't just the policemen who sat in there, especially on Saturday afternoons, with the stove going in winter and the fan in summer and the door open to let in the pleasant air on an in-between day like today. Colonel Box would be there—in fact, they could already hear the wheeze he made, the long-drawn-out after-effects of his asthmatic laughter. He was a relative of Jimmy's, but there was a coolness in the family because he did not approve of Jimmy's father's marriage. He spoke to Jimmy, when he recognized him, in a surprised, ironic tone of voice. "If he ever offers you a quarter or anything, you say you don't need it," Jimmy's mother had told him. But Colonel Box had never made such an offer.

Also, Mr. Pollock would be there, who had retired from the drugstore, and Fergus Solley, who was not a half-wit but looked like one, because he had been gassed in the First World War. All day these men and others played cards, smoked, told stories, and drank coffee at the town's expense (as Bud's father said). Anybody wanting to make a complaint or a report had to do it within sight of them and probably within earshot.

Run the gantlet.

They came almost to a stop outside the open door. Nobody had noticed them. Colonel Box said, "I'm not dead yet," repeating the final line of some story. They began to walk past slowly with their heads down, kicking at the gravel. Round the corner of the building they picked up speed. By the entry to the Men's Public Toilet there was a recent streak of lumpy vomit on the wall and a couple of empty bottles on the gravel. They had to walk between the refuse bins and the high watchful windows of the Town Clerk's office, and then they were off the gravel, back on the square.

"I got money," Cece said. This matter-of-fact announcement brought them all relief. Cece jingled change in his pocket. It was the money his mother had given him after he washed up the dishes, when he went into the front bedroom to tell her he was going out. "Help yourself to fifty cents off the dresser," she had said. Sometimes she had money, though he never saw his father give her any. And whenever she said "Help yourself" or gave him a few coins, Cece understood that she was ashamed of their life, ashamed for him and in front of him, and these were the times when he hated the sight of her (though he was glad of the money). Especially if she said that he was a good boy and he was not to think she wasn't grateful for all he did.

They took the street that led down to the harbor. At the side of Paquette's Service Station there was a booth from which Mrs. Paquette sold hot dogs, ice cream, candy, and cigarettes. She had refused to sell them cigarettes even when Jimmy said they were for his Uncle Fred. But she didn't hold it against them that they'd tried. She was a fat, pretty woman, a French Canadian.

They bought some licorice whips, black and red. They meant to buy some ice cream later when they weren't so full from dinner. They went over to where there were two old car seats set up by the fence under a tree that gave shade in summer. They shared out the licorice whips.

Captain Tervitt was sitting on the other seat.

Captain Tervitt had been a real captain, for many years, on the lake boats. Now he had a job as a Special Constable. He stopped cars to let the children cross the street in front of the school and kept them from sledding down the side street in winter. He blew his whistle and held up one big hand, which looked like a clown's hand, in a white glove. He was still tall and straight and broad-shouldered, though old and white-haired. Cars would do what he said, and children, too.

At night he went around checking the doors of all the stores to see that they were locked and to make sure that there was nobody inside committing a burglary. During the day he often slept in public. When the weather was bad he slept in the library and when it was good he chose some seat out-of-doors. He didn't spend much time in the Police Office, probably because he was too deaf to follow the conversation without his hearing aid in, and like many deaf people he hated his hearing aid. And he was used to being solitary, surely, staring out over the bow of the lake boats.

His eyes were closed and his head tilted back so that he could get the sun in his face. When they went over to talk to him (and the decision to do this was made without any consultation, beyond one resigned and dubious look) they had to wake him from his doze. His face took a moment to register—where and when and who. Then he took a large old-fashioned watch out of his pocket, as if he counted on children always wanting to be told the time. But they went on talking to him, with their expressions agitated and slightly shamed. They were saying, "Mr. Willens is out in Jutland Pond," and "We seen the car," and "Drowned." He had to hold up his hand and make shushing motions while the other hand went rooting around in his pants pocket and came up with his hearing aid. He nodded his head seriously, encouragingly, as if to say, "Patience, patience," while he got the device settled in his ear. Then both hands up—be still, be still—while he was testing. Finally another nod, of a brisker sort, and in a stern voice—but making a joke to some extent of his sternness—he said, "Proceed."

Cece, who was the quietest of the three—as Jimmy was the politest and Bud the mouthiest—was the one who turned everything around.

"Your fly's undone," he said.

Then they all whooped and ran away. The jolt of freedom, the joy of outrage, the uttermost trespass.

Their elation did not vanish right away. But it was not something that could be shared or spoken about: they had to pull apart.

Cece went home to work on his hideaway. The cardboard floor, which had been frozen through the winter, was sodden now and needed to be replaced. Jimmy climbed into the loft of the garage, where he had recently discovered a box of old Doc Savage maga-zines that had once belonged to his Uncle Fred. Bud went home and found nobody there but his mother, who was waxing the din-ing-room floor. He looked at comic books for an hour or so and then he told her. He believed that his mother had no experience or authority outside their house and that she would not make up her mind about what to do until she had phoned his father. To his surprise, she immediately phoned the police. Then she phoned his father. And somebody went to round up Cece and Jimmy.

A police car drove in to Jutland from the township road, and all was confirmed. A policeman and the Anglican minister went to see Mrs. Willens.

"I didn't want to bother you," Mrs. Willens was reported to have said. "I was going to give him till dark."

She told them that Mr. Willens had driven out to the country yesterday afternoon to take some drops to an old blind man. Some-times he got held up, she said. He visited people, or the car got stuck.

Was he downhearted or anything like that? the policeman asked her.

"Oh, surely not," the minister said. "He was the bulwark of the choir."

"The word was not in his vocabulary," said Mrs. Willens.

Something was made of the boys' sitting down and eating their dinners and never saying a word. And then buying a bunch of licorice whips. A new nickname—Deadman—was found and set-tled on each of them. Jimmy and Bud bore it till they left town, and Cece—who married young and went to work in the elevator—saw it passed on to his two sons. By that time nobody thought of what it referred to.

The insult to Captain Tervitt remained a secret.

Each of them expected some reminder, some lofty look of injury or judgment, the next time they had to pass under his uplifted arm, crossing the street to the school. But he held up his gloved hand, his noble and clownish white hand, with his usual benevolent compo-sure. He gave consent.

Proceed.

II. Heart Failure

"Glomerulonephritis," Enid wrote in her notebook. It was the first case that she had ever seen. The fact was that Mrs. Quinn's kidneys were failing, and nothing could be done about it. Her kidneys were drying up and turning into hard and useless granular lumps. Her urine at present was scanty and had a smoky look, and the smell that came out on her breath and through her skin was acrid and ominous. And there was another, fainter smell, like rotted fruit, that seemed to Enid related to the pale lavender-brown stains appearing on her body. Her legs twitched in spasms of sudden pain and her skin was subject to a violent itching, so that Enid had to rub her with ice. She wrapped the ice in towels and pressed the packs to the spots in torment.

"How do you contract that kind of a disease anyhow?" said Mrs. Quinn's sister-in-law. Her name was Mrs. Green. Olive Green. (It had never occured to her how that would sound, she said, until she got married and all of a sudden everybody was laughing at it.) She lived on a farm a few miles away, out on the highway, and every few days she came and took the sheets and towels and nightdresses away to wash. She did the children's washing as well, brought everything back freshly ironed and folded. She even ironed the ribbons on the nightdresses. Enid was grateful to her—she had been on jobs where she had to do the laundry herself, or, worse still, load it onto her mother, who would pay to have it done in town. Not wanting to offend but seeing which way the questions were tending, she said, "It's hard to tell."

"Because you hear one thing and another," Mrs. Green said. "You hear that sometimes a woman might take some pills. They get these pills to take for when their period is late and if they take them just like the doctor says and for a good purpose that's fine, but if they take too many and for a bad purpose their kidneys are wrecked. Am I right?"

"I've never come in contact with a case like that," Enid said.

Mrs. Green was a tall, stout woman. Like her brother Rupert, who was Mrs. Quinn's husband, she had a round, snub-nosed, agreeably wrinkled face—the kind that Enid's mother called "potato Irish." But behind Rupert's good-humored expression there was wariness and withholding. And behind Mrs. Green's there was yearning. Enid did not know for what. To the simplest conversation Mrs. Green brought a huge demand. Maybe it was just a yearning for news. News of something momentous. An event.

Of course, an event was coming, something momentous at least in this family. Mrs. Quinn was going to die, at the age of twenty-seven. (That was the age she gave herself—Enid would have put some years on it, but once an illness had progressed this far age was hard to guess.) When her kidneys stopped working altogether, her heart would give out and she would die. The doctor had said to Enid, "This'll take you into the summer, but the chances are you'll get some kind of a holiday before the hot weather's over."

"Rupert met her when he went up north," Mrs. Green said. "He went off by himself, he worked in the bush up there. She had some kind of a job in a hotel. I'm not sure what. Chambermaid job. She wasn't raised up there, though—she says she was raised in an orphanage in Montreal. She can't help that. You'd expect her to speak French, but if she does she don't let on."

Enid said, "An interesting life."

"You can say that again."

"An interesting life," said Enid. Sometimes she couldn't help it—she tried a joke where it had hardly a hope of working. She raised her eyebrows encouragingly, and Mrs. Green did smile.

But was she hurt? That was just the way Rupert would smile, in high school, warding off some possible mockery.

"He never had any kind of a girlfriend before that," said Mrs. Green.

Enid had been in the same class as Rupert, though she did not mention that to Mrs. Green. She felt some embarrassment now because he was one of the boys—in fact, the main one—that she and her girlfriends had teased and tormented. "Picked on," as they used to say. They had picked on Rupert, following him up the street calling out, "Hello, Rupert. Hello, Ru-pert," putting him into a state of agony, watching his neck go red. "Rupert's got scarlet fever," they would say. "Rupert, you should be quarantined." And they would pretend that one of them—Enid, Joan McAuliffe, Marian Denny—had a case on him. "She wants to speak to you, Rupert. Why don't you ever ask her out? You could phone her up at least. She's dying to talk to you."

They did not really expect him to respond to these pleading overtures. But what joy if he had. He would have been rejected in short order and the story broadcast all over the school. Why? Why did they treat him this way, long to humiliate him? Simply because they could.

Impossible that he would have forgotten. But he treated Enid as if she were a new acquaintance, his wife's nurse, come into his house from anywhere at all. And Enid took her cue from him.

Things had been unusually well arranged here, to spare her extra work. Rupert slept at Mrs. Green's house, and ate his meals there. The two little girls could have been there as well, but it would have meant putting them into another school—there was nearly a month to go before school was out for the summer.

Rupert came into the house in the evenings and spoke to his children.

"Are you being good girls?" he said.

"Show Daddy what you made with your blocks," said Enid. "Show Daddy your pictures in the coloring book."

The blocks, the crayons, the coloring books were all provided by Enid. She had phoned her mother and asked her to see what things she could find in the old trunks. Her mother had done that, and brought along as well an old book of cutout dolls which she had collected from someone—Princess Elizabeth and Margaret Rose and their many outfits. Enid hadn't been able to get the little girls to say thank you until she put all these things on a high shelf and announced that they would stay there till thank you was said. Lois and Sylvie were seven and six years old, and as wild as little barn cats.

Rupert didn't ask where the playthings came from. He told his daughters to be good girls and asked Enid if there was anything she needed from town. Once she told him that she had replaced the light bulb in the cellarway and that he could get her some spare bulbs.

"I could have done that," he said.

"I don't have any trouble with light bulbs," said Enid. "Or fuses or knocking in nails. My mother and I have done without a man around the house for a long time now." She meant to tease a little, to be friendly, but it didn't work.

Finally Rupert would ask about his wife, and Enid would say that her blood pressure was down slightly, or that she had eaten and kept down part of an omelette for supper, or that the ice packs seemed to ease her itchy skin and she was sleeping better. And Rupert would say that if she was sleeping he'd better not go in.

Enid said, "Nonsense." To see her husband would do a woman more good than to have a little doze. She took the children up to bed then, to give man and wife a time of privacy. But Rupert never stayed more than a few minutes. And when Enid came back downstairs and went into the front room—now the sickroom—to ready the patient for the night, Mrs. Quinn would be lying back against the pillows, looking agitated but not dissatisfied.

"Doesn't hang around here very long, does he?" Mrs. Quinn would say. "Makes me laugh. Ha-ha-ha, how-are-you? Ha-ha-ha, off-we-go. Why don't we take her out and throw her on the manure pile? Why don't we just dump her out like a dead cat? That's what he's thinking. Isn't he?"

"I doubt it," said Enid, bringing the basin and towels, the rubbing alcohol and the baby powder.

"I doubt it," said Mrs. Quinn quite viciously, but she submitted readily enough to having her nightgown removed, her hair smoothed back from her face, a towel slid under her hips. Enid was used to people making a fuss about being naked, even when they were very old or very ill. Sometimes she would have to tease them or badger them into common sense. "Do you think I haven't seen any bottom parts before?" she would say. "Bottom parts, top parts, it's pretty boring after a while. You know, there's just the two ways we're made." But Mrs. Quinn was without shame, opening her legs and raising herself a bit to make the job easier. She was a little bird-boned woman, queerly shaped now, with her swollen abdomen and limbs and her breasts shrunk to tiny pouches with dried-currant nipples.

"Swole up like some kind of pig," Mrs. Quinn said. "Except for my tits, and they always were kind of useless. I never had no big udders on me, like you. Don't you get sick of the sight of me? Won't you be glad when I'm dead?"

"If I felt like that I wouldn't be here," said Enid.

"Good riddance to bad rubbish," said Mrs. Quinn. "That's what you'll all say. Good riddance to bad rubbish. I'm no use to him anymore, am I? I'm no use to any man. He goes out of here every night and he goes to pick up women, doesn't he?"

"As far as I know, he goes to his sister's house."

"As far as you know. But you don't know much."

Enid thought she knew what this meant, this spite and venom, the energy saved for ranting. Mrs. Quinn was flailing about for an enemy. Sick people grew to resent well people, and sometimes that was true of husbands and wives, or even of mothers and their children. Both husband and children in Mrs. Quinn's case. On a Saturday morning, Enid called Lois and Sylvie from their games under the porch, to come and see their mother looking pretty. Mrs. Quinn had just had her morning wash, and was in a clean nightgown, with her fine, sparse, fair hair brushed and held back by a blue ribbon. (Enid took a supply of these ribbons with her when she went to nurse a female patient—also a bottle of cologne and a cake of scented soap.) She did look pretty—or you could see at least that she had once been pretty, with her wide forehead and cheekbones (they almost punched the skin now, like china doorknobs) and her large greenish eyes and childish translucent teeth and small stubborn chin.

The children came into the room obediently if unenthusiastically. Mrs. Quinn said, "Keep them off of my bed, they're filthy."

"They just want to see you," said Enid.

"Well, now they've seen me," said Mrs. Quinn. "Now they can go."

This behavior didn't seem to surprise or disappoint the children. They looked at Enid, and Enid said, "All right, now, your mother better have a rest," and they ran out and slammed the kitchen door.

"Can't you get them to quit doing that?" Mrs. Quinn said. "Every time they do it, it's like a brick hits me in my chest."

You would think these two daughters of hers were a pair of rowdy orphans, wished on her for an indefinite visit. But that was the way some people were, before they settled down to their dying and sometimes even up to the event itself. People of a gentler nature—it would seem—than Mrs. Quinn might say that they knew how much their brothers, sisters, husbands, wives, and children had always hated them, how much of a disappointment they had been to others and others had been to them, and how glad they knew everybody would be to see them gone. They might say this at the end of peaceful, useful lives in the midst of loving families, where there was no explanation at all for such fits. And usually the fits passed. But often, too, in the last weeks or even days of life there was mulling over of old feuds and slights or whimpering about some unjust punishment suffered seventy years earlier. Once a woman had asked Enid to bring her a willow platter from the cupboard and Enid had thought that she wanted the comfort of looking at this one pretty possession for the last time. But it turned out that she wanted to use her last, surprising strength to smash it against the bedpost.

"Now I know my sister's never going to get her hands on that," she said.

And often people remarked that their visitors were only coming to gloat and that the doctor was responsible for their sufferings. They detested the sight of Enid herself, for her sleepless strength and patient hands and the way the juices of life were so admirably balanced and flowing in her. Enid was used to that, and she was able to understand the trouble they were in, the trouble of dying and also the trouble of their lives that sometimes overshadowed that.

But with Mrs. Quinn she was at a loss.

It was not just that she couldn't supply comfort here. It was that she couldn't want to. She could not conquer her dislike of this doomed, miserable young woman. She disliked this body that she had to wash and powder and placate with ice and alcohol rubs. She understood now what people meant when they said that they hated sickness and sick bodies; she understood the women who had said to her, I don't know how you do it, I could never be a nurse, that's the one thing I could never be. She disliked this particular body, all the particular signs of its disease. The smell of it and the discoloration, the malignant-looking little nipples and the pathetic ferret-like teeth. She saw all this as the sign of a willed corruption. She was as bad as Mrs. Green, sniffing out rampant impurity. In spite of being a nurse who knew better, and in spite of it being her job—and surely her nature—to be compassionate. She didn't know why this was happening. Mrs. Quinn reminded her somewhat of girls she had known in high school—cheaply dressed, sickly-looking girls with dreary futures, who still displayed a hard-faced satisfaction with themselves. They lasted only a year or two—they got pregnant, most of them got married. Enid had nursed some of them in later years, in home childbirth, and found their confidence exhausted and their bold streak turned into meekness, or even piety. She was sorry for them, even when she remembered how determined they had been to get what they had got.

Mrs. Quinn was a harder case. Mrs. Quinn might crack and crack, but there would be nothing but sullen mischief, nothing but rot inside her.

Worse even than the fact that Enid should feel this revulsion was the fact that Mrs. Quinn knew it. No patience or gentleness or cheerfulness that Enid could summon would keep Mrs. Quinn from knowing. And Mrs. Quinn made knowing it her triumph.

Good riddance to bad rubbish.

When Enid was twenty years old, and had almost finished her nurse's training, her father was dying in the Walley hospital. That was when he said to her, "I don't know as I care for this career of yours. I don't want you working in a place like this."

Enid bent over him and asked what sort of place he thought he was in. "It's only the Walley hospital," she said.

"I know that," said her father, sounding as calm and reasonable as he had always done (he was an insurance and real-estate agent). "I know what I'm talking about. Promise me you won't."

"Promise you what?" said Enid.

"You won't do this kind of work," her father said. She could not get any further explanation out of him. He tightened up his mouth as if her questioning disgusted him. All he would say was "Promise."

"What is all this about?" Enid asked her mother, and her mother said, "Oh, go ahead. Go ahead and promise him. What difference is it going to make?"

Enid thought this a shocking thing to say, but made no comment. It was consistent with her mother's way of looking at a lot of things.

"I'm not going to promise anything I don't understand," she said. "I'm probably not going to promise anything anyway. But if you know what he's talking about you ought to tell me."

"It's just this idea he's got now," her mother said. "He's got an idea that nursing makes a woman coarse."

Enid said, "Coarse."

Her mother said that the part of nursing her father objected to was the familiarity nurses had with men's bodies. Her father thought—he had decided—that such familiarity would change a girl, and furthermore that it would change the way men thought about that girl. It would spoil her good chances and give her a lot of other chances that were not so good. Some men would lose interest and others would become interested in the wrong way.

"I suppose it's all mixed up with wanting you to get married," her mother said.

"Too bad if it is," said Enid.

But she ended up promising. And her mother said, "Well, I hope that makes you happy." Not "makes him happy." Makes *you*. It seemed that her mother had known before Enid did just how tempting this promise would be. The deathbed promise, the self-denial, the wholesale sacrifice. And the more absurd the better. This was what she had given in to. And not for love of her father, either (her mother implied), but for the thrill of it. Sheer noble perversity.

"If he'd asked you to give up something you didn't care one way or the other about, you'd probably have told him nothing doing," her mother said. "If for instance he'd asked you to give up wearing lipstick. You'd still be wearing it."

Enid listened to this with a patient expression.

"Did you pray about it?" said her mother sharply.

Enid said yes.

She withdrew from nursing school; she stayed at home and kept busy. There was enough money that she did not have to work. In fact, her mother had not wanted Enid to go into nursing in the first place, claiming that it was something poor girls did, it was a way out for girls whose parents couldn't keep them or send them to college. Enid did not remind her of this inconsistency. She painted a fence, she tied up the rosebushes for winter. She learned to bake and she learned to play bridge, taking her father's place in the weekly games her mother played with Mr. and Mrs. Willens from next door. In no time at all she became—as Mr. Willens said—a scandalously good player. He took to turning up with chocolates or a pink rose for her, to make up for his own inadequacies as a partner.

She went skating in the winter evenings. She played badminton.

She had never lacked friends, and she didn't now. Most of the people who had been in the last year of high school with her were finishing college now, or were already working at a distance, as teachers or nurses or chartered accountants. But she made friends with others who had dropped out before senior year to work in banks or stores or offices, to become plumbers or milliners. The girls in this group were dropping like flies, as they said of each other—they were dropping into matrimony. Enid was an organizer of bridal showers and a help at trousseau teas. In a couple of years would come the christenings, where she could expect to be a favorite godmother. Children not related to her would grow up calling her Aunt. And she was already a sort of honorary daughter to women of her mother's age and older, the only young woman who had time for the Book Club and the Horticultural Society. So, quickly and easily, still in her youth, she was slipping into this essential, central, yet isolated role.

But in fact it had been her role all along. In high school she was always the class secretary or class social convener. She was well liked and high-spirited and well dressed and good-looking, but she was slightly set apart. She had friends who were boys but never a boyfriend. She did not seem to have made a choice this way, but she was not worried about it, either. She had been preoccupied with her ambition—to be a missionary, at one embarrassing stage, and then to be a nurse. She had never thought of nursing as just something to do until she got married. Her hope was to be good, and do good, and not necessarily in the orderly, customary, wifely way.

At New Year's she went to the dance in the Town Hall. The man who danced with her most often, and escorted her home, and pressed her hand good night, was the manager of the creamery—a man in his forties, never married, an excellent dancer, an avuncular friend to girls unlikely to find partners. No woman ever took him seriously.

"Maybe you should take a business course," her mother said. "Or why shouldn't you go to college?"

Where the men might be more appreciative, she was surely thinking.

"I'm too old," said Enid.

Her mother laughed. "That only shows how young you are," she said. She seemed relieved to discover that her daughter had a touch of folly natural to her age—that she could think twenty-one was at a vast distance from eighteen.

"I'm not going to troop in with kids out of high school," Enid said. "I mean it. What do you want to get rid of me for anyway? I'm fine here." This sulkiness or sharpness also seemed to please and reassure her mother. But after a moment she sighed, and said, "You'll be surprised how fast the years go by."

That August there were a lot of cases of measles and a few of polio at the same time. The doctor who had looked after Enid's father, and had observed her competence around the hospital, asked her if she would be willing to help out for a while, nursing people at home. She said that she would think about it.

"You mean pray?" her mother said, and Enid's face took on a stubborn, secretive expression that in another girl's case might have had to do with meeting her boyfriend.

"That promise," she said to her mother the next day. "That was about working in a hospital, wasn't it?"

Her mother said that she had understood it that way, yes.

"And with graduating and being a registered nurse?"

Yes, yes.

So if there were people who needed nursing at home, who couldn't afford to go to the hospital or did not want to go, and if Enid went into their houses to nurse them, not as a registered nurse but as what they called a practical nurse, she would hardly be breaking her promise, would she? And since most of those needing her care would be children or women having babies, or old people dying, there would not be much danger of the coarsening effect, would there?

"If the only men you get to see are men who are never going to get out of bed again, you have a point," said her mother.

But she could not keep from adding that what all this meant was that Enid had decided to give up the possibility of a decent job in a hospital in order to do miserable backbreaking work in miserable primitive houses for next to no money. Enid would find herself pumping water from contaminated wells and breaking ice in winter washbasins and battling flies in summer and using an outdoor toilet. Scrubboards and coal-oil lamps instead of washing machines and electricity. Trying to look after sick people in those conditions and cope with housework and poor weaselly children as well.

"But if that is your object in life," she said, "I can see that the worse I make it sound the more determined you get to do it. The only thing is, I'm going to ask for a couple of promises myself. Promise me you'll boil the water you drink. And you won't marry a farmer."

Enid said, "Of all the crazy ideas."

That was sixteen years ago. During the first of those years people got poorer and poorer. There were more and more of them who could not afford to go to the hospital, and the houses where Enid worked had often deteriorated almost to the state that her mother had described. Sheets and diapers had to be washed by hand in houses where the washing machine had broken down and could not be repaired, or the electricity had been turned off, or where there had never been any electricity in the first place. Enid did not work without pay, because that would not have been fair to the other women who did the same kind of nursing, and who did not have the same options as she did. But she gave most of the money back, in the form of children's shoes and winter coats and trips to the dentist and Christmas toys.

Her mother went around canvassing her friends for old baby cots, and highchairs and blankets, and worn-out sheets, which she herself ripped up and hemmed to make diapers. Everybody said how proud she must be of Enid, and she said yes, she surely was.

"But sometimes it's a devil of a lot of work," she said. "This being the mother of a saint."

Then came the war, and the great shortage of doctors and nurses, and Enid was more welcome than ever. As she was for a while after the war, with so many babies being born. It was only now, with the hospitals being enlarged and many farms getting prosperous, that it looked as if her responsibilities might dwindle away to the care of those who had bizarre and hopeless afflictions, or were so irredeemably cranky that hospitals had thrown them out.

This summer there was a great downpour of rain every few days, and then the sun came out very hot, glittering off the drenched leaves and grass. Early mornings were full of mist—they were so close, here, to the river—and even when the mist cleared off you could not see very far in any direction, because of the overflow and density of summer. The heavy trees, the bushes all bound up with wild grapevines and Virginia creeper, the crops of corn and barley and wheat and hay. Everything was ahead of itself, as people said. The hay was ready to cut in June, and Rupert had to rush to get it into the barn before a rain spoiled it.

He came into the house later and later in the evenings, having worked as long as the light lasted. One night when he came the house was in darkness, except for a candle burning on the kitchen table.

Enid hurried to unhook the screen door.

"Power out?" said Rupert.

Enid said, "Sh-h-h." She whispered to him that she was letting the children sleep downstairs, because the upstairs rooms were so hot. She had pushed the chairs together and made beds on them with quilts and pillows. And of course she had had to turn the lights out so that they could get to sleep. She had found a candle in one of the drawers, and that was all she needed, to see to write by, in her notebook.

"They'll always remember sleeping here," she said. "You always remember the times when you were a child and you slept somewhere different."

He set down a box that contained a ceiling fan for the sickroom. He had been in to Walley to buy it. He had also bought a newspaper, which he handed to Enid.

"Thought you might like know what's going on in the world," he said.

She spread the paper out beside her notebook, on the table. There was a picture of a couple of dogs playing in a fountain.

"It says there's a heat wave," she said. "Isn't it nice to find out about it?"

Rupert was carefully lifting the fan out of its box.

"That'll be wonderful," she said. "It's cooled off in there now, but it'll be such a comfort to her tomorrow."

"I'll be over early to put it up," he said. Then he asked how his wife had been that day.

Enid said that the pains in her legs had been easing off, and the new pills the doctor had her on seemed to be letting her get some rest.

"The only thing is, she goes to sleep so soon," she said. "It makes it hard for you to get a visit."

"Better she gets the rest," Rupert said.

This whispered conversation reminded Enid of conversations in high school, when they were both in their senior year and that earlier teasing, or cruel flirtation, or whatever it was, had long been abandoned. All that last year Rupert had sat in the seat behind hers, and they had often spoken to each other briefly, always to some immediate purpose. Have you got an ink eraser? How do you spell "incriminate"? Where is the Tyrrhenian Sea? Usually it was Enid, half turning in her seat and able only to sense, not see, how close Rupert was, who started these conversations. She did want to borrow an eraser, she was in need of information, but also she wanted to be sociable. And she wanted to make amends—she felt ashamed of the way she and her friends had treated him. It would do no good to apologize—that would just embarrass him all over again. He was only at ease when he sat behind her, and knew that she could not look him in the face. If they met on the street he would look away until the last minute, then mutter the faintest greeting while she sang out "Hello, Rupert," and heard an echo of the old tormenting tones she wanted to banish.

But when he actually laid a finger on her shoulder, tapping for attention, when he bent forward, almost touching or maybe really touching—she could not tell for sure—her dark thick hair that was wild even in a bob, then she felt forgiven. In a way, she felt honored. Restored to seriousness and to respect.

Where, where exactly, is the Tyrrhenian Sea?

She wondered if he remembered anything at all of that now.

She separated the back and front parts of the paper. Margaret Truman was visiting England, and had curtsied to the Royal Family. The King's doctors were trying to cure his Buerger's disease with Vitamin E.

She offered the front part to Rupert. "I'm going to look at the crossword," she said. "I like to do the crossword—it relaxes me at the end of the day."

Rupert sat down and began to read the paper, and she asked him if he would like a cup of tea. Of course he said not to bother, and she went ahead and made it anyway, understanding that this reply might as well be yes in country speech.

"It's a South American theme," she said, looking at the crossword. "Latin-American theme. First across is a musical . . . *garment*. A musical garment? Garment. A lot of letters. Oh. Oh. I'm lucky tonight. Cape Horn!

"You see how silly they are, these things," she said, and rose and poured the tea.

If he did remember, did he hold anything against her? Maybe her blithe friendliness in their senior year had been as unwelcome, as superior-seeming to him, as that early taunting?

When she first saw him in this house, she thought that he had not changed much. He had been a tall, solid, round-faced boy, and he was a tall, heavy, round-faced man. He had worn his hair cut so short, always, that it didn't make much difference that there was less of it now and that it had turned from light brown to gray brown. A permanent sunburn had taken the place of his blushes. And whatever troubled him and showed in his face might have been just the same old trouble—the problem of occupying space in the world and having a name that people could call you by, being somebody they thought they could know.

She thought of them sitting in the senior class. A small class, by that time—in five years the unstudious, the carefree, and the indifferent had been weeded out, leaving these overgrown, grave, and docile children learning trigonometry, learning Latin. What kind of life did they think they were preparing for? What kind of people did they think they were going to be?

She could see the dark-green, softened cover of a book called "History of the Renaissance and Reformation." It was secondhand, or tenthhand—nobody ever bought a new textbook. Inside were written all the names of the previous owners, some of whom were middle-aged housewives or merchants around the town. You could not imagine them learning these things, or underlining "Edict of Nantes" with red ink and writing "N.B." in the margin.

Edict of Nantes. The very uselessness, the exotic nature of the things in those books and in those students' heads, in her own head then and Rupert's, made Enid feel a tenderness and wonder. It wasn't that they had meant to be something that they hadn't become. Nothing like that. Rupert couldn't have imagined anything but farming this farm. It was a good farm, and he was an only son. And she herself had ended up doing exactly what she must have wanted to do. You couldn't say that they had chosen the wrong lives or chosen against their will or not understood their choices. Just that they had not understood how time would pass and leave them not more but maybe a little less than what they used to be.

"Bread of the Amazon," she said. "Bread of the Amazon?"

Rupert said, "Manioc?"

Enid counted. "Seven letters," she said. "Seven."

He said, "Cassava?"

"Cassava? That's a double 's'? Cassava."

Mrs. Quinn became more capricious daily about her food. Sometimes she said she wanted toast, or bananas with milk on them. One day she said peanut-butter cookies. Enid prepared all these things—the children could eat them anyway—and when they were ready Mrs. Quinn could not stand the look or the smell of them. Even jello had a smell she could not stand.

Some days she hated all noise; she would not even have the fan going. Other days she wanted the radio on, she wanted the station that played requests for birthdays and anniversaries and called people up to ask them questions. If you got the answer right you won a trip to Niagara Falls, a tankful of gas, or a load of groceries or tickets to a movie.

"It's all fixed," Mrs. Quinn said. "They just pretend to call somebody up—they're in the next room and already got the answer told to them. I used to know somebody that worked for a radio, that's the truth."

On these days her pulse was rapid. She talked very fast in a light, breathless voice. "What kind of car is that your mother's got?" she said.

"It's a maroon-colored car," said Enid.

"What *make?*" said Mrs. Quinn.

Enid said she did not know, which was the truth. She had known, but she had forgotten.

"Was it new when she got it?"

"Yes," said Enid. "Yes. But that was three or four years ago."

"She lives in that big rock house next door to Willenses'?"

"Yes," said Enid.

"How many rooms it got? Sixteen?"

"Too many."

"Did you go to Mr. Willen's funeral when he got drownded?"

Enid said no. "I'm not much for funerals."

"I was supposed to go. I wasn't awfully sick then, I was going with Herveys up the highway, they said I could get a ride with them and then her mother and her sister wanted to go and there wasn't enough room in back. Then Clive and Olive went and I could've scrunched up in their front seat but they never thought to ask me. Do you think he drownded himself?"

Enid thought of Mr. Willens handing her a rose. His jokey gallantry that made the nerves of her teeth ache, as from too much sugar.

"I don't know. I wouldn't think so."

"Did him and Mrs. Willens get along all right?"

"As far as I know, they got along beautifully."

"Oh, is that so?" said Mrs. Quinn, trying to imitate Enid's reserved tone. "Bee-you-tif-ley."

Enid slept on the couch in Mrs. Quinn's room. Mrs. Quinn's devastating itch had almost disappeared, as had her need to urinate. She slept through most of the night, though she would have spells of harsh and angry breathing. What woke Enid up and kept her awake was a trouble of her own. She had begun to have ugly dreams. These were unlike any dreams she had ever had before. She used to think that a bad dream was one of finding herself in an unfamiliar house where the rooms kept changing and there was always more work to do than she could handle, work undone that she thought she had done, innumerable distractions. And then, of course, she had what she thought of as romantic dreams, in which some man would have his arm around her or even be embracing her. It might be a stranger or a man she knew—sometimes a man whom it was quite a joke to think of in that way. These dreams made her thoughtful or a little sad but relieved in some way to know that such feelings were possible for her. They could be embarrassing, but were nothing, nothing at all compared with the dreams that she was having now. In the dreams that came to her now she would be copulating or trying to copulate (sometimes she was prevented by intruders or shifts of circumstances) with utterly forbidden and unthinkable partners. With fat squirmy babies or patients in bandages or her own mother. She would be slick with lust, hollow and groaning with it, and she would set to work with roughness and an attitude of evil pragmatism. "Yes, this will have to do," she would say to herself. "This will do if nothing better comes along." And this coldness of heart, this matter-of-fact depravity, simply drove her lust along. She woke up unrepentant, sweaty and exhausted, and lay like a carcass until her own self, her shame and disbelief, came pouring back into her. The sweat went cold on her skin. She lay there shivering in the warm night, with disgust and humiliation. She did not dare go back to sleep. She got used to the dark and the long rectangles of the net-curtained windows filled with a faint light. And the sick woman's breath grating and scolding and then almost disappearing.

If she were a Catholic, she thought, was this the sort of thing that could come out at confession? It didn't seem like the sort of thing she could even bring out in a private prayer. She didn't pray much anymore, except formally, and to bring the experiences she had just been through to the attention of God seemed absolutely useless, disrespectful. He would be insulted. She was insulted, by her own mind. Her religion was hopeful and sensible and there was no room in it for any sort of rubbishy drama, such as the invasion of the Devil into her sleep. The filth in her mind was in her, and there was no point in dramatizing it and making it seem important. Surely not. It was nothing, just the mind's garbage.

In the little meadow between the house and the riverbank there were cows. She could hear them munching and jostling, feeding at night. She thought of their large gentle shapes in there with the money musk and chicory, the flowering grasses, and she thought, They have a lovely life, cows.

It ends, of course, in the slaughterhouse. The end is disaster.

For everybody, though, the same thing. Evil grabs us when we are sleeping; pain and disintegration lie in wait. Animal horrors, all worse than you can imagine beforehand. The comforts of bed and the cows' breath, the pattern of the stars at night—all that can get turned on its head in an instant. And here she was, here was Enid, working her life away pretending it wasn't so. Trying to ease people. Trying to be good. An angel of mercy, as her mother had said, with less and less irony as time went on. Patients and doctors, too, had said it.

And all the time how many thought that she was a fool? The people she spent her labors on might secretly despise her. Thinking they'd never do the same in her place. Never be fool enough. No.

Miserable offenders, came into her head. *Miserable offenders.*
Restore them that are penitent.

So she got up and went to work; as far as she was concerned, that
was the best way to be penitent. She worked very quietly but steadily through the night, washing the cloudy glasses and sticky plates
that were in the cupboards and establishing order where there was
none before. None. Teacups had sat between the ketchup and the
mustard and toilet paper on top of a pail of honey. There was no
waxed paper or even newspaper laid out on the shelves. Brown
sugar in the bag was as hard as rock. It was understandable that
things should have gone downhill in the last few months, but it
looked as if there had been no care, no organization here, ever. All
the net curtains were gray with smoke and the windowpanes were
greasy. The last bit of jam had been left to grow fuzz in the jar, and
vile-smelling water that had held some ancient bouquet had never
been dumped out of its jug. But there was a good house still, that
scrubbing and painting could restore. But what could you do about
the ugly brown paint that had been recently and sloppily applied to
the front-room floor?

When she had a moment later in the day she pulled the weeds
out of Rupert's mother's flower beds, dug up the burdocks and
twitch grass that were smothering the valiant perennials.

She taught the children to hold their spoons properly and to say
grace.

> Thank you for the world so sweet,
> Thank you for the food we eat . . .

She taught them to brush their teeth and after that to say their
prayers.

"God bless Mama and Daddy and Enid and Aunt Olive and
Uncle Clive and Princess Elizabeth and Margaret Rose." After that
each added the name of the other. They had been doing it for quite
a while when Sylvie said, "What does it mean?"

Enid said, "What does what mean?"

"What does it mean 'God bless'?"

❑ ❑ ❑ ❑

Enid made eggnogs, not flavoring them even with vanilla, and fed them to Mrs. Quinn from a spoon. She fed her a little of the rich liquid at a time, and Mrs. Quinn was able to hold down what was given to her in small amounts. If she could not do that, Enid spooned out flat, lukewarm ginger ale.

The sunlight, or any light, was as hateful as noise to Mrs. Quinn by now. Enid had to hang thick quilts over the windows, even when the blinds were pulled down. With the fan shut off, as Mrs. Quinn demanded, the room became very hot, and sweat dripped from Enid's forehead as she bent over the bed attending to the patient. Mrs. Quinn went into fits of shivering; she could never be warm enough.

"This is dragging out," the doctor said. "It must be those milk-shakes you're giving her, keeping her going."

"Eggnogs," said Enid, as if it mattered.

Mrs. Quinn was often now too tired or weak to talk. Sometimes she lay in a stupor, with her breathing so faint and her pulse so lost and wandering that a person less experienced than Enid would have taken her for dead. But at other times she rallied, wanted the radio on, then wanted it off. She knew perfectly well who she was still, and who Enid was, and she sometimes seemed to be watching Enid with a speculative or inquiring look in her eyes. The color was long gone from her face and even from her lips, but her eyes looked greener than they had in the past—a milky, cloudy green. Enid tried to answer the look that was bent on her.

"Would you like me to get a priest to talk to you?"

Mrs. Quinn looked as if she wanted to spit.

"Do I look like a Mick?" she said.

"A minister?" said Enid. She knew this was the right thing to ask, but the spirit in which she asked it was not right—it was cold and faintly malicious.

No. This was not what Mrs. Quinn wanted. She grunted with displeasure. There was some energy in her still, and Enid had the feeling that she was building it up for a purpose. "Do you want to talk to your children?" she said, making herself speak compassion-ately and encouragingly. "Is that what you want?"

No.

"Your husband? Your husband will be here in a little while."

Enid didn't know that for sure. Rupert arrived late some nights, after Mrs. Quinn had taken the final pills and gone to sleep. Then he sat with Enid. He always brought her the newspaper. He asked what she wrote in her notebooks—he noticed that there were two—and she told him. One for the doctor, with a record of blood pressure and pulse and temperature, a record of what was eaten, vomited, excreted, medicines taken, some general summing up of the patient's condition. In the other notebook, for herself, she wrote many of the same things, though perhaps not so exactly, but she added details about the weather and what was happening all around. And things to remember.

"For instance, I wrote something down the other day," she said. "Something that Lois said. Lois and Sylvie came in when Mrs. Green was here and Mrs. Green was mentioning how the berry bushes were growing along the lane and stretching across the road, and Lois said, 'It's like in "Sleeping Beauty." ' Because I'd read them the story. I made a note of that."

Rupert said, "I'll have to get after those berry canes and cut them back."

Enid got the impression that he was pleased by what Lois had said and by the fact that she had written it down, but it wasn't possible for him to say so.

One night he told her that he would be away for a couple of days, at a stock auction. He had asked the doctor if it was all right, and the doctor had said to go ahead.

That night he had come before the last pills were given, and Enid supposed that he was making a point of seeing his wife awake before that little time away. She told him to go right in to Mrs. Quinn's room, and he did, and shut the door after him. Enid picked up the paper and thought of going upstairs to read it, but the children probably weren't asleep yet; they would find excuses for calling her in. She could go out on the porch, but there were mosquitoes at this time of day, especially after a rain like the afternoon's.

She was afraid of overhearing some intimacy or perhaps the suggestion of a fight, then having to face him when he came out.

Mrs. Quinn was building up to a display, of that Enid felt sure. And before she made up her mind where to go she did overhear something. Not the recriminations or (if it was possible) the endearments, or perhaps even weeping, that she had been half expecting, but a laugh. She heard Mrs. Quinn weakly laughing, and the laughter had the mockery and satisfaction in it that Enid had heard before but also something she hadn't heard before, not in her life—something deliberately vile. She didn't move, though she should have, and she was at the table still, she was still there staring at the door of the room, when he came out a moment later. He didn't avoid her eyes—or she his. She couldn't. Yet she couldn't have said for sure that he saw her. He just looked at her and went on outside. He looked as if he had caught hold of an electric wire and begged pardon—who of?—that his body was given over to this stupid catastrophe.

The next day Mrs. Quinn's strength came flooding back, in that unnatural and deceptive way that Enid had seen once or twice in others. Mrs. Quinn wanted to sit up against the pillows. She wanted the fan turned on.

Enid said, "What a good idea."

"I could tell you something you wouldn't believe," Mrs. Quinn said.

"People tell me lots of things," said Enid.

"Sure. Lies," Mrs. Quinn said. "I bet it's all lies. You know Mr. Willens was right here in this room?"

III. Mistake

Mrs. Quinn had been sitting in the rocker getting her eyes examined and Mr. Willens had been close up in front of her with the thing up to her eyes, and neither one of them heard Rupert come in, because he was supposed to be cutting wood down by the river. But he had sneaked back. He sneaked back through the kitchen not making any noise—he must have seen Mr. Willens's car outside before he did that—then he opened the door to this room just easy, till he saw Mr. Willens there on his knees holding the thing up to her eye and, he had the other hand on her leg to keep his balance.

He had grabbed her leg to keep his balance and her skirt got scrunched up and her leg showed bare, but that was all there was to it and she couldn't do a thing about it, she had to concentrate on keeping still.

So Rupert got in the room without either of them hearing him come in and then he just gave one jump and landed on Mr. Willens like a bolt of lightning and Mr. Willens couldn't get up or turn around, he was down before he knew it. Rupert banged his head up and down on the floor, Rupert banged the life out of him, and she jumped up so fast the chair went over and Mr. Willens's box where he kept his eye things got knocked over and all the things flew out of it. Rupert just walloped him, and maybe he hit the leg of the stove, she didn't know what. She thought, It's me next. But she couldn't get round them to run out of the room. And then she saw Rupert wasn't going to go for her after all. He was out of wind and he just set the chair right side up and sat down in it. She went to Mr. Willens then and hauled him around, as heavy as he was, to get him right side up. His eyes were not quite open, not shut either, and there was dribble coming out of his mouth. But no skin broke on his face or bruise you could see—maybe it wouldn't have come up yet. The stuff coming out of his mouth didn't even look like blood. It was pink stuff, and if you wanted to know what it looked like it looked exactly like when the froth comes up when you were boiling the strawberries to make jam. Bright pink. It was smeared over his face from when Rupert had him face down. He made a sound, too, when she was turning him over. *Glug-glug.* That was all there was to it. *Glug-glug* and he was laid out like a stone.

Rupert jumped out of the chair so it was still rocking, and he started picking up all the things and putting each one back where it went in Mr. Willens's box. Getting everything fitted in the way it should go. Wasting the time that way. It was a special box lined with red plush and a place in it for each one of his things that he used and you had to get everything in right or the top wouldn't go down. Rupert got it so the top went on and then he just sat down in the chair again and started pounding on his knees.

On the table there was one of those good-for-nothing cloths, it was a souvenir of when Rupert's mother and father went up north to see the Dionne Quintuplets. She took it off the table and wrapped it around Mr. Willens's head to soak up the pink stuff and so they wouldn't have to keep on looking at him.

Rupert kept banging his big flat hands. She said, Rupert, we got to bury him somewhere.

Rupert just looked at her, like to say, Why?

She said they could bury him down in the cellar, which had a dirt floor.

"That's right," said Rupert. "Where are we going to bury his car?"

She said they could put it in the barn and cover it up with hay.

He said too many people came poking around the barn.

Then she thought, Put him in the river. She thought of him sitting in his car right under the water. It came to her like a picture. Rupert didn't say anything at first, so she went into the kitchen and got some water and cleaned Mr. Willens up so he wouldn't dribble on anything. The goo was not coming up in his mouth anymore. She got his keys, which were in his pocket. She could feel, through the cloth of his pants, the fat of his leg still warm.

She said to Rupert, Get moving.

He took the keys.

They hoisted Mr. Willens up, she by the feet and Rupert by the head, and he weighed a ton. He was like lead. But as she carried him one of his shoes kind of kicked her between the legs, and she thought, There you are, you're still at it, you horny old devil. Even his dead old foot giving her the nudge. Not that she ever let him do anything, but he was always ready to get a grab if he could. Like grabbing her leg up under her skirt when he had the thing to her eye and she couldn't stop him and Rupert had to come sneaking in and get the wrong idea.

Over the doorsill and through the kitchen and across the porch and down the porch steps. All clear. But it was a windy day, and, first thing, the wind blew away the cloth she had wrapped over Mr. Willens's face.

Their yard couldn't be seen from the road, that was lucky. Just the peak of the roof and the upstairs window. Mr. Willens's car couldn't be seen.

Rupert had thought up the rest of what to do. Take him to Jutland, where it was deep water and the track going all the way back and it could look like he just drove in from the road and mistook his way. Like he turned off on the Jutland road, maybe it was dark and he just drove into the water before he knew where he was at. Like he just made a mistake.

He did. Mr. Willens certainly did make a mistake.

The trouble was, it meant driving out their lane and along the road to the Jutland turn. But nobody lived down there and it was a dead end after the Jutland turn, so just the half mile or so to pray you never met anybody. Then Rupert would get Mr. Willens over in the driver's seat and push the car right off down the bank into the water. Push the whole works down into the pond. It was going to be a job to do that, but Rupert at least was a strong bugger. If he hadn't been so strong they wouldn't have been in this mess in the first place.

Rupert had a little trouble getting the car started because he had never driven one like that, but he did, and got turned around and drove off down the lane with Mr. Willens kind of bumping over against him. He had put Mr. Willens's hat on his head—the hat that had been sitting on the seat of the car.

Why take his hat off before he came into the house? Not just to be polite but so he could easier get a clutch on her and kiss her. If you could call that kissing, all that pushing up against her with the box still in one hand and the other grabbing on, and sucking away at her with his dribbly old mouth. Sucking and chewing away at her lips and her tongue and pushing himself up at her and the corner of the box sticking into her and digging her behind. She was so surprised and he got such a hold she didn't know how to get out of it. Pushing and sucking and dribbling and digging into her and hurting her all at the same time. He was a dirty old brute.

She went and got the Quintuplets cloth where it had blown on to the fence. She looked hard for blood on the steps or any mess on the porch or through the kitchen, but all she found was in the front room, also some on her shoes. She scrubbed up what was on the floor and scrubbed her shoes, which she took off, and not till she had all that done did she see a smear right down her front. How did she come by that? And the same time she saw it she heard a noise that turned her to stone. She heard a car and it was a car she didn't know and it was coming down the lane.

She looked through the net curtain and sure enough. A new-looking car and dark green. Her smeared-down front and shoes off and the floor wet. She moved back where she couldn't be seen, but she couldn't think of where to hide. The car stopped and a car door opened, but the engine didn't cut off. She heard the door shut and then the car turned around and she heard the sound of it driving back up the lane. And she heard Lois and Sylvie on the porch.

It was the teacher's boyfriend's car. He picked up the teacher every Friday afternoon, and this was a Friday. So the teacher said to him, Why don't we give these ones a lift home, they're the littlest and they got the farthest to go and it looks like it's going to rain.

It did rain, too. It had started by the time Rupert got back, walking home along the riverbank. She said, A good thing, it'll muddy up your tracks where you went to push it over. He said he'd took his shoes off and worked in his sock feet. So you must have got your brains going again, she said.

Instead of trying to soak the stuff out of that souvenir cloth or the blouse she had on, she decided to burn the both of them in the stove. They made a horrible smell and the smell made her sick. That was the whole beginning of her being sick. That and the paint. After she cleaned up the floor, she could still see where she thought there was a stain, so she got the brown paint left over from when Rupert painted the steps and she painted over the whole floor. That started her throwing up, leaning over and breathing in that paint. And the pains in her back—that was the start of them, too.

After she got the floor painted she just about quit going into the front room. But one day she thought she had better put some other cloth on that table. It would make things look more normal. If she didn't, then her sister-in-law was sure to come nosing around and say, Where's that cloth Mom and Dad brought back the time they went to see the Quints? If she had a different cloth on she could say, Oh, I just felt like a change. But no cloth would look funny.

So she got a cloth Rupert's mother had embroidered with flower baskets and took it in there and she could still smell the smell. And there on the table was sitting the dark-red box with Mr. Willens's things in it and his name on it and it had been sitting there all the time. She didn't even remember putting it there or seeing Rupert put it there. She had forgot all about it.

She took that box and hid it in one place and then she hid it in another. She never told where she hid it and she wasn't going to. She would have smashed it up, but how do you smash all those things in it? Examining things. Oh, Missus, would you like me to examine your eyes for you, just sit down here and just you relax and you just shut the one eye and keep the other one wide open. Wide open, now. It was like the same game every time, and she wasn't supposed to suspect what was going on, and when he had the thing out looking in her eye he wanted her to keep her panties on, him the dirty old cuss puffing away getting his fingers slicked in and puffing away. Her not supposed to say anything till he stops and gets the looker thing packed up in his box and all and then she's supposed to say, "Oh, Mr. Willens, now, how much do I owe you for today?"

And that was the signal for him to get her down and thump her like an old billy goat. Right on the bare floor to knock her up and down and try to bash her into pieces. Dingey on him like a blow-torch.

How'd you've liked that?

Then it was in the papers. Mr. Willens found drowned.

They said his head got bunged up knocking against the steering wheel. They said he was alive when he went in the water. What a laugh.

IV. Lies

Enid stayed awake all night—she didn't even try to sleep. She could not lie down in Mrs. Quinn's room. She sat in the kitchen for hours. It was an effort for her to move, even to make a cup of tea or go to the bathroom. Moving her body shook up the information that she was trying to arrange in her head and get used to. She had not undressed, or unrolled her hair, and when she brushed her teeth she seemed to be doing something laborious and unfamiliar. The moonlight came through the kitchen window—she was sitting in the dark—and she watched a patch of light shift through the night, on the linoleum, and disappear. She was surprised by its disappearance and then by the birds waking up, the new day start-ing. The night had seemed so long and then too short, because nothing had been decided.

She got up stiffly and unlocked the door and sat on the porch in the beginning light. Even that move jammed her thoughts together. She had to sort through them again and set them on two sides. What had happened—or what she had been told had happened—on one side. What to do about it on the other. What to do about it—that was what would not come clear to her.

The cows had been moved out of the little meadow between the house and the riverbank. She could open the gate if she wanted to and go in that direction. She knew that she should go back, instead, and check on Mrs. Quinn. But she found herself pulling open the gate bolt.

The cows hadn't cropped all the weeds. Sopping wet, they brushed against her stockings. The path was clear, though, under the riverbank trees, those big willows with the wild grape hanging on to them like monkeys' shaggy arms. Mist was rising so that you could hardly see the river. You had to fix your eyes, concentrate, and then a spot of water would show through, quiet as water in a pot. There must be a moving current, but she could not find it.

Then she saw a movement, and it wasn't in the water. There was a boat moving. Tied to a branch, a plain old rowboat was being lifted very slightly, lifted and let fall. Now that she had found it, she kept watching it, as if it could say something to her. And it did. It said something gentle and final.

You know. You know.

When the children woke up they found her in bountiful good spirits, freshly washed and dressed and with her hair loose. She had already made the jello crammed with fruit that would be ready for them to eat at noon. And she was mixing batter for cookies that could be baked before it got too hot to use the oven.

"Is that your father's boat?" she said. "Down on the river?"

Lois said yes. "But we're not supposed to play in it." Then she said, "If you went down with us we could." They had caught on at once to the day's air of privilege, its holiday possibilities, Enid's unusual mix of languor and excitement.

"We'll see," said Enid. She wanted to make the day a special one for them, special aside from the fact—which she was already almost certain of—that it would be the day of their mother's death. She wanted them to hold something in their minds that could throw a redeeming light on whatever came later. On herself, that is, and whatever way she would affect their lives later.

That morning Mrs. Quinn's pulse had been hard to find and she had not been able, apparently, to raise her head or open her eyes. A great change from yesterday, but Enid was not surprised. She had thought that great spurt of energy, that wicked outpouring talk, would be the last. She held a spoon with water in it to Mrs. Quinn's lips, and Mrs. Quinn drew a little of the water in. She made a mewing sound—the last trace, surely, of all her complaints. Enid did not call the doctor, because he was due to visit anyway later that day, probably early in the afternoon.

She shook up soapsuds in a jar and bent a piece of wire, and then another piece, to make bubble wands. She showed the children how to make bubbles, blowing steadily and carefully until as large a shining bladder as possible trembled on the wire, then shaking it delicately free. They chased the bubbles around the yard and kept them afloat till breezes caught them and hung them in the trees or on the eaves of the porch. What kept them alive then seemed to be the cries of admiration, screams of joy, rising up from below. Enid put no restriction on the noise they could make, and when the soapsud mixture was all used up she made more.

The doctor called when she was giving the children their lunch—jello and a plate of cookies sprinkled with colored sugar and glasses of milk into which she had stirred chocolate syrup. He said he had been held up by a child's falling out of a tree and he would probably not be out before suppertime. Enid said softly, "I think she may be going."

"Well, keep her comfortable if you can," the doctor said. "You know how as well as I do."

Enid didn't phone Mrs. Green. She knew that Rupert would not be back yet from the auction and she didn't think that Mrs. Quinn, if she ever had another moment of consciousness, would want to see or hear her sister-in-law in the room. Nor did it seem likely that she would want to see her children. And there would be nothing good about seeing her for them to remember.

She didn't bother trying to take Mrs. Quinn's blood pressure anymore, or her temperature—just sponged off her face and arms and offered the water, which was no longer noticed. She turned on the fan, whose noise Mrs. Quinn had so often objected to. The smell rising from the body seemed to be changing, losing its ammoniac sharpness. Changing into the common odor of death.

She went out and sat on the steps. She took off her shoes and stockings and stretched out her legs in the sun. The children began cautiously to pester her, asking if she would take them down to the river, if they could sit in the boat, or if they found the oars could she take them rowing. She knew enough not to go that far in the way of desertion, but she asked them, Would they like to have a swimming pool? Two swimming pools? And she brought out the two laundry tubs, set them on the grass, and filled them with water from the cistern pump. They stripped to their underpants and lolled in the water, becoming Princess Elizabeth and Princess Margaret Rose.

"What do you think," said Enid, sitting on the grass with her head back and her eyes shut—"what do you think, if a person does something very bad, do they have to be punished?"

"Yes," said Lois immediately. "They have to get a licking."

"Who did it?" said Sylvie.

"Just thinking of anybody," said Enid. "Now, what if it was a very bad thing but nobody knew they did it? Should they tell that they did and be punished?"

Sylvie said, "I would know they did it."

"You would not," said Lois. "How would you know?"

"I would've seed them."

"You would not."

"You know the reason I think they should be punished?" Enid said. "It's because of how bad they are going to feel, in themselves.

Even if nobody did see them and nobody ever knew. If you do something very bad and you are not punished you feel worse, you feel far worse, than if you are."

"Lois stold a green comb," Sylvie said.

"I did not," said Lois.

"I want you to remember that," Enid said.

Lois said, "It was just laying the side the road."

Enid went into the sickroom every half hour or so to wipe Mrs. Quinn's face and hands with a damp cloth. She never spoke to her and never touched her hand, except with the cloth. She had never absented herself like this before with anybody who was dying. When she opened the door at around half past five she knew there was nobody alive in the room. The sheet was pulled out and Mrs. Quinn's head was hanging over the side of the bed, a fact that Enid did not record or mention to anybody. She had the body straightened out and cleaned and the bed put to rights before the doctor came. The children were still playing in the yard.

"July 5. Rain early A.M. L. and S. playing under porch. Fan off and on, complains noise. Half cup eggnog spoon at a time. B.P. up, pulse rapid, no complaints pain. Rain didn't cool off much. R.Q. in evening. Hay finished.

"July 6. Hot day, vy. close. Try fan but no. Sponge often. R.Q. in evening. Start to cut wheat tomorrow. Everything 1 or 2 wks ahead due to heat, rain.

"July 7. Cont'd heat. Won't take eggnog. Ginger ale from spoon. Vy. weak. Heavy rain last night, wind. R.Q. not able to cut, grain lodged some places.

"July 8. No eggnog. Ginger ale. Vomiting A.M. More alert. R.Q. to go to calf auction, gone 2 days. Dr. says go ahead.

"July 9. Vy. agitated. Terrible talk.

"July 10. Patient Mrs. Rupert (Jeanette) Quinn died today approx. 5 P.M. Heart failure due to uremia. (Glomerulonephritis.)"

Enid never made a practice of waiting around for the funerals of people she had nursed. It seemed to her a good idea to get out of the house as soon as she decently could. Her presence could not help being a reminder of the time just before the death, which might have been dreary and full of physical disaster, and was now going to be glossed over with ceremony and hospitality and flowers and cakes.

Also, there was usually some female relative who would be in place to take over the household completely, putting Enid suddenly in the position of unwanted guest.

Mrs. Green, in fact, arrived at the Quinns' house before the undertaker did. Rupert was not back yet. The doctor was in the kitchen drinking a cup of tea and talking to Enid about another case that she could take up now that this was finished. Enid was hedging, saying that she had thought of taking some time off. The children were upstairs. They had been told that their mother had gone to Heaven, which for them had put the cap on this rare and eventful day.

Mrs. Green was shy until the doctor left. She stood at the window to see him turn his car around and drive away. Then she said, "Maybe I shouldn't say it right now, but I will. I'm glad it happened now and not later when the summer was over and they were started back to school. Now I'll have time to get them used to living at our place and used to the idea of the new school they'll be going to. Rupert, he'll have to get used to it, too."

This was the first time that Enid had realized that Mrs. Green meant to take the children to live with her, not just to stay for a while. Mrs. Green was eager to manage the move, had been looking forward to it, probably, for some time. Very likely she had the children's rooms ready and material bought to make them new clothes. She had a large house and no children of her own.

"You must be wanting to get off home yourself," she said to Enid. As long as there was another woman in the house it might look like a rival home, and it might be harder for her brother to see the necessity of moving the children out for good. "Rupert can run you in when he gets here."

Enid said that it was all right, her mother was coming out to pick her up.

"Oh, I forgot your mother," said Mrs. Green. "I forgot about that snappy little car."

She brightened up and began to open the cupboard doors, checking on the glasses and the teacups—were they clean for the funeral?

"Somebody's been busy," she said, quite relieved about Enid now and ready to be complimentary.

Mr. Green was waiting outside, in the truck, with the Greens' dog, General. Mrs. Green called upstairs for Lois and Sylvie, and they came running down with some clothes in brown paper bags. They ran through the kitchen and slammed the door, without taking any notice of Enid.

"That's something that's going to have to change," said Mrs. Green, meaning the door-slamming. Enid could hear the children shouting their greetings to General and General barking excitedly in return.

Two days later Enid was back, driving her mother's car herself. She came late in the afternoon, when the funeral would have been well over. There were no extra cars parked outside, which meant that the women who had helped in the kitchen had all gone home, taking with them the extra chairs and teacups and the large coffeepot that belonged to their church. The grass was marked with car tracks and some dropped crushed flowers.

She had to knock on the door now. She had to wait to be asked in.

She heard Rupert's heavy, steady footsteps. She spoke some greeting to him when he stood in front of her on the other side of the screen door, but she didn't look into his face. He was in his shirtsleeves, but was wearing his suit trousers. He undid the hook of the door.

"I wasn't sure anybody would be here," Enid said. "I thought you might still be at the barn."

Rupert said, "They all pitched in with the chores."

She could smell whiskey when he spoke, but he didn't sound drunk.

"I thought you were one of the women come back to collect something you forgot," he said.

Enid said, "I didn't forget anything. I was just wondering, how are the children?"

"They're fine. They're at Olive's."

It seemed uncertain whether he was going to ask her in. It was bewilderment that stopped him, not hostility. She had not prepared herself for this first awkward part of the conversation. So that she wouldn't have to look at him, she looked around at the sky.

"You can feel the evenings getting shorter," she said. "Even if it isn't a month since the longest day."

"That's true," said Rupert. Now he opened the door and stood aside and she went in. On the table was a cup without a saucer. She sat down at the opposite side of the table from where he had been sitting. She was wearing a dark-green silk-crêpe dress and suède shoes to match. When she put these things on she had thought how this might be the last time that she would dress herself and the last clothes she would ever wear. She had done her hair up in a French braid and powdered her face. Her care, her vanity, seemed foolish but were necessary to her. She had been awake now three nights in a row, awake every minute, and she had not been able to eat, even to fool her mother.

"Was it specially difficult this time?" her mother had said. She hated discussion of illness or deathbeds, and the fact that she had brought herself to ask this meant that Enid's upset was obvious.

"Was it the children you'd got fond of?" her mother said. "The poor little monkeys."

Enid said it was just the problem of settling down after a long case, and a hopeless case of course had its own strain. She did not go out of her mother's house in the daytime, but she did go for walks at night, when she could be sure of not meeting anybody and having to talk. She had found herself walking past the walls of the county jail. She knew there was a prison yard behind those walls where hangings had once taken place. But not for years and years. They must do it in some large central prison now, when they had to do it. And it was a long time since anybody from this community had committed a sufficiently serious crime.

Sitting across the table from Rupert, facing the door of Mrs. Quinn's room, she had almost forgotten her excuse, lost track of the way things were to go. She felt her purse in her lap, the weight of her camera in it—that reminded her.

"There is one thing I'd like to ask you," she said. "I thought I might as well now, because I wouldn't get another chance."

Rupert said, "What's that?"

"I know you've got a rowboat. So I wanted to ask you to row me out to the middle of the river. And I could get a picture. I'd like to get a picture of the riverbank. It's beautiful there, the willow trees along the bank."

"All right," said Rupert, with the careful lack of surprise that country people will show, regarding the frivolity—the rudeness, even—of visitors.

That was what she was now—a visitor.

Her plan was to wait until they got out to the middle of the river, then to tell him that she could not swim. First ask him how deep he thought the water would be there—and he would surely say, after all the rain they had been having, that it might be seven or eight, or even ten, feet. Then tell him that she could not swim. And that would not be a lie. She had grown up in Walley, on the lake, she had played on the beach every summer of her childhood, she was a strong girl and good at games, but she was frightened of the water, and no coaxing or demonstrating or shaming had ever worked with her—she had not learned to swim.

He would only have to give her a shove with one of the oars and topple her into the water and let her sink. Then leave the boat out on the water and swim to shore, change his clothes, and say that he had come in from the barn or from a walk and found the car there, and where was she? Even the camera if found would make it more plausible. She had taken the boat out to get a picture, then somehow fallen into the river.

Once he understood his advantage, she would tell him. She would ask, Is it true?

If it was not true, he would hate her for asking. If it was true— and didn't she believe all the time that it was true?—he would hate her in another, more dangerous way. Even if she said at once—and meant it, she would mean it—that she was never going to tell.

She would speak very quietly all the time, remembering how voices carry out on the water on a summer evening.

"I am not going to tell, but you are. You can't live on with that kind of secret."

You cannot live in the world with such a burden. You will not be able to stand your life.

If she had got so far, and he had neither denied what she said nor pushed her into the river, Enid would know that she had won the gamble. It would take some more talking, more absolutely firm but quiet persuasion to bring him to the point where he would start to row back to shore.

Or, lost, he would say "What will I do?" and she would take him one step at a time, saying first, "Row back."

The first step in a long, dreadful journey. She would tell him every step and she would stay with him for as many of them as she could. Tie up the boat now. Walk up the bank. Walk through the meadow. Open the gate. She would walk behind him or in front, whichever seemed better to him. Across the yard and up the porch and into the kitchen.

They will say goodbye and get into their separate cars and then it will be his business where he goes. And she will not phone the Police Office the next day. She will wait and they will phone her and she will go to see him in jail. Every day, or as often as they will let her, she will sit and talk to him in jail, and she will write him letters as well. If they take him to another jail she will go there; even if she is allowed to see him only once a month she will be close by. And in court—yes, every day in court, she will be sitting where he can see her.

She does not think anyone would get a death sentence for this sort of murder, which was in a way accidental, and was surely a crime of passion, but the shadow is there, to sober her when she feels that these pictures of devotion, of a bond that is like love but beyond love, are becoming indecent.

Now it has started. With her asking to be taken on the river, her excuse of the picture. Both she and Rupert are standing up, and she is facing the door of the sickroom—now again the front room—which is shut.

She says a foolish thing.

"Are the quilts taken down off the windows?"

He doesn't seem to know for a minute what she is talking about. Then he says, "The quilts. Yes. I think it was Olive took them down. In there was where we had the funeral."

"I was only thinking. The sun would fade them."

He opens the door and she comes around the table and they stand looking into the room. He says, "You can go in if you like. It's all right. Come in."

The bed is gone, of course. The furniture is pushed back against the walls. The middle of the room, where they would have set up the chairs for the funeral, is bare. So is the space in between the north windows—that must have been where they put the coffin. The table where Enid was used to setting the basin, and laying out cloths, cotton wool, spoons, medicine, is jammed into a corner and has a bouquet of delphiniums sitting on it. The tall windows still hold plenty of daylight.

"Lies" is the word that Enid can hear now, out of all the words that Mrs. Quinn said in that room. *Lies. I bet it's all lies.*

Could a person make up something so detailed and diabolical? The answer is yes. A sick person's mind, a dying person's mind, could fill up with all kinds of trash and organize that trash in a most convincing way. Enid's own mind, when she was asleep in this room, had filled up with the most disgusting inventions, with filth. Lies of that nature could be waiting around in the corners of a person's mind, hanging like bats in the corners, waiting to take advantage of any kind of darkness. You can never say, Nobody could make that up. Look how elaborate dreams are, layer over layer in them, so that the part you can remember and put into words is just the bit you can scratch off the top.

When Enid was four or five years old she had told her mother that she had gone into her father's office and that she had seen him sitting behind his desk with a woman on his knee. All she could remember about this woman, then and now, was that she wore a hat with a great many flowers on it and a veil (a hat quite out of fashion even at that time), and that her blouse or dress was unbuttoned and there was one bare breast sticking out, the tip of it disappearing into Enid's father's mouth. She had told her mother about this in perfect certainty that she had seen it. She said, "One of her fronts was stuck in Daddy's mouth." She did not know the word for breasts, though she did know they came in pairs.

Her mother said, "Now, Enid. What are you talking about? What on earth is a front?"

"Like an ice-cream cone," Enid said.

And she saw it that way, exactly. She could see it that way still. The biscuit-colored cone with its mound of vanilla ice cream squashed against the woman's chest and the wrong end sticking into her father's mouth.

Her mother then did a very unexpected thing. She undid her own dress and took out a dull-skinned object that flopped over her hand. "Like this?" she said.

Enid said no. "An ice-cream cone," she said.

"Then that was a dream," her mother said. "Dreams are sometimes downright silly. Don't tell Daddy about it. It's too silly."

Enid did not believe her mother right away, but in a year or so she saw that such an explanation had to be right, because ice-cream cones did not ever arrange themselves in that way on ladies' chests and they were never so big. When she was older still she realized that the hat must have come from some picture.

Lies.

She hadn't asked him yet, she hadn't spoken. Nothing yet committed her to asking. It was still *before*. Mr. Willens had still driven himself into Jutland Pond, on purpose or by accident. Everybody still believed that, and as far as Rupert was concerned Enid believed it, too. And as long as that was so, this room and this house and her life held a different possibility, an entirely different possibility from the one she had been living with (or glorying in—however you wanted to put it) for the last few days. The different possibility was coming closer to her, and all she needed to do was to keep quiet and let it come. Through her silence, her collaboration in a silence, what benefits could bloom. For others, and for herself.

This was what most people knew. A simple thing that it had

taken her so long to understand. This was how to keep the world habitable.

She had started to weep. Not with grief but with an onslaught of relief that she had not known she was looking for. Now she looked into Rupert's face and saw that his eyes were bloodshot and the skin around them puckered and dried out, as if he had been weeping, too.

He said, "She wasn't lucky in her life."

Enid excused herself and went to get her handkerchief, which was in her purse on the table. She was embarrassed now that she had dressed herself up in readiness for such a melodramatic fate.

"I don't know what I was thinking of," she said. "I can't walk down to the river in these shoes."

Rupert shut the door of the front room.

"If you want to go we can still go," he said. "There ought to be a pair of rubber boots would fit you somewhere."

Not hers, Enid hoped. No. Hers would be too small.

Rupert opened a bin in the woodshed, just outside the kitchen door. Enid had never looked into that bin. She had thought it contained firewood, which she had certainly had no need of that summer. Rupert lifted out several single rubber boots and even snow boots, trying to find a pair.

"These look like they might do," he said. "They maybe were Mother's. Or even mine before my feet got full size."

He pulled out something that looked like a piece of a tent, then, by a broken strap, an old school satchel.

"Forgot all the stuff that was in here," he said, letting these things fall back and throwing the unusuable boots on top of them. He dropped the lid and gave a private, grieved, and formal-sounding sigh.

A house like this, lived in by one family for so long a time, and neglected for the past several years, would have plenty of bins, drawers, shelves, suitcases, trunks, crawl spaces full of things that it would be up to Enid to sort out, saving and labelling some, restoring some to use, sending others by the boxload to the dump. When she got that chance she wouldn't balk at it. She would make this house into a place that had no secrets from her and where all order was as she had decreed.

He set the boots down in front of her while she was bent over unbuckling her shoes. She smelled under the whiskey the bitter breath that came after a sleepless night and a long harsh day; she smelled the deeply sweat-soaked skin of a hard-worked man that no washing—at least the washing he did—could get quite fresh. No bodily smell—even the smell of semen—was unfamiliar to her, but there was something new and invasive about the smell of a body so distinctly not in her power or under her care.

That was welcome.

"See can you walk," he said.

She could walk. She walked in front of him to the gate. He bent over her shoulder to swing it open for her. She waited while he bolted it, then stood aside to let him walk ahead, because he had brought a little hatchet from the woodshed, to clear their path.

"The cows were supposed to keep the growth down," he said. "But there's things cows won't eat."

She said, "I was only down here once. Early in the morning."

The desperation of her frame of mind then had to seem childish to her now.

Rupert went along chopping at the big fleshy thistles. The sun cast a level, dusty light on the bulk of the trees ahead. The air was clear in some places, then suddenly you would enter a cloud of tiny bugs. Bugs no bigger than specks of dust that were constantly in motion yet kept themselves together in the shape of a pillar or a cloud. How did they manage to do that? And how did they choose one spot over another to do it in? It must have something to do with feeding. But they never seemed to be still enough to feed.

When she and Rupert went underneath the roof of summer leaves it was dusk, it was almost night. You had to watch that you didn't trip over roots that swelled up out of the path, or hit your head on the dangling, surprisingly tough-stemmed vines. Then a flash of water came through the black branches. The lit-up water near the opposite bank of the river, the trees over there still decked out in light. On this side—they were going down the bank now, through the willows—the water was tea-colored but clear.

And the boat waiting, riding in the shadows, just the same.

"The oars are hid," said Rupert. He went into the willows to locate them. In a moment she lost sight of him. She went closer to the water's edge, where her boots sank into the mud a little and held her. If she tried to, she could still hear Rupert's movements in the bushes. But if she concentrated on the motion of the boat, a slight and secretive motion, she could feel as if everything for a long way around had gone quiet.

Carolyn Cooke

The Twa Corbies

From *The Gettysburg Review*

Mony a one for him makes mane,
But nane sall ken whar he is gane;
O'er his white banes, when they are bare,
The wind sall blaw for evermair.
—Anonymous, from "The Twa Corbies"

OH, MURDER," said my sister-in-law, who frightens me, passing crackers on a plate. "Crackers *and* cheese. Oh, this is murder. And what extra*ordinary* cheese—"

"It's Kraft mild cheddar from the Lil Peach," I said, to plug her up.

"Mild cheddar. Why, it isn't sharp at all! Extraordinary how they get the sharpness *out* of it. Of course we all get sharper as we get older, isn't that true?"

Because she laughs, it's clear Gay has meant this as a joke.

"I find myself duller as I age," I said.

"Not you, Billy. You have a rapier wit, just like Tad. More so. Isn't that so, Tad?"

But Tad had set his pink stuffed chair on fire again. Smoke rose up around his legs. Tad looked anciently collegiate in his khakis and pin-striped shirt and blue blazer and his bow tie. He looked essentially the same as he had looked in college—handsome, self-indulgent, remote. But his face was red-spotty, and his blue eyes were full of smoke.

"Tad, dear, you're on fire," Gay said. She spoke to Tad as if he were there.

She got up and slapped the cushions with her hands to get the smoke down. Tad submitted, oblivious, smoking. He smoked his cigarette down to the end; he held the end of it close to his lips until the ember fell from the hard pads of his fingers. Since he fell down those stone stairs at Duxbury, smoke was all he remembered how to do—tip back his chin in two fingers and watch the smoke roll out of his nose. The act of smoking recovered for my brother the effect of thoughtful intelligence, reminded him, perhaps, of his old instinct for pleasure. But all his mind was gone. If you said, "Would you like me to turn up the radio, Tad?" he would say, "I'd rather have a cigarette."

I was once a great supporter of the tobacco farmer myself; I owe a debt to that smoky world. It was my only vice, really, apart from starting cocktails, like sunset in spring, a minute earlier every day. Before my bypass eighteen years ago, the anesthesiologist said he would like me better as a nonsmoker, and I was coward enough to stop. Still, at night I dream of smoking; I wake every morning and think I have given in.

Tad's chair smoldered on; even Gay could not completely put it out. She had flung so much water on it she had soaked the old feather cushions, and they had a burnt hair smell that reminded me of our mother, Tad's and mine, a suffragette, standing over an iron stove and burning pinfeathers off a chicken.

Gay slapped the cushions down, then swiveled around to the end table and cut a square of cheese and fit it on a cracker—"Have some of Billy's *mahvellous* cheese, Tad, dear." Tad was lighting a fresh cigarette, and Gay had to hunch absurdly with the cheesed cracker on her palm, balls of bone hugging the blades of her back, arrayed in a lounging pajama printed with clubs and spades.

Why, you're nothing but a pack of cards, I thought. She was outrageously thin, either decadently voguish or gravely ill. Tad puffed out smoke and accepted the cracker. Smiling out at us, aware of being quizzed, he took an obedient bite and chewed.

"Very good," he said. "Cheese."

My mission was mercy, to baby-sit my brother while Gay went to the hospital for what she called "a little checkup." It seemed to me, surely, that she would never be released. Who would have the authority to release her? She should have unloaded Tad to an asylum years ago, sold her house, and gone to a Home. Now look where we were. She had saved his life, brought him back from the dead. Dr. Wesley had said himself, "If he survives, Tad will be a vegetable all his life." And yet Gay had fought for his life! She had spoiled him so that no nursing home would have him, letting him wake up and go to bed whenever it pleased him, letting him smoke. And now look at her—anyone could see she was in trouble. Last month, leaning into a cupboard for a carton of cigarettes, Gay had broken three ribs. The mailman found her on the kitchen floor two days later when he noticed the box was full. "We were getting hungry here, weren't we, Tad?" Gay—still on her back on the kitchen floor—cackled when the mailman found her. Tad asked for ice cream. While Gay lay invalid, he sat in his pink chair with his carton of Pall Malls and blew smoke rings in the face of death— death by absurdity.

"Look here, you had better write down the name of the hospital on a pad before you go," I said.

Gay laughed hilariously. "Oh, Billy, you wag! So if I don't come home, you're going to come and get me, is that a deal?" Truly, she terrified me. She passed peanuts in a blue glass bowl.

"I was simply," I said. Simply what? My fingers searched the bowl for nuts.

Her fingers scratched my arm like chalk. "You were simply concerned. Isn't he adorable, Tad?"

In her blue painted kitchen, while I dumped the ice and gin at the bottoms of our two glasses into the old copper sink, Gay dumped a jar of apricot preserves over a roast chicken. She poured hollandaise sauce into a gravy boat.

I stepped into the airless mahogany dining room, which smelled of tarnished silver. "Put out your cigarette, Tad," I said, and sat down at the table. He was like a child, a certain petulant obedience I recognized from fifty years teaching in the middle school—though I had learned the technique as an older brother first. In my college days, in the larger lectures, smoking by a teacher was not any cause for comment. This dates me, I realize. We all smoked then—Pall Malls, Lucky Strikes. I kept an ashtray in the shelf of the lectern for when I recited poetry in Oral English. Poems, cigarettes.

It is some years now since I was there. They have admitted girls, who no doubt clamor for Emily Dickinson and the lady-suicides. I say, let them go. I say, bring on Walter Savage Landor, bring on "Lord Randall" and "The Twa Corbies." Bring on—in season— Ernest Lawrence Thayer!

Tad smiled and said, "I'd like a plate of chocolate ice cream."

"Would you serve the rice, Tad, dear?" Gay twittered, and set down a casserole and a spoon before him. Tad picked up a plate and spooned rice onto it. When Gay walked back into the dining room with a basket of rolls, Tad had just transferred the entire casserole to the first dinner plate.

"Tad, what a generous heart you are!" Gay said hilariously. "Shouldn't we give some of the casserole to each person?"

"You were having rice," Tad said.

"But then, dear, what would be left for you and Billy?" Gay asked. She divided the rice among three plates, her hand spread over Tad's on the spoon.

"We could have a plate of chocolate ice cream," Tad said.

"The ice cream is for dessert, dear," Gay said. "Look, Tad, I have asparagus too, with hollandaise sauce." She shook shreds of chicken over the plates and set them down in front of us.

"May I have a cigarette then?" He reached into his jacket pocket and pulled out his pack of Pall Malls.

"Remember we agreed, no smoking at the dinner table," Gay said.

"I'll be going along to bed then. Goodnight," he said, and stood up.

"Oh, mercy," Gay said. "What are we going to do with you, Tad?" He left.

I had assumed with Tad out of the way that we would speak frankly and realistically. Instead Gay brought down two cut-glass cordial glasses from her sideboard and struggled with a bottle of wine.

"I'm not much of a traveler in the wine world," I confessed. "I would make another martini, with your permission."

"Would you, darling Billy?" Gay cried girlishly.

She talked nonstop. "My aerobics class is perfectly *mah-vellous.* Why, we leap and run in place—what a workout, I'm sure! And the people are fascinating! We have a veterinarian and a biologist. Did you know that quail migrate south for the winter on foot, in single file down the sides of mountains? Isn't that simply extraordinary? I told Tad about it—he was so surprised." Her hand, suspended from a raised elbow throughout this speech, held a fork with a few grains of rice on it. Rice fluttered down off the fork as she spoke until none was left. Then Gay moved the fork into her mouth and went through a pantomime of chewing and swallowing—nothing.

"Simply *mah-vellous,"* she said, a lie and a habit, but with gin and a hot dinner I forgave her.

She sprinkled cigarette ash onto her uneaten supper, talking, talking. Her arms cut the air like scissors. She was not a smoker, particularly, but an actress, an ancient coquette.

Much later, I found myself, after several cocktails, wandering upstairs in my BVDs and my raincoat, looking for the john. Here was a linen closet. Here were Gay and Tad, cadaverous on their backs under a white sheet. A shadow moved along the wall, and Gay sat up. "Billy, what a delightful surprise. Move your legs, Tad. Billy has come to sit with us. Isn't it just like camping out, sitting up late, talking in the moonlight, having cigarettes?" she said.

Tad's eyes opened.

I stepped back in horror. "I was merely going to make my final statement," I said. The toilet and the claw feet of the bathtub bloomed up through an open door across the hall.

I slept guiltily on the pallet in Gay's sewing room. In the morning Gay clattered downstairs, ready for the hospital in a sleeveless dress and high heels. We each sat over a cup of coffee and a toasted frozen waffle on a plate. Tad smoked through breakfast. I had the sense, as Gay applied red lipstick in the mirror by the door and hooked a powder-blue purse over her bone arm, that I would not see her again. My spirit flailed protests as she rolled her car backward into the road, heedless of traffic, and drove away.

A clock I could not see thumped out seconds. Flung back in his pink easy chair, Tad lit a cigarette. I walked a turn through the kitchen, dining room, and living room—a circular pattern that led nowhere. The telephone on a table reminded me that I had not got the name of the hospital from Gay.

I dried the three cups and saucers, the three plates and the silverware, and left everything upside down on the drainboard. I passed the morning supervising Tad's smoking and reading some amusing pieces from the old magazines I had brought along for Gay. My memory is feeble enough that any good reading seems fresh.

At noon I told Tad I would take him to lunch. He stood up and pocketed his cigarettes and lighter, and we walked out the door without overcoats, two old men with as little baggage as when we were boys.

Gay's house was on a sharp corner near the town line, twelve stone steps straight down to the road. I held tight to the iron rail, which had rattled loose from years. Tad undulated abreast of me, his blazer sleeve hooked in mine.

The bottom stair met the road blindly; cars sped around a curve at forty-five miles an hour. Tad and I waited on the bottom stair, our woolen elbows almost touching. The stones were slick with yellow maple leaves, and I mistook for a speeding car the rush of the world that seemed to welcome us. Then, impatient, I pulled Tad out to a quiet place, and a roulette wheel of Thunderbirds and produce trucks spun dizzily past us on their way to the green squares of the old outer farms. I breathed the needly scent of pine sprill, the mossy autumn dander on the ground. A pulse sang in my neck.

Tad weighted my arm, pulling me down into the road. Then

thrillingly close, without a breath of warning, a red Cadillac rushed by, brushing the outer leaves of Gay's English ivy on the wall.

We were spared, not smashed; the heels of our loafers held to the bottom stone. My heart roared life in my ears, but how could I be glad? My life is a shuck, and I did not think of Tad as a life.

I untwined my arm from his and left him standing in the road. It seemed the only sensible thing, with Gay gone; otherwise, he would end up in a Home, wild and uncomprehending, not allowed to smoke. For a moment it seemed a simple thing, a rectification of an earlier mistake, Gay's mistake in bringing him back from the dead. I backed up onto the stone stairs again, flattened myself into the English ivy on the old dirt wall. I considered climbing the stairs to read a few pages of my book while I waited, but this seemed coldblooded, and the stairs were difficult and dangerous. I would say, when asked, that Tad must have wandered off.

Tad, sensing himself alone in the road, reached into his pocket and removed his lighter and a Pall Mall.

The maple leaves haunted my dim eyes—they looked like bicyclists. Tad's cigarette mixed tobacco smoke with the old smell of burning leaves. He was full alive, standing in the road at the edge of death, smoking a cigarette, and no car came.

No car came and ran him down or pulled him into its path. I closed my eyes in a sort of prayer, and heard no shriek of brakes, no sound of metal on bone. No car came at all. Traffic had stopped suddenly on this well-used route when I put my brother in its path. Unable to hear or see any car that might be around the corner, I made a jump of faith into the road. I gave us both up and brought us stiffly to the other side, single file, like quail down the mountainside, heading south with Tad behind me.

No guilt haunted me—setting my brother out this way in the road. I could not recognize myself, pressed against Gay's ivy on the dirt wall, waiting. But I have not recognized myself for years. Only Tad, lighting a cigarette, seemed real; his face, unlit by any sense of danger or betrayal, seemed more familiar than my own. What had I done? Maybe nothing.

We walked slowly through the town, past the Walgreen's where, two weeks before, Kay Kilcannon had been hit and killed on the sidewalk by a woman on a motorcycle.

I worried us across the street, all arms and elbows, then we slid into the two slick sides of a red-cushioned booth at Brigham's. The waitress handed us menus tacky with pancake syrup. "I would like a hamburg and a cup of coffee," I told her.

"I would like a plate of chocolate ice cream," Tad said.

"I don't suppose you have the slightest idea what's going on," I said when the waitress had finally left.

"No, no," said Tad, pulling his Pall Malls out of his jacket pocket and shaking the pack.

Nothing came out but some tobacco and lint.

"Here, here, let me do that for you," I said. I took the pack and his Zippo lighter from him, shook out the pack and nothing fell out. The weight of the Zippo felt familiar in my hand, the metal smooth under the wide blue flame.

Though the lunch would be my treat, of course, I would tell Gay about the cigarettes. They didn't carry Pall Malls. I pointed to a pack of my old brand under the glass and paid the girl. When I returned to our table with the new pack, Tad already had a cigarette burning in his lips. I recalled Gay telling me how he had become quite cagey, hiding smokes all over himself.

"It doesn't matter if you smoke—the usual considerations don't apply to you, do they?" I asked.

"Mmmm-mmm," Tad nodded his head, dragging on his cigarette and watching the smoke drift.

"Tell me, Tad, do you remember the accident at all, falling down the stairs? Do you remember our mother?"

"Where is Gay?" he said, and leaned back while the waitress slid a silver dish of ice cream somewhere between us. Tad held his cigarette between two fingers while he spooned up his ice cream. When he finished and the waitress came to take the dish away he said, "I'll have more ice cream."

"Certainly, sir," she said, and she was gone before I could stop her.

The next time Tad asked for more ice cream, I took out my wallet and asked for the bill.

"Shall I get the ice cream first?" the waitress asked, confused.

"Of course not. Can't you see this man is five years old?" I scoffed.

"I might go along to bed then," Tad said.

But he was only reaching for his pack of cigarettes and his Zippo. We walked back to Gay's—neither of us spoke. We got across the road safely, no thanks to me, and up the stone stairs. We climbed to the second floor, and I left him there and went to my cot in the sewing room. I lay there looking at a ball of Tad's socks next to Gay's sewing machine. When I got up an hour later, I saw Tad from the corner of my eye—unrolled on the chenille bedspread, his brown shoes stuck up like boards on the bed. The ordinariness of the scene surprised me: a conjugal bedroom, Gay's glass and silver jars, a basket of scarves, bottles of eau de Cologne and aftershave on the bureau, Tad's blazer hung on a valet in one corner.

That night I believe he missed her.

"Where is Gay?" he said when he woke up.

"Do you know who I am, Tad?" I asked him, but he would not say.

"Where is Gay? Gay!" he called. He went through every room in the house, leaning heavily on her fragile, old wicker end tables, old, rotten painted chairs. Finally, he came back into the living room where I was sitting in a rocking chair, reading and drinking a martini. He hung in the door.

"Tell Gay I need her now."

"Gay will be back tomorrow. There is nothing to eat," I said clearly.

"I'll be in the car then," he said.

A thrill buzzed through me. *Down the stairs and into the road.*

"The hell with you," I said, and returned to my book.

But he just sat down in his chair and pulled out a half-smoked cigarette from under the seat cushion. He smoked for an hour, facing me with his head tipped back, looking as if he might laugh or smile, or as if he thought he had one up on me.

Tad went to bed early—it couldn't have been after six o'clock. I was still reading when he came down again at about nine, dressed in a fresh shirt and slacks, and demanded breakfast.

"Go back to bed, Tad," I said.

"I want Gay," he said.

"You've been spoiled," I said.

"You pushed me," he said.

"Don't be silly, Tad," I said.

"You did push. I want to see Gay," he insisted. He went off and disappeared, then he came back wearing nothing.

This was too much. I stood up and faced him down the way we used to play—stink eye. "You aren't going anywhere," I said.

His eyes, watery and old, looked back into mine. "But get the blue pajamas," he said.

I had hoped she would return before sunset so I could cut out early, but by the time Gay's key scratched in the door, I was a prisoner of the dark. She looked poorly, and more gaunt, and moved a vase of vivid plastic flowers from the piano to the cocktail table. She seemed like a body from which the spirit had fled, but this was conjecture. She flitted like a moth, and I imagined her clinging to a drape and dying upright, crumbling into yellow powder when I reached out to feel if she was cold. She snatched at my hand and her fingers felt like dust. "Oh, Billy, how delightful of you to take Tad to Brigham's for lunch!" she said, and even her voice sounded dry.

When Gay was gone I would list the house with Hunneman, send the few good things to auction at Skinner, and give the rest to the junkman. At my age I have no interest in Tad's artifacts.

She brought out the gin bottle and I forgave her for lateness. I stirred martinis for Gay and me in a smaller flower vase, poured ginger ale for Tad into a jelly glass. I found no cupboards for glassware or food, only batteries and cocktail napkins and beeswax candles and cracked cups filled with ballpoint pens and cartons of Pall Malls.

"Well, you have been to the doctor," I said, opening the subject.

"Oh, Billy, how good of you to ask. Everything is just fine, thank you." She bustled over chicken pot pies, which we ate out of their tins off TV trays in the living room, then Gay surprised me by offering cordials. "Let's sit, let's have a cordial. Shall I turn on the radio? Tad just loves music, don't you, Tad?"

My eye had hung since yesterday on the pack of cigarettes I had bought for Tad—my old brand—and the hunger had grown in me until, with Gay smoking too, and Tad, I finally got up and picked up the pack to shake out a smoke and revisit that old haunt one more time.

But once again the pack was empty.

When Gay came tottering back on her high heels with the tiny glasses of gin, I spoke rather sharply to her about it. "Before I forget, I might ask you to make good on this pack I bought for Tad yesterday. He's run through it already," I told her.

She put down the drinks and rummaged through her purse and then through her wallet and finally extracted a dollar bill and two quarters.

"Is this enough?"

"That should cover it," I said. I was rather rough on Gay for the rest of the evening, I'm afraid, so annoyed was I with myself for almost smoking, for giving in now when I had not given in before.

I woke from a dream in which I was stuck in Tad's pink chair, smoking cigarette after cigarette, breathing greedily the smoke into my lungs, puffing out "The Cremation of Sam McGee" to a roomful of students. I woke guilty on the cot in Gay's sewing room. My pillow smelled of old smoke. I walked down the uneven hall in darkness, barefoot in BVDs and my tan raincoat, to the open door of the bath. A chain hung down from a burning naked bulb, and under it stood Gay with her back toward me in a thin nightgown printed over with delphiniums, the bone bumps of the blades of her back rising as she heaved herself up from the chenille bathmat to the window ledge with her arms on the towel bar. Her leg bent in on itself like a chicken wing. The old double-hung window opened unevenly over the flagstones twenty feet below, and it dawned on me at last that she was about to leap out of the window, that she was trying to do herself in.

The black shadow of her head turned and unfolded itself hugely from the wall. She straddled the window like a scarecrow.

"Gay!" I said.

She turned to me, all attentive, as if I had asked her to pass a plate of chicken.

"Do you need to use the loo, Billy? I'll be right out," she said. With two hands she pulled her legs down, one at a time, from the ledge. Sounds came forth, like joints popping. Through the fabric of her nightgown, in the harsh light of the bulb, I saw the violent crosshatching of her bones.

She climbed down, obedient. I stood in the doorway, an old man in BVDs and a raincoat, a toothbrush hanging in my hand to brush away the taste of ashes. I read the names on the bottles and jars lined up on the ceramic back of the toilet: Nail Polish Remover, Cold Cream, After Bath Splash, a glass jar filled with cotton balls, marked "cotton balls," all of which reminded me, with a pang, of the women of my generation, most of whom are now dead.

My arms flew up—in fear—as Gay slid by me like a card.

"Don't kiss me, I'm covered in creams," she said.

I saw in the darkness the sick glow of her face and the white spectral palms she held up to ward me off.

And this was how, having failed to do in my brother, I saved my sister-in-law's life, then brushed my teeth and went to bed. In the morning I went home to familiar ground and left them as they were.

Arthur Bradford

Catface

From *Epoch*

1. Room for Rent

THE DISABILITY PAYMENTS were being cut down since, according to their doctor, I was getting better. I had been without work for months and needed money so I decided to share my place and split the cost. My place was small. They called it a "studio apartment" which meant it was only one room. The kitchen was set off in the corner and my little bed sat over against the opposite wall. It was a cozy arrangement.

My first roommate was a guy named Thurber. He breathed very heavily through his nose and when he spoke the words came out in high-pitched squeaks. Thurber moved quickly with jerks and twists like spasms and for a while I thought he was diseased. He had dark circles under his eyes. Before he moved in I had placed two small green plants on the windowsill but once Thurber saw these he pitched them out the window. "Damn plants!" he yelled after them. Later on I brought in a larger spider plant and he screamed at me, "Get that fucking plant out of here!"

Thurber had answered my ad for "roommate-wanted" by show-ing up at my door with his bags. I am a somewhat meek person and I let him stay even though I was suspicious of his shifty appearance. Thurber said he was a good cook and would prepare fine meals for me. I said great, I like good food as much as the next guy. As it turned out Thurber hardly ever cooked and when he did he made a chaotic mess which sat there for days until I cleaned it up myself. Thurber's taste in food was always too hot for my palate and his dishes usually looked nothing like whatever he said they were supposed to be. "This is Lemon Chicken," he once said. But the food in question looked more like baked beans, or maybe some kind of Sloppy Joe.

Thurber snored loudly too and this was finally why he had to leave. "Thurber," I said, "you snore like a pig and I can't sleep. Perhaps you should find somewhere else to go."

"I don't snore," replied Thurber, but he left sometime the next afternoon. As he packed up his stuff he casually slipped several pieces of my clothing into his bag. He also took a brand new toothbrush of mine and a large lamp. I was standing right there watching him.

My next roommate was a woman named Cynthia who claimed to have some children which she kept at her sister's house. I never saw them. Cynthia read three or four magazines a day and it wasn't until a few weeks of living with her that I learned about her hooking business. When I was gone she would take men into our place and give them head for ten to twenty dollars apiece. According to her she never had real sex with them and I'm inclined to believe this because I have been in whorehouses before and they have a certain electricity to them. It's in the air. I never felt this electric feeling when I walked into my home. A man who lived next door told me about all the male visitors and so that night I said to Cynthia, "What's going on here?"

She said, "Oh, I just give them blowjobs for money."

After Cynthia, Clyde moved in and he only stayed for three days. He had a large duffel bag full of clothes but he never changed outfits once since I knew him. He liked his blue jeans and T-shirt I guess. Two guys with toothpicks in their mouths showed up on Clyde's third day and they stood in the doorway staring at Clyde for quite some time before one said, "Let's go, Clyde."

❏ ❏ ❏ ❏

Jimmy moved in next and he was quite a card. He told jokes to me all the time and some of them were very funny. I remember one in particular about a rabbit working in a gas station which had me laughing off and on for hours.

"You should be a comedian, Jimmy," I once said.

"That's what they all say," he said.

As far as I could tell Jimmy helped out a man who took bets on college sporting events. I'm not nosy and I don't pry into the lives of other people. Jimmy had simply told me that he was "in sports management."

I appreciated Jimmy's sense of humor a lot and then one day Jimmy did something which made me appreciate him even more. He brought in a small orange tent and set it up right inside the apartment. He put his blankets and pillow in there and said, "See, this way I have my own room."

Jimmy and his tent had been in the apartment for nearly two months when we heard a loud knock on the door. "It's me, Thurber," said the voice behind the door. It was high pitched, whining even.

"Come on in, Thurber," I said, but I did not get up to open the door for him.

Thurber rattled the handle a little bit and then whacked the door with his hand. It was locked. I still didn't get up and so after a while he went away.

Jimmy said, "I know some friends of mine who could kick that guy's ass."

"That would be nice," I said.

A few days later Thurber came into our apartment. He let himself in with a set of keys he had kept from before. His lip was fat and purple and both his eyes were black.

"I need to wash up," he said.

Thurber limped over to the sink and splashed water all over the place. "A group of men kicked my ass for no reason," he said.

"If you had keys," I said, "why didn't you let yourself in before?"

"I never even met those fuckers before in my life." Thurber was covered in water, pink from his own blood. He looked terrible. His hair was greasy and his clothing was matted with dirt.

"You look terrible," I said.

Thurber spied a group of potted plants by the window and lunged at them. His skinny arm knocked them over so the dirt spilled onto the carpet.

"Why is there a tent in here?" he asked me.

Jimmy answered him from inside. "It's my tent, asshole," he said.

Thurber looked down at the tent which had just spoken to him. He seemed a little surprised.

"You're kidding me."

"No," said Jimmy's voice, "and those were my friends who kicked your ass. I asked them to do it."

Thurber was amazed. He stumbled around and stuttered a bit and then walked out the door. He left drops of water all over the place and a putrid smell which lingered in the air for a while. The plants lay overturned on the carpet.

"Keep me posted on any developments with this Thurber fruit-cake," said Jimmy one day as he packed his bag.

"I'm going away for a while so I won't be around," he said.

"Okay fine," I said and then that day I found myself a pet dog. I didn't know how long Jimmy would be away and so I wanted some company. I have always wanted a dog.

The dog I found had only three legs. He was missing a front one so he hopped forward on one paw. Like most three-legged dogs this dog managed quite well for himself and I didn't feel sorry for him at all. While Jimmy was gone the dog and I went out for frequent walks and once I got a citation for not having a leash on my pet.

"I'm really sorry about this, officer. It will never happen again," I said, and I meant it. I want no trouble with the law. I used a piece of rope instead of a leash though.

Once when we returned from a walk we found Thurber sitting inside the apartment with a man we all knew as "Catface." Catface was a guy who had some sort of medical problem which made his face very shiny and flat. His eyes were only little slits. His nose was small and flattened and his ears were tiny and crumpled up. I had once thought that Catface was the victim of a bad accident with fire but then someone told me that this was not the case. He was born like that.

"Hello, Thurber," I said, "Hello, Catface." We all called him Catface. There was no hiding it.

Thurber, I noticed, had been eating my food. It was in a bowl next to where he sat. The funny thing about it was he had chosen some food I had intended to feed to the dog.

"You've eaten the dog's food." I said.

Thurber said, "Your dog only has three legs."

"I know that," I said.

"Where's the guy who lives in the tent?" asked Thurber.

I hadn't noticed this before but now I saw that stupid Thurber had dismantled Jimmy's tent and scattered it all over the floor.

"Oh, you shouldn't have done that," I said. I looked at Catface to see if he had been part of the destruction.

"If he had been inside that thing he would have been in a lot of trouble," said Thurber. "Catface would have tore him apart."

Catface nodded in agreement.

"Listen," I said, "I wish you two hadn't come in here and messed up Jimmy's stuff. Now we have to clean it up before he gets back."

"Where is he?" asked Thurber.

"I don't know," I answered.

Thurber and Catface decided to leave. On the way out Catface patted my dog.

"How are you, Catface?" I asked. I hadn't seen him in a while. In fact, I had never spoken to him before, but I think he knew who I was.

"I'm doing okay," said Catface.

When Jimmy returned a few days later he did not notice what Thurber and Catface had done because I had cleaned the whole mess up. He laid his stuff down on a chair and said to me, "I'd like you to meet my friend Robyn."

In walked this woman with straight red hair and a large ring through the tip of her nose.

"That's a nice ring," I said.

Robyn said, "Thank you."

I introduced Jimmy and Robyn to the dog and Jimmy told a joke about a three-legged dog who ran a Laundromat. After he was done and we all chuckled Jimmy said, "Robyn and I are going to step out for a while."

They didn't get back until it was almost morning and the dog barked loudly when they walked in. Robyn made a hissing sound through her teeth which shut him up right away.

It wasn't until late in the afternoon that Jimmy and Robyn crawled out of the tent. Robyn was completely naked and I saw that she had several tattoos including one of a wicked snake which coiled up her thigh. Again the dog barked at them and again Robyn hissed. I found my piece of rope and took the dog for a walk so as to give Jimmy and Robyn some time to themselves.

We wandered around for hours and didn't get back until after dark. Inside the apartment I discovered that Robyn and Jimmy had lit about a hundred candles. The candles were melting and wax was dripping everywhere. I could feel the heat.

"This is something else," I said.

Jimmy and Robyn were sitting on my bed. "I heard about what that fuckface Thurber did to my tent," said Jimmy.

"I haven't seen him since that," I said.

"Robyn has placed a hex on him," said Jimmy. "His life will never be the same."

I was not let in on the specifics of Robyn's hex. I knew only that it involved many candles and would eventually make Thurber very miserable.

"Is it working?" I asked Robyn after a few days had passed.

"Oh yes," she said, and then she muttered something about how "all sheep do cometh yonder."

"Do you worship Satan?" I asked her.

"No, I do not," she said.

□ □ □ □

Jimmy and Robyn decided to go out one afternoon and I was instructed to keep the candles burning. They had been gone only about ten minutes when Thurber burst in. He looked worse than I had ever seen him. He was sweaty and his teeth were black.

"And what is going on here?" he yelled.

"Hello, Thurber," I said.

"What is this voodoo bullshit? Huh?"

"Jimmy's friend Robyn is interested in this," I said. The dog growled at Thurber. I had never seen someone so close to death. Thurber's skin was a pale green. He had lost weight and so his ratty clothes were falling off him.

Thurber began knocking the candles over with wild sweeps of his thin arms. I was worried he would start a fire. He soon became winded though and had to stop.

"Jimmy will be upset about this," I said.

Thurber coughed and collapsed onto the floor. I went over to his smelly body and saw that he was still breathing. I dragged him out the door, down the stairs, and onto the street where I left him lying.

At some point Thurber must have gotten up and left because Jimmy and Robyn did not see him on their way in. They did however see the waxy mess he had left behind when he knocked over the candles. Robyn exclaimed, "He hath come."

That night Robyn spent several hours smearing paint and make-up all over Jimmy's body. When she was done Jimmy looked like an animal of the jungle.

"Go forth," she said to Jimmy. "Seek ye the lamb."

Jimmy walked out the door naked, covered in the paint of many colors.

"Now what is a person going to think when they see that?" I asked.

Robyn placed a finger over her lip and she said, "Shhh . . ."

We waited up for Jimmy but dawn came and he did not return. Robyn let the candles die out.

"My work is done here," she said to me.

"Where is Jimmy?" I asked.

"He shall never return."

Robyn searched in her bag and produced a piece of fruit. It was dark, as if it had been ripe too long.

"Here," she said, holding the fruit out to me. "Eat of this and ye shall transcend."

It was strange fruit, long and wrinkled. On its skin there were tiny hairs. I ate it and it tasted good.

I went walking with the dog in the early morning. The air was cold and I had to face away from the sun as it rose up. It was too bright. We limped along, me and the three-legged dog. I was feeling better. On the empty street I came across Catface. He too was wandering around.

"Hello, Catface," I said.

"I understand you are looking for a roommate," said Catface.

"Yes I am," I said.

2. Mutants

I took my three-legged dog for a walk in the park today. He is a happy dog in spite of his lack of a front leg. He gets along just fine. When we go out someone usually comes up to me and wants to know how it happened. I don't know the real answer but often I come up with some good tales about how a bear nipped it off in the woods or how when he was a puppy he got too close to a bandsaw. The truth is I got him this way. He was limping around outside my place and I took him in. I was lonely at the time (I still am) and I figured I needed a pet.

So today I was walking with him and this woman approached me with real wide eyes. She said, "Hey, you got a dog with only three legs."

I said, "That's right."

The woman kept looking at me from different angles, like she wasn't sure if I was really there, like maybe I was an illusion, a mirage, I don't know. She said, "I too have a dog."

"With three legs?" I inquired.

"No," she said, "she's got all four."

Just then a chubby little hound waddled up to us, tail wagging, tongue hanging out. "This is Esmeralda," said the woman.

"Nice name," I said.

We watched together as Esmeralda and my three-legged dog frolicked about on the grass. That Esmeralda sure was a flirt! Then I turned to the lady and said, "Is your dog fixed?" By that I meant had the dog been given an operation so that it could no longer reproduce.

The woman said, "Oh no. Of course not. Do you believe in that?"

"Oh, I don't know," I said. I didn't know. Perhaps we should leave our dogs alone, let them breed as they please.

The dogs were getting along famously. They licked and bit and clawed and chomped at each other's faces. "This is nice that they are playing," I said.

"Yes," said the woman. I then got a close look at her. I wouldn't mind being with her, I thought. She had a soft face with a kind of European look to it, possibly Polish. Her eyes were sad and she had brown curly hair. She was no looker, to be sure, but I would have all the same.

She then asked me, "Do you know a lot about dogs?"

"Well, I know a little bit," I said. "About as much as anyone else."

"Esmeralda has had some puppies," she said. "Would you like to see them?"

I said, "Yes, I sure would." Puppies!

The woman led me back to her small apartment. It looked out over an enormous parking lot. She said the lights from the lot shined in her windows at night so that the whole place sort of glowed.

"Must be hard to sleep," I ventured.

"Yes, it is," she said after giving it some thought.

She took me to a little back room where the puppies were strewn about on the floor. It was dark in there because she had hung a bedsheet over the window. All that I could see were small black lumps. The room was filled with a stale, organic odor, the pungent smell of milky puppy breath perhaps. Esmeralda wandered in and lay down amongst the squirming mass. Tiny whimpers rose into the air, little sniffles and cries of recognition. My dog stood cautiously behind us in the doorway.

"How about turning on a light?" I said. I couldn't see the little critters. They only appeared to be balls of fur.

Before she flicked on the light switch the woman said to me, "Now, I think there might be something wrong with them . . ."

What an understatement that was. The little pups were mutants! Deformed! They crawled about on mere nubs instead of legs. Some were missing limbs all together. One clump of three of them were attached at the sides—a three way Siamese twin!

I stood there dumbfounded. What a collection of misfits! "These puppies are deformed," I finally said. One of them had no eyes. Where the sockets should have been there was just skin, flat and covered with fur. What strange creature had Esmeralda come across?

The woman looked at me worried. "I know that they are wrong," she said. "I know most puppies don't come out like that. I already knew that."

My dog began a low growl from behind us. "Grrrrrr," he said. Esmeralda just lay among them, a proud mother.

"Well," I said, "I don't know what to tell you. I don't think some of them will survive." One forlorn pup had squirmed his way into a corner of the room. He was equipped with a set of four furry fins instead of legs. Flippers maybe, like those of a sea tortoise.

The low "grrrrrr" sound from behind us continued. I decided to step aside so that my dog could examine the mutants himself. He growled louder but ventured forth into the bodies all the same.

"Your dog," said the woman, "is abnormal also." She looked at me for some sort of confirmation, as if knowledge of this fact shared would ease her soul.

And I said, "Yes, this is true." I reached out and took her hand, soft and clammy, into mine. She gripped me tight.

My dog wandered amongst the whimpering pups, sniffing at them, on occasion giving one a gentle lick. Esmeralda maintained her motherly glow. I moved closer to the woman. I still didn't know her name. I put my arm around her and felt her bony shoulders. A nice warmth arose from them.

"Do you want to go into the other room?" I asked.

She nodded and we left the dogs to their sniffing and strange little grunts and squeaks. We went into her bedroom and there I removed her clothing, half expecting to find some gross scar or hidden limb beneath it all. She was normal though, with white skin and funny ribs which stuck out, making her look more slender than she really was. I sucked on her nipple and she let out a little moan, high-pitched, surprised, excited.

3. Catface and the Little Dogs

I had been living with Catface for a few weeks now. He kept strange hours, preferring to sleep during the day and leaving me alone at night. I'm not sure what he did with himself while he was away. He was employed part-time down at one of the warehouses as a security guard, I believe. I had taken to visiting my woman friend Christine in the daytime, while he slept. Christine lived by herself with a room full of mutant puppies. Each morning I would make my way over there with my three-legged dog and we would tend to the little creatures. They needed constant care and supervision. Some of the more able pups had grown feisty and they were giving the others trouble, shutting them out from Esmeralda's milking breasts and nipping at their helpless nubs in a cruel mockery of puppy play. I suggested separating them but Christine would not have it. "They are a family," she said.

One day I returned to the apartment and Catface was singing in his sleep. It was a silly song about a cottontail rabbit named "Squeak." I had at first assumed that Catface was awake as he sung this tune but when I moved closer I saw that his freaky cat eyes were shut. He wore an impish grin and his voice was pitched in a high falsetto, like a girl's. This is how the ditty went:

> I am a cottontail rabbit named Squeak
> and I hop and play all day.
> Everywhere I go

the kids are sure to follow
because Squeak is here to stay!

What a songbird that Catface was! I had never seen him so animated. He swung his round head from side to side in joyful exuberance as he chirped away. I took his singing as a sign that he had grown comfortable here and I was pleased about that.

When Catface woke up it was dark. He rubbed his little slits for eyes and gazed about the room.

"How's Squeak?" I asked him.

"What?" he said.

I began to sing his song: *"I am a cottontail rabbit named Squeak and I hop and play all day . . ."*

Catface seemed confused. "What the hell is that?" he asked.

Was he really unaware of his own childish banter? Perhaps he was embarrassed and only feigning ignorance. I decided to let it drop. I said, "Oh, it's nothing."

"Okay, fine," said Catface. He rose up from his bed, fully clothed, as was his habit. He did occasionally change his outfits but never before he went to sleep. He even kept his socks on. That night he was wearing what is known as "double denim"—blue jeans and a blue jean shirt. He was quite a stylish guy.

Catface stretched out his long arms and he said, "My family is coming to town."

"Oh, really?" I said. His family! I didn't know Catface had any relatives at all, much less a whole family.

"They are coming through town on business," he said. "They'll be here for a few days."

"Excellent," I said. "Can I meet them?"

"Yes, you may," said Catface.

I wanted to ask him if they too possessed catfaces, but I felt it would be inappropriate. I would find out soon enough.

Esmeralda was growing weary of the constant nipping and tugging from her puppies. One day she got up and walked away from them, causing a great deal of commotion in the puppy room. They yipped and barked until we went in there ourselves with bottles of milk in hand. Christine had named each of the puppies after the Greek gods. I couldn't keep them all straight. There was Hermes with the furry flippers and there was Adonis with no eyes. There was Aphrodite with a cyclops eye and Athena with the nubs for legs. The three way Siamese twins were simply called "The Weird Sisters" after the three witches in the play by Shakespeare called "Macbeth."

The little mutants were growing larger and soon they would have to do without their mother's milk. "What plans do you have for these puppies?" I asked Christine.

She said, "I believe God has delivered them to me. I have accepted it as my mission to care for them all."

What a notion! This woman was going to live out her life with a dozen mutant dogs. I had, in more private moments, envisioned a happy future for Christine and myself. A small house in the country perhaps, with that frisky Esmeralda and my three-legged dog, and maybe one or two of the mutants. But the whole lot of them? I began to question my fanciful dreams.

When I arrived home that day Catface was at it again with his singing. I said to myself, "I've got to get some material proof of this." So I went to my neighbor's place and borrowed his small tape recorder. I taped Catface singing, *"Oh, I am Squeak the cottontail. Won't you come and play with me?"* He sang it over and over.

That night, when Catface woke up, I said to him, "Boy, do I have something for you."

I played the tape for him and he said, "What the fuck is that?"

I said, "It's you singing."

"No, it's not," he said.

"Don't you remember this song?" I asked him. I turned up the volume on the tape player. It sounded ridiculous, like a psychotic young child.

Catface said, "Is this your idea of a joke?"

I gave up and turned the tape player off. "It's not a joke," I said. "It's you." I went back downstairs to return the tape player to my neighbor, but I kept the tape for myself.

❑ ❑ ❑ ❑

When I got back upstairs Christine and Esmeralda were in the apartment. Christine was sobbing and Catface had his hand on her shoulder in a comforting gesture. Christine looked up at me and said, "The puppies are gone. Someone has taken them."

"That's awful," I said. "Why would someone do that?"

"I wish you had told me they were special puppies," said Catface. "I just wish I had known about that."

"I'm sorry," I said, "I thought I'd told you."

"Well you didn't."

It occurred to me then that Catface and Christine had never met. I said, "Catface, this is Christine."

"I know that," said Catface.

Christine wiped her eyes with a hanky which Catface had given her. She said, "And you didn't tell me that Gerard had a catface."

I looked at Catface. "Your name is Gerard?" I said.

"Yes, it is," he said.

We all got together and tried to think of what to do about the missing puppies. Catface and Christine seemed unusually comfortable with one another. At several points he boldly took her frail hands into his. I wondered if they were forming some kind of allegiance against me because I had not informed them of each other's mutation secrets.

We filed a police report and posted notices all over the neighborhood. They said, in big block letters, "WHO STOLE THE PUPPIES?" The intruder had left Christine's apartment a mess. He rifled through everything, but the only objects he ended up stealing were the puppies, all twelve of them. I imagined this must have been quite a caper. Christine's clothes were scattered about everywhere, and, in a particularly eerie touch, the house plants had been uprooted and flung against the walls.

"Do you suppose Thurber is back in town?" I asked Catface.

"I think it is possible," he said.

That night Catface, Christine, and I took a bus out to the fairgrounds to see Catface's family. It turned out they were working for a traveling carnival. Catface had said only that they "worked in the show," so I couldn't be sure what that meant. As we walked onto the fairgrounds Christine and Catface held hands and I tried to ignore that.

The carnival was lit up in a spectacular display of lighting technology. The rides soared towards the heavens glistening with robust colors and magical sounds. There were shouts and screams coming from all directions and the wind carried with it a distinct odor of sugar and flaming beef. I hadn't been to such an event since I was a small child and I must confess I was struck with awe.

Catface took it all in stride however and he led us calmly through the masses. He seemed suddenly at home in this land of glitz and grandeur. We walked by the Pickled Punk Show, a tent which claimed to have the bodies of freak babies preserved in jars. "There's no real flesh in there," said Catface. "It's just photographs. They outlawed the jars years ago."

Christine said, "I see."

For a dollar we could have entered a tent where a drug-crazed maniac stuffed a python down his throat. There was a man who could hammer six-inch nails into the nostrils of his nose. There was a fire eater and a sword swallower and of course, there was a fat lady. Catface led us past them all. "It's all real," he said.

We entered a red tent pitched behind the hubbub and commotion. Catface went in first and he was greeted with cries of, "Gerard! Hooray, it's Gerard!" I followed Christine and watched as a whole family of them mobbed around my friend Catface. Yes, they had catfaces too. There was the big Papa, sitting in his chair, shiny flat face and all. There was the mama, plump as well, with her hair done up in a bun so that you could see her little crumpled ears. "How nice that they have found each other," I thought. The kids, four of them, dashed about with enormous grins on their little cat faces. They leapt upon their big brother and showered him with love. "Gerard is here! Gerard is here!" they cried out. Of course they did not call him "Catface" as I had foolishly expected.

Catface introduced Christine and me to his jovial family and we all sat down for some tea. Mama Catface poured the potent brew and it tasted like nothing I had ever drunk before. "This is delicious," I said.

"Why, thank you," she said.

It turned out that Catface's family ran this show. Far from being mere freaks on display, as I had crassly hypothesized, they were the Big Bosses. The freaks had to answer to them! "Oh, we started out as performers," said Papa Catface, "but a little business sense changed that in a hurry." He chuckled and the children gathered about him at his feet.

Catface asked, "Where's Maria?"

His mother answered, "Oh, she's out and about. She'll be back soon."

Mama Catface turned to Christine and me and she said, "Maria is Gerard's twin sister."

A twin sister. My God, the secrets old Catface had kept from me. And he had been upset over my not telling him about Christine's puppies. "I'd like to meet Maria," I said.

"Oh, she'd like you," said Mama Catface and I was glad to hear that.

Then a normal looking young man walked in and he went over to whisper something in Papa Catface's ear. Papa Catface nodded and he said, "Send him in."

The man left and Papa Catface said to us, "Someone has come with a business proposition."

There was a bustling about outside. I heard the familiar yips of young canines and then the horrible high-pitched whine of a voice which could only come from the man we all knew as Thurber. He burst into the tent with an enormous burlap sack slung over his shoulder. His skinny body was covered in dust and grime.

"Get away from me!" he was saying. "I don't need your god-damn help!"

Thurber plunked the squirming sack down on the floor. He looked up and saw big Papa Catface first, then Catface, and then me.

"Hello, Thurber," I said.

"What the hell are you doing here?" he said to me.

Christine rushed forward and opened up Thurber's sack. The little puppies came spilling out, squealing with delight and joy. She said, "Oh, my little darlings," and they jumped upon her, licking at her face.

Catface stood up and walked towards Thurber.

"Well hello, Catface," said Thurber.

"My name is Gerard," said Catface.

Thurber's dirty face was filled with anger and confusion. "What's going on here?" he said.

"You stole these puppies," said Catface.

"I did not," said Thurber. "I bought them off a merchant on the street."

Catface said, "Get out," and Thurber stood there for a moment trying to think of something else to say. His weasel-like eyes darted around the tent. I could see him trying to take it all in. Poor Thurber. He must have thought he'd hit upon a gold mine with those freak puppies, and now this.

Finally Thurber said, "Forget it," and he left.

Catface knelt down and he nestled his face into the mass of puppy bodies. They licked at him and he said, "Oh, what lovely creatures."

We all sat and watched as Catface let the puppies crawl over him. He laughed like a child and spoke to them in a crazy little voice. "Oh, what nice puppies," he chirped. "Oh, what wonderful little puppies." That voice! It was Squeak the Rabbit! But I did not tell him so.

The Catfaces invited us to stay for dinner, a scrumptious feast of rice and beans. We ate it up as the mutant pups played around our feet. When the meal began to wind down, Catface took Christine by the hand and said, "Let's go for a walk."

I was left alone with the family of the catfaces and in the awkward silence which followed, the woman known as Maria walked in. She had shiny golden hair and a face just like a cat.

Mama Catface introduced us. She said, "Maria, I'd like you to meet a friend of Gerard's." We shook hands.

Then Maria smiled at me and she said, "Would you like to come with me to see the fairgrounds?"

And I said, "Yes, I sure would."

Andre Dubus

Dancing After Hours

From *Epoch*

EMILY MOORE was a forty-year-old bartender in a town in Massachusetts. On a July evening, after making three margaritas and giving them to Kay to bring to a table, and drawing four mugs of beer for two young couples at the bar wearing bathing suits and sweatshirts and smelling of sun screen, she went outside to see the sun before it set. She blinked and stood on the landing of the wooden ramp that angled down the front wall of the bar. She smelled hot asphalt; when the wind blew from the east, she could smell the ocean here, and at her apartment, and sometimes she smelled it in the rain, but now the air was still. In front of the bar was a road, and across it were white houses and beyond them was a hill with green trees. A few cars passed. She looked to her right, at a grassy hill where the road curved; above the hill, the sun was low and the sky was red.

Emily wore a dark blue shirt with short sleeves and a pale yellow skirt; she had brown hair, and for over thirty years she had wanted a pretty face. For too long, as a girl and adolescent then as a young woman, she had believed her face was homely. Now she knew it was simply not pretty. Its parts were: her eyes, her nose, her mouth, her cheeks and jaw, and chin and brow; but, combined, they lacked the mysterious proportion of a pretty face during Emily's womanhood in America. Often, looking at photographs of models and actresses, she thought how disfiguring an eighth of an inch could be, if a beautiful woman's nose were moved laterally that distance, or an eye moved vertically. Her body had vigor, and beneath its skin were firm muscles, and for decades her female friends had told Emily they envied it. They admired her hair too: it was thick and soft and fell in waves to her shoulders.

Believing she was homely as a girl and a young woman had deeply wounded her. She knew this affected her when she was with people, and she knew she could do nothing but feel it. She could not change. She also liked her face, even loved it; she had to: it held her eyes and nose and mouth and ears; they let her see and hear and smell and taste the world; and behind her face was her brain. Alone in her apartment, looking in the mirror above her dressing table, she saw her entire life, perhaps her entire self, in her face, and she could see it as it was when she was a child, a girl, a young woman. She knew now that most people's faces were plain, that most women of forty, even if they had been lovely once, were plain. But she felt that her face was an injustice she had suffered and, no matter how hard she tried, she could not achieve some new clarity, could not see herself as an ordinary and attractive woman walking the earth within meeting radius of hundreds of men whose eyes she could draw, whose hearts she could inspire.

On the landing outside the bar, she was gazing at the trees and blue sky and setting sun, and smelling the exhaust of passing cars. A red van heading east, with a black man driving and a white man beside him, turned left from the road and came into the parking lot. Then she saw that the white man sat in a wheelchair. Emily had worked here for over seven years, had never had a customer in a wheelchair, and had never wondered why the front entrance had a ramp instead of steps. The driver parked in a row of cars facing the bar, with an open space of twenty feet or so between the van and the ramp; he reached across the man in the wheelchair and closed the window and locked the door, then got out and walked around to the passenger side. The man in the wheelchair looked to his right at Emily and smiled; then, still looking at her, he moved smoothly backward till he was at the door behind the front seat, and turned his chair to face the window. Emily returned the smile.

The black man turned a key at the side of the van; there was the low sound of a motor, and the door swung open. On a lift, the man in the wheelchair came out and, smiling at her again, descended to the ground. The wheelchair had a motor, and the man moved forward onto the asphalt, and the black man turned the key, and the lift rose and went into the van and the door closed.

Emily hoped the man's injury was not to his brain as well; she had a long shift ahead of her, until one o'clock closing, and she did not want the embarrassment of trying to speak to someone and listen to someone whose body was anchored in a chair and whose mind was afloat. She did not want to feel this way, but she knew she had no talent for it, and she would end by talking to him as though he were an infant, or a dog. He moved across the parking lot, toward the ramp and Emily. She turned to her right, so she faced him and the sun.

The black man walked behind him, but did not touch the chair. He wore jeans and a red tee shirt. He was tall and could still be in his twenties, and he exercised: she guessed with medium weights and running. The man in the moving chair wore a pale blue shirt with the cuffs rolled up twice at his wrists, and tan slacks, and polished brown loafers. Emily glanced at his hands, their palms up and fingers curled and motionless on the armrests of his chair; he could work the chair's controls on the right armrest, but she knew he had not polished the loafers; knew he had not put them on his feet either, and had not put on his socks, or his pants and shirt. His clothes fit him loosely and his body looked small; *arrested,* she thought, and this made his head seem large, though it was not. She wanted to treat him well. She guessed he was in his mid-thirties, but all she saw clearly in his face was his condition: he was not new to it. His hair was brown, thinning on top, and at the sides it was combed back and trimmed. Someone took very good care of this man, and she looked beyond him at the black man's eyes. Then she pulled open the door, heard the couples in bathing suits and the couples at tables and the men at the dartboard; smells of cigarette smoke and beer and liquor came from the air-conditioned dark; she liked those smells. The man in the chair was climbing the ramp, and he said: "Thank you."

His voice was normal, and so was the cheerful light in his eyes, and she was relieved. She said: "I make the drinks too."

"This gets better."

He smiled, and the black man said: "Our kind of place, Drew. The bartender waits outside, looking for us."

Drew was up the ramp, his feet close to Emily's legs; she stepped inside, her outstretched left arm holding the door open; the black man reached over Drew and held the door, and said: "I've got it."

She lowered her arm and turned to the dark and looked at Rita, who was watching from a swivel chair at the bar. Rita Bick was thirty-seven years old, and had red hair in a ponytail, and wore a purple shirt and a black skirt; she had tended bar since late morning, grilled and fried lunches, served the happy hour customers, and now was drinking a straight-up Manhattan she had made when Emily came to work. Her boyfriend had moved out a month ago, and she was smoking again. When Emily had left the bar to see the evening sun, she had touched Rita's shoulder in passing, then stopped when Rita said quietly: "What's so great about living a long time? Remote controls?" Emily had said, "What?" and Rita had said: "To change channels. While you lie in bed alone." Emily did not have a television in her bedroom, so she would not lie in bed with a remote control, watching movies and parts of movies till near dawn when she could finally sleep. Now Rita stood and put her cigarette between her lips and pushed a table and four chairs out of Drew's path, then another table and its chairs, and at the next table she pulled away two chairs, and Drew rolled past Emily, the black man following, the door swinging shut on the sunlight. Emily watched Drew moving to the place Rita had made. Rita took the cigarette from her lips, and looked at Drew.

"Will this be all right?"

"Absolutely. I like the way you make a road."

He turned his chair to the table and stopped, his back to the room, his face to the bar. Rita looked at Emily, and said: "She'll do the rest. I'm off."

"Then join us. You left two chairs."

Emily was looking at the well-shaped back of the black man when he said: "Perfect math."

"Sure," Rita said, and went to the bar for her purse and drink. Emily stepped toward the table to take their orders, but Kay was coming from the men at the dartboard with a tray of glasses and beer bottles, and she veered to the table. Emily went behind the bar, a rectangle with a wall and a swinging door to the kitchen at one end. When Jeff had taught her the work, he had said: "When you're behind the bar, you're the ship's captain; never leave the bar, and never let a customer behind it; keep their respect." She did. She was friendly with her customers; she wanted them to feel they were welcome here and were missed if they did not come in often. She remembered the names of the regulars, their jobs and something about their families, and what they liked to drink. She talked with them when they wanted her to, and this was the hardest work of all; and standing for hours was hard, and she wore runner's shoes, and still her soles ached. She did not allow discourtesy or drunkenness.

The long sides of the bar were parallel to the building's front and rear, and the couples in bathing suits faced the entrance and, still talking, glanced to their right at Drew. Emily saw Drew notice them; he winked at her, and she smiled. He held a cigarette between his curled fingers. Kay was talking to him and the black man, holding her tray with one arm. Emily put a Bill Evans cassette in the player near the cash register, then stepped to the front of the bar and watched Kay in profile: the left side of her face, her short black hair, and her small body in a blue denim skirt and a black silk shirt. She was thirty and acted in the local theater and performed on nights when Emily was working, and she was always cheerful at the bar. Emily never saw her outside the bar, or Rita either; she could imagine Rita at home because Rita told her about it; she could only imagine about Kay that she must sometimes be angry, or sad, or languid. Kay turned from the table and came six paces to the bar and put her tray on it; her eyelids were shaded, her lipstick pale. Emily's concentration when she was working was very good: the beach couples were talking and she could hear each word and Evans playing the piano and, at the same time, looking at Kay, she heard only her, as someone focusing on one singer in a chorus hears only her, and the other singers as well.

"Two margaritas, straight up, one in a regular glass because he has trouble with stems. A Manhattan for Rita. She says it's her last."

Dark-skinned, black-haired Kay Younger had grey-blue eyes, and flirted subtly and seriously with Rita, evening after evening when Rita sat at the bar for two drinks after work. Rita smiled at Kay's flirting, and Emily did not believe she saw what Emily did: that Kay was falling in love. Emily hoped Kay would stop the fall, or direct its arc toward a woman who did not work at the bar. Emily wished she were not so cautious, or disillusioned; she longed for love, but was able to keep her longing muted till late at night when she lay reading in bed, and it was trumpets, drums, French horns; and when she woke at noon, its sound in her soul was a distant fast train. Love did not bring happiness, it did not last, and it ended in pain. She did not want to believe this, and she was not certain that she did; perhaps she feared it was true in her own life, and her fear had become a feeling that tasted like disbelief. She did not want to see Rita and Kay in pain, and she did not want to walk into their pain when five nights a week she came to work. Love also pulled you downhill; then you had to climb again to the top, where you felt solidly alone with your integrity, and were able to enjoy work again, and food, and exercise, and friends. Kay lit a cigarette and rested it on an ashtray, and Emily picked it up and drew on it and put it back; she blew smoke into the ice chest and reached for the tequila in the speed rack.

The beach couples and dart throwers were gone, someone sat on every chair at the bar, and at twelve of the fifteen tables, and Jeff was in his place. He was the manager, and he sat on the last chair at the back of the bar, before its gate. A Chet Baker cassette was playing, and Emily was working fast and smoothly, making drinks, washing glasses, talking to customers who spoke to her, punching tabs on the cash register, putting money in it, giving change, and stuffing bills and dropping coins into the brandy snifter that held her tips. Rita brought her empty glass to Emily; it had been her second Manhattan and she had sipped it, had sat with Drew and the black man while they drank three margaritas. There were no windows in the bar, and Emily imagined the quiet dusk outside and Rita in her purple shirt walking into it. She said: "Jeff could cook you a steak."

"That's sweet. I have fish at home. And a potato. And salad."

"It's good that you're cooking."

"Do you? At night?"

"It took me years."

"Amazing."

"What?"

"How much will it takes. I watch TV while I eat. But I cook. If I stay and drink with these guys, it could be something I'd start doing. Night shifts are better."

"I can't sleep anyway."

"I didn't know that. You mean all the time?"

"Every night, since college."

"Can you take a pill?"

"I read. Around four I sleep."

"I'd go crazy. See you tomorrow."

"Take care."

Rita turned around and waved at Drew and the black man and walked to the door, looking at no one, and went outside. Emily imagined her walking into her apartment, listening to her telephone messages, standing at the machine, her heart beating with hope and dread; then putting a potato in the oven, taking off her shoes, turning on the television to bring light and sound, faces and bodies into the room.

Emily had discipline: every night she read two or three poems twice, then a novel or stories till she slept. Eight hours later she woke and ate grapefruit or a melon, and cereal with a banana or berries and skimmed milk, and wheat toast with nothing on it. An hour after eating, she left her apartment and walked five miles in fifty-three minutes; the first half mile was in her neighborhood, and the next two were on a road through woods and past a farm with a meadow where cows stood. In late afternoon she cooked fish or chicken, and rice, a yellow vegetable and a green one. On the days when she did not have to work, she washed her clothes and cleaned her apartment, bought food, and went to a video store to rent a movie, or in a theater that night watched one with women friends. All of this sustained her body and soul, but it also isolated her: she became what she could see and hear, smell and taste and touch; like and dislike; think about and talk about; and they became the world. Then, in her long nights, when it seemed everyone on earth was asleep while she lay reading in bed, sorrow was tangible in the dark hall to her bedroom door, and in the dark rooms she could not see from her bed. It was there, in the lamplight, that she knew she could never bear and love children; that tomorrow would require of her the same strength and rituals of today; that if she did not nourish herself with food, gain balancing peace of soul with a long walk, and immerse herself in work, she could not keep sorrow at bay, and it would consume her. In the lamplight she read, and she was opened to the world by imagined women and men and children, on pages she held in her hands, and the sorrow in the darkness remained but she was consoled, as she became one with the earth and its creatures: its dead, its living, its living after her own death; one with the sky and water, and with a single leaf falling from a tree.

A man at the bar pushed his empty glass and beer bottle toward Emily, and she opened a bottle and brought it with a glass. Kay was at her station with a tray of glasses, and said: "Rita left."

"Being brave."

Emily took a glass from the tray and emptied it in one of two cylinders in front of her; a strainer at its top caught the ice and fruit; in the second cylinder she dipped the glass in water, then placed it in the rack of the small dishwasher. She looked at each glass she rinsed and at all three sides of the bar as she listened to Kay's order. Then she made piña coladas in the blender, whose noise rose above the music and the voices at the bar, and she made gin-and-tonics, smelling the wedges of lime she squeezed; and made two red seabreezes. Kay left with the drinks and Emily stood facing the tables, where the room was darker, and listened to Baker's trumpet. She tapped her fingers in rhythm on the bar. Behind her was Jeff and she felt him watching her.

Jefferson Gately was a tall and broad man who had lost every hair on top of his head; he had brown hair on the sides and back, and let it grow over his collar. He had a thick brown moustache with gray in it. Last fall, when the second of his two daughters started college, his wife told him she wanted a divorce. He was shocked. He was an intelligent and watchful man, and at work he was gentle, and Emily could not imagine him living twenty-three years with a woman and not knowing precisely when she no longer wanted him in her life. He told all of this to Emily on autumn nights, with a drink after the bar closed, and she believed he did not know his wife's heart, but she did not understand why. He lived alone in a small apartment, and his brown eyes were often pensive. At night he sat on his chair and watched the crowd and drank club soda with bitters; when people wanted food he cooked hamburgers or steaks on the grill, potatoes and clams or fish in the fryers, and made sandwiches and salads. The bar's owner was old and lived in Florida and had no children, and Jeff would inherit the bar. Twice a year he flew to Florida to eat dinner with the old man, who gave Jeff all his trust and small yearly pay raises.

In spring Jeff had begun talking differently to Emily, when she was not making drinks, when she went to him at the back of the bar. He still talked only about his daughters and the bar, or wanting to buy a boat to ride in on the river, to fish from on the sea; but he sounded as if he were confiding in her; and his eyes were giving her something: they seemed poised to reveal a depth she could enter if she chose. One night in June he asked Emily if she would like to get together sometime, maybe for lunch. The muscles in her back and chest and legs and arms tightened, and she said, "Why not," and saw in his face that her eyes and voice had told him "No," and she had hurt him.

She had hurt herself too, and she could not say this to Jeff: she wanted to have lunch with him. She liked him, and lunch was in daylight and not dangerous; you met at the restaurant and talked and ate, then went home, or shopping for groceries or beach sandals. She wanted to have drinks and dinner with him too; but dinner was timeless, there could be coffee and brandy, and it was night and you parted to sleep; a Friday dinner could end Saturday morning, in a shower that soothed your skin but not your heart that had opened you to pain. Now there was AIDS, and she did not want to risk death for something that was already a risk, something her soul was too tired to grapple with again. She did not keep condoms in her apartment because two winters ago, after one night with a thin, pink-faced, sweet-eyed man who never called her again, she decided that next time she made love she would know about it long before it happened, and she did not need to be prepared for sudden passion. She put her box of condoms in a grocery bag, and then in a garbage bag, and on a cold night after work she put the bag on the sidewalk in front of her apartment. In a drawer, underneath her stacked underwear, she had a vibrator. On days when most of her underwear was in the laundry basket, the vibrator moved when she opened and closed the drawer, and the sound of fluted plastic rolling on wood made her feel caught by someone who watched, someone who was above this. She loved what the vibrator did, and was able to forget it was there until she wanted it, but once in a while she felt shame, thinking of dying, and her sister or brother or parents finding the vibrator. Sometimes after using it she wept.

It was ten-fifteen by the bar clock that Jeff kept twenty minutes fast. Tonight he wore a dark brown shirt with short sleeves, and white slacks; his arms and face and the top of his head were brown with a red hue from the sun, and he looked clean and confident. It was a weekday, and in the afternoon he had fished from a party boat. He had told Emily in winter that his rent for a bedroom, a living room, a kitchen, and bathroom was six hundred dollars a month; his car was old; and until his wife paid him half the value of the house she had told him to leave, he could not buy a boat. He paid fifteen dollars to go on the party boat and fish for half a day, and when he did this he was visibly happier. Now Emily looked at him, saw his glass with only ice in it, and brought him a club soda with a few drops of bitters; the drink was the color of Kay's lipstick. He said: "I'm going to put wider doors on the bathroom." Their faces were close over the bar so the woman sitting to the right of Jeff could not hear unless she eavesdropped. "That guy can't get in."

"I think he has a catheter. His friend took something to the bathroom."

"I know. But the next one in a chair may want to use a toilet. He likes Kay. He can feel everything, but only in his brain and heart."

She had seen Drew talking to Kay and smiling at her, and now she realized that she had seen him as a man living outside of passion. She looked at Jeff's eyes, feeling that her soul had atrophied; that it had happened without her notice. Jeff said: "What?"

"I should have known."

"No. I had a friend like him. He always looked happy and I knew he was never happy. A mine got him, in Vietnam."

"Were you there?"

"Not with him. I knew him before and after."

"But you were there."

"Yes."

She saw herself face-down in a foxhole while the earth exploded as close to her as the walls of the bar. She said: "I couldn't do that."

"Neither could I."

"Now, you mean."

"Now, or then."

"But you did."

"I was lucky. We used to take my friend fishing. His chair weighed two hundred and fifty pounds. We carried him up the steps, and lifted him over the side. We'd bait for him, and he'd fold his arms around the rod. When he got a bite we'd reel it in. Mike looked happy on a boat. But he got very tired."

"Where is he now?"

"He died."

"Is he the reason we have a ramp?"

"Yes. But he died before I worked here. One winter pneumonia killed him. I just never got to the bathroom doors."

"You got a lot of sun today."

"Bluefish too."

"Really?"

"You like them?"

"On the grill. With mayonnaise and lemon."

"In foil. I have a grill on my deck. It's not really a deck. It's a landing outside the kitchen, on the second floor. The size of a closet."

"There's Kay. I hope you had sunscreen."

He smiled and shook his head, and she went to Kay, thinking they were like that: they drank too much, they got themselves injured, they let the sun burn their skin, they went to war. The cautious ones bored her. Kay put down her tray of glasses, and slid two filled ashtrays to Emily, who emptied them in the garbage can. Kay wiped them with a paper napkin and said: "Alvin and Drew want steak and fries. No salads. Margaritas now, and Tecates with the meal."

"Alvin."

"Personal care attendant. His job."

"They look like friends."

"They are."

Emily looked at Jeff, but he had heard and was standing; he stepped inside the bar and went through the swinging door to the kitchen. Emily rubbed lime on the rims of glasses and pushed them into the container of thick salt, scooped ice into the blender and poured tequila, and imagined Alvin cutting Drew's steak, sticking the fork into a piece, maybe feeding it to him; and that is when she knew that Alvin wiped Drew's shit. Probably as Drew lay on his bed, Alvin lifted him and slid a bedpan under him, then he would have to roll him on one side to wipe him clean, and take the bedpan to the toilet. Her body did not shudder, but she felt as if it shuddered; she knew her face was composed, but it seemed to grimace. She heard Roland Kirk playing tenor saxophone on her cassette, and words at the bar, and voices from the tables; she breathed the smells of tequila and cigarette smoke, gave Kay the drinks, then looked at Alvin. Kay went to the table and bent forward to place the drinks. Drew spoke to her. Alvin bathed him somehow too, kept his flesh clean for his morale and health. She looked at Alvin for too long; he turned and looked at her. She looked away, at the front door.

□ □ □ □

It was not the shit. Shit was nothing. It was the spiritual pain that twisted her soul: Drew's helplessness, and Alvin reaching into it with his hands. She had stopped teaching because of pain: she had gone with passion to high school students, year after year, and always there was one student, or even five, who wanted to feel the poem or story or novel, and see more clearly because of it. But Emily's passion dissolved in the other students. They were young and robust, and although she knew their apathy was, above all, a sign of their being confined by classrooms and adolescence, it still felt like apathy. It made Emily feel isolated and futile, and she thought that if she were a gym teacher or a teacher of dance, she could connect with her students. The women and men who coached athletic teams or taught physical education or dance seemed always to be in harmony with themselves and their students. In her last three years she realized she was becoming scornful and bitter, and she worked to control the tone of her voice, and what she said to students, and what she wrote on their papers. She taught without confidence or hope, and felt like a woman standing at a roadside, reading poems aloud into the wind as cars filled with teenagers went speeding by. She was tending bar in summer and finally she asked Jeff if she could work all year. She liked the work, she stopped taking sleeping pills because when she slept no longer mattered, and, with her tips, she earned more money. She did not want to teach again, or work with teenagers, or have to talk to anyone about the books she read. But she knew that pain had defeated her, while other teachers had endured it, or had not felt it as sharply.

Because of pain she had turned away from Jeff, a man whom she looked forward to seeing at work. She was not afraid of pain; she was tired of it; and sometimes she thought being tired of it was worse than fear, that losing fear meant she had lost hope as well. If this were true, she would not be able to love with her whole heart, for she would not have a whole heart; and only a man who had also lost hope, and who would settle for the crumbs of the feast, would return her love with the crumbs of his soul. For a long time she had not trusted what she felt for a man, and for an even longer time, beginning in high school, she had deeply mistrusted what men felt for her, or believed they felt, or told her they felt. She chronically believed that, for a man, love was a complicated pursuit of an orgasm, and its evanescence was directly proportionate to the number of orgasms a particular man achieved, before his brain cleared and his heart cooled. She suspected this was also true of herself, though far less often than it was for a man.

When a man's love for Emily ended, she began to believe that he had never loved her; that she was a homely fool, a hole where the man had emptied himself. She would believe this until time healed the pain. Then she would know that in some way the man had loved her. She never believed her face was what first attracted these men; probably her body had, or something she said; but finally they did like her face; they looked at it, touched it with their hands, kissed it. She only knew now, as a forty year old woman who had never lived with a man, that she did not know the truth: if sexual organs were entities that drew people along with them, forcing them to collide and struggle, she wanted to be able to celebrate them; if the heart with intrepid fervor could love again and again, using the sexual organs in its dance, she wanted to be able to exalt its resilience. But nothing was clear, and she felt that if she had been born pretty, something would be clear, whether or not it were true.

She wanted equilibrium: she wanted to carry what she had to carry, and to walk with order and strength. She had never been helpless, and she thought of Drew: his throbless penis with a catheter in it, his shit. If he could not feel a woman, did he even know if he was shitting? She believed she could not bear such helplessness, and would prefer death. She thought: *I can walk. Feed myself. Shower, Shit in a toilet. Make love.* She was neither grateful nor relieved; she was afraid. She had never imagined herself being crippled, and now standing behind the bar she felt her spine as part of her that could be broken, the spinal cord severed; saw herself in a wheelchair with a motor, her body attenuating, her face seeming larger; saw a hired woman doing everything for her and to her.

Kay's lighter and cigarettes were on the bar; Emily lit one, drew on it twice, and placed it on the ashtray. Kay was coming out of the dark of the tables, into the dim light at the bar. She picked up the cigarette and said: "Oh look. It came lit."

She ordered, and Emily worked with ice and limes and vodka and gin and grapefruit juice and salt, with club soda and quinine water, and Scotch and bottles of beer and clean glasses, listening to Roland Kirk, and remembering him twenty years ago in the small club on the highway, where she sat with two girl friends. The place was dark, the tables so close to each other that the waitresses sidled, and everyone sat facing the bandstand, and the blind black man wearing sunglasses. He had a rhythm section and a percussionist, and sometimes he played two saxophones at once. He grinned, he talked to the crowd, his head moving as if he were looking at them. He said: "It's nice, coming to work blind. Not seeing who's fat or skinny. Ugly. Or pretty. Know what I mean?"

Emily knew then, sitting between her friends, and knew now, working in this bar that was nearly as dark as the one where he played; he was dead, but here he was, his music coming from the two speakers high on the walls, coming softly. Maybe she was the only person in the bar who heard him at this moment, as she poured gin; of course everyone could hear him, as people heard rain outside their walls. In the bar she never heard rain or cars, or saw snow or dark skies or sunlight. Maybe Jeff was listening to Kirk while he cooked. And only to be kind, to immerse herself in a few seconds of pure tenderness, she took two pilsner glasses from the shelf and opened the ice chest and pushed the glasses deep into the ice, for Alvin and Drew.

Kirk had walked the earth with people who only saw. So did Emily. But she saw who was fat or ugly, and if they were men she saw them as if through an upstairs window. Twenty years ago, Kirk's percussionist stood beside him, playing a tambourine, and Kirk was improvising, playing fast, and Emily was drumming with her hands on the table. Kirk reached to the percussionist and touched his arm and stepped toward the edge of the bandstand. The percussionist stepped off it and help up his hand; Kirk took it and stepped down and followed the percussionist, followed the sound of the tambourine, playing the saxophone, his body swaying. People stood and pushed their tables and chairs aside, and clapping and exclaiming, followed Kirk. Everyone was standing, and often Kirk reached out and held someone's waist, and hugged. In the dark they came toward Emily, standing with her friends. The percussionist's hand was fast on his tambourine, he was smiling, he was close, then he passed her and Kirk was there. His left hand encircled her, his hand pressing her waist; she smelled his sweat as he embraced her so hard she lost balance and stood on her toes; she could feel the sound of the saxophone in her body. He released her. People were shouting and clapping, and she stepped into the line, held the waist of a man in front of her; her two friends were behind her, one holding her wait. She was making sounds but not words, singing with Kirk's saxophone. They weaved around tables and chairs, then back to the bandstand, to the drummer and the bass and piano players, and the percussionist stepped up on it and turned to Kirk, and Kirk took his hand and stepped up and faced the clapping, shouting crowd. Then Kirk, bending back, blew one long high note; then lowered his head and played softly, slowly, some old and sweet melody. Emily's hands, raised and parted to clap, lowered to her sides. She walked backward to her table, watching Kirk. She and her friends quietly pulled their table and chairs into place, and sat. Emily quietly sat, and waitresses moved in the dark, bent close to the mouths of people softly ordering drinks. The music was soothing, was loving, and Emily watched Kirk and felt that everything good was possible.

It would be something like that, she thought now, *something ineffable that comes from outside and fills us; something that changes the way we see what we see; something that allows us to see what we don't.*

She served four people at the bar, and Jeff came through the swinging door with two plates and forks and knives, and went through the gate and around the bar to Alvin and Drew. He stood talking to them; Alvin took the plate Jeff had put in front of Drew, and began cutting the steak. Jeff came to the bar, and Emily opened two bottles of Tecate and pulled the glasses out of the ice chest. Jeff said: "Nice, Emily."

Something lovely spread in her heart, blood warmed her cheeks, and tears were in her eyes, then they flowed down her face, stopped near her nose, and with the fingers of one hand she wiped them, and blinked and wiped her eyes and they were clear. She glanced around the bar; no one had seen. Jeff said: "Are you all right?"

"I just had a beautiful memory of Roland Kirk."

"Lucky man." He held the bottle necks with one hand, and she put the glasses in his other hand; he held only their bottoms, to save the frost.

"I didn't know him. I saw him play once. That's him now."

"That's him? I was listening in the kitchen. The oil bubbled in time."

"My blood did, that night."

"So you cry at what's beautiful?"

"Sometimes. How about you?"

"It stays inside. I end up crying at silly movies."

He brought the beer to Alvin and Drew, and stood talking; then he sat with them. A woman behind Emily at the bar called her name, and the front door opened and Rita in a peach shirt and jeans came in, and looked at Drew and Alvin and Jeff. Then she looked at Emily and smiled and came toward the bar. Emily smiled, then turned to the woman who had called; she sat with two other women. Emily said: "All around?"

"All around," the woman said.

Emily made daquiris in the blender and brought them with both hands gripping the three stems, then went to Rita standing between two men sitting at the bar. Rita said: "Home sucked." She gave Emily a five dollar bill. "Dry vermouth on the rocks with a twist."

Emily looked at Jeff and Alvin and Drew; they were watching and smiling. She poured Rita's drink and gave it to her and put her change on the bar, and said: "It's a glorious race."

"People?" Rita said, and pushed a dollar toward Emily. "Tell me about it."

"So much suffering, and we keep getting out of bed in the morning."

She saw the man beside Rita smiling. Emily said to him: "Don't we?"

"For some reason."

"We get hungry," Rita said. "We have to pee."

She picked up the vermouth and went to Jeff and Alvin and Drew; Jeff stood and got a chair from another table. Alvin stuck Drew's fork into a piece of meat, and placed the fork between Drew's fingers and Drew raised it to his mouth. He could grip the French fries with his fingers, lift them from the plate. Kay went to their table and, holding her tray of glasses against her hip, leaned close to Rita and spoke, and Rita laughed. Kay walked smiling to the bar.

When Alvin and Drew finished eating, Drew held a cigarette and Rita gave him a light. Emily had seen him using the lighter while Rita was at home. He could not quite put out his cigarettes; he jabbed them at the ashtray and dropped them and they smoldered. Sometimes Alvin put them out, and sometimes he did not, and Emily thought about fire, where Drew lived, then wondered if he were ever alone. Jeff stood with their empty plates and went to the kitchen, and she thought of Drew, after this happened to him, learning each movement he could perform alone, and each one he could not; learning what someone else had to help him do, and what someone else had to do for him. He would have learned what different people did not like to do. Alvin did not smoke, or he had not tonight. Maybe he disliked touching cigarettes and disliked smelling them burning to the filter in an ashtray, so sometimes put them out and sometimes smelled them. But he could empty bags of piss, and wipe shit. Probably he inserted the catheter.

Two summers ago a young woman came to work as a bartender, to learn the job while doing it. Jeff worked with her, and on her first three days the noon crowd wanted fried clams, and she told Jeff she could not stand clams but she would do it: she picked them up raw and put them in batter and fried them and they nauseated her. She did not vomit but she looked all through lunch as if she would. On the fourth day Jeff cooked, but when she smelled the frying clams while she was making drinks, she could see them raw and feel them in her hands and smell them, and she was sick as she worked and talked with customers. She had learned the essential drinks in four days and most of the rare ones, and Jeff called a friend who managed a bar whose only food was peanuts to make the customers thirsty, and got her a job.

So, was anyone boundless? Most of the time, you could avoid what disgusted you. But if you always needed someone to help you simply live, and that person was disgusted by your cigarettes, or your body, or what came out of it, you would sense that disgust, be infected by it, and become disgusted by yourself. Emily did not mind the smell of her own shit, the sight of it on toilet paper and in the water. There was only a stench if someone else smelled it, only disgust if someone else saw it. Drew's body had knocked down the walls and door of his bathroom; living without this privacy, he also had to rely on someone who did not need him to be private. It was an intimacy babies had, and people like Drew, and the ill, and dying. And who could go calmly and tenderly and stoutly into his life? For years she had heard married women speak with repugnance of their husbands: their breath, their farts, their fat stomachs and asses, their lust, their golf, their humor, their passions, their loves. Maybe Jeff's wife was one of these; maybe she had been with him too long; maybe he brought home too many fish.

Kirk said: *Know what I mean?* To love without the limits of seeing; so to love without the limits of the flesh. As Kirk danced through the crowd, he had hugged women and men, not knowing till his hand and arm touched their flesh. When he hugged Emily, she had not felt like a woman in the embrace of a man; she melded; she was music.

Alvin stood and came to the bar and leaned toward her and said: "Are we close to a motel?"

"Sure. Where did you come from?"

"Boston."

"Short trip."

"First leg of one. He likes to get out and look around." He smiled. "We stopped for a beer."

"I'm glad you did. You can use the bar phone."

She picked up the telephone and the book beside the cash register and put them on the bar. She opened the yellow pages. Alvin said: "We need the newest one."

"Are the old ones bad?"

"Eye of a needle."

"Are you with him all the time?"

"Five days a week. Another guy takes five nights. Another, the weekend, day and night. I travel with him."

"Have you always done this work?"

"No. I fell into it."

"How?"

"I wanted to do grand things. I read his ad, and called him."

"What grand things?"

"For the world. It was an abstraction."

Now the bar was closed and they had drawn two tables together; Emily was drinking vodka and tonic, Louis Armstrong was playing, and she listened to his trumpet, and to Drew; he was looking at her, his face passionate, joyful.

"You could do it," he said. "It's up in Maine. They teach you for—what?" He looked at Alvin. "An hour?"

"At most."

Kay said to Alvin: "Did you do it?"

"No. I don't believe in jumping out of airplanes. I don't feel good about staying inside of one either."

"Neither do I," Emily said.

"You could do it," Drew said, watching Emily. He was drinking beer, but slowly, and he did not seem drunk. Alvin had been drinking club soda since they ate dinner. "You could come with me. They talk to you, then they take you up." Emily saw Drew being carried by Alvin and other men into a small airplane, lowered into a seat, and strapped to it. "They told me there was a ground wind. They said if I was a normal, the wind wouldn't be a problem. But—"

Jeff said: "They said 'a normal'?"

"No. What the guy said was: with your condition you've got a ninety percent chance of getting hurt." Drew smiled. "I told him I've lived with nine to one odds for a long time. So we went up in their little plane." Emily could not imagine being paralyzed, but she felt enclosed in a small plane; from inside the plane she saw it take off. "The guy was strong, very confident. Up in the air he lifted me out of the seat and strapped me to him. My back to his chest. We went to the door of the plane, and I looked at the blue sky."

"Weren't you terrified?" Emily lit one of Drew's cigarettes and placed it between his fingers. When she had cleaned the bar and joined them at the table, she had told him and Alvin her name. Drew Purdy. Alvin Parker. She shook their hands, Alvin rising from his chair; when Drew moved his hand upward, she had inserted hers between his fingers and his palm. His hand was soft.

"It felt like fear," Drew said. "But it was adrenaline. I didn't have any bad pictures in my head: like the chute not opening. Leaving a mess on the ground for Alvin to pray over. Then he jumped; we jumped. And I had this rush, like nothing I had ever felt. Better than anything I ever felt. And I used to do a lot, before I got hurt. But this was another world, another body. We were free-falling. Dropping down from the sky like a hawk, and everything was beautiful, green and blue. Then he opened the chute. And you know what? It was absolutely quiet up there. I was looking down at the people on the ground. They were small, and I could hear their voices. I thought I heard Alvin. Probably I imagined that. I couldn't hear words, but I could hear men and women and children. All those voices up in the sky."

Emily could see it, hear it, and her arms and breast wanted to hug him because he had done this; her hand touched his, rested on his fingers, then she took his cigarette and drew on it and put it between his fingers and blew smoke over his head.

Kay said: "I think I'd like the parachute. But I couldn't jump out of the plane."

Drew smiled. "Neither could I."

"I don't like underwater," Rita said. "And I don't like in the air."

"Tell them what happened," Alvin said.

"He didn't think I should do it."

"I thought you should do it on a different day, after what he told you. I thought you could wait."

"You knew I couldn't wait."

"Yes." Alvin looked at Emily. "It's true. He couldn't."

"I broke both my legs."

"No," Emily said.

Jeff said: "Did you feel them?"

Rita was shaking her head; Kay was watching Drew.

"No," Drew said. "They made a video of it. You can hear my legs break. The wind dragged us, and I couldn't do anything with my legs."

"He was laughing the whole time," Alvin said. "While the chute was pulling them on the ground. He's on top of the guy, and he's laughing and shouting, 'This is great, this is great.' And on the video you can hear his bones snapping."

"When did you know?" Jeff said.

"On the third day. When my feet were swollen, and Alvin couldn't get my shoes on."

"You never felt pain?" Rita said.

"Not like you do. It was like a pinball machine, this little ball moving around. So in the hospital they sent me a shrink. To see if I had a death wish. If a normal sky dives and breaks some bones, they don't ask him if he wanted to die. They ask quads. I told him if I wanted to die, I wouldn't have paid a guy with a parachute. I told him it was better than sex. I told him he should try it."

"What did he say?" Jeff said.

"He said he didn't think I had a death wish."

Rita said: "How did you get hurt?"

"Diving into a wave."

"Oh my God," Emily said. "I love diving into waves."

"Don't stop." He smiled. "You could slip in the shower. I know a guy like me, who fell off his bed. He wasn't drunk; he was asleep. He doesn't know how he fell. He woke up on the floor, a quad."

She was sipping her third drink and smoking one of Rita's cigarettes, and looking over Jeff's head at the wall and ceiling, listening to Paul Desmond playing saxophone with Brubeck. Rita's face was turned to Kay, and Emily could only hear their voices; Jeff and Alvin and Drew were planning to fish. She looked at them and said: "Paul Desmond—the guy playing sax—once lost a woman he loved to an older and wealthier man. One night he was sitting in a restaurant, and they came in, the young woman and the man. Desmond watched them going to their table and said: 'So this is how the world ends, not with a whim but a banker'."

Rita and Kay were looking at her.

"I like that," Drew said.

"He was playing with a T. S. Eliot line. The poet. Who said 'April is the cruelest month.' That's why they called him T. S."

They were smiling at her. Jeff's eyes were bright.

"I used to talk this way. Five days a week."

"What were you?" Drew asked.

"A teacher."

She was looking at Drew and seeing him younger with strong arms and legs, in a bathing suit, running barefoot across hot sand to the water, his feet for the last time holding his weight on the earth, his legs moving as if they always would, his arms swinging at his sides; then he was in the surf, running still but very slowly in the water; the cold water thrilled him, cleared his mind; he moved toward the high waves; he was grinning. Waves broke in front of him and rushed against his waist, his thighs, his penis. A rising wave crested and he dived into it as it broke, and it slapped his legs and back and turned him, turned him just so, and pushed him against the bottom.

Alvin asked Rita to dance, and Kay asked Jeff. They pushed tables and chairs and made a space on the floor, and held each other, moving to Desmond's slow song. Emily said: "When this happened to you, who pulled you out of the water?"

"Two buddies. They rode in on the wave that got me. They looked around and saw me. I was like a big rag doll in the water. I'd go under, I'd come up. Mostly under."

"Did you know how bad it was?"

"I was drowning. That's what I was afraid of till they came and got me. Then I was scared because I couldn't move. They put me on the beach, and then I felt the pain; and I couldn't move my legs and arms. I was twenty-one years old, and I knew."

Last night Emily had not worked and yesterday afternoon she had gone to the beach with a book of stories by Edna O'Brien. She had rubbed sunscreen on her body and had lain on a towel and read five stories. When she finished a story she ran in the surf, and dived into a wave, opened her eyes to the salt water, stood and shook her hair and faced the beach, looking over her shoulder at the next wave coming in, then dived with it as it broke, and it pushed and pulled her to the beach, until her outstretched hands then her face and breasts were on sand, and the surf washed over her.

John Coltrane was playing a ballad, and Jeff looked at her and said: "Would you like to dance?"

She nodded and stood, walking around tables, and in the open space turned to face him. Rita and Alvin came and started to dance. Emily took Jeff's hand and held him behind his waist, and they danced to the saxophone, her breasts touching his chest; he smelled of Scotch and smoke; his moustache was soft on her brow. She looked to her left at Drew: he had turned the chair around, and was watching. Now Kay rose from her chair and stood in front of him; she bent forward, held his hands, and began to dance. She swayed to the saxophone's melody, and her feet moved in rhythm, forward, back, to her sides. Emily could not see Drew's face. She said: "I don't know if Kay should be doing that."

"He jumped from an airplane."

"But he could feel it. The thrill anyway. The air on his face."

"He can feel Kay too. She's there. She's dancing with him." He led Emily in graceful turns toward the front wall, so she could see Drew's face. "Look. He's happy."

Drew was smiling; his head was dancing: down, up to his right, down, up to his left. Emily looked at Jeff's eyes and said: "You told me your friend always looked happy and you knew he was never happy."

"It's complicated. I knew he couldn't en*joy* being a quad. I knew he missed his body: fishing, hunting, swimming, dancing, girls, just *walk*ing. He probably even missed being a soldier, when he was scared and tired, and wet and hot and thirsty and bug-bit; but he was whole and strong. So I say he was never happy, he only looked happy. But he had friends; and he had fun. It took a lot of will for him to have fun. He had to do it in spite of everything. Not because of everything."

He turned her and dipped: she was leaning backward and only his arms kept her balanced; he pulled her up and held her close.

"On a fishing boat I lose myself. I don't worry about things. I just look at the ocean and feel the sun. It's the ocean. The ocean takes me there. Mike had to do it himself. He couldn't just step onto a boat and let the ocean take him. First he had to be carried on. Anybody who's helpless is afraid; you could see it in his eyes, while he joked with us. I'm sure he was sad too, while we carried him. He was a soldier, Emily. That's not something he could forget. Then out on the ocean, he couldn't really hold the rod and fish. And his body was always pulling on him. He had spasms on the boat, and fatigue."

Coltrane softly blew a low note and held it, the drummer tapping cymbals, and the cassette ended. Emily withdrew her hand from Jeff's back, but he still held hers, and her right hand. He said: "He told me once: 'I wake up tired.' His body was his enemy, and when he fought it he lost. What he had to do was ignore it. That was the will. That was how he was happy."

"Ignore it?"

"Move beyond it."

He released her back and lowered her hand, and shifted his grip on it and held it as they walked toward the table, then Jeff stopped her. He said: "He had something else. He was grateful."

"For what?"

"That he wasn't blown to pieces. And that he still had his brain."

They walked and at the table he let go of her hand and she stood in front of Drew, and said: "You looked good."

Kay sat beside Rita; Jeff and Alvin stood talking.

"My wife and I danced like that."

"Your wife? You said—" Then she stopped; a woman had loved him, had married him after the wave crippled him. She glanced past him; no one had heard.

"Right," he said. "I met her when I was like this."

"Shit."

He nodded. She said: "Would you like a beer?"

"Yes."

She walked past the table, then stopped and looked back; Drew was turning his chair around, looking at her now, and he said: "Do you have Old Blue Eyes?"

"Not him," Rita said.

"He's good to dance to," Kay said.

"I've got him," Emily said. "Anybody want drinks?"

She went behind the bar and made herself a vodka and tonic. Kay and Rita came to the bar, stood with their shoulders and arms touching, and Emily gave them a Tecate and a club soda, and they brought them to Drew and Alvin. They came back and Emily put in the Sinatra cassette and poured vermouth for Rita and made a salty dog with tequila for Kay. While she was pouring the grapefruit juice, Kay said to Rita: "Can you jitterbug?"

"Girl, if you lead I can follow."

Kay put her right hand on Rita's waist, held Rita's right hand with her left, then lifted their hands and turned Rita in a circle, letting Rita's hand turn in hers; then, facing each other, they danced. Kay sang with Sinatra:

> "Till the tune ends
> We're dancing in the dark
> And it soon ends"

Emily sang:

> "We're waltzing in the wonder
> Of why we're here
> Time hurries by, we're here
> And gone—"

Emily watched her pretty friends dancing, and looked beyond them at Jeff and Alvin, tapping the table with their fingers, watching, grinning; Drew was singing. She smiled and sang and played drums on the bar till the song ended. Then she poured Jeff a Scotch on ice and went to the table with it, and he stood and pulled out the chair beside him, and she sat in it.

She looked at Drew. She could not see pallor in the bar light, but she knew from his eyes that he was very tired. Or maybe it was not his eyes; maybe she saw his fatigue because she could see Jeff's friend, tired on the fishing boat, talking and laughing with Jeff, a fishing rod held in his arms. Rita and Kay sat across from her, beside Alvin. Emily leaned in front of Jeff and said to Drew: "How are you?"

"Fine."

Her right knee was touching Jeff's thigh, her right arm resting on his, and her elbow touched his chest. For a moment she did not notice this; then she did; she was touching him as easily as she had while dancing, and holding his hand coming back to the table. She said to Drew: "You can sleep late tomorrow."

"I will. Then we'll go to Maine."

"You're *jump*ing again?"

"Not this time. We're going to look at the coast. Then we'll come back here and fish with Jeff."

She looked at Jeff, so close that her hair had touched his face as she turned. She drew back, looking at his eyes, seeing him again carrying a two hundred and fifty pound wheelchair with a man in it up the steps to the wharf, and up the steps to the boat: Jeff and Alvin and someone else, as many men as the width of the steps would allow; then on the boat at sea, Jeff standing beside Drew, helping him fish. She said: "Really? When."

"Monday," Jeff said.

She sat erectly again and drank and glanced at Kay and Rita in profile, talking softly, smiling, their hands on the table holding cigarettes and drinks.

Sinatra was singing "Angel Eyes," and Kay and Rita were dancing slowly, and Jeff and Alvin were in the kitchen making ham and cheese sandwiches. Kay was leading, holding Rita's hand between their shoulders, her right hand low on Rita's back; they turned and Emily looked at Rita's face: her eyes were closed. Her hand was lightly moving up and down Kay's back, and Emily knew what Rita was feeling: a softening thrill in her heart, a softening peace in her muscles; and Kay too. She looked at Drew.

"You danced with your wife, you—" She stopped.

"Are you asking how we made love?"

"No. Yes."

"I can have an erection. I don't feel it. But you know what people can do in bed, if they want to."

Looking at his eyes, she saw herself with the vibrator.

"I was really asking you what happened. I just didn't have the guts."

"I met her at a party. We got married, we had a house. For three years. One guy in a *hun*dred with my kind of injury can get his wife pregnant. Then, wow, she was. Then on New Year's Eve my wife and my ex-best friend came to the bedroom, and stood there looking down at me. I'd thought they spent a lot of time in the living room, watching videos. But I never suspected till they came to the bed that night. Then I knew; just a few seconds before she told me the baby was his, I knew. You know what would have been different? If I could have packed my things and walked out of the house. It would have hurt; it would have broken my heart; but it would have been different. On the day of my divorce it was summer, and it was raining. I couldn't get into the courthouse, I couldn't go up the steps. A guy was working a jackhammer on the sidewalk, about thirty yards away. The judge came down the steps in his robe, and we're all on the sidewalk, my wife, the lawyers. My lawyer's holding an umbrella over me. The jackhammer's going and I can't hear and I'm saying: 'What? What did he say?' Then I was divorced. I looked up at my wife, and asked her if she'd like Chinese lunch and a movie."

"Why?"

"I couldn't let go."

She reached and held his hand.

"Oh, Drew."

She did not know what time it was, and she did not look at the clock over the bar. There was no music. She sat beside Jeff. Drew had his sandwich in both hands; he bit it, then lowered it to the plate. Alvin was chewing; he looked at Drew, then as simply as if Drew's face were his own, he reached with a paper napkin and wiped mustard from Drew's chin. Drew glanced at him, and nodded. *That's how he says thank you,* Emily thought. One of a hundred ways he would have learned. She picked up her sandwich, looked across the table at Kay and Rita chewing small bites, looked to her right at Jeff's cheek bulging as he chewed. She ate, and drank. Kay said: "Let's go to my house, and dance all night."

"What about your neighbors?" Rita said.

"I don't have neighbors. I have a house."

"A whole house?"

"Roof. Walls. Lawn and trees."

"I haven't lived in a house since I grew up," Rita said.

"I've got to sleep," Drew said.

Alvin nodded.

"Me too," Jeff said.

Rita said: "Not me. I'm off tomorrow."

"I won't play Sinatra," Kay said.

"He *is* good to dance to. You can play whatever you want."

Jeff and Alvin stood and cleared the table and brought the plates and glasses to the kitchen. Drew moved his chair back from the table and went toward the door, and Emily stood and walked past him and opened the door. She stepped onto the landing, and smelled the ocean in the cool air; she looked up at stars. Then she watched Drew rolling out and turning down the ramp. Kay and Rita came, and Jeff and Alvin. Emily turned out the lights and locked the door and went with Jeff down the ramp. At the van, Emily turned to face the breeze, and looked up at the stars. She heard the sound of the lift and turned to see it coming out of the van. Kay leaned down and kissed Drew's cheek, and Rita did; they kissed Alvin's cheek, and Jeff shook his hand, then held Drew's hand and said: "Monday."

"We'll be here."

Emily took Alvin's hand and kissed his cheek. Jeff pointed east and told him how to drive to the motel. Emily held Drew's hands and leaned down and pressed her cheek against his; his face needed shaving. She straightened and watched Drew move backward onto the lift, then up into the van, where he turned and went to the passenger window. Alvin, calling Goodnight, got into the van and started it and leaned over Drew and opened his window. Drew said: "Goodnight, sweet people."

Standing together, they all said Goodnight and waved, held their hands up till Alvin turned the van and drove onto the road. Then Kay looked at Emily and Jeff.

"Come for just one drink."

Emily said: "I think it's even my bedtime. But ask me another night."

"And me," Jeff said.

"I will."

"I'll follow you," Rita said.

"It's not far."

They went to their cars, and Rita drove behind Kay, out of the parking lot, then west. Emily watched the red lights moving away, and felt tender, hopeful; she felt their hearts beating as they drove.

"Quite a night," she said.

"It's beautiful."

She looked at him; he was looking at the stars. She looked west again; the red lights rose over a hill and were gone. She looked at the sky.

"It is," she said. "That's not what I meant."

"I know. Do you think if Drew was up there hanging from a parachute, he could hear us?"

"I don't know."

He looked at his watch.

"You're right," he said. "It's four o'clock."

He walked beside her to her car; she unlocked it and opened the door, then turned to face him.

"I'm off Monday," she said. "I want to go fishing."

"Good."

She got into the car and closed the door and opened the window and looked up at Jeff.

"The bluefish are in," he said. "We'll catch some Monday."

"You already have some. Let's eat them for lunch."

"Today?"

"After we sleep. I don't know where you live."

"I'll call and tell you. At one?"

"One is fine," she said, and reached through the window and squeezed his hand. Then she drove east, smelling the ocean on the wind moving her hair.

Matthew Klam

The Royal Palms

From *The New Yorker*

LAST WINTER, we went on vacation to the Caribbean. When the plane landed, we were so exhausted we could barely lift our bags. We checked in at the hotel, and got rid of the suitcases, and without unpacking went out the gate to look at the casino. A guard pointed us in the opposite direction from the beach, down a little dirt road, a five-minute walk from the hotel gate.

The casino was a small white stucco building, with bars on the windows and a brown wooden sign. There were some German tourists in there, and I overheard a couple of Americans talking, but the rest of the faces in the room were either friendly employees or locals—whatever, black people, people from there. I played blackjack, and I was on a roll. Winning relaxes me; at some point in the night I was up two thousand dollars. Diane played the slot machines, going all night without a hit, waiting for me to finish. I cashed out because the place was closing. It was just after one in the morning. We were practically the last ones in there, definitely the last white ones in the place. They paid out my winnings and I followed Diane to the door.

I had a buzz on. I put the money in the belly of my shirt, because I couldn't carry it all in my pockets. It was half the cost of the trip, although that wasn't an issue. Two guys came out of the casino behind us, local guys, and we nodded to them and they went to their car. They pulled it around in our direction. Diane looked back and saw the car; she looked at me—there was that funny moment—and then she started running down the road.

The car came up behind us. It took me a second to figure out what was going on. Diane had a ten- or twenty-yard lead on me—she's a fast runner, she was a gymnast in high school—and I started running with all this goddam money bouncing around, but I couldn't keep up. I was telling her to wait for me, and yelling at her not to run, because it would only make things worse, incriminate us or attract their attention, although she did have a point. The car kept slowing down, because the road was in terrible shape. I was running as fast as possible, Diane's white pants disappearing in the dark in front of me, the money bouncing around everywhere in my shirt. Lights from the hotel loomed in front of us now, the car bounding into those barrel-size humps and potholes, its headlights leaping across us and up into the trees. I could hear the thumping of the engine—it was an old Jeep and it sounded like a washing machine—but the noise came both from right behind me and from far away, echoing through the woods. I was chugging now, gaining on Diane. I could see the hotel guard, asleep in his shack.

We got to the gate and the guard sat up. The car pulled up alongside us, and the two guys looked over at us, and we looked at them. The guard had a shotgun. He went and spoke to the driver. Then they turned around and drove away. I had been happy back there at the blackjack table, beating the slit-eyed dealer, but with the sudden heat and the run down the road, the airplane food and the funny smell of this fertile jungle, I wanted to puke.

We were staying in a bungalow beside the main building, one of a row of cottages in the trees along the beach. Diane went into the bathroom without a word. I was so freaked that I didn't know what to do. I didn't want that cash in there with us, so after she went to sleep I walked around back, behind the cabin, and buried the money in the sand. It was dark.

Then I got into bed. I listened to Diane breathe. I couldn't tell if she was asleep or not, and I'd become afraid of that lately, of not knowing—and of how it didn't matter. We hadn't had sex since Thanksgiving. Diane said her ass was too fat. We hadn't enjoyed each other's company now in a long time, and before this trip there were nights when we didn't speak. Earlier that day, standing in line at the airport with all our luggage, she said to me, "I'm fat. I feel ugly."

I said, "We're going on a great vacation, so try to have fun."

She said, "You hate me." I didn't know what to say. I did hate her, partly, she was right, but not for being fat: Diane is small and cute, everything on her is round and full anyway. But I was taking it very seriously that she was repulsed by me, that she stopped me anytime I tried to touch her.

I still felt love for her, too, but we didn't have the same outlook anymore. And I didn't like listening to her complain all the time. My life was going the way I always thought it should—I mean my job, and money. The contracts I'd sold last quarter were huge, my company had just bought a smaller firm and merged, we were booming—and I had nobody to tell that to. Diane's job was a total disappointment, or so she claimed, though she could never be specific. She mentioned getting a master's in something, or learning to make jewelry, but that might be too complicated. At home, she ate frozen Snickers bars in bed. She made Kool-Aid every night and chugged it from the pitcher. I hadn't seen Diane in her underwear in months, or her bare shoulders or her pretty chest, or her pale, round thighs: she said she was flab, pure jello; she said her potbelly hung over the waist of her skirt. At night she'd put on her big yellow sweatshirt that came down to her knees; she'd pull the hood up over her head and tie the string and get into bed and turn off the lights. It got so bad that I couldn't even kiss her—she'd laugh or cover her lips and say, "I have to wax my mustache." We had more money now, and sometimes we discussed doing something new, either kids or a new house; neither one felt like the natural thing, but what were we going to do next? Something was missing. We needed the next phase, and we needed what was missing to get to the next phase. I didn't know whether to be worried or not.

The next morning I went out to get the money I'd buried in the sand. As I was digging, I saw it all again in my mind, the little jeep turning and then Diane running. Who knows what those guys wanted—they probably thought we were crazy—but it occurred to me then that she'd never looked back. What if I'd tripped? Maybe I missed something, but I felt terrible then, remembering: Diane, running away from me. The money was all wet; I'd packed it in a plastic bag, and a jogger who walked by wondered if it was shell-fish I had caught.

I had the hotel clerk change it into big bills and put it in the vault. He assured me that nothing bad had ever happened here, and never would, that I was perfectly safe. The natives were friendly, he said; I should forget it and begin to enjoy myself.

The food area was a vast tented pavilion, with plush, oversized chairs and an enormous breakfast buffet of all different kinds of exotic food. I had the cook make me an omelette. He was dark black, like the guys from the night before. I looked over at Diane, who had a couple of orange slices and a banana on her plate. I said, "Hey, come on, eat something. We're on vacation." She said she didn't want to get too full.

As we walked to the water, I said I liked her new straw hat. She said, "If you stare at my gut I will kill you."

I rubbed some sunscreen on. The beach was totally empty. Where the hell was everybody? "Jesus Christ," I said to Diane, "this is some fucking resort."

At lunch the place was full, though, and then the crowd came to the beach, and later that afternoon there was a softball game and we joined in. I got a hit that went over the shortstop's head. Diane pitched for the other team and did great. That evening we ate pasta and shellfish. They had drummers in the pavilion, but we were too tired to stay for more than a minute, and I slept that night the way you'd hope to sleep on vacation—like a five-year-old kid with no troubles. I dreamed about my base hit and woke up to birds singing outside the window. We had pancakes for breakfast, and later the staff organized a big tug-of-war and a sack race, and we met some more of the other guests. Our team won the sack race but lost the tug-of-war.

We claimed a spot for ourselves on the beach. Every morning you could find us there. We spent our day swimming, napping, baking in the sun. After a couple of days your eyes don't fight the land-scape. The beach was gorgeous; it started at the dock and wound along for half a mile, narrow in some places, funnelling into a rocky point with a jetty. The ocean was blue—deep, brilliant tur-quoise—except that at noon, with the sun directly overhead, it turned the color of tin. Low tide left lumps of seaweed like piles of old, wet wigs; guys came by with rakes and took them away. On the rim of the beach there were big palm trees to lie under. It was cool in the shade. If you waved to one of the staff guys, he'd bring you a chaise.

We got used to it. I figured out how you adjust your chaise without chopping off a finger. Where to go to eat lunch, which way to the Tiki Bar. I found a shortcut through the pricker bushes to the cottage. It's a resort, so it's yours as much as it is anybody's. You know some other people now, so you say hello. I sat there staring at the water and thought back to my life: breakfast meetings, angry clients, me in a rage at the office, somebody crying, somebody quit-ting, me driving back home wondering what kind of mood we'll both be in that night—days come in like the surf, and I'm sand, I'm the rocks, and it pounds me.

Diane bought a flowered bikini in the hotel store. She looked fine, but she wrapped a towel around her waist whenever she stood up. Her hair looked shiny in the sun. Her skin was getting darker. Then the sun would go behind a cloud, she'd tuck her hair behind her ear and turn a page, the wind would come up off the ocean—and I'd see her nipples through the fabric of her bathing suit and I'd have to look away. Her body was soft, round peaches. I'd think, Don't rush it. That would be stupid. I wondered what the hell we were going to do.

We were having lunch one day under the big top, and this couple came up and introduced themselves. Their names were Rick and Joanie. They had just got there the night before, and were staying in the bungalow right next to ours, it turned out. Our table was empty, and we invited them to sit. He was an outdoor-type guy, tall and athletic, with a mustache—he had on a black tank top, with smooth, flat muscles underneath it—and she was tall and fit with sandy blond hair, like him. They were already tan. They hadn't got their plates yet, so we told them what was good on the buffet and what to steer clear of, and what they run out of every day, and like that.

Rick said, "Have you tried the goatfish?" He told us the fish was a delicacy here. When they came back with food, they had some of that fish on their plates, and brought an extra piece for us to try.

They lived in northern Florida. Joanie was an actress. She said she did a lot of local television commercials. She had huge teeth and a big, wide smile. When we stood up, later, I realized she was about a foot taller than me. Rick sold powerboats; he had two dealerships and a third one on the way. He had broad shoulders and big hands, a thin nose and smooth skin, and a steel diving watch on his left wrist. I'm not that tall, or as good-looking as some guys, but I'm not an ugly fucking freak or anything. These two were perfect, though. They looked like models, big models who lifted weights. They had a boy, five, and a girl, two, and they showed us pictures of them, and Rick had a picture of himself on his Harley, giving the thumbs-up. I said they must still be exhausted from the flight, but Rick pulled his hair back in a rubber band and said he'd already reserved a court for paddle tennis later.

He asked me what I thought of the fish. I said it was good. Rick said they really knew how to cook it here; it tasted like butter.

The next morning I was walking down the beach and I saw Rick. He said, "Hey, neighbor, where you going?"

I said, "Nowhere," and Rick said, "I'm going fishing. Come on." I'd never been fishing. I ran back to our suite. Diane was taking a nap. I didn't know what to bring. I grabbed my Swiss Army knife and left a note: "Didn't want to wake you up, honey—Rick and I went fishing."

The resort chartered a boat twice a week to take people out, and besides us there were seven or eight other guests on board. It headed toward the horizon, loud and stinking of diesel fuel. Then they shut the engine off and everybody dropped their lines. It was amazing out there. Rick fished. I didn't fish. I watched the other people.

I saw a couple of sailboats and some birds—it was quiet this far from shore—and if you stared over the side into the water you could make out the bottom, thirty or forty feet down. Rick kept taking things out of his pockets: a piece of gum, a chunk of bait, a pill from a bottle of medicine, a visor, a box of Tic-Tacs. He put on sunscreen and smoothed his mustache. Then his rod snagged—it was so bent I thought he would snap it—and he pulled a fish right out of the water, a beautiful, flat, wide fish, shimmering aquamarine color. It had incredible skin. He held it up; it was flipping around like crazy. I'd never seen a fish like that. I wasn't sure if he wanted to keep it or throw it back, but he laid it on the deck and stepped on it and stuck a knife into its head. Then he threw it in a Ziploc bag.

"That, right there," he said, "is good eating." I watched as the interior of the bag fogged over with moisture. I think the fish was still moving.

I said, "Is it dead?"

He said, "What do you mean?"

"Would you kill it, please?"

He said, "It's dead."

"Is that goatfish?"

"That? No."

We had beers from a cooler and watched the other people fish. There was a woman across from us wearing a thing like a black slip and drinking a Coke. Rick said, "Look at her. She's incredible. My dick's been hard the whole day."

She looked like "Breakfast at Tiffany's"—that actress with the skinny neck. I smiled at her. She smiled back. "Guess what," Rick said. "She wants to fuck you." They started the engine again, and we cruised along the water, spray coming over the side and hitting us. He kept staring at the woman. She flipped her long black hair, talking with the captain, and turned her beautiful ass in our direction. She was small and had a little waist and tan shoulders. Her legs were perfect. He said, "What I'd do to get my rocket off in her." The boat was turning around then. We headed back.

They let us out at the dock, a little way from the buildings and the people lying out on the sand. We came walking up the beach with Rick's fish, and Rick went someplace to clean it. The women, Joanie and Diane, were lying side by side.

"Look at this," Diane said, and sat up to show me the back of her head. "Joanie did this to my hair." It was all braided in teeny rows. She was excited.

"That's great, honey," I said. "Thanks, Joanie."

She said, "No problem." She was propped up on her elbow, with her free hand covering her eyes like a visor. She squinted into the sun, smiling hopefully.

"Here," I said, and tossed her my baseball hat.

"Thanks," she said, and pulled it down and swung her ponytail out the back. I looked at Diane—her mouth was hanging open in surprise. Did she want my hat for herself? I guess so.

She slid down to wipe the sand off her feet, and I knelt beside her and kissed her. I took her hand and held it. I ducked down and kissed her neck. She giggled and said to Joan, "Maybe I should get my ears pierced." Joanie was staring down the beach looking for her husband. She was already very tan, and had a great body—a taut, swimmer's body, trim and lanky; she had beautiful bosoms, and her hip bones jutted up so nicely you could've hung Christmas ornaments on them. I kissed Diane's throat, and held her little braids in my hand. She jerked her head away. "My hair's filthy," she said. Joan looked down the blanket at us, over the delicate arch of her pelvis, and smiled.

The four of us sat together at dinner that night, and drank wine. I ate this fish stew in a flaky pie crust, and after dinner the staff built a bonfire on the beach and we took another bottle of wine and went down there.

They'd dragged big logs over for us to sit on, and I sat down next to the guy stoking the fire. It was chilly out. The fire was heating up one side of my face, making it swell, and the sea breeze hit me on the other side and it felt numb. The local guys were talking to each other a mile a minute—it was totally unintelligible—and across the circle I saw Diane chatting with a couple we'd met on the airport van.

Our vacation was half over. On the whole, things were better.

Was that what Diane thought, too? Or had she stopped loving me, and couldn't say so? I kept wondering if this was the end. I was sitting in a jolly crowd of people. I sipped my wine. Rick was standing over on the side, talking with the woman from the boat; he opened her beer for her with a thing on his key chain and took a swig. The girl laughed. Joanie was two feet away from them. She still had that dopey smile plastered on her face. She sat Indian style on the sand, looking tan and tired, watching the fire.

After a minute, Rick sat down. He was wearing white tennis shorts and a flannel shirt with the sleeves ripped off and I thought, What kind of guy brings a ripped shirt with him on vacation? It was cold out, and everybody else was wearing jackets. He didn't seem cold. The fire glowed in his golden hair. He had dimples next to his mouth, and he wore his hair long and curly. He moved down the log right next to me. He was tan as hell, his arm muscles were like knotted brown wood. Rick had the looks—handsome and strong and cool at the same time, that was him. Like those guys you knew in high school who had it all. He probably used to drive a Camaro with a surfboard on it.

On the other side of the circle there were two hotel guys playing guitars. They weren't good or terrible, but one guy had a nice voice. Rick asked me how everything was; we talked about home, how it seemed like a million miles away. I started to tell him about my problems, my rotten sex life with Diane. I don't know why—people do funny things on vacation.

He listened, staring into the fire. I tried to keep the descriptions as vague as possible, and then I thought, fuck it—some stupid boat dealer from the Everglades who I'm never gonna see again, so what if he knows my wife has a mustache? He said he understood. He was, it turned out, totally cool. We talked about how married people get along together. He rubbed his chin. "That's all normal," he said. "You have to work around it."

So, as Diane and I walked back to our suite, I grabbed some matches and asked for a candle from the front desk. Following Rick's advice, I gave Diane a neck rub, and put some warm water in a bowl and got a washcloth. I washed her neck and shoulders with the cloth. She asked me what I was doing, and I told her to be quiet. I washed her hands and her fingers; I untied her sandals and washed the tops of her feet. She said, "That feels good." I put some lotion on her elbows. She let me undress her. I took her shirt off, and her bra; I undid her shorts and pulled them off. She lay down and smiled, and I took the cloth and rubbed it in slow circles over her entire body.

I loved her, I still knew that. This was my princess here. We weren't going to die from this. I sat beside her, and we talked about the trip so far, the dinners, the bonfire, those guys in the jeep who were trying to kill us. She'd signed up for a windsurfing lesson for later in the week and was all excited about going. I put some moisturizer on her shoulders, and brushed her hair, and then I took all my clothes off and lay there next to her. We seemed happy. She was cute as hell. In the past four days, the sun had made her hair lighter. Her arms and legs were dark, her tummy was a lighter shade of tan; where the bikini had been was pure white. I mentioned a few things about life at home, how we needed to make some changes, to plan for the future. Diane had her arm under her head, and every few minutes she shut her eyes. Her eyelids were almost white against her tan face. When I asked her if she was sleepy she said no. We stayed like that for a while.

It reminded me of a scene out of high school—the candle on the table, both of us buzzed on wine, my dick wanging around between us. I looked down the length of her body, and put my hand on her. She didn't move. I was thinking the way I had in high school, too—like I would do anything just to touch her. She yawned. I pictured doing it to her even if she passed out. Diane said, "Excuse me." I was dying to fuck my wife. I was sizzling. As soon as I tried something—I moved myself against her, and put my lips on her neck—she jumped back and a look crossed her face; she said my beard was scratchy. And then she started talking a mile a minute about the woman in the cabin next to Joan's who'd seen an iguana, how it ran across her foot and disappeared into the woods, and we lay there, nobody saying a word now. In a few more minutes, I heard her breathing change. The candle was still going, flickering alongside us. She'd fallen asleep.

❏ ❏ ❏ ❏

The next day, as we were eating our jambalaya for lunch, they came by. Joanie asked Diane if she wanted to go shopping. Diane said yes, and Rick said he'd rented mountain bikes and heard of some trails that went up into the hills, if I was interested. I didn't feel like it, and with everybody gone I went into our room and called my office. I turned on my computer and faxed them some stuff, and spent an hour on the phone with our comptroller—we'd had a scare with a big supplier, but it was O.K. now. I returned some other calls. Everything was fine. At four o'clock, I looked up. The day was ending. There were three days left of our vacation, it had flown by, and what the fuck was I doing crapping around inside?

I walked toward the hotel's plaza, feeling pale and tired. My hands were sweaty. I hated myself for missing the sun, and now the ocean was calm, and the breeze had died. Salt covered everything— stones, leaves, the spotlights sticking up every five feet in the ground. I walked back and forth between the tennis courts and the place where we usually sat on the beach. There were some Euro-pean-looking dudes in our spot, wearing little Speedos; I felt like walking up to them and kicking in their skulls. I didn't see anyone I knew, as if a whole crew of fresh guests, all ghostly white and uncomfortable, had come in the night before and replaced the old ones. A woman stood next to me with her baby, changing its diaper in the middle of the plaza, stinking up the joint with her kid's smelly dump. When I finally saw a familiar face go by—the kitchen-staff guy who made my omelettes—I was so relieved I almost hugged him. He was carrying a three-foot-long fish—a tuna, he said, seventy pounds; it had just come off a boat. I followed him to an outdoor kitchen, and while he cut it up I asked him about growing up on the island.

A little later I was sitting in the hotel lobby, reading the newspa-per, when Rick came in with his bicycle. He had on tight black bicycle-rider pants, and his thick, muscular legs were all tan and defined, with big veins on his calves. He said the ride had been great, and showed me on a map where he'd gone. Then he pulled me up by the arm with his iron grip and yanked off his sun-glasses—he had a raccoon stripe of white where the glasses had been. Talking low, he told me there were guys out there living forty feet up in the trees, pot growers with machine guns who almost shot him but then took him in and befriended him. He said they were the nicest guys, and he talked with them and smoked pot and sang reggae. They gave him a tour of their jungle hideout. They'd made crude musical instruments out of tin boxes and wire, and they had their feet propped up on crates of ammo. He said, "One of them went to Oxford."

I said, "Great."

He said, "They ship the pot out in these carved heads, the dark wood carving this area is known for, called *obiko*. Joanie was supposed to buy one when she went into town today. They stuff the shit into a hollowed-out part of the heads and ship them around the world."

I said, "Is that so?"

Rick said, "Listen, come back up with me tomorrow. You can't believe the view."

I said, "Not in a million years."

"I'm taking Joanie," he said.

"You're not taking Joanie up there. They'll gang-rape her."

"They're the friendliest people in the world. They gave me dope. They had piles of it lying around." He started to reach into his bicycle pants, in the middle of the lobby. He said, "I got it here somewhere."

"Rick—what the fuck are you doing?" I said, and grabbed his hand.

He said, "Possession of marijuana is not a crime here. And even if it is, they want the tourists to smoke it."

Diane asked Rick to tell the whole story again at dinner. I was sick of it and said nothing. I was going gambling again at that little shack. It was "casino night," whatever that meant. Rick came with me. I agreed on the condition that he leave his wacky weed at home. Diane stayed with Joanie. There was a lounge singer in the night club, and they went to see his act.

The casino was busier that night. There were lines for the slot machines and a crowd at every table. I played blackjack. I ate about a thousand pounds of salty cashews, and didn't drink. Rick stood next to me, and after an hour a seat opened up at the table and he decided to play.

"I'll be your wingman," he said, stacking his chips in ten-dollar piles.

Blackjack is pretty simple: you need some luck, you need to be able to add up to twenty-one, and like that. I've seen all kinds of systems, basic card counting, charts guys carry with statistical analysis; I've seen guys with backers—professionals—and I've seen people asked to leave casinos for various offenses. Rick bet erratically, in no particular pattern; I couldn't tell if he had any experience at all, and I watched him rip through his bank and go back to the cashier for more chips. He talked to himself and filled up on vodka, and when his bank was gone he went back another time. I couldn't bear to look. He bummed a cigarette off somebody, and mentioned going waterskiing in the morning, and told me how he gave up smoking, cold turkey, on New Year's Day. "This is my first puff in a month," he said.

I said, "If you get rid of that hand, you might not lose as fast." He ignored me.

Meanwhile, I did well. I'm good at math, and blackjack is a lot of math. At one point, the dealer aimed his finger at me and said, "You're tough," and I shrugged. I felt like David Hasselhoff. I pointed back at him, and then didn't say a word except when I needed a card. Rick was out, he'd played like an imbecile, and he stayed to watch me, hunched over in his skintight rugby shirt.

I took a card. The dealer split a pair of eights. I watched all the stupid people around me losing money, and a little later a new dealer took over, and I cashed in almost nine hundred bucks. I won, and the house lost. As we walked back to the hotel—it wasn't even midnight, and it was cool and breezy like every other night since I'd arrived—Rick asked me to give him his money back. It was five hundred dollars. He said, "Please, buddy." I tried to tell him that the money he lost was no longer his money—it was the bank's—and what I had was different money, not his. He started explaining: he said he'd been drunk, the rules were different here from the ones in the casino he played in, whatever. I said to him,

"Why don't you go for a swim?" He said no. He begged me. I started laughing and pretended to play the violin. He told me Joanie had refused to let him take money for gambling, but he'd taken it anyway, and now he'd blown it, and he needed the money before we got back or she'd kill him. I said no. He asked me one more time. "What do I look like?" I said. "Get an advance on your credit card."

We got to Rick and Joanie's cabin. I could hear the women inside. I said to him, "Next time you gamble you need to have a figure in your head, a top amount you can lose," but he told me to shut up. Then he opened the door, and we went inside.

The women said the lounge singer was great, and started dancing around the bed. Diane had ordered two pizzas from room service, and there was food all over the place. Rick sat in a chair in the corner with his hat on backward. He looked fried, as if he got a sunburn on the bike that day. Diane and I went to our room.

We were in bed with the lights off when Rick knocked at the door. I went outside and stood on the paved path with him. The moon was shining on the water. He'd been crying. I could see where the discussion was about to go. He wore wrinkled blue boxers and white socks. He'd taken his hat off, and I noticed he had hives on his forehead, probably from riding his bike through the jungle.

He said he felt like crap inside. He said he loved me, he told me he was so surprised to find a friend at one of these places that he couldn't believe his luck. "You know what I mean?" he said. I saw that the light was on in their room, which meant Joanie probably knew he'd lost the money. He was talking about the fish we'd caught together. "There's nothing like fishing with your friend," he said. His oratory didn't seem to be rounding any corner. There were so many different stupid things about this moment, now he was telling me how he got ripped off buying some Krugerrands, I wanted him to shut the fuck up, I didn't know what to do, I went back into my bungalow and got five hundred dollars from the night's winnings and handed it to him. I said, "Here."

He said, "Thank you."

I didn't answer him. I thought he was full of shit.

He went back in and shut the door. I stood there, outside my doorway, furious at myself. His light went off. I distinctly heard him say something to Joanie. I waited another minute. I didn't hear anything else.

My watch said 2 A.M. A mosquito came up and bit my eyelid, but I didn't feel like going inside yet. I was sweating. Right next door, if I needed them, were my new friend Rick and his piece-of-ass wife. And in my bungalow I had my own no-fuck, don't-touch wife sleeping off her pizza pies. I had a view of the ocean, the seaborne air, mountains in back of me, jungles full of tree-climbing pot freaks. In the moonlight, there were swans or storks, maybe pelicans, gliding above the calm sea, looking for a fish to spear.

The next day was perfect, like all the others. Diane and I swam and read our books and lay on the beach. Joanie appeared at lunch and joined us; she looked tired, and the three of us said almost nothing as we ate. I asked about Rick, and she shrugged, and from then on we baked in the sun, watching the water. Joanie told us she'd talked to her kids that morning; their grandpa had made them spaghetti sandwiches, and they loved it. We swam, and later Joanie said Rick was probably playing tennis, and at dinner, when we still didn't see him, she said he was exhausted and had never woken up from his nap.

We said good night and went to bed. This time it was Diane who started up. She kissed me and I kissed her back. I held her tits. She opened my shorts and massaged me with a feathery touch of her fingertips, kind of teasing.

It went on for, I don't know, a while. There was all this circling, circling—had she forgotten how to do everything? She was doing a terrible job. I couldn't stand it anymore, I shoved her out of the way and started rubbing myself. It was not a good scene—not loving, if you know what I mean, not the expression of the subtle union between two people. And then Diane started to cry. She said she felt like a failure in every way—I was ready to agree—and then she went the other way and said I didn't know her anymore, that I'd forgotten how it used to be when we were crazy about each other, that now I didn't give a fuck about anything but making money. She cried and I held her. I regretted whacking off like that, I admitted it made everything worse. But I didn't really care. Without any more fighting, we both fell asleep.

First thing Friday morning, Diane went off to that windsurfing lesson in the bay. Joanie and I sat on the beach and talked. There was still no sign of Rick.

I told her about my business. She said it sounded fascinating. She told me there was a soap opera based in Miami that she was thinking of trying out for. We went swimming. I blew bubbles out my nose, and it cracked her up. Breakfast ended at eleven, and neither of us did anything about it. Eventually I got up and bought us apples at the commissary.

Rick showed up around noon, all sweaty in a tennis outfit and a purple baseball hat with the name of the resort stitched across it. I'd actually missed having him around. Rick's eyes were so green they almost glowed, from all that time in the sun. He was grinning again. Joanie asked if he was hungry; he said no. He had a white plastic bucket and a fishing rod; he went over near the dock and began surfcasting.

Joanie was looking at me. I didn't know what she meant. I said, "What are you smiling for?"

She said, "I'm such a fucking idiot."

Diane came back. She was all excited. She sat in the sand and told us how she got the Windsurfer going—it was tricky—and how the instructor, Philippe, and she and two others went way out into the ocean. She said she'd never had so much fun in her life. The group had had to turn back because the weather was starting to change, but not before they spotted a giant sea turtle, swimming alongside them. She said, "It was huge and gray—it had slimy bumps on its back." I looked off to the horizon, but I couldn't see anything, just a few clouds in a long line above the water.

Diane jumped up to go say hello to Rick over by the dock. They started chatting, and soon she was holding the rod and Rick was leaning around her, showing her how to draw it back with his long, bronze muscles. Rick was tall and broad-shouldered, and Diane was looking up at him. You could hear them laugh. Joanie sat beside me, blinking into the hazy sun, her lips coated in a thick film of sunblock. After a few minutes, I laid my head down, and when I looked up Diane and Rick were gone. I took my shirt off and fell asleep.

I woke up to the wind kicking sand, just the way Philippe had said. My mouth was dry. The sun was gone.

The beach was empty. I sat up, my face mashed into wrinkles from the towel. Joanie had passed out, too, curled up beside me in her bikini bottoms and my gray T-shirt. I sat back and looked at her small pink feet, the calluses on her heels and toes, her smooth, hairless thighs, the faint hint of veins beneath the skin. The stretched back of her red bikini bottoms across her dynamite ass. It was so pretty I wanted to cry. She yawned, reaching her long, thin arms up, and I saw her bikini top lying next to her on the towel.

Joanie sat up on her knees, beside me. "Where did they go?" she said. I didn't know. She'd knotted my shirt so it rode high up on her rib cage. I reached across and pulled the knot. She watched me. My hand slipped underneath the T-shirt, and I felt my palm across her stomach. There was sand stuck on her leg, and I watched her braless boobs moving against the inside of my shirt. I saw her swallow. I felt her breathe.

Diane came walking up the beach from the direction of the jetty. She said she was tired, and did I want to come take a nap with her. A second later, we were walking down the beach to our room. Joanie didn't have time to respond.

Diane closed the blinds. I sat down and untied my sneakers. She stepped between my legs and put her tongue against my teeth. She knelt, and yanked off my bathing suit and flung it on the lampshade. I was so excited I started to shake. I sat back on the bed, flustered. She took off her bottoms, standing in front of me, and kissed my throat. I kept looking for marks on her from Rick—a sign of use on my wife's body—but I was so turned on after all this time that I was seeing spots. The place where her bikini had been was glowing. She held my head. I rubbed my face against her stomach.

We lay down and started to do it. She seemed fine, I guess. She was digging it. It was the same old Diane. I held her sweet face.

She said, "It's nice to see you smile again." Finally, we were grooving.

When it was over, I went into the bathroom and got a glass of water. My groin was raw. She lay on her stomach, breathing.

I sat beside her and rubbed my hand across the top of her ass, as fine as silk.

She said, "I can't move."

"So don't."

"You're the best lover in the world," she said, and turned over and held me. "I promised Rick I'd go fishing, on that boat you guys went on." She looked at me. "Is it all right if I try it? It's our last day."

I said, "Absolutely." She squeezed my body. I hugged her back, as hard as she was hugging me.

"You feel so good," she said, and I said, "Um-hmm." The next second she was standing on one leg, trying to get into her panties. She said, "Thank you."

"For what?"

"For being so wonderful to me."

"No problem," I said. She ran around the room, looking for clothes. She took my baseball hat and fitted it on her head. I was still in bed. She leaned down next to me.

"You're the perfect husband." She gave me a kiss, pulling my lips with her teeth.

"O.K.," I said. She took the camera and flew out the door.

It was four o'clock. I was on my own. I thought of going back to find Joanie on the beach. I flipped open my briefcase, and then shut it, and got up and showered and left the bungalow.

I stopped by the Tiki Bar for a last drink. Jimmy, the bartender, was there, washing the bar off with a hose. The woman from the boat came, and we said hello. I hadn't seen her since the bonfire that night.

She was wearing a bikini, and wore a little leather belly bag clipped around her waist. She wiggled her ass onto the next bar-stool and lit a smoke and said, "Jim, what do I want?" He shovelled ice into the sink, waiting for her to answer. She said, "Rum-and-Coke, my favorite."

"I'm going back to Baltimore on Sunday. I miss my cats," she told me. She'd been here at least a week. She said, "They bill this place as a singles' resort, but I didn't see any singles here. Just me. And a couple of Swedish guys in G-strings."

I said, "How many cats?"

"Two. They're probably dead by now. My sister's been feeding them."

I was thinking about Diane. The perfume smell of her hair, the velvet softness of her baby skin. We got so close. She was floating all around me.

"I bet they're O.K.," I said. "Don't get depressed."

"I'm sick of this Tiki Bar," the woman said. I thought about Diane and Rick—what was she doing? I pictured them fishing and talking and doing whatever else you do on a boat. Diane and I were in some new place together, and I thought of how it had to keep being new, or else we were doomed. More people came. Here I was, sitting around, depressed. That's because you are a loser, I said to myself. I sipped my daiquiri. It tasted like ice cream. The woman from Baltimore was staring at me. She tapped her cigarette, waiting for me to say something else. I had nothing to say. I stared out at the water as the time passed in long sips. Out beyond the beach, I saw the cruiser pulling back into the harbor.

I said, "Hey—you like lawyers?" She asked why. "My cousin Walt is a lawyer. He's good-looking. He lives in Baltimore."

She said, "Really?"

"He has his own firm. He's loaded."

"Wow."

Walt had a lisp. He talked like Popeye. But he also had muscles and owned a house on two acres in the suburbs.

"Walt's a great guy," I said. "He'd love you." She smiled and put out her cigarette. "I'll call him when we get back."

She gave me a business card from her belly bag. "Something to look forward to," she said.

Diane and Rick came back. They'd seen dolphins, they said. Diane looked beautiful. I wanted to hold her and touch her again.

Rick had caught three fish. He was carrying them in a little cooler filled with ice. The long one he called a "dagger fish." He didn't know its real name. His jaw was cocked in a big smile. I stared at his straw-colored curls.

Diane sure seemed happy now. What had happened? I didn't have a clue. I thought of all the different combinations. I didn't panic—why the fuck should you panic? While I'm thinking this, though, Rick winked at the barstool next to me, at the woman, and she smiled and blushed. Diane looked at me and I looked at her and Rick. I still don't know what was going on. He showed me the other two fish; he wanted to take them home in dry ice and smoke them, and send them to me in the mail. I said, "I do not accept dead fish in the mail," and finished my drink. Diane came over and grabbed me. I put my arm around her and held her tight. The cook ended up broiling the fish for dinner. Rick bought all the wine.

"Here's to us," he said, "and fuck the mortgage." He was all smiles, and our happiness continued. Later in the evening, I found out they were a lot more than that five hundred dollars behind; they had debts at home, too. It was painful. Probably all he needed to avert disaster was some sane advice, a speck of financial insight. I could give him that. I told him to call me before he made any God-awful decisions.

We drank and ate till midnight, and went swimming naked while the ladies crawled around looking for shells by the light of the moon. The next morning, we rode with them to the airport, through that beautiful countryside. I was looking at everything, and it was so nice, because we were leaving.

Kiana Davenport

The Lipstick Tree

From *Story*

THEY RAN SILENTLY in single file, the bush so thick they moved by intuition. By morning they would be missed in their village, and by noon they would dwell in the mouths of elders as curses. Darkness hid a wall of matted spiderwebs that flung them backward to the ground, and Kona wept because she was young and terrified. Eva comforted her, and they lay still watching flying foxes like rags in brief ellipses through the trees.

"We're going to die," Kona said.

Eva shook her gently. "No, we're going to be famous." What she meant was that they were going to be remembered, and hated.

Smelling the stench from a nearby village—rotting vegetation, rancid pig fat, the smoke of old fires mixed with human and animal waste—reminded her of home. For a moment something buckled inside her, but Eva was strong, knowing whatever she would become, she was becoming now in flight.

Through fog, lights flickered on the river.

"They're hunting *puk-puks,*" she whispered, guiding her cousin toward the banks of the Sepik, where torches danced.

Exhausted, missing her bed of banana leaves, Kona slid down to earth and dozed. Eva sat beside her, watching men in dugouts, poised with spears. Near mudflats, red, glowing discs—crocodile eyes—blinked up at blazing *pitpit* cane. In the dark a man knew the size of a crocodile by the distance between the eyes. Once her father had killed a seven-foot *puk-puk* with only a bamboo spike. Its tail tasted like fish meat and the hide brought a very good price.

Now she lay back thinking of Agnes, whose clan belonged to her father's, so the girls had grown up like sisters. Two years older than Eva, at sixteen Agnes had married and borne her first son. Clan-women had helped her build a small grass hut for birthing, staying nearby in the bush, shouting advice but keeping a distance when she went into labor. Touching her during childbirth would pollute their minds and hands, preventing them from looking at, or cooking for, their husbands.

Observing the taboo of female blood, no man witnessed childbirth for fear of dying or going insane. Only Eva crept close that day, watching Agnes moan, squatting with her head in her hands. After several hours, she screamed. Seeing the baby's head pop out between her legs, Eva fainted.

After the birth of her son, Agnes' head was shaved and dyed with scarlet seeds from the lipstick tree. When her boy was four years old, he was taken away, raised in the men's house so spells would not be cast on him by his mother. Agnes lived with the women in low pig houses made of *pitpit* cane with thatched roofs. There the women slept in semicircles at the end of each hut, with pig stalls along one wall down the middle. When husbands felt the urge to mate, they called their wives into the bush, then returned to sleep in the men's house. Out of sorrow and terrible frustration, sometimes women fell asleep coddling piglets, even nursing them.

Eva watched Agnes grow swayback from load-bearing and child-carrying and digging in the yam fields, while clan-men lay around discussing bride prices, paybacks, and politics. Eva wondered if this was her future—a life of squatting in the bush, of hookworm and tattooed cheeks, and flesh caked with animal fat to ward off night chill and malarial mosquitoes.

This was the legacy of the women of the Sepik, the seven-hundred-mile-long river coiling from northern slope mountain ranges in central New Guinea down through lowlands of the interior and out to the Pacific Ocean on the country's northeast coast. Just north of Australia, it was a country whites called "Stone Age," "The Last

Unknown," where they were still addressed as "Masta" and "Missus."

Eva had been a bright child, crawling too early, walking and talking too soon. In primary mission-school, she had taken each English word on her tongue like a sacrament. By secondary school she saw that the white man's language was her passport to the outside world. But before she could even envision that world, one day she woke bleeding.

She was washed and oiled, adorned with shells and plumes of bird of paradise, and led into the center of the village. Though not beautiful, Eva was known to be clever and would graduate from secondary school. Her father proudly paraded her in front of village men, dark skin gleaming like wet bark, her kinky hair like luminous coils.

"My daughter is now a woman ready for betrothal. Intelligent, hardworking, and virtuous. Prepare your bride price, fatten your pigs, collect your salt wheels and gold-lip pearl shells. Bring your offerings to our home."

When Eva told Agnes she would soon marry, Agnes wept for her. "Pray for a girl, so you have something to love."

On the night of Eva's first mating with her husband, and ever after, he whispered chants to protect him from the potency of the female who bled without being wounded, who gave birth to other humans, whose power could shrivel his unprotected soul.

One day Eva watched Agnes with her second son, now two years old, walking toward the river, a slow serenity in her stride. She turned back once, waved to Eva through the trees, and plunged into the Sepik. Eva dropped her digging stick and ran toward the river. Crocodiles sunning in the shallows lifted their heads and in slow sighs stretched out chubby, childlike legs ending in claws. Pushing off from mudflats, they drifted, heads submerged. Agnes surfaced, holding her son up like an offering, and a large croc shot forward.

Her head bobbed as the current swept her along. A shiver ran down the tail of the reptile as it lunged into the depths, then shot up with Agnes in its jaws. The son floated momentarily then was pulled under, water around them boiling red. Eva screamed, and could not stop.

Police arrive, shooting *puk-puks* from their launch, then slit their bellies wide. They found eels, herons, a brass trumpet, a camera, a Bible, a dog. They did not find Agnes or her child. The funeral feast continued for weeks taking on the air of a celebration. Agnes' family, ghostly gray in mourning ash, received six slain pigs from her husband's family, plus yams and taros, bananas and sweet potatoes, the last installment of her bride price.

After that, Eva wept each time her husband called her to the bush. Three times she stole from her village and hid in the Lutheran Mission Church.

"I don't want a child," she told the reverend's wife. "I don't want my head painted red like a slave."

Three times her husband, Ernest, dragged her home. The reverend's wife suggested Eva go away from her village to the large coastal town of Wewak, north of where the Sepik met the Pacific Ocean. There she could study to become a nurse's aide, or one day even a nursing sister at the Lutheran Mission Hospital.

"My husband will write you a letter of recommendation," she said. "You're very bright, Eva. There's nothing here for you."

It was such a large idea, she needed time to think, to gather her nerve. By then she had graduated from secondary school and worked as cleaning girl at the hotel in Si-Siara, an old river station two swamps over from her village that drew tourists and foreign traders looking for totemic masks and *kunda* drums made by local tribes. The hotel was clean but decrepit, twenty rooms with exploding wallpaper and rusted light switches.

The owner was a burly Australian with the lashless eyes of a squid, reeking of insect repellent and cigars. Eva suspected, like all whites who settled in her country, he was full of unwholesome secrets. Yet he was married to a New Guinea woman as black as slate, whom he did not beat or scold, and when he talked to Eva he was kind. She had been working there several weeks when he took her aside.

"You're a good worker and a smart girl, you savvy? But guests are goin' on about you."

Eva stepped back, frightened. "Why, Masta? I do not steal."

He sniffed, fluttering his nostrils. "Use a bit of scent now and again. Or I shall have to let you go."

Other cleaning girls showed her their bottles of deodorant. At the pharmacy where jars were labeled "For Heartworm," "For Tapeworm," "For Malaria," she purchased a bottle with a pink, roll-on top. That night she pulled it from her string bag, stoking it in the dark. She had never owned perfume. Next day she bathed in a stream, and dreamily slid on the sticky wax that smelled like stale gardenias.

Scouring a toilet bowl at the hotel, Eva ran her hands over the graceful curve of its belly, flushing it repeatedly. One day she stopped relieving herself in the bush. The toilet, like her new perfume, became a habit. Sometimes, changing barely wrinkled sheets, she thought of the plaited grass sleeping-mats in her village, shared by humans and animals month after month until they shredded.

She watched elders of her clan who bathed only when it rained, who wore white man's hand-me-downs until they turned to rags. She studied her mother, head bowed from a life of carrying her *bilum*—the string bag of burden—hanging down her back from a braided strap across her head. Through the decades she had carried infants in her *bilum,* firewood, arrows and spears during tribal wars. Her mother had even fought in wars. She had never seen her bathe.

Sometimes Eva buried her face in hotel bath towels, inhaling the wonderful odors, and thought affectionately of her grandmother in her short grass skirt, and her grandfather in his "arse grass" and banana leaf penis-wrapper, and how they loosed in the air around them a rich, forlorn rottenness. Yet, her grandfather could split the skull of a wild boar at forty feet with a simple wooden arrow. And her grandmother had once hypnotized a python, dragging it home like a thick garden hose. What white woman could do that?

One day Eva stood watching a cousin serve Australian expatriates in the dining room. The white men sat over lunch observing two educated natives discussing upcoming elections of a new prime minister of Papua New Guinea. The natives were eating pork ribs, loudly crunching the bones. On the walls overhead, photos of earlier days showed tribes of cannibals holding up shrunken heads.

Nervously, the Aussies lit up cigarettes, exhaling profoundly, turning the pictures on the walls into dreams. Eva's tribe was descended from the people on the walls; she had once discussed it with her grandfather.

"Do you remember eating human flesh when you were young, grandfather?"

He answered slowly in Pidgin, *"Time ee got man belong kaikai small no more by and by man ee full up."* When there was man to eat, only a little bit would fill you up.

"But *yu laik em kaikai* white man?" Eva asked. But you liked eating the flesh of the white man?

He shook his head, making a face. *"Meat belong im stink too muss."*

She reflected sadly on how her people were now paid as waiters to serve the white men they once ate.

She was nineteen then, and one day she watched her grandmother, tiny as a pygmy, running down the road. Having borne ten children, old age had come to her as a luxury. Never still, feet calloused and hard as horns, she was always scurrying off to market with yams or freshly caught bats and eels.

"Grandmother," Eva asked, "are you happy?"

The woman cocked her head like a bird, as if considering the question, patted Eva's cheek, spat out a jet of betel-nut juice, and went cackling and spinning down the road. Sometimes Eva found her squatting with other ancient women—teeth rotten, lips and gums like open wounds from chewing betel-nut—weaving their *bilums,* or pounding sago. Work was their life, what they took pride in. It was their only voice.

She grew up listening to these women gossip in the fields, watching them help each other in childbirth and child burial. In the heads of each woman of each clan were libraries of encyclopedic lore, local legends, knowledge of plants and animals, and the twenty kinds of soil along the Sepik. These were the daughters of memory, the true prophets and seers who protected the fertility of the land.

"They have power," the reverend's wife said. "Their secret is, they share. If you go into the white man's world, Eva, this is what you will miss. White women don't share." She had said it wistfully, and there was alcohol on her breath.

The woman was Canadian, married to an Australian of Scottish descent, and they had lived on different missionary posts along the Sepik for over ten years. Eva became her part-time mother's helper while she was in mission-school, and she insisted Eva call her Margaret, rather than "Missus."

Only fifteen years older than Eva, her face had already surrendered. Direly thin, she seemed to be wearing away. When there was news on the wireless of tribal wars in the highlands and pack-rapes by roving "rascals," Margaret's face turned bloodless. This was when Eva noticed the smell of alcohol and suspected she had been too long away from her own kind.

One night, half-asleep in the pig house, Eva heard her husband call her name, and followed him outside. Though he had gone to mission-school like Eva, he had no curiosity about the world. Mostly he and his clan-men lounged in the *haus tambaran,* the spirit house, smoking and storytelling, or stalking the jungle for small game. The smell of beer was heavy on his breath as Ernest knelt over her. Undoing his shorts, he suddenly froze; she had not washed the deodorant from her underarms. His slap was like fire across her cheek.

"You smell of white man," he cried. "How many you been sleeping with, whore!"

He pummeled her stomach and chest with his fists, slapped her face repeatedly until she bled. Women carried her back to the pig house, rubbing her wounds with heated plant stems that numbed the pain.

"You're taking on white man's ways," her mother said in the language of their tribe. "Making your husband look like he 'have no bones.' " It was an old expression that meant a man was not a man. "Stay home in the fields, where you belong."

"Why is it wrong to want to learn?" Eva cried. "My wages go to my husband and father, and still I am beaten!"

For two weeks she washed off the deodorant before she reached home. One day she forgot and men sniffed as she passed them in her village. That night Ernest beat her again, leaving her bleeding in the bush. Slowly, painfully, she turned her head toward the Sepik, just visible through the trees.

Margaret told her that downriver ninety miles, where the Sepik met the Pacific, was where the world began. Great costal towns where ships the size of villages docked. Towns peopled with Anglos and Malaysians and Chinese, clanless places with no rules where a woman could become anything she wanted to be. Eva pictured herself in a place where no one would watch her, where she could slowly and carefully grow. But she was only nineteen, she had never even crossed the river. She rolled over in the dark.

The hotel owner warned her twice, but she would not use deodorant again. Guests complained that she smelled like wildlife, and the day she was fired, she sat weeping in Margaret's kitchen.

"Resign yourself," Margaret said softly. "Or go away from here."

"How?" Eva cried. "And why must I leave my people? Why can't things just change? I am not the only unhappy one. Why do you think Agnes gave herself to the *puk-puks?*"

Margaret shuddered, looking longingly toward the cupboard where she kept a bottle.

"My dear, don't you think I know? I watch your women giving up. Poison. The rivers. Or they throw themselves over gorges, taking their infants with them. Ten years of this, look at me. People think I'm fifty." Her gaze drifted, then returned. "Stay here, Eva. Help me with the children. Then one day we'll take you to the mission-hospital at Wewak. You can begin medical training." She took her hand. "I could use the company."

Eva was afraid. Moving into the mission-house with Margaret and Reverend Burns would be desertion of her husband. Ernest would be shamed. Bad feelings would grow between the clans. He had borrowed pigs to pay Eva's bride price and had not yet paid it back. There would be tension between the reverend and the villagers. Ernest might kidnap her, take her home, but not divorce her. He might take another wife, he could take many wives, and keep her as valuable labor.

When she told him she had been fired, he beat her again.

"You are my shame. A joke on me. You do not work in fields with the women. Cannot hold a job with white men. Cannot give me a child!"

She closed her eyes with each blow, hoping she was dying. Near dawn, someone gently lifted her head.

"Be still," her cousin, Kona, whispered. "Elders forbid us to come for you. Your mother cried all night."

She poured something bitter between Eva's lips, wiping insects from her wounds.

Eva moaned, trying to stand. "I thought I died."

"We'll both die here," Kona whispered. "Eva, you must help me run away. You're more clever than I. They're marrying me to a man who worked his last two wives to death."

Kona was fifteen. Her beauty had drawn the attention of many suitors, pressing her father to name how many pigs and gold-lip shells he required for her hand.

For five days Eva lay feverish, infected wounds covered with medicinal leaves and plant stems. On the sixth day she went back to work in the fields, thinking constantly of Wewak, wondering how she would be strong enough to leave her village.

One day she stood by the river gathering kindling. Crocodiles were sunbathing on mudflats, and a large one turned, gazing at her, eyelids opening and closing voluptuously. Eva moved closer, and three *puk-puks* slid almost lazily into the water, floating invisibly but for their snouts. Only the large one remained, contemplating her. Suddenly it trembled from snout to tail, a terrible prolonged shudder.

She had often spied on *puk-puks,* the graceful, swirling waterdance of their courtship. Her father said they fetched back millions of years, that they were as old as earth itself. Revered by her people as patron saints of war and hunting, their heads were carved on weapons and prows of dugout canoes. In initiation rites, men's bodies were scarred to resemble crocodile scales.

Slowly, she approached the huge reptile, moving into the water to her knees. Reaching her hand out, she felt an obsessive need to touch it, to stroke its head. It shuddered again, opened its jaws and, hugely, audibly, sighed.

Eva splashed forward. "Agnes, is it you!"

Recognizing the other, she was wrenched out of herself, and for a moment wondered if she were insane. Then slowly, thoughtfully, she rested her hand on its head, its scales like cold, wet stones.

"Are you finally at peace?" she whispered. "Oh, I am so much like you."

The crocodile sighed again, its eyes fixed dreamily on Eva.

"I will live for both of us," she whispered. "I will break away."

Two days later, elections were held for the new prime minister of Papua New Guinea. The man favored by the people lost. Suspecting rigged elections, natives rioted across the country. Stores were looted and burned, women raped by roving packs of "rascals." Nine people were speared to death, one of them Margaret's husband, Reverend Burns, leaving a supply store upriver from Si-Siara. By the time the news reached Eva, a police launch had already docked in town, but no one could penetrate the reverend's house.

Eva was there when they finally broke down the door; inside it was like a tomb. Then Margaret's baby cried and they found her and her three children, hiding in a closet under clothes. She pointed a cocked revolver at the district chief of police, a big, muscular native, and they saw she was gone, just gone. Hearing the news of her husband on the wireless, she had finally snapped.

Eva moved through the crowd and knelt before her, talking softly about dinner, and bathing the children, and maybe a nice, cool drink, until Margaret handed over the revolver like a child. Days later, a mile outside town where a coral airstrip had been left from World War II, a bush-plane lifted her and her children out of the jungle, circling once over tribes wailing with grief. With Margaret gone, Eva felt her chance at another life was over.

Resigned now, she watched clan-women with bellies huge as if from deep, long inhalations. Each year, as rhythmically as the seasons, women swelled, then expelled their babies, had their heads shaved, and their skulls dyed red. Sometimes infants, in turn, swelled—first feet, then legs and stomach—vomiting worms, the mother pulling them from the infant's throat as it suffocated and died. If not worms, then malaria, pneumonia. In one year, twenty-three infants had died. In a second inhalation, it seemed, the women's bellies swelled again, and the cycle repeated itself, death and birth made routine by repetition.

At night, in the fertile smell of the pig house, Eva felt larvae dropping from the thatched roof, insects gnawing, pigs snuffling. She held her head and wept.

"You look at us with shame," her grandmother whispered.

"No," she cried. "I only wanted to learn a better life."

"It is all the same," the old woman said. "You learn new ways, this becomes that. But it is all the same."

An older, childless couple settled into the mission, big, doughy Brits, at first too stunned to talk. Reverend Hart had florid skin punished by the sun; during services a girdle of sweat grew steadily down his trousers. Sometimes his wife stood near Eva, wheezing, smelling of white shoe polish, and Eva knew they would not become friends.

But one day the woman gave her an envelope with her name on it. "We found this in the desk with things they left behind. I know you helped Margaret with the children. Perhaps she left you something."

Eva walked slowly along the river, stroking the white square in her pocket, her senses so alerted the jungle came at her in twos—a snake choking down another snake, tails slamming in duet, a pig gnawing the skull of another pig, trees suckling each other, fighting for oxygen. She sat down in a broth of orange mist.

It was a letter addressed to the director of the Lutheran Mission Hospital at Wewak, a friend of Margaret's husband, recommending Eva for internship there as medical aide. The letter was signed, but words were crossed out, as if Reverend Burns had planned to draft another version.

"But it is signed!" she cried, hugging the letter, and it seemed the jungle around her loosened its grip. Fog retreated, snow egrets rose in a column, and a dying sun on huge lotus lilies made the river a floating tapestry.

Desperate, Eva sought out the hotel owner's wife, Suliana. She was from a village near the capital city of Port Moresby where native women went to university and wore lip rouge, and even lived alone.

Eva showed her the letter. "Please help me. I want to be . . . a modern woman."

Suliana smoked a cheroot and rubbed her wedding band. "I have watched you, Eva. You're a bright girl. If you leave, you can never come back."

"Why?" she cried. "I don't want to give up my family forever."

"You would return educated, wearing shoes. Your clan would still be wearing mud. What would you say to them? What would you talk about?" She shook her head. "The river flows one way. This I have learned."

Finally, when she felt Eva was sure, she sent a runner downriver to a hamlet called Pondi. "That is where you will cross the Sepik."

All of that week the people of her village prepared for a *Sing-Sing,* officially welcoming the new reverend and his wife. That night would come back to Eva in memory and dreams, the rhythmical stamping and chanting of men drenched in pig fat, steaming like panthers, faces caked in reds and blues and yellows from plant dye and ash.

Legs tasseled in cassowary feathers, crescents of gold-lip pearl shell blazing on their chests, in feathered headdresses and bone nose-plugs, they moved in waves to great thunking heartbeats of slit-gong drums, while women stood aside, swaying with their infants. For hours, bodies whirled, voices chanted, finally climaxing in the sacrifice of the pigs, a prolonged, baffling shower of blood and squeals. In the light of cane-grass torches, Reverend Hart and his wife lifted their heads and closed their eyes, as if waiting to be impaled.

The night before, Eva had squatted beside her mother and grandmother, watching them sleep. Her mother had slowly sat up, handing her a rag wrapped around a handsome, gold-lip pearl shell carved in the shape of a crescent. This was precious currency. No words were exchanged, but she knew her daughter was going.

Now Eva sat with her tribe in firelight, people glowing with the drippings of slaughter. She moved to her father, touching his arm

ringed with boar tusks, his kinky hair exploding with trapped fire-
flies. He would be the angriest, the most unforgiving. She looked at
Ernest, he would find better wives. Then she sat beside her grandfather picking lice from his arse grass, snapping them between his
nails.

She asked him how the pig was, and he proudly held up a large
hunk of pork, as if he had given birth to it. *"Em bilong mi!"* All of
this is mine!

She wrapped her arms around his thin shoulders, hugging him,
then turned toward her grandmother squatting in a circle with her
cronies, little sun-dried birds thoughtfully smoking their pipes.
When she was very young her grandmother had dragged her
through the bush at night, to stare through the windows of a white
man's house lit electrically by generator. They had stood there for
hours until he tapped a switch—a miracle—dousing the mysterious
light within. Her grandmother had clapped her hands to her
mouth, gasping with fear and wonder. Now Eva looked at her, and
could not speak.

The old woman shook her head, knowing. "You will see. This
becomes that. It is all the same."

She held her hands before her navel as if she'd caught a frog,
then reached inside her waistband, drawing forth an object
wrapped in cobwebs, pressing it on Eva. An ancient watch face,
hands long gone, where rust and lice hung captive. She had carried
it for years.

"Time!" she whispered, stroking the watch as if it contained
Eva's future. Then she patted Eva's face, and cried.

She and Kona ran hard, in fog so thick the villages they passed
were soft and blurred like velvet. Stopping for breath, they could
still hear the chanting of their village. By now the drums had
reached an otherworldly density, clans dancing with ancestral spirits.

Kona suddenly fell to her knees, sobbing. "My family will be
shamed. They'll slaughter my piglets. Apinum and Pawpaw. There
are no trees in the city, no mango and dragon plums. Who'll give us

plant herbs when we're sick? Who'll give payback when we're insulted?"

Eva shook her viciously. "You fool. Wewak's a town, not a big city. There are trees, and a marketplace. We're not going to Sydney across the bloody ocean!"

"*You* will one day," Kona cried. "What then will become of me?"

Eva dragged her forward, continuing downriver, avoiding swamps like aspic quivering in their path. They walked all night and slept all day in rain that resurrected sewage, and woke beneath a dozing python, like giant bracelets hanging from a branch. Since noon, news of their runaway had echoed on slit-gong drums through the jungle. They walked again the next night, paralleling the river, but avoiding the shore and possible search parties in dugouts from their tribe.

Through the hours Eva sustained herself on what Margaret had said. "Feed your mind. Live up to your capacity."

Then she remembered Suliana's words. "You leave the Sepik. It never leaves you."

On the third night they reached the village of Pondi, where a dugout would come to take them across the river. Hiding in the cleft of a banyan tree, they slept fitfully, finally so welted with mosquito bites, they dived into the Sepik. The village was quiet, fast asleep, and in the darkness Eva saw the outline of a boy paddling a canoe. He drifted closer, calling her name.

"Yes," she cried. "We are ready!"

She swam to shore, gathering her things, then waded to the dugout, pulling Kona behind her. But Kona was no longer there, her voice already drifting, calling back from shore.

"Forgive me! I am not brave enough." In the dark they heard her sobs.

The boy stopped paddling, but Eva urged him from behind. "Go! We must go on."

If they were not across the river by first light, they would be intercepted. Eva's husband would take her back to her village as forced labor. Standing carefully, she took an oar, helping point the dugout toward deep waters. Stars shifted, the night deepened, and

Kona's cries grew dim. The current fought them, pulling them downriver, so the trip across took almost all night.

In that time Eva fought against the ineffable softness of river fog, like second skin to her, knowing she would never again sleep beside the steamy breath of these waters, or hear the haunting, eerie insistence of bamboo flutes, or feel orphaned piglets draw tenderness from her like fluid. But no man would ever beat her again, of this she was sure.

They paddled silently until contours grew out of the boy's black silhouette, and Eva saw it was a young woman near her age. Night eased, the shore stepped forward, and bats like huge, brown pods hung quivering in trees of a village called Wara.

The girl turned to her. "You're safe. In another district."

By running away to another district, she had officially divorced her husband. By divorcing him, she had renounced her clan.

Stepping ashore, the girl pointed toward the jungle.

"Follow the dirt path up the mountain. One day's walk, you reach a rusting bunker. Downhill, another day, the coast. Climb the bunker, you'll see Wewak, the Pacific Ocean!"

Between Wara and Wewak lay forty miles of swamp, flat bush country, jungle-covered mountain. Eva looked back at the Sepik, shaking, then flung herself against the girl. They held each other, then the girl stepped back. "Hurry. My village wakes."

"Why did you do this?" Eva whispered. "For me, a stranger?"

"It's too late for me. I have children." She handed her some local currency. "*Kina,* from Suliana." Then she pushed her foward. "Go. Become something."

For two hours, Eva moved swiftly, looking neither left or right. She was bright and ambitious, she told herself. Wewak would be easy. The only hard thing would be talking to people. Then she crawled under a bush and sobbed. At day's end she reached the bunker. In the dark, she pulled an old sweater from her *bilum,* falling asleep wrapped in the smell of her childhood.

At dawn she woke and climbed the bunker, a lookout point left from World War II. Fog slowly lifted and, looking down, she shuddered. In the distance was Wewak, tall, hard-edged buildings jangled with sunlight, a harbor suckled by giant ships. Beyond it, the Pacific, melting into the world. She thought of all the things ahead, shoes aching to be worn, shelves of books waiting to be read, and she was breathless.

Beside a stream, she washed her face, smoothed her hair, and inventoried her *bilum*. The reverend's letter of recommendation, a few *Kina,* a gold-lip pearl shell. Deodorant, a rusty watch. She had never owned so much.

She climbed to the top of the bunker again, and studied the horizon, seeing herself decanted into the future, going even further than Wewak. One day she would have her legs and cross the sea, and walk boulevards of great cities. Asleep alone in the white man's world, she would dream of deep river and remembered soil, and *puk-puks* dancing in the shallows. She would hear the *kunda* drums, and smell the odor of her tribe. And she would wake in birdless dawns, knowing she lived only in the tears of the daughters of memory.

Breaking a seed from a lipstick tree, she touched it to her mouth, delicately rouging her lips, then started down the mountain.

Ian MacMillan

The Red House

From *The Gettysburg Review*

SO MAYBE now it's down to the woods.

"I shoveled the gutters, washed milk pails." The way he looks now at the table, no wonder men in town call him The Chimp. "I'm goin' to the woods."

A snort. Looks up from an oily dismantled carburetor on the plastic tablecloth crisscrossed white and red, his creased, stubbly face blank. Grins. "Honey on your stinger?"

"No, just walkin'." Sort of told him from the edge three times that it's the float lever shaft, that it's bent, or lost, or sheared off, but he won't pick up the clue and so that old tractor won't ever work right. Right there in the Operator's Manual. But the last time he had that look, you say that once more and you'll lose some teeth.

Out. The woodshed walls gray melting clapboard sliding down toward the stone foundation whose concrete melted long ago in snow and heat, snow and heat. Decay.

Swish through the timothy down the hill toward the woods ahead bobbing with the rhythm of walking. Beyond the woods, more woods, dark rounded humps vanishing in the bluish haze. The Chimp. Early in the summer he dragged a dead cow by a back leg to the back of the pasture, and the skin stripped where it slid over the rocky, dry soil, and it rotted there, melted in the sun into a lake of maggots, and the smell went all the way to town. Hey, what's that stink? I don't know.

Turn. The house roof sags, rusted corrugated sheeting, window frames bending away from square, porch posts leaning away from plumb. Decay. Beyond the house the barn and stalls. Every year The Chimp buys a piglet and raises it nine months and every year he cuts its throat in June and takes it to Mr. Evans to cut up and in a week you look at a cooked rib and remember. That you ran in the grass with the piglet, sweet-smelling and fast, who saw you and said hello with a heh heh heh heh heh low in his throat. That when it was two hundred pounds, you stood at the pen and it said heh heh heh and you said you don't know nothin' about your throat bein' cut. You don't know nothin' and I don't know nothin' and he don't know nothin' and on it goes, maggots and slit throats, summer into summer.

Deanna Branch. Just past the spring in the looming pine needle floored woods by the red house.

The first time. Walking toward the fence past the red house and there the dense blue of jacket and white face. A smirk. Oooo, The Chimp's kid. "What you doin' here?"

Red faced. "Uh, just walkin'."

"Walkin' where?"

"Nowhere. Just walkin' is all it is."

The second time. "Hey, what you got with this place?"

"Nothin'. I was just here lookin' at the old house. Gonna rebuild it." First time that idea ever came. "Gonna get me roofing, two-by-fours, all that."

"Really?"

Third time. Hotter and she was in the woods wearing a T-shirt and shorts. Sneakers, red puffballs above her heels. "Hey, it's you again. Where's your hammer?" When she moved the breasts rolled inside there. When she turned her breasts paused a split second before following her. Deanna Branch.

Walking. Jounce, jounce, jounce, flesh bouncing in gravity. Down the hill to the logroad that vanishes into the trees, a dark tunnel lit at the opening by floating dust. Like a mine entrance. The leafed tube leading to the red house. Grandaddy Chimp dead a long time. Decayed in the cemetery. Brothers too, not dead but gone fourteen years, gone without saying anything into the service and no letters or phone calls since. Can't write letters anyway. Chimp's kids can't read like The Chimp and Mrs. Chimp can't read. Brothers gone fourteen years and the afterthought walking toward the leafed tunnel. Only strange dreamlike figures, looming above when you were two. But why? Because Jimmy has a scar on his leg from the thrust of a pitchfork when he was twelve, because Ricky has a misshapen nose from The Chimp's fist when he was thirteen. Never saw that though. Kids at school knew. Because they are covered with scars from beatings, from being The Chimp's kids.

The Chimp. Why? Because he is bowlegged and stocky and short and has long, hairy arms. Because he has a long, drooping face with a big lower lip. Because he slaps the shit out of anyone who drops anything. Because when he is mad he pinches the side, so that you are caught in a nightmare of pain. Because he can't read, never could. Because he can't write a check, never could. Because he hates any kid in his house to read or go to school, even though when he takes his papers to the village to Mr. Steele the postmaster for Mr. Steele to do all his paperwork and taxes, his long, drooping chimp face has on it a look of simpering helpless want, well, here I am again and by Jesus I can't figure this out, never could, and Mr. Steele says aww, it ain't no trouble for me, Bob. Because even when he watched TV and words come on the screen, you better not practice like you did by reading them out loud, so you mouth them softly to yourself: Just do it. Don't try this with any plugged in razor. Buy now interest free with low monthly payments. Speeds clocked on test track only. Third and II.

Into the tunnel. Cool, tree-smelling with shafts of dusty light slanting to the rotted leaves. Just a few hundred yards, the bubbling spring with the lump of water in the middle quickly changing shape with the upward current a little like the fountain in the hall at school. The water cold, and another fifty yards the red house. Not red now, red fifty years ago but decayed now, perforated, clapboards sliding like the woodshed, sheetmetal roofing full of holes through which thin spears of light come, dotting the rotted floor and the rusted stove.

Weeks after the cow was dragged back there and the bloat was gone, the skin draped over the bones, the maggots glistening around the edges. A week later a lake of them. And up behind the barn the faint stain of the pig's blood. Heh heh heh.

The spring, just off the logroad hidden down in the dead leaves, tiny cliffs of green moss at the edges, a cone of clear water with the lump dancing in the middle. On knees and up it sweeps, dip, and drink, the cold metallic water colder than at school.

Hate school, love school.

Hate it for the smell of manure and turned milk and gasoline and pinesap in the clothes, the girls and boys sniffing insults behind the back. Hate it for the nurse who finds ticks in the scalp, nits in the hair, who puts Gentian Violet on impetigo so it is worn like a purple badge on the cheek. Hate it for the sound of their voices: hoo-hoo-hoo-hoo-haaah! and the monkey scratch of the ribs.

Love it for the books: in the quiet study hall words words words. National Geographic. Vertebrate Paleontology. Life Beneath the Sea. Best the big dictionary. Precarious is an old silo about to tip over. Precarious is The Chimp on the tractor on a side hill turning up so that one huge wheel leaves the ground for a split second. Unblemished is Deanna Branch's face. Unblemished is the lump of water dancing in the little conical pool. Words.

And The Chimp: you'll quit when you're sixteen because I say so. You'll quit because I need the help and that's all there is to it. You'll quit.

Oh yes the help. In May Brownie had a shit-sodden tail and you tied it by its long, wet end hair to a pipe beam so you could milk her the cow who couldn't be milked by machine and then you turned her out and she walked away from her tail in the sound of a metallic bong leaving it hanging tied there, dark empty skin, the cow walking out with a thin red stick for a tail, slick and sharp at the end. And the beating went on for five minutes (I forgot! I forgot!), strap, fist, some with a little piece of two by four (I forgot!), a kick in the ribs that still leaves a shadow all this time, bloody nose and hair pulled out. Oh yes the help.

No more school. Nothing. Only a medical book out of the dumpster behind the bus garage that last day, hidden now in the red house because The Chimp won't have it. The Family Medical Guide. Waste of time. A lot of goddam idling. Cutaways of human bodies and pictures of acne and clubfoot and rickets (The Chimp, probably) and uteruses and vaginas and penises and livers and spinal columns and hearts. Pictures of different kinds of decay: rheumatoid arthritis and cancer and something of the liver. Uh-oh, the body's precarious health. How many thousands of miles of veins and arteries? How many crucial organs floating in that tissue? The heart, auricles and ventricles and valves and arteries as thick as garden hoses. Even The Chimp has them. Blood goes from the auricle to the ventricle. Words.

Only fifty yards up through the trees, the red house, the tangled brush surrounding the foundation, the overgrown roses and burdocks, the faint impressions near the front where wagons once sat. Inside the house, rotted furniture on the sagging floor, kitchen things, and in a bedroom or maybe some kind of pantry a box and inside the box the Medical Guide. A kind of flutter in the chest. Words. Peritonitis. Plasma. Pelvis. Prenatal. Duodenum. Dilation. Deltoid.

Deanna Branch. As many miles of veins and arteries as the body of The Chimp's kid. A uterus and mammary glands, a heart with four chambers, a stomach leading to a small intestine and after that to a large intestine, the whole thing a slick, glistening twenty-four feet long. Suppose you stretched one human out that way? All the miles of veins and arteries, and the digestive system stretched out in a line so that you could walk along it and see the protective membrane, the surrounding veins, globules of fat. Lay one out, teeth lined up, eyes sitting side by side, jawbone here, one ear on one side and one on the other, between which lies the complicated little chambered system that affects balance. The semicircular canal.

Renal failure.

Up ahead the red house. Emerging with the jouncing rhythm of walking it leans, doorway still straight while the corner beams up and down are off plumb so that clapboard has popped loose and fallen, hinged at the doorway and pointing just a little down toward the corner. A house from a dream. Big hewn granite stones for steps leading to the front door, as level as pools of water.

Stop. Listen. Deanna Branch. Only birds, a jay, in the distance the swish swish of a deer scraping past brush, groaning, breathing trees, and the soft, hushed breeze in the treetops.

The red house. Those boards, gray and mossy on the bottom edges, were once red, because in the little cracks you can see it, the paint faded into a dull salmon, and then if you pull a board a little away from the doorframe, you can see the red inside, as if painted yesterday.

The house pauses in a hush like a breath held. There are clicking sounds, sounds of wood fibers sliding against each other in a slow, painful groan. The floor seems to inflate as it begins to rise, as if the basement were a huge lung gradually drawing air. The clapboards, all still and at their years of angles, shudder and just visibly begin to close up like closing scissors, the pivots where nails still hold pop-ping and snapping as the gray wood moves. Window frames shriek as the heavy beams move slowly toward plumb, above which corru-gated steel pings, surface shimmering like gasoline on water, the rust drawing inward toward its origin, closing up in a galvanized advance, the sheets sliding back into place at the edges, snaking into line and silvering in the sunlight, the blotches of rust that were nails receding into themselves revealing the perfect circles of nailheads, and as the clapboards line in, their seams go narrow until they become black lines from which the oxidized salmon of ancient paint creeps outward, brightening, advancing across the newing wood like a rapid virus, reddening and growing brighter. Brush grows backwards, shrinking into infancy and revealing windows that creep up like inverted sheets of falling water, beyond which, just visible inside, a rug spreads like a growing viral blotch on the floor that oozes gray to brown, the stain and varnish materializing like a photograph emerging out of a chemical solution, centered by the rug of brightening geometric shapes, and flowers.

"I'll get me a saw and hammer, nails, that kind of shit."

What is it today? Renal failure. Reach through the open window to the box, topped with faded oilcloth. In the list of tiny words in the back. What is a renal? Read read read. A word is either one thing, or can mean something you can't touch, not a thing but a   . Precarious.

But Deanna Branch. Page sixty-six. "Development of the breast: Left, rudimentary ducts in infancy and childhood; Center, elongation of ducts and tissue growth; Right, adult breast with milk-secreting lobules." Lobule.

Shirt hit by something. Burdock. Away thirty feet she stands smiling. "Hey, what you readin'?"

"Nothin'." Put it away and slide off toward the corner of the house. She comes up. Jeans, a halter. Adult breast with milk-secreting lobules.

Pull the burdock off. "Each little spike has a hook on the end. You ever see that?"

"L'me see," she says. Hand the burdock to her.

Studies it, squinting. "Yeah, I see them. Neat."

Stoops and pulls a pack of Marlboros from her sock. "I come here to smoke. So far away not even the dog smells it."

"The tar is no good for you."

"Shove it," and she giggles. "Brought you something else too." Digs in her jeans pocket. Nails. A handful of them. Holds the nails out, drops them into your hand.

"Hey, thanks." Hot nails. From the heat of her tissue, the hot tissue of her thigh.

"Where's the hammer?"

"I ain't got it yet." Put the hot nails on a gray windowsill.

Lights the cigarette with a paper match, slides the book back into the cellophane, puts the pack back in her sock. The first big puff inflates her chest, smoke billows from her mouth and nose. "So what you like on TV?"

"Nothin'. My dad's always watchin' cowboy movies and wrestlin'." And he doesn't let anyone touch his little remote device. Nobody. Knows only a couple of the buttons but won't let anyone touch it. Channel up, channel down, off, on. Of menu and setup and res/mem and prog and clear he knows nothing.

"I like Beverly Hills."

"Who's she?"

Laughs so hard that she begins to cough, the veins in her neck bulging, breasts shaking.

"What's so funny?" Face hot, scalp prickling.

"It's a place, not a girl."

"Oh."

Down below the fully developed uterus, ovaries and fallopian tubes rest inside the pelvic bones, all encased in skin and denim. No congenital malformations. A generally healthy development including the widening of the pelvis. More smoke. Every vein and every capillary now constricting, reducing body heat, especially in the extremities.

"I like to read."

Laughs again. Then, "No no no. I'm not teasing. It's just that like, like you say the weirdest things."

"I was just sayin' that because I don't watch a lot of TV. I like words so I read, anything, I don't care."

"Well, that's good."

"I want to read every book ever written."

"In English you mean. But there's like millions of them. I mean," and a gesture at the trees. "Like—" Smokes, looking.

Red face again, scalp prickling.

Words coming through smoke, "Kids at school make fun of you." So? Kids at school made fun of all of us. We're trash.

Why here? That feeling of not caring. So just say it.

"I'm The Chimp's kid."

Funny look. Turns, walks a little along the gray, decaying wood, looks in a window. "There's a real sort of new looking enamel pot in there."

"We don't have real washin' machines and stuff. So my clothes smell like woodsmoke an' cowshit."

Now a funnier look. Like she made a mistake by being—what is the word? Frank. Frank is a name and frank is a way of talking and franking has something to do with stamps.

"I could wash some of your clothes."

"Your ol' man wouldn't care for that. 'Hey what is this Chimp clothes doin' in the washer?'"

"He wouldn't say that."

Then it's up a sapling, ten, twelve feet, then higher until it bends like a fishing rod, and hanging, yell "Hoo-hoo-hoo-hoo-haah!" so that the sound vanishes into the woods while she seems to watch it vanish, and hanging by one arm scratch the ribs, and drop the ten feet shhh-thump in the leaves. Laugh.

"You make fun of yourself." Sits, looking. Puts the cigarette out in the wet, mulchy soil under the leaves, grinds it with the heel of her sneaker. "I never made fun of you."

"Nobody in my family could read."

"Like, what's that got to do with—"

"So I like to read. I'm gonna fix up this house and fill it with books." First time that idea ever came.

Looks. "I've got books too. You want some?"

"All you can spare. And paint it red. Was red once."

And fill it with books. Almost like a feeling of shock. Undecay it and fill it with books. Oh Jesus what an idea.

Her arms folded around her knees, the largest joints in her body. Cornered again because of that look on her face.

"What?"

"I was thinking. I could help you sort of, you know, like with the house. An old house like this, I'd bet it has a good frame still."

"This house has good bones."

Bruise expanding outward from the eye socket. Study it, the reddishness in the eye-white, a little scrape where The Chimp's fist hit. Then the side-pinch. You gonna be late again? No. You sure? Yeah, I'm sure. Cause if you are I'll beat the shit outta you. I won't be late. Damn fool, go to the woods without a gun—what the hell you do out there? Walk around is all—walking is all it is. But this time something hangs like smoke around the whole thing, around the picture of The Chimp swinging and then the sickening, silver flash of sudden pressure in the sinuses and the dizziness. Are you really allowed to do that? Or is there some other shadow of something hanging around all this and all she can say is don't be late for stuff, you know how he gets. But how he gets is still the question, if you are caught where you are and Ricky and Jimmy were caught where they were and the pigs were caught year by year and the sun went up and went down and that was all it was. Nobody knows nothin'.

Why does black paint on the back of a mirror make it silver on the other side? Not silver, it's—reflective. Some paint fell off and you can see through a hazy hole.

A bruise is a contusion caused by blows or falls that break small vessels under the skin without breaking the surface. Discoloration is temporary.

Up to the barn, into the smell of watery summer manure and hay and the molasses smell of grain, the smell of wood and milk and sweaty cowhide. All up in the pasture now, only an hour ago the breathing and soft stomping on cement and the hiss chuck hiss chuck of the machines and the looks on their faces when you dumped the grain down in front of their wet, slick noses, their eyes all misty with pleasure from the molasses taste of the grain, deep pools like wells their eyes, as if you could look inside and see space itself. And an hour from now after the scrape scrape of shoveling the watery, maggot-speckled manure into the shit-spreader and washing the pails and machines scrape scrape with the wad of bright coiled steel, the red house.

Running down the hill toward the woods. Wind pressing the eyes, heart high in the chest, the feet hardly on the ground at all. Thump thump thump, speed increasing as if you fly, the dead timothy and bright rocks and the woods ahead a blur, a jouncing smear of color.

And swoosh into the tunnel, all the way up the logroad past the shimmering spring to the clearing bouncing in the distance and up then to the red house and there she sits, books on her knees.

"Hey, I brought you these. What happened to your eye?"

No breath. "How . . . what . . . uh, door."

Slamming auricles and ventricles. Eyes running—produced by the lacrimal apparatus. "I'm a little, uh, lachrymose."

Sitting. Her ball-and-socket joints permit that flexibility and range of motion, because the rounded head of the femur fits into a cup-shaped cavity in the hipbone called the acetabulum. So her thighs can be up against her chest, while the reproductive organs inside the pelvic cavity rest unblemished.

Breathe. Hold out a hand and she places the biggest on it. American College Dictionary. Open it to—quarter. "Jesus, it takes up a half a page, tiny letters."

"What?"

"The word *quarter.*"

"So? A fourth, a coin, part of a football game."

"But look look look, number twenty, 'a place to stay, residence, or lodgment, esp. in military use, the buildings, houses,' and so on and so on. There are forty meanings."

"Really?"

"Where'd you get this?"

"Basement. Nobody wants it."

"I don't have anything to—hey, what's *esp?*"

"Hey, like forget it. No big deal." Cigarettes out now.

"I can't take this without—"

"Build me a nice room where I can smoke, dude."

A nice room. The gray, sliding boards still there, the sagging floor still sagging, and if it rained, then what would happen to the dictionary, the medical book?

Another book held out, encircled by billowing smoke. Take it. Modern Timber Engineering—Scofield-O'Brien. Chapter I: "Structure and Characteristics of Wood. Wood differs from most other structural materials in that it is made up of cells—hollow tubes, many times as long as they are wide."

"If you like books so much, why'd you quit school?"

"My dad needs help here."

Looking up through the window past the rotted ceiling into the beams. Then the smell of smoke. Close, can feel the funny tangible shadow of her.

"What you looking at?"

"Look here," pointing to page seventy-four—Truss Types. "That looks like a . . . fan truss or a king post truss."

"You're crazy."

Close. Can see every eyelash, the blondish down on her upper lip, the subtle pulsing of veins in the neck. Or is it arteries? Soft tissue surrounding the shoulder joints, which are really three separate joints acting together, permitting the great range of flexibility of motion.

"Do you have a hammer?" From her voice box.

"There's a broken one in there." Pointing. Leans over into the window and looks, her hands on the sill, profile of breasts and stomach stark against the gray wood.

"Somethin' to do. A smoking room, I mean that's—"

You would start up above the ceiling, up in the trusses to make sure they are all right, but the house has good bones. You would start up there. "Okay, I'm gonna climb up there and check the trusses." Hoo hoo hah.

Baling. Ahead pulling the baler The Chimp on the bigger tractor, eating windrow after windrow, the hay pounded into the box where the heavy knives shear it off and thunk thunk thunk it is pounded out the square chute, the knotting mechanism no good on one side. Sit there in the billowing cloud of chaff and wait until the bale is just so and tie a square knot with the twine before it fouls in the tying box, over and under same side, no granny knots or they will explode, no hesitation because even with the square knot tied too late the bales will look like amber bananas. And then it will be the slap to the head, the pinch on the side.

No red house today. No Deanna Branch the perfect specimen of muscle and bone and organs and fissures and tunnels and chambers and tubes and secretions of enzymes and oils and lobules, all together in the unblemished finishment of healthy womanhood. No king post truss, no joint A and joint B, no nails for clapboards that close up like scissors into their places while only two hundred yards away past the green amber blocks of hay the newer house sags, Mother in the kitchen walking across a sagging floor so that glasses in the cupboard tinkle and the table vibrates. While only two hundred yards away wood rots, softens, fungus and moss working inward, dry rot obscuring square corners, beetles boring holes and planting grubs in the basement beams, fingerprints of rust on the stovepipe deepening until threads of smoke ooze out like tiny snakes. Slowly it melts, clapboards opening like scissors, paint fading, beams bending downward in the basement until cracks appear and widen, and then one of them breaks, fibers opening, so that the rest open and follow.

No red house today, dude.

"You can't leave until you're eighteen."

"I didn't say I would."

"They did, so why wouldn't you?"

Look. Funny expression The Chimp has, hands still gripping the taut baling twine, the bale still poised on his knee. Then up it goes onto the wagon. Follows it, pauses with his hand on his back. "Shit." Disk problem maybe?

"I think I know how to fix the knotter."

"The shit you do."

"I watched how the other one worked. It—"

"Leave it the hell alone."

The Chimp. Has his way and that's that, dude. Leave everything the hell alone. Cut up the red house for firewood probably. First time that idea came. True though. The red house. Toast.

But you can't burn words.

Through the woods upper body rocking back and forth like a game-legged person walking, something heavy in front of her gripped with both hands, rocking and stomping, her hair swinging under her chin back and forth. Gasping for breath. Stops. "Hey, gimme a hand with this!"

Stands there with hands on hips—not hips but larger outside bones of the pelvic cavity since to put your fists on your hips would mean them sliding down your thighs. Closer. A bead of sweat has left her armpit and, leaving a bright trail out of the edge of white deodorant, hovers like a shimmering diamond just above the side strap of her halter. To halt what? Fabric now so insignificant compared to the weight and substance of what is halted inside. Shorts today, revealing the long, pale thighs that vanish into the tubes of the shorts' legs, up just a little more to the other stuff standing straight on in a transparent display of bilateral symmetry. Two of each thing. Except for all the single things in the middle.

"It's paint."

"Really?"

"Red, like you said. Barn paint. My dad said take it, it's getting so old the can'll rot."

Carry it the rest of the way. Strong, she must be, because this is five gallons almost. Strong biceps and long muscles in the back. From her house? Jesus.

In the shade, sitting by the red house. "Jeez, this is beginning to look good."

"Well, I replaced some beams inside, from old barn junk from the pile over there." Point. In those burdocks and weeds, in that tangle of old rose bushes, a foundation full of boards, some good. "The book only shows examples of a flat howe truss, but I used the picture for the end joints."

"Cool."

"Siding from the barn junk goes on top instead of that old sheeting. Piece of cake. Make a stovepipe outta roof sheeting."

Misty, distant look. "You know, I looked it up. There isn't a restaurant within twenty miles of here."

"Really? Isn't the cafeteria a kind of restaurant?"

"No. We're like in the middle of nowheresville."

"Isn't the hotel bar in town a restaurant?"

"It's a flophouse for old drunks is what it is. I never realized—" Hugs the knees, her chin propped, so that her head moves with each word. "We're out of it. Here I am sitting here by this old red house . . . Jesus, now even *I'm* seeing it red when it isn't." Stands up now, hands on pelvic bones. "Don't you want to go someplace? I mean far away? Those girls at school, they go where they want, they rent videos, they—"

Stops. Where? Or why? "I want—" like a funny swirl of something in the head, a circling, a sweeping cyclonelike movement inward toward, "what it is, is that we're in the middle of decay." Sits again, squints. "I mean, we're at the bottom of a V of decay and now we're going to undecay." First time that idea ever came.

"I think you went right past me there, dude."

"That's why this house is going to sort of go backward away from it."

"But what do you want?"

"Nothin'. Only to see the"—Jesus, again like something clarifying in the air, something moving in the head, feeling the brain—"the design of things, that's what it is. See inside things. A truss, a knotter on a baler, the human body." Another one, Jesus. That is it, the design of things.

Looking down, sort of into her halter almost, down at her lap. "Uh-oh." Laughs.

Redfaced. Caught. The idea that she sees the idea is awful, like nakedness. "Did you know that a pillar of bone is much stronger than reinforced concrete?"

A shake of the head, that funny look as if she is examining the tiny movement of chemicals through the various wires and tubes of your brain. Awful, like nakedness.

"Girls' bodies too I bet."

"Lighter and more flexible too. Bones I mean."

"Like, oh my *god!*" in a squeak. "Hey, which room is mine?"

Step to the window. Her breath behind, the sort of electrical field of her substance tickling your back. Of bone and muscle, body heat, and the aroma of her, somewhere between sweat and apples. "Right here I think," pointing inside. The best room.

"Cool."

"You can smoke in there, read—"

A hand on your side—"Oops." Almost fell. The buzz of the contact of hand on side—still there.

"Watch out for nails."

Looks down at the dead leaves. "Sure thing, dude."

A tattoo of sensation, the handprint on the side, and all through the milking and then sitting there in the dark living room while The Chimp watches wrestling and up-downs channels, you wait for words to come on the screen like you used to—use as directed with diet plan, individual weight loss may vary, world television premiere, handcrafted pottery bowl with chopsticks—the handprint a strange good burning on the side, as if it would be visible there, a little redder than the skin outside it, the touch of her flesh against his flesh, the result an oozing of that touch down below making a boner that just won't go away until you make it go away later in the dark when they won't hear, when the cows and birds and insects won't hear. The tattoo of Deanna Branch, who in a frontal transparency has what looks like a funny tree in her stomach, the ovaries out and hanging off single branches.

Sit and watch her, scrape scrape scrape on the pot while under your hand the carburetor stain blotches the tablecloth. Mother. Once a long-tailed pollywog called a sperm bit its way into one of her eggs and out you came covered with a cheesy material called vernix, out you came knowing nothing. Just do it. Funny prickling of fear.

"Ma, I'm tired of gettin' beat up for nothin'."

"Don't drop stuff." Turns from the sink and rubs her hands on the two gray spots on her apron.

"It's like he's tryin' to make me leave when I'm eighteen."

Stares, like the peculiar, precarious beginning of an idea mosquitoes around her ear. "He don' mean no real harm."

"A pitchfork is harm."

"Who tol' you that?"

"Everybody knows."

"The shit they do."

Funny, open look, like she's thinking now.

"I'm fixin' up the red house and putting books inside."

"What red house?"

"Grampa's."

"Don't you go gettin' ideas. He'll—"

"Ideas is what I'm getting. I read. I read like crazy."

"If he finds out—"

"He will. That's my place. Tell him I won't leave when I'm eighteen if he leaves it alone. Tell him I won't leave if he lets me show him how to fix the carburetor for the Ford. Tell him I'm gonna fix the knotter on the baler or at least show him how. Tell him if he punches me again, I'll stand outside the house and read a book at the top of my lungs night and day until he goes nuts. Tell him that. Tell him I'm finished with being The Chimp's kid."

"You watch your mouth."

"You gonna tell him?"

Nothing. Looking as if what is sitting at the table is a thing from another planet, almost scared she looks, as if she has to watch her back because the thing is going to put a knife in it when she isn't looking. Or knock her over the head with a dictionary.

To the woods, the red house, Deanna Branch if she isn't already in school, running down the hill with the soaring feeling of it—it's out of the bag now, you're in trouble now, dude, he's gonna kill you, but it's out of the bag now with the soaring feeling to the red house, the woods. Stand outside and read at the top of your lungs until he goes out of his mind. Mouth words to the TV—2.9 APR no dealer markup, make brass shine like new coming soon to a theater near you—mouth words so loud that he'll learn them too whether he wants to or not.

In the bouncing, shifting plane of vision it comes into view, the corner nearest red almost above the window, the planking from the barn tight as anything on the beams of the roof with the king post trusses.

Out of breath. Deanna Branch, nope.

Shit.

So, more paint then. Least if the brush isn't so goddam hard that it'd be more like a pancake flipper. What word is that? Spatula. Hoo-hah!

And bingo, even before the can is open, up she comes, same shorts and halter for her mammary glands with their milk-secreting lobules.

"Know how I knew you were here?"

"No."

"I heard you crashin' through the woods like a bull."

"I told my ma this house is mine. Hey, when do you go back to school?"

"Week."

"Hell, we'll be finished by then."

"I don't wanna go back. Makes me wanna walk outta my skin, dude."

Stop. Everything held like a photograph for a split second. The skin lies in a heavy pile on the ground, the largest organ of the body, and there she stands, glistening red, musculature crisscrossed by almond-shaped muscles and thin, powerful ribbons of pale tendon, eyeballs huge in their wet sockets.

"What?"

"I . . . I saw you without your skin."

"Oh, that again." Thinks. Uh-oh, an idea of some kind. Stares away at an idea just coming out from behind a tree. "C'mere."

"Why? I mean, aren't we gonna work on the house?"

Looks, hands on her hips. "I want to show you something about the design of things."

"Wait a minute."

"When I heard you comin', I went and hid in the bushes just to see if you'd go for the medical book. I know which pages you like 'cause the edges are all dirty. The part about girls' bodies. C'mere."

Hate it. Flushed face and shaky knees. Hate it. Caught. Caught doin' something dirty. "No."

"I won't hurt you."

Like the ground tips, trees lean, the sun jerks over a little, and the swirl spirals inward and the smell of sweat and fear billows out of the shirt top like stale breath.

"At school they talk about it all the time. The town girls, and what do I get to talk about? How I went and picked flowers for my mom? Changed my little sister's nasty diapers?"

"Actually, the best ideas I ever got were when I was talkin' to you."

"Okay, like here we go again. I mean like jeez Louise, what the hell does that mean?"

"I—"

"All I wanted was just to . . . I mean, it isn't like it's something I like *plan* to talk about, all right?"

"What do you want me to do?"

"C'mere is all I said."

Step, step, crunch leaves. Awful, like the time the teacher said stand at the front of the class and tell us blah blah blah. No control. The muscles just don't work.

"Give me your hand."

Laugh. What, do you unscrew it? Or does it just pop off?

"C'mon."

Takes it by the wrist with her right hand. Pull back. "C'mon, I'm not going to bite you. Jeez. Close your eyes."

Red black, sight through the lids. When the hand touches flesh there is no question, the softness and warm liquidity, the weight, the electrical current of living human tissue with the faint, precarious blipping of a rapid heartbeat. Faster than your own. The hand gripping the wrist pulls it tighter on the flesh, and the eyes open to her face staring back, mouth open, a look of experimental awe, eyes boring straight into a face with the same expression. Lifts the wrist a little, mashes the hand around in little circles, and the index finger feels the harder rounded edge of pectoral muscle, deeper down the surface of a rib. Then the wrist is released, and the hand departs slowly, the soft tissue following it until the last contact is gone. Back goes the halter.

Giggles. "Scared you? You scared?"

"Yeah." Heart slamming, even blips the vision brighter with each beat. "I mean . . . yeah, scared."

"It's like no big deal after all. I just wanted to show you something about, you know."

"Design."

"Can we work on the house now?"

The face so sort of normal, little hairs on the upper lip reflecting sunlight in tiny amber and golden needles. Calmer now. Raise the hand and smell it.

"What?" Laughing, shaking her head.

"I couldn't help it."

"You *smelled* your *hand?*"

Look away, think. Nothing to think. "You ever heard of narcolepsy?" Her face held still, a mask of wonder on the edge of laughing. "Or catalepsy? How they put epsy on the ends of things?"

"Uh-oh, here we go again."

Always know by the way The Chimp sort of circles that he's getting ready to swing. The idea backs away, the idea holds up a hand and tucks the Operator's Manual under the arm and, "Look, all I'm sayin' is that of all the parts on the table I didn't see no float lever shaft."

"Get high and mighty with me an' I'll clean your clock."

"All I'm sayin' is that without the float lever shaft you can't put it back together."

Sneers. "You read that in there?"

"Yeah, I read it in here." Hold it out. Hey, it won't bite. "If we can't find it, we can make one out of a piece of wire or a little nail or something."

"You think you're hot shit don't you."

"No. But that isn't the problem. Listen to this—"

Circles a little, looking, that wounded anger on his Chimp face. Oh does he hate it, does he ever hate the idea that there's an idea in front of him.

" 'Engine backfires but will not start. This symptom indicates that the spark plugs are not firing in their proper order, either due to the ignition high tension system being shorted, the spark plug wires being transposed, or the camshaft out of time. Perform the following operations in the order given.' That might be the problem."

Surprise on The Chimp's face. "L'me see that."

Hand it to him.

"Where's it say that?"

Point, "Here, 'Engine backfires but will not start.' That's what that says."

"No shit."

"That's what it says."

"So what are these operations?"

"We put the carburetor back together first."

"What about that thing, that—"

"We'll make one."

The Chimp thinking. The idea of beating up on the little Chimp gone, like smoke in the wind. Thinking, churning something through the brain like food in a stomach. You don't know nothin' and then you know there's somethin' you don't know and that's where it all starts. Holds the lower lip between a dirty, grime-blackened thumb and a dirty, grime-blackened finger, pulls on it a little. "So how much more schoolin' would you hafta have to do the paper stuff, milk check and taxes and all that shit? How much more?"

"I can do it now."

"The shit you can."

"No, I can do it. You wouldn't hafta take it down to Mr. Steele. I can do it easy."

"Like shit you can."

In the red house. The Medical Guide. Nothing about weight, or heat. Nothing about the bright secret buzz of electricity. Nothing about the power of human tissue to scare. Nothing about the awful tickling surge of some strange, complicated system of racing liquids built into the design that squirt around every cell and tickle every organ and vein, all four chambers of the heart with its precarious blipping. Nothing about standing so close and being engulfed by the vapor of her presence, by the contact with one body part radiating inside into all the secret tubes and chambers and valves and membranes and filters and tiny assembly lines of cells.

Three-thirty has to be, the way the sun slants in through the paneless window onto the gray, dusty floor.

Dictionary—go for the page even before the idea of going for it has formed, and there it is a third of a column long.

"Don't close it."

Up from the chair, heart slamming. "Jesus."

"School sucks. You shoulda heard those girls."

Turn, heart still slamming.

"Don't touch it—I wanna see what you looked up. What girl's body part did you look up today?"

As if the heart sort of exploded right out of the chest cavity sending bits of lung and bone pinwheeling through the air and going splat, some sticking to the wall, some arcing out the open window hole to land in the leaves outside. A grenade made of tissue, blam.

"What's the matter?"

"I . . . you scared me."

"I got you these."

Books. Focus now, the same halter and shorts, she has changed out of her school clothes. Take the books, the hand holding them leaking electricity through the pages and covers into your own, electricity from the whole of her body, from every corner having passed through every part, having made every single hair sort of glow like a tungsten filament. Little Women and Exploring Poetry, hot from her hands.

"Thanks."

"What were you looking up?"

Move toward it and she tries to go around, laughing. Been eating mint candy, she has. It's in her breath, going in and out of her lungs and then into your nose, proof that you breathe her breath.

"By the way, Little Women isn't about midgets."

"Oh." And they will go in alphabetical order even though there are only five of them, all lined up neatly on the shelf like shoulder to shoulder, Dictionary one side, Modern Timber Engineering on the other.

Nothing to do now. Caught again. Leaning over, her hands on either side of the Dictionary palms down, the long muscles of her back making the valley of her spine, the denim depressing the flesh in a circle around her waist. Apples and mint, and the hushed odor of mysterious enzymes evaporating on her skin.

"It's nothin' I was just—"

"Shh."

Finger moves down the first column and you are caught, standing at attention as if waiting to be shot, as if the next words will be hoo hah! as if she will laugh and run, something to tell the oh my gosh girls. Like, would you believe what—

Finds the word love and stands up, face stilled with a dumbstruck wonder, the idea exploring her brain like little hands feeling their way while she holds still feeling them, the little hands making something like a sculpture that the backs of her eyes seem to follow, to watch. Then it forms and she blinks, her mouth slowly opening in the formation of a word.

"Uh-oh."

Mary Gaitskill

Comfort

From *Fourteen Hills*

DANIEL SAT at the dining table in his San Francisco apartment watching his girlfriend read and contemplating sex with her. They had just eaten dinner, and at his elbow were the pungent remains of the feast: tiny bones, wet trails of sour cream, lemon juice and scraps of mashed fish skin. He was supposed to be composing sheet music for himself but he was too seduced by Jacquie in the armchair, encoiled in a blanket, holding a book in her small stubby hands. As she read, her gold-brown eyes moved intently back and forth, giving off a spark of private frisson. Half-hidden under her lowered lids, the movement of her eyes reminded him of a leopard, glimpsed as it slips quietly through the underbrush. He'd decided to write just a few more bars when the phone rang.

"Probably somebody we don't want to talk to," said Jacquie.

It was Daniel's brother calling from Iowa. "Hello *Albert*," said Daniel, looking at Jacquie with mild accusation.

"Dan," said Albert, "something bad happened."

"What?"

"Mom had a car crash. She's alive but she's really hurt. She's broken her neck and smashed her pelvis." He paused, breathing heavily. "And she also broke some ribs."

Daniel gasped with pain. Jacquie glanced at him; the concern in her eyes felt almost sharp.

The rest of the evening was a feverish melding of misery and sensual tenderness. Jacquie held his head against her breast and stroked him as pain moved through his mind and body in slow, consistent waves. At moments, the pain seemed to blur together with the contours of Jacquie's body, to align itself with her warmth and care, as if by soothing it, she actually made it greater. Even then, he loved her embrace, her presence, her comfort.

But later, when he thought about it, he did not quite remember the way Jacquie had comforted him. Much stronger in his memory was the conversation they'd had later that night. They were lying in the dark on their narrow single bed. Jacquie held him from behind, one strong arm firmly around his chest, her dry feet pressed against his. She spoke against his back, her voice muffled, her breath a warm puff against his skin. "Your family gets in a lot of car crashes, don't they?"

He opened his eyes. "Yes," he said. "So do a lot of people. There's car crashes all over America all the time."

"Well, there was the one with the whole family in it when you were a little kid, and then the one when your father drove into the fence, and then the one where your mother got hit in the parking lot, and now this. That seems like a lot for one family."

"What are you trying to say?"

"I'm not trying to say anything. I just noticed it."

"My mother's lying in the hospital with half her bones broken and you just noticed that."

Jacquie took her arm away from him, and turned the other way.

For a moment rage towered over his misery, then subsided into exhausted bewilderment. There is something wrong with her, he thought. They had been together for two years; this was not the first time he had had this thought.

He flew to Iowa the following day.

He had not been in his brother's suburban house before; he found it bland and characterless and he was glad of that. A more decoratively expressive home might've piqued his sensibility and made him feel worse.

Albert was a pharmacist. Together he and his wife Rose reminded Daniel of two colored building blocks made to illustrate solidity, squareness and rectangularness for children, the kind of blocks that, when picked up, turn out to be practically weightless and not solid at all. Apart from Rose, Albert became heavier, more sullen. His problems expressed themselves in his heavy brows. His hands took on a morose, defensive character. The brothers were eight years apart in age. They had never been close and they had become less close in adulthood.

On the night of Daniel's arrival, they sat at the kitchen table eating Mexican take-out and trying to comfort each other. Their words were difficult and, on the surface, irrelevant to comfort. Their halting conversation would've been small talk but for the emotional current moving under it, sometimes rising to fill whole strings of words with mysterious feeling, then subsiding to a barely felt pulse. Rose sat forward attentively, as though she were silently monitoring the unspoken current. When they got up from the table they all hugged, mostly touching shoulders and hands. Albert hugged as though part of him wanted the embrace and part of him wanted to get it over with. When his face came away, Daniel saw Albert's left eye staring over Daniel's shoulder, wild, bright, and oddly furtive.

All night he lay awake in his hard little guest bed, thinking about his mother. He remembered her serving dishes of yogurt and cut fruit for dessert. He remembered her sitting with her feet up on the couch, painting her false fingernails pink. She was wearing her nightgown and he could see that her knees were rough and that veins had flowered on her legs. Her hair was a manic knot of curls. She looked at her watch often. He could see all these images but he could not feel them. He turned them this way and that, trying to feel his mother. She used to sit across the table from their father, working her jaws stiffly and minutely. "Daniel," she said. "I want you to ask your father where he was last night." For five years preceding the divorce, his mother and father had addressed each other primarily through their children. Although when it got truly ugly his mother would drop the circuity and scream at her husband straight on. Daniel brought his hard guest pillow to his side and hugged it. "Mother," he said.

It was already dark when they drove to the hospital. Daniel cracked the car window and the winter air drew his cigarette smoke out like a thin ghost. He saw square porches, bricked-in flower boxes and shiny black lampposts standing in puzzled isolation before entrance walks; the familiar landscape soothed the itch of memory. He hoped they would pass the church, the stained-glass windows of which he and his friends had smashed with rocks when they were in the sixth grade. The day after they'd done it, he'd heard his mother on the phone, discussing the incident, which had destroyed thousands of dollars worth of stained glass. She had speculated, as had the papers, about the rise of juvenile crime and what it meant. Daniel had felt embarrassed and slightly disoriented, as though he had nothing to do with the maniac who had destroyed the church windows.

"You must have been very angry."

Jacquie had said that when he'd told her about it.

"I was just being a kid," he'd returned.

"A very angry kid."

He'd rolled his eyes.

The ugliness of the hospital seemed appropriate and that pleased him. The lounge was furnished with smudged plastic chairs, a vinyl couch with a strip of masking tape on it and a candy machine. There were people sitting in varied attitudes of unhappiness. Daniel looked at them. One man looked back. His hair was standing up and his hands appeared numb. He looked as though he might say something hostile. Daniel looked away.

A girl with a bitter mouth and blue eye shadow that deepened violently in the crease of her eyelids handed them purple guest passes. A female voice, enlarged and blurred by a loudspeaker, clouded the hall. The elevator bore them up. They entered a room. Daniel saw a person he didn't identify as his mother until Albert said, "Mom?"

Tufts of pale, silken hair floated from her partially shaved head. Blue veins lumped her scalp. The skin on her face and neck was lax, yet stiff as old papier-mâché. A ghostly array of bottles hung from metal poles around her bed. Little rubber tubes were taped against her arms. A thick rubber hose protruded from her distended mouth like a visual bray of anger. She was held erect by a brace at her back. It was a minute before he noticed that holes had been drilled into the frontal bone on either side of her forehead, and that metal rods had been driven into the holes. Her head was suspended in a metal hoop centered by the rods. Her eyes were closed. Her breath rasped. Daniel thought, "Frankenstein." He began to sweat.

"You can talk to her, Dan," said Rose. "She's sedated, but she understands."

Albert sat in a chair beside the bed and touched the papery arm. "We brought Daniel, Mom. He's here from California."

The eyes opened. It was her.

Daniel's ears were suddenly filled with internal noise. A tremulous black fuzz blocked his vision. "I'll be right back," he said. "I have to go to the bathroom." He stumbled out, palming the bumpy wall of the hallway. He banged his shins on a bench and sat on it, dropping his head between his knees. The fuzz parted to reveal an expanse of gold-flecked tile.

"Daniel?" Rose's voice. "Are you all right?"

When they got back from the hospital, their father called to talk to Daniel. He invited him out to have dinner, without Albert and Rose. His father preferred taking them out to dinner one at a time, a preference neither brother questioned. They rarely went out as a group.

Before hanging up, his father said he was involved in a new business. His last venture, importing tropical fish, had lasted two months.

"It's some weird thing to do with videos now," said Albert. "Something about videos for tourists in hotel rooms."

"That sounds viable," said Daniel.

"If he can hold it together," said Albert. "Which I doubt."

It was understandable that Albert would say this; their father never succeeded in his business ventures. Still, the comment annoyed Daniel and he changed the subject. "Has he seen Mom often?"

"Yeah," said Albert. "He's been good that way." He sighed and stiffly stretched in a hard, ungiving little chair. "He was there the first night they brought her in. All Mom's family were there and I guess it was a bad scene. It might've been better if Rose and I were there but we didn't arrive until after the blow-out."

With a sort of angry relish, Albert told his second-hand version of the story. When their father had arrived in the waiting room, no one in the family could tell him what exactly had happened to their mother, what condition she was in or where she was, apparently because they had been given inadequate information by the doctors and were too timid to press for more. Their father had roared around the waiting room cursing and calling them all "sheep," Aunt Pauline had wept and Uncle Jimmy had called their father a "bastard." Eventually their father had forced the hospital staff to be more communicative—to the secret relief of all, Albert hypothesized.

"Once again, Dad does the thing everybody wants done but no one will do," said Daniel.

"Yep," said Albert. A smile of unhappy vindication made his dull eyes glint. "Later, after we got there, Grandpa came up to Dad and tried to make up but Dad told him to fuck off, literally."

"Oh man." But Daniel felt a little flutter of triumph, even though he thought it was mean to say fuck off to an old guy whose daughter had just been smashed to shit.

Jacquie thought his father was handsome but mean. "He looks like Johnny Carson," she said. "Too bad he's such a prick."

"Don't call my dad a prick," said Daniel. "You don't know what you're talking about. My dad's a good guy."

"He tortured your mother and he abandoned you and your brother, psychologically. That's not a good guy."

"Have you ever heard the phrase 'get on with your life'?"

"Yeah," snapped Jacquie. "And I've seen what passes for life among the general population."

"Oh, excuse me. Everything's got to be perfect, everyone's got to be perfect."

They tried to scoot to the far ends of the bed, but it was so mushy in the center that they rolled together anyway.

Daniel and his father went to a seafood restaurant. It was an expensive restaurant with deep red carpeting, brown paneled walls and shiny tin decor meant to evoke railroads. Waiters wearing their names on plastic cards came to the table, folded their hands and recited the names of fish.

His father sat away from the table, his long legs crossed, a cigarette lax in his fingers. He wore an expensive suit. His eyes were harsh and watchful, his thin mouth downwardly taut. As they ate, he described his new idea, which involved the production of informational videos made specifically for people who have to stand in line, at the post office or the DMV or any place else where lines are formed.

"I was thinking maybe you could represent us in San Francisco." His father's eyes shifted up. "If you're interested."

"I've never done that kind of work before."

"That doesn't matter. You'd be a natural." His father speared a slice of lobster meat with a tiny aluminum pick. "The next time you start worrying about your career as a musician, I want you to do this. Just put on your best suit. Then go stand in front of a full-length mirror and take a good look at yourself. Just see what a good impression you make. You'll always have that. Whatever happens, with your music or anything else, you can always sell." He drew on his cigarette, his eye-wrinkles tensing. "Although you'd have to cut your hair."

No matter how thoroughly his father failed, Daniel saw him as a suave gambler vested with sneering cool. The ridiculous tropical fish business, the trips to South America, the drunken squabbles with surly young girlfriends in motel restaurants, the seedy hotel rooms, the dirty socks that must surely be under the beds of the wifeless—it all merely added to his allure. Even the vision of his father rising from a badly scrambled bed in a box-shaped hotel room and staggering into the bathroom to vomit gave him a pang of admiration and love.

When he was a teenager, his father had said to him, "You're the son I don't worry about at all. You're a cat that lands on its feet. You could be stuck in the middle of the desert and you'd find your way."

They dabbed their shrimp with lemon and delicately ate it with toothpicks.

"How did your mother look when you saw her?"

"Well, as a matter of fact . . ." He hesitated and, to his dismay, smiled. "It was horrible. I almost fainted." His smile was watery, his lips felt weak—why was he smiling at all? He had exposed a tender spot. "I had to leave the room."

"It is horrible." His father vigorously uncrossed his legs. "Horrible and unfair. After all she's suffered." He neatly separated some lobster meat from its shell and then lost interest in it. "You know we had a bad relationship. That marriage was ruined by her family." He grabbed his fork, put it down again. "But I'll tell you something. Your mother and I are still close in a way I've never been with another woman. We're still man and wife, even if we never speak to each other again." He chewed rapidly and lightly, then swallowed. "Marriage means something to me and so does family."

"Me too," said Daniel.

His father looked up. "I still can't believe that idiot family of hers. Sitting there letting nurses tell them what to do." He snorted and poked his tongue around in his mouth. "What a bunch of sheep."

"How is Raye?" asked Daniel. "Do you still see her?"

"Oh yeah." His father smiled, a little archly. "She's crazy as always. Last time I saw her we went to some restaurant, pretty late at night. She had coffee and she poured about four sugars into it. I told her it wasn't a good idea to eat so much sugar and she said, 'What the fuck do you know about health? You alcoholic old asshole.'"

It was late when they left the restaurant. The night cold reached

in through Daniel's nose and seized his lungs. Buildings and cars
looked stunned and abandoned in the intense cold. His father's big
car shuddered in the wind, its rusted, corrugated ass-end stuck out
from the other cars, proud and devastated. They got in the car and
sat silently for several minutes while his father worked to make the
engine turn over, grunting slightly as if he were lifting a heavy
object. Windblown snow rose up from heaped, dirty embankments
to scud through the parking lot in clouds. Daniel felt suddenly,
deeply connected to his father and this place. He thought of Jacquie, thought of showing her the connection as if it were something
he could hand her. He pictured her looking at it, an expression of
understanding slowly altering her face.

When he got home he called Jacquie. Her voice softened the sharp,
sudden line of connection between him and his father. She was glad
to hear from him; she had thought he was still mad at her for
wondering aloud about all the accidents in his family.

"No," he said, "I'm not mad." He had been, but now he could
not remember his anger. He was trying to make the feeling-world
of him and Jacquie congruent with the feeling-world he had experienced with his father.

"I'm sorry," she said. "I realized it must've sounded cold. But
that's not how I meant it."

"It's okay. You were just freaked out." He imagined Jacquie,
sitting invisible in the car with him and his father, feeling his
father. He felt certain that if they knew each other as he knew
them individually they would love each other. That certainty
crested, subsided and broke up into different feelings.

"I talked about it with my therapist," she continued. "I told her
about this thing that happened when I was a kid. I mean, in relation to what I said to you about the accident."

He barely listened to her; he was too involved in thoughts of
being with her on their bed, massaging the little bones between her
breasts. These bones were spare and they gave slightly if he pressed
hard. She loved to have them rubbed, especially the places in between the bones. Massaging her there made him feel her secret
frailty, made him feel privileged that she let him do it.

"We were going to the ice cream social at my school," she said, "which naturally I liked because it meant a ton of ice cream and cake. But as we were pulling out of the driveway, we ran over our cat, Midnight. She was up under the wheel and she didn't get out in time. It was awful because when we got out we saw her hips were crushed, but she was still moving reflexively, trying to get up."

He stopped imagining and listened, alert and puzzled.

"I said, 'Look, she's still alive,' and my mother said, 'No, it's just reflex,' and my sisters immediately began to sob. But I didn't."

"Do you think you were shocked?"

"I don't know. I don't think so. I think I just wanted to go get ice cream. We went to the ice cream social and I sat there and packed it in. My sisters were too upset to eat, but not me. I remember thinking it was weird even then."

"It is weird, don't you think?"

"No. And neither does my therapist."

He sighed and stuck his feet in front of a furnace vent made of metal strips and dark, heat-breathing slits. "What did your therapist say?"

"That I was probably not as oriented toward the sensate as my sisters. That I probably had a very practical and cerebral turn of mind as a child and that simple death didn't seem terrible to me. Like, the cat's dead, there's nothing we can do, so let's go have our ice cream."

"But it's normal to care about pets."

"It wasn't that I didn't care. I just had a different set of responses than the conventional one."

He recognized the therapist's voice in that last phrase.

"Actually I remember getting more upset about Midnight's brother, Walnut. He was obviously very distraught when he saw her body. He walked around the house for days, looking for her and meowing. That did seem sad to me. Partly because he didn't understand what had happened and we couldn't explain it to him."

He got off the phone feeling okay. But later that night he lay in bed, wide awake and furious at Jacquie. It was weird for a kid to eat ice cream over the body of a squashed pet. It was even weirder for her to tell him a story like that in such close proximity to his mother's terrible car accident in which *her* hips were crushed.

He visited his mother every day during the ten days he stayed in Iowa. He got used to the thin hoop haloing her impaled head. The tube came out of her mouth and her eyes began to show expression—usually a dull and cantankerous one. Cards and flowers proliferated in her room. Daniel notice with irritation that nothing had come from Jacquie.

Finally she was able to talk. "How is Jacquie?" she asked.

"Pretty good."

"That's good. She's a nice girl." Her voice was devoid of inflection, flat and invulnerable. There was an undercurrent of grudging bitterness in it, as if she had concluded some time ago that there was no hope for her, but that she was willing to pretend otherwise so that you wouldn't feel depressed, and that this pretense was a nuisance. Daniel realized with discomfort that she had talked like this for years. "Has she started acting classes yet?"

"No. She hasn't saved enough money."

"Oh." Her eyes shifted vaguely around the room. "She is a nice girl." Her hand began to twitch on the rumpled bed sheet. He put his hand out to still it. It felt like an injured and panicking bird. His hand sweated and he wondered if it repelled her. No, he thought. Just hold her hand.

"Has Harry been to see you?" he asked. Harry was a talkative gynecologist she had been dating for the last three months.

"Oh yes. Several times. I think he's afraid of running into your father."

"How is he?"

"Oh, he's Harry. He's incredibly Harry." She smiled and her eyes wrinkled elfishly. He saw for a second the pert little girl that smiled at him from old black and white photos in the family album. "Tell me about your music," she said.

He told her about his one steady job in a dark little bar with a crippled neon sign that blinked Free Crabs—Jazz Nite. He told her about playing in the park and being chased by cops. He told her about the time the famous piano player had told him he was "the death." He wasn't sure what it meant to her. It could seem seedy and pathetic.

He finished talking and they were quiet. She whispered, "Honey, I'm so glad you're here. Let's just sit quietly together now."

The flat rasp of her voice made the endearment strangely poignant to him. He shifted his sweating fingers, stretched them to air them out and then took her hand again. The room was a lulling beige and cream terrain permeated by the muted hum of the building. He listened to it and became aimlessly thoughtful. He thought of Mrs. Harris, whose son had been killed in an amusement park accident several years before. The son had been an acquaintance of his. He had liked him, and yet, when confronted with the weeping Mrs. Harris, he'd been embarrassed and hadn't known what to do. He wished he could see Mrs. Harris again, so that he could hold her and console her.

His mother opened her eyes. "I've never felt so much pain before in my life," she said. "It's unbelievable." She closed her eyes again.

Daniel stroked the length of her arm with his hand. When he was little and he had a headache, his father would put his hands on either side of his head and say, "I'm drawing the pain out of your head and into my hands." He would stand over Daniel with his hands firm on his skull, a terrible look of concentration on his face. Then he would step away and say, "Now your headache is gone." Daniel would still have a headache, but it didn't matter. He loved it when his father came to take the headache away.

He held his mother's shoulders, watching her face for signs of relief. Her face sagged, her eyes were peevishly closed. It struck him that this was only an extreme form of her habitual expression. She always seemed to be suffering in some remote, frozen way. He had been so used to it that he hadn't recognized it as suffering. He didn't think she did either. It seemed to be her natural state. It seemed natural in part because of her courage, which was also habitual. He thought of her driving on the highway, dressed in her checked business suit, drumming her fingers on the wheel and moving her lips in silent conversation with herself.

The door opened. A dark-haired nurse with a still face came in, pushing a small metal machine. His mother poked one eye open and regarded the nurse like an animal from within a lair. The nurse told her she had to do a test, extract something. "It won't be painful," said the nurse.

"Bullshit," snapped his mother.

That night Daniel thought of calling Jacquie again, after Albert and Rose were in bed. But he was still mad at her about the cat story, and half afraid that if he called again she'd say something else that would piss him off. He sat alone at the kitchen table picking at a powdered donut. He felt he was learning something important, something to do with families and with himself that he needed to sort out. But when he imagined telling Jacquie about it, he imagined her becoming antagonistic. She often got that way on the subject of families generally.

Once she had gone to visit her married sister, Angeline. She had come home upset about the way Angeline's husband had treated their three-year-old, Kimberly. She was upset as a child would be, agitated and disbelieving. It was Easter time. Kimberly had brought her parents painted eggs that she had done in daycare. She had wanted to eat them and her father wouldn't let her because he didn't think they were free-range chicken eggs. Kimberly cried and threw an egg on the floor. Her father spanked her.

"She'll get over it," said Daniel. "Kids understand rules."

"It's not just that," said Jacquie. "He disrespects her all the time. She'll run up to him and show him something and he'll say, in baby talk, 'Oh, look at what Kim has,' and then look over her head at me and roll his eyes and say, 'Really interesting, huh?' That's wrong, Daniel. It's totally confusing for her."

"Maybe he's embarrassed to be talking baby talk in front of you. Like you'll think he's uncool or something."

"That's no excuse. She's going to grow up and have all kinds of problems with men and nobody will understand why. Not even her."

"Oh, come on. Basically, they love her, so they have margin for error. Kids grow themselves up anyway."

"That's why the world is so shitty. Kids are growing themselves up, i.e., never really growing up. Because what's called love and nurturance in most families is so small and inadequate—"

"Loving doesn't mean being perfect."

"Jesus Christ, I'm not talking about perfect, I'm just talking about respect and kindness for your own kids. You think that's too much?"

He didn't, but something in her words annoyed him. She was looking at him like a stray animal with wounded eyes and a snappish air. It was ridiculous. Jacquie was a strong girl. She had square shoulders and a tough, full ass. She took dance and karate lessons. She lifted weights at a gym. Competence and gumption seemed built right into her. Most of the time he could see her gumption in the animal vibrance of her gold eyes. But sometimes her eyes would reflect a sense of stubborn injury that he could not understand. It was an expression that seemed to regard competence and gumption as contrivances that, while they kept her going, had nothing to do with who she really was inside. As if who she was had been determined by circumstances beyond her control and that she resented it.

The look aggravated him. But it also made him sense something in her that he couldn't grasp and therefore titillated him. He could feel the look in a different way when they had sex. They would embrace and he'd feel her engage him from the surface of her skin to the secrecy of her hidden female organs. But there always came a moment when he stopped feeling her. She held him close, but she was somewhere else. He would look at her face and see it twisted away from him, her eyes closed as if she were looking at the inside of her own head in horror and fascination and need. There would be a moment of cerebral tension like a fishing line pulled taut, and then he would feel her slowly return. She would open her eyes and look at him and clasp his hand, her ardent palm open on his, her expression clear and triumphant.

He thought of asking her why she went away from him, of trying to make her stay. But then he wouldn't have the pleasure of her return, that clasping hand meeting his in a declaration of secret victory.

"You say you don't like those things and every time I turn around you're eating another one." Albert stood in the kitchen door in his pajamas, blinking.

"I know, it's funny. I'd never eat them at home."

Albert went to the refrigerator to get a drink from his water jar. He was only thirty-five and he already walked like an exhausted man in late middle age.

The last time he went to see his mother, he went with his father. In spite of what his father had said in the restaurant about how close he was with Daniel's mother, there was a sense of overwhelming discomfort between them. It was clear that they were both sad, but they seemed to be sad in separate, restricted ways, as though they were hoarding it. His mother's mouth was sarcastic, as though she found it ridiculous to be suffering before her ex-husband. His father was gentle, but the gentleness was excruciating. He didn't say anything to her about his new business. They didn't refer to the past or to her family. They talked about the accident, about Albert and Rose, and a little about the country club they once belonged to. When Daniel talked, he felt that he was, in a more advanced and subtle form, serving the same function as he had when they relayed messages through him.

They had been in the room for about half an hour when two interns came in. They said they needed to do a brief examination. One of them asked, "Are you Mr. Belmont?" Daniel's father said yes. "And you're the son. Then you can stay if you want. This will only take a few minutes." Then, with gestures that would have been rapacious had they been less efficient, they stripped the sheet from Daniel's mother, jerking up her gown to expose her lower body. Her pelvic bones stuck out like horns. Her pubic hair was thin and snarled. "Whoops, sorry," said an intern. He pulled down her gown and absently patted her belly. "All in the family."

Jesus Christ, thought Daniel.

His mother smiled like a bitter doll. "Oh hello, doctors. You might be interested to know that Mr. Belmont and I have not been married for ten years."

His father didn't say anything.

It was strange to be back in San Francisco, having dinner with Jacquie in the apartment again. He told her about how difficult it had been to see his mother that first time, and how he had almost fainted. He told her about his father and how he had routed the relatives in the hospital waiting room. He told her how his mother had said "bullshit" to the nurse. She listened attentively; he had the impression that she didn't know what to say. She worked on her sweet potato with inordinate delicacy. Her gold eyes subtly glimmered with inchoate thoughts or feelings. He wanted to tell her about the moment he'd had with his father, but it was too far away from him now.

"Could you tell me again why your grandparents hate your father?" she asked. "I know you've told me, but I can't remember exactly."

"Mostly because my father is more adventurous than they are. When my father worked for my grandfather, he had a lot of ideas. He wanted to expand the business into something bigger than this little local thing, and my grandfather just wanted to keep it the way it was. They were arguing about it, and then my grandfather found out that my father was expanding production in certain branches of the company. So he fired him."

"Really? I thought it was something different. I thought you told me that your father lost the company money, and that's why he fired him."

"I told you that's what Grandpa said. You weren't listening to me."

She tilted her head toward her plate in a vaguely deferential way. "I always wondered how your father could possibly be angry at them."

"I want to ask you something," he said.

"What?"

"Why didn't you send my mother a card?"

She looked startled. "Well, from what you said, I thought she'd be too bad off to read it, or even know about it. Actually, I looked at some cards today but they were all really ugly. I'll look at a better store tomorrow."

"You think she cares what the card looks like?"

"If I'm going to send a card I want it to be a good one."

"You don't understand at all." He stood up and walked away from the table. "You're just thinking about yourself and about the impression you're going to make. The point isn't a cute card and a cute comment inside it. You're right, of course, she's too bad off to look at it. She can hardly fucking move."

"It wasn't about making an impression." Jacquie's voice was going high and stricken. "Sending cards isn't something I usually ever do. I was going to send one to your mom because what else am I going to do? But it's a stupid inadequate way of saying anything to anybody."

"That's not the point. The point of all these stupid cards on her table is one thing. They're all signed 'love.' That's it. Every time she sees another card signed 'love' she knows somebody else is behind her, caring about her. That's what counts. And last week was the time to send it. Of course it's inadequate. It's still better than nothing. Do you know how much pain she's in? They've got her so sedated she can hardly talk and she's still in pain. And you don't send her a card?"

For a moment she seemed to hover between emotions, her face shadowed by expressions too pale and quick to recognize. Then her features went into an afflicted flinch. She covered her face with her hands and he knew she was crying. This was what he had wanted to see, but now he felt sorry, even though she wasn't crying much.

"It's not that I don't care about your mother. I just didn't want to send a card that didn't mean anything. I hate cards. I wanted to send her a letter, but I knew she couldn't read it." She wiped her face, lifted her head and faced him. "I was going to send her a book after she gets better. I have it picked out. It's not that I wasn't thinking of her."

He sat down next to her and put his arm across her shoulders. "I know you care about my mother," he said. He paused. "You've just never been in this kind of situation before and you don't know how to respond." Her quivering slowed and he felt her listening. "I used to be like that. Something like this is so awful that you don't know how to react, and part of you is worried about how you're going to look. But the important thing is just to say that you care, somehow. It doesn't matter if it's not exactly right. You just do it."

She looked up at him. "But I can't think that way, Daniel. If I make a gesture I want it to be real. Especially if the situation is really bad. It seems insulting to act out of convention. It's like saying, 'Have a nice day.' It isn't connected to anything."

He dropped his arm from her shoulder and turned away. He thought of himself alone in Albert's guest room, holding his pillow and saying, "Mother." He felt defeated and cold. "I can't hear this stuff again," he said. "I just can't. It's fucking therapy talk and I can't believe you're saying it now."

There was a moment of silence. With a soft rubbing noise she embraced him from behind. "I'm sorry, Daniel," she said. "God, I'm sorry."

He felt her heart, moving in loud, hyperextended beats against his back. He felt her intensely in the heat and solidity of her body, felt who she was underneath her silly, snobbish words; a fullness of woman, an abundant expanse of heart and life and comfort. He turned into her embrace and held her. He could be patient with her, he thought. He could help her see what things were really like, wean her away from the mysterious aggrievement that led her to recite platitudes borrowed from therapists. He took her chin in thumb and forefinger and tried to tip her head so that he could see her face. She resisted, avoiding his fingers and poking her head more firmly into his chest. He thought she might be crying again so he sat quietly with her. He felt clear and curiously maternal.

She shifted in his arms and reached up to hold his face in her hands. "You're such a darling," she said. She disengaged herself, got up and went into the bathroom. He heard the dull ruffle of toilet paper unraveling from its roll, the hiss and squish of a dainty nose-blow. She emerged into the room again, moving in a familiar gait of authority and confidence in her strong body. But her face, half-turned away from him, was strained, diminished and searching for something that he didn't know, something that had nothing to do with him, nothing at all.

Robert Morgan

The Balm of Gilead Tree

From *Epoch*

I WOULDN'T SAY I noticed a thing unusual at first. There were airplanes coming in and taking off most of the day, and the new road was right under their path. It was the height of tourist season, and the sun was so bright you didn't want to glance up at the sky anyway. I wanted to look into the shade of the trees beyond the highway construction, and forget about the awful heat, and the headache I'd had all day.

"Hey look at that," Roy hollered. He was pulling up surveyor's markers and throwing them into the foreman's pickup. "He's going to hit."

I looked to where he pointed. The airliner was coming in from the south, probably the flight from Atlanta. It was a DC-9 with its flaps down, slowing for landing. I knew what kind of plane it was because I had flown on them when I was in the service. With the sun high in the sky you couldn't see much else about the plane. It was near two o'clock and I still had that heavy feeling from eating my bologna sandwiches too fast. And the headache wouldn't go away. I wished I had some asprin.

"He's going to do it," Brad said. Brad stopped with a load of dirt in his shovel raised about a foot off the ground. My eyes stung with sweat and the bright light, but I saw it too. It was one of those little private planes—bigger than a Piper Cub, a Cessna—coming from the west and headed directly toward where the airliner was going.

"My God," Joey, the foreman, said. He was tinkering with his transit beside the pickup. "I don't believe it," he said. I guess everybody on the job was looking up there, except maybe the earthmover and bulldozer drivers who couldn't hear anything and had to keep their eyes on the grading markers.

"I God," I said, sounding like my Uncle Albert without meaning to. It just came out.

"He ain't going to do it," Roy said.

It felt like electric shock jolted through me as the little plane came on. It stretched on and on toward the airliner, seeming to rip the sky in front of it.

"The Lord have mercy," Joey said.

It didn't seem possible. I expected the big plane to turn aside, or the little plane to bank and dive, or suddenly climb. But both pilots must have been blind. It all happened in a second or two, but it seemed to take hours. I couldn't watch. I had flown in planes in the army, all the way to Vietnam and back, and I thought of those people up there, in the clean air conditioning, just having finished lunch and thinking they were about to arrive in the mountains. Women in their fine clothes and perfume and men in business suits and doubleknits in the middle of August, and kids with toys in their laps.

"I God," I said, and raised my shovel like I was trying to push the little plane away. Dirt slid off the blade onto my sweaty arms and chest just as the two planes touched and turned into a fireball bigger than the sun. I don't remember if there was any noise or not. Maybe the sound of the motors continued even after the collision.

The fire just hung there in the sky for a second, and then the two planes pulled apart. The little Cessna went down like somebody had dropped it. It fluttered into pieces that wobbled. I didn't see it hit except out of the corner of my eye because I was watching the DC-9 as it swung away from the impact in a steep curve, carrying the fire on its back, but not spiraling.

"They's people falling," Roy said. And sure enough, we saw the dots and little figures thrown from the burning plane. At first it looked like debris from the explosion, but you could see the tiny arms and legs.

"God-damn," Brad said.

Suddenly the tail of the plane broke off and more people spilled like seeds out of pod. And the two main sections of the aircraft dropped like somebody had pitched them. They fell among scraps and burning pieces all the way down the sky. I thought at first they were falling right on top of us, but as they descended it was clear they were going to the south, further down the new roadway. As they fell the pieces seemed to get further and further away, and by the time they hit in showers of fire, they looked about two miles down the road, down the river of red clay and machinery.

"God-damn," Brad said again.

"Let's go," Roy said. He jumped into the cab of the foreman's pickup and started the engine. Brad and me threw down our shovels and climbed into the back.

"Hey," Joey called. But Roy ignored him. Roy and Joey had been playing a game of chicken all summer. Roy would see how much he could get away with without being fired. Joey would see if he could act superior to Roy by not losing his temper and not cussing. We had all gone to high school together and played football together. But Joey had stayed out of the draft by taking a course in engineering at the community college, and when we got out of the service he was foreman on the new highway job.

The roadbed was graded dirt, and Roy had to swing the pickup around bulldozers and fuel tanks and piles of crushed rock. Some of the earthmovers were still working and we almost hit one as it lurched across the bed with its belly full of dirt and both front and back engines blasting diesel smoke.

"Watch out," Brad hollered, and beat on the cab with his fist. But what we had to worry about most was other vehicles racing down the soft roadbed. Dozens of people on the job site headed just where we were. And people from town and from the shopping centers had seen the crash and were driving in the same direction.

"People is going crazy," Brad said.

We had to hold on because Roy was hitting rocks and bumps and piles of dirt that hadn't been smoothed. The new road looked like bomb craters in places, a shelled zone. Roy hit a caterpillar track that had been left rusting in the dirt, but he kept going. It was further to the crash than we had thought.

The first body we came to, Roy slammed on the brakes. A farm truck loaded with hampers of polebeans roared past us raising the orange dust. "Damn buzzards," Brad called after it. Nobody but those building the road were supposed to be on the site. The headache pulsed like a strobe light under my hardhat.

Roy got to the body first. It was an elderly woman with blue-looking hair. She was lying on her side with a shoulder drove into the ground. Her glasses lay in the dirt nearby, looking like they had been tossed there. Her dress was thrown up over her thighs and you could see the straps of her garter belt.

Roy rolled her over and felt for her pulse. Her eyes were open and a thin line of blood ran from the corner of her mouth. "She's dead," he said.

"No shit," Brad said. "She just fell a mile out of the sky."

"Excuse me for being so obvious," Roy said. "I forgot to be subtle."

I bent down to look at her, and when I straightened up I felt dizzy from my headache and the blinding sun. Cars and pickups, jeeps and tractors, whined over the rough dirt toward the black smoke of the wreck. I saw another body about a hundred yards ahead, right at the edge of the highway cut, half in the weeds. "Can't do her any good," I said, and started running. I tried to think of what first aid I could remember from the army, in case any of the bodies were still alive. I glanced back at Roy and Brad and they had started going through the old woman's pockets and purse. For the first time it came to me why so many people were running to the crash. We all wanted to get there first, before any authorities arrived and secured the area. I ran up the bank to the edge of the construction.

It was the body of a businessman that lay half in the weeds and half in the graded dirt. There's a sad dry look to dirt and weeds in late summer, and the body had fallen right against some blackberry briars. The berries were ripe and splattered and I couldn't tell at first what was berry juice and what was blood. The man was lying face down in the weeds and I rolled him over. The face was mashed in a little, nose flattened, and the eyes popping out with dirt and trash stuck to them. He was dead as a door bolt. There wasn't a thing I could do for him. A bad smell rose from the body, like it had just farted. His suitcoat had been ripped at the arms, maybe by the explosion or by the wind when he was falling. I lifted his wrist to feel the pulse and his watch was cold as if it had been in a refrigerator. It was still cool from the air conditioning in the plane.

I was really sweating from the heat and running, and from the headache. I reached into his coat pocket to get his wallet. I knew businessmen did not keep wallets in their hip pockets, but in their breast pockets. I thought, I'll just see what his name is. He had this fancy wallet made of madras cloth and rimmed with gold on the corners. I opened it and there was his driver's license and a bunch of credit cards and pictures of kids. The license said "Jeremy Kincaid," and the address was in Aiken, South Carolina. I looked in the bill compartment and there was a sheaf of twenties, and behind them a couple of fifties and a single hundred. I thought, I'll just leave this here for his wife and kids. And then I thought, somebody else will go and take it. Might as well be me.

The whole road was crawling with people far as I could see. More were arriving in trucks and cars, on motorcycles. In the distance I could hear a siren, and then the donkey horn of a firetruck. The bills felt cool and new. Cold cash I thought. A cool million, as they say. It amazes me sometimes how people have already thought of everything. I took out the bills and put the wallet back in the coat. His family will get all the insurance money, I thought. And none of this would ever get back to them anyway. I folded the bills like pages of a little book and slid them in the pocket of my sweaty jeans. Then I thought of the credit cards and reached back into the wallet for the shiny plastic. But I saw they were useless. I'd have to forge Mr. Kincaid's signature on any charges, and I didn't want any of that.

"Hot damn," I said and stood up. The headache crashed down on me. I'd had headaches ever since I got back from the army. I wished I had some cool headache powders, some Stanback or aspirin. People swarmed over every inch of the highway, among the earthmovers and bulldozers, backhoes, between piles of dirt and holes dug for culverts. Somebody had left a tractor running.

I saw there was no way to look further in the highway site. The smoke of the wreck seemed to come from a field or apple orchard to the left, toward the Dana Road. I ran out through the weeds in that direction. The blackberry briars reached out and clawed as I passed. I had to stomp down catbriars and hogweeds, big ironweeds and the first goldenrods. I could see people ahead running out through the brush and into the trees, like they were racing each other.

Cold cash, I kept saying to myself in the terrible heat. I thought of cool sharp-edged bills that would slice a finger. I thought of a whole plateful of fifty dollar bills served like a feast, and the filling station I would buy to get out of construction work, and the mechanics courses I would take at the community college. Ever since I got out of the army I'd had to work so hard I couldn't make use of the GI Bill. I thought of my girlfriend Diane in her cool lavender shorts and how we could get married and build a beauty shop next to the filling station and she could get out of the hot basement at Woolworth's. Diane was the prettiest woman I'd ever seen, and we had been engaged since last year. I thought of us under the cool sheets at night. She deserved a beauty shop and I deserved a filling station. Enough for a down-payment, and the bank would loan us the rest.

Suddenly I saw somebody bent over in the weeds ahead of me. It looked like an animal pawing carrion, a big dog or a bear. But it was a man's back rising and falling. I was going to run around him. I didn't care what he was doing. But he had already heard me and looked around. He was a big red-faced fellow that was almost bald, and he was wearing the gray uniform of a delivery man. I think it was a bread company. He was one of those men who drive bread trucks.

"Hot dog," he said. He was going through the pockets of a boy and had found a wallet. He had the boy's watch already and he was fumbling with bills in the fold of the wallet. "Hot dog," he said. "What a way to get a case of chiggers."

I ran around him still headed toward the smoke, and he looked at me like he wanted to stop me, like he didn't want anybody to get ahead of him. "Hey boy," he hollered. "You ain't trying to hog it all for yourself are you?" I ignored him and ran on.

There was a fence with a hedgerow in front of me, and I was looking for an easy way through the barbed wire when I saw the body in a post-oak tree. The body was caught in the limbs about twelve feet off the ground. Some of the branches had broke but the body was stuck there. I thought of climbing the tree. I grabbed the ends of a limb and tried to shake it loose. But the body had lodged between the branches and would not slide off.

I looked around for a stick or pole to push it loose. The bald-headed man in the uniform was running toward me and I figured if I could just get the body down before he reached the fence it was mine. There was a dead poplar sapling leaning in the hedgerow and I jumped on it with both feet. But it didn't break; it was still rooted in the dirt.

"Hey hog," the bread truck driver hollered. "You can't claim all of them." He had a look in his eyes, like he didn't hardly care what he was doing.

"You stay away," I said.

"*You* stay away," he said. He reached up for the oak limb and tried to shake the body loose. He shook the tree like he was trying to make acorns fall.

The second time I jumped on the poplar it broke. I snapped off the tip and had a pole about ten feet long. "You stand back, bastard," the bald-headed man said. He took a hawk-bill knife out of his back pocket. It was the kind of knife you use to cut out cardboard or linoleum.

"I'll cut your balls off," he said, holding the knife with one hand and jerking the oak limb with the other. I swung the pole and hit him on the back of the head. He went down like a sandbag in the weeds. "Bastard yourself," I said, but he was out cold.

With the pole I knocked the body in the tree loose and it fell almost beside the bread truck driver. The arms and legs were turned wrong, where they had been broke when they hit the post-oak. The man looked about seventy and was wearing a Hawaiian shirt. There wasn't more than forty dollars in his billfold, but he had a book of traveler's checks in his pocket. I tried to think if you could spend traveler's checks, but they were already signed in one corner and I threw them in the weeds. I was about to run on when I noticed the great bulge in the bald man's uniform pocket. I reached in and pulled out what must have been a wad of a hundred twenty dollar bills. I would leave him his wallet and whatever he had that was his. But I would take the wad because he had threatened me with the knife.

On the other side of the hedgerow was a bunch-bean field. It had been standing in water earlier in the summer and most of the vines had turned yellow. The ground looked painted with baked silt, like the bottom of a dried puddle. There were suitcases and overnight bags fallen among the vines, most of them busted open. I looked through some of them, but they were mostly just shirts and blouses, hairbrushes, women's shoes. I didn't even see any jewelry.

There was a piece of blackened airplane lying in the row, still smoking. It smelled of burnt fuel. It looked like a piece of the DC-9 with a shattered window.

There was a whole lot of sirens now, coming from all directions. And there were voices, and horns honking. I knew the police would arrive any time. I heard a helicopter coming from somewhere. That really reminded me of the army. But at no time in Nam had I seen this many bodies.

There was a woman on her knees in the bean rows near the creek, and I thought she must be picking over a body or a suitcase. I saw her out of the corner of my eye and avoided going in that direction. But after I went through ten or fifteen pieces of luggage and found only one purse with seventy dollars in it I looked her way again. She hadn't moved, and she was leaning in a peculiar way. Her back was twisted.

I ran over there and saw the strangest thing I'd seen all day. She was sunk in the soft dirt by the creek up to her knees. She had fallen out of the sky standing up and drove into the ground like a stake. Her face was stretched from the impact. Her necklace had broke off and was lying in the dirt. It looked like diamonds. I didn't see a pocketbook. It spooked me to look at her face with the eyes pushing out. My headache thundered louder. I grabbed up the necklace and ran on.

To go toward the smoke of the wreck I had to cross the creek. The stream was low from the late summer drought and almost hidden by weeds. Mud from the highway construction lined the banks, and the creek itself seemed one long pool through the level bottomland. It was green stagnant water, a dead pool, like a coma of water poisoned by bean spray and weed killer. There was no easy way to cross. A snake slid down a limb and plopped into the water. A scum like green hair and paint floated on the top.

I didn't see any way to cross except walk right into the creek, so I splashed in. I was halfway across and the water up to my chest when I bumped into something. The body must have been floating just under the surface for when I touched it it turned over and the face shot right up in my face. It was a man whose head had been burned and his brains had busted out. I pushed the body away and crossed the creek quick as I could.

I climbed up the other bank brushing moss and green scum off my jeans. The water smelled sour but I didn't pay it any mind. When I broke through the tall weeds I was at the edge of a field of apple trees. The wreck was burning still further on, beyond another hedgerow. I could hear people hollering and sirens in that direction. I figured I would stay away from where the crowd was. The orchard seemed to be full of bodies and pieces of the wreck.

It was a young orchard which meant there were wide spaces around trees and you could see a long way between rows. There were dozens of people picking through the rows. I figured if I moved quick through the trees I wouldn't be any more noticeable than the rest. I hoped I didn't see anybody I knew. I hoped I didn't see Roy and Brad again.

The orchard had been plowed once that summer, which meant there was an open break of red dirt around each of the trees. The ground had baked hard and rough. Weeds rose right out of the unplowed ground into the limbs of the tree. The trees were loaded with green apples. The spray looked white and silver on the fruit. I had been raised in an apple orchard down near Saluda and it sickened me to think of the sweat that had gone into that grove.

You grafted and fertilized, pruned and waited, sprayed and plowed, and still a late frost or early frost, a beetle or fungus, drought or wet summer, could ruin you. A hailstorm, a flood, a plane crash, a drop in the market price, could wipe you out. You have to fight, I said to myself. I thought of the filling station and the beauty shop I would build.

The sirens were getting closer, and growing in number. It sounded like all the firetrucks and patrol cars and ambulances in the world were screaming and wailing. I was glad I had got off the road, but I had to work fast. The firetruck horns were blasting toward the column of smoke and car horns answered the sirens.

"Clear the area, clear the area," a voice thundered out of the sky. I looked up and saw the chopper. It was the sheriff's chopper, the one they used to look for marijuana fields in the mountain coves.

"Clear the area, clear the area," the voice boomed again, rattled by static on the loudspeaker. I could feel the wind off the blades washing over the apple trees, fluttering leaves and shaking green apples. For a second I thought they were going to land and try to arrest me. I kept my head down in case they were taking pictures. The heat of the wind and the pulse of my headache made me feel I had slipped through a time warp. If they landed I could try to run for the woods at the other end of the orchard. Then I realized they couldn't land among the apple trees. They were trying to scare people away from the wreck.

The helicopter tilted and swung away ahead of me. I gave it the finger; but there wasn't much time. I ran around a tree and there was this old couple in Bermuda shorts bent over a body. Their straw hats and sunglasses told me they were tourists from Miami. The mountains had been overrun by retirees from south Florida ever since I was a kid. They filled up the streets and highways with their long Cadillacs, driving in the middle of the road. "They come up here with a dollar and one shirt and don't change either," my Uncle Albert liked to say. I God.

They were crouching over the body and the old woman jumped when she heard me coming. She had on thick red lipstick and makeup. "We were just trying to see if we could help," she said.

"You go right ahead," I said.

"Is there nothing anybody can do?" the man said. He was holding his right hand behind his back. He must have taken the wallet from the body and hadn't had time to slip out the bills.

"We're just trying to help," the woman said. "These could be our family. They could be somebody's family."

"You all help yourself," I said. I ran past them and they watched me in horror, expecting to be mugged.

There was a piece of the private plane lying up against an apple tree. It was a part of the cockpit. The fuselage had been sheared like it was cut with a torch. The metal was blackened but not burning. I thought I saw a face behind the window and I ran closer. It was a face, and I lifted the torn section of the plane to free the body. But I instantly wished I had left it alone. It was a little boy about eight years old. The half of his face I had seen through the window was unmarked, but the other half had been sliced off by the impact. The kid never saw what hit him. Nothing I had glimpsed in the infantry was more sickening. I dropped the section of the Cessna and ran.

"You will clear the area," a voice said over a bullhorn. It was from a police car cruising around the perimeter of the orchard. "Looters will be arrested." I crouched down behind an apple tree until the flashing lights were past. It made me think of those preacher's cars with loudspeakers, one horn pointing forward and one backward on top of the car.

Got to fight, I said to myself. You've got to fight. It's what I said to myself for a whole year in the army. It's what I said to myself as a boy working in the orchard, in the heat and mud and stinging spray.

"We're sweeping the area and arresting looters," the loudspeaker crackled.

There were bodies and pieces of bodies all over the orchard. I ran quick as I could from one to the other, avoiding the people like it was a game of hide-and-seek. Flies were finding the torn limbs in the weeds.

There was a beautiful stewardess still in pieces of her uniform, but she didn't have either jewelry or a billfold on her. She had fallen into the lower limbs of a spreading apple tree and looked like she had gone to sleep there.

Some bodies were naked, but I avoided those, not only because I knew there wouldn't be any money on them but because it was embarrassing to get close. I didn't want to be seen looking at naked corpses, and I didn't want to see myself doing it either.

My pockets were stuffed with cash, some of it slightly burned, some of it bloody, some of it dirty. Some of the money had been soaked in diesel fuel. I found more and more businessmen, but most of them had credit cards and little money. The women carried more cash in their purses. I threw away a lot of traveler's checks. I found bodies that had already been searched.

I was nearing the edge of the orchard and getting closer to the smoke and the gathering sirens. There was another hedgerow, and then a field where the main part of the wreck seemed to have come down.

"Clear the area immediately," the bullhorn blasted. "All looters will be arrested. It is a Federal offense to tamper with an airplane crash."

I dashed out of the orchard and across the haulroad. A pink ladies' purse lay in the brush against the hedgerow. I was about to reach for the handle when a black bullet shot in front of my face. And then I saw the hornet's nest about the size of a peck bucket behind the purse. The falling pocketbook had knocked off a section of the nest and the hornets boiled out of the hole. They hummed and shocked the air like ten thousand volts.

The purse was made of soft pink leather. I just knew it was full of money. But it was dangerous to get near a nest that big, especially if they were all riled up. Ten hornet stings can kill you, can put you to sleep forever. There must have been a thousand in that nest.

"Everybody clear the area," the loudspeaker said. "Only members of the volunteer fire department should be in the area. They will be wearing red armbands. All others will be arrested."

I thought I might have ten minutes before they got to me. The cruiser with flashing lights was circling back on the haulroad. I wiped the sweat out of my eyes and watched the hornets circle. The handbag lay among the weeds and baked late summer dirt.

As I broke a twig off the tree above my head and brought it to my lips I smelled the aroma. It was balm of Gilead. The bright spicy smell woke me up from the heat and reminded me of the tree by the old house down at Saluda. The twig smelled like both medicine and candy.

Somebody was coming. There were voices and it sounded like the volunteer firemen were already sweeping the area. Of course they would take everything they could find for themselves, same as the cops would. Wasn't any reason to leave the money for them, money that would never get to heaven or hell with the owners, or to the rightful heirs.

I had heard boys brag about breaking off a limb with a hornet's nest on it and running down the mountainside so fast the hornets couldn't sting them. But I never believed them. A hornet can fly faster than the eye can see, and these were already boiling. I didn't have any smoke to blow on them, and I couldn't wait till dark. And I didn't have a cloth to throw over them either.

I took the red bandanna off my neck and wrapped it around my left hand and wrist. The hardhat would protect part of my head. I grabbed the handle of the purse and jerked away, but the first hornet popped me on the shoulder and another got me on the elbow. I ran hard as I could through the weeds. A hornet sting always hits you in two stages. First the prick of the stinger, and then the real pain of the poison squirting home. A hornet must release its venom with powerful pressure because it always feels like you've stopped a bullet or had a bone broke and your flesh rings with the pain. I got hit twice more.

I ran along the haulroad like a scalded dog until I didn't hear the hornets circling anymore. There were voices on the other side of the ditch and I dropped down behind a sumac bush. The heat was terrible. It magnified the pain of the stings and speeded the ache of the poison through me. A hornet sting makes your bones and joints feel sick. It makes you feel old with rheumatism.

But my headache didn't seem as bad. I had heard people say you could cure a headache with a bee sting, but I never believed it. Most likely the hurt of the sting makes you forget the headache. But there was no doubt the throb in my head was fading. I thought of the cool frosty powders of aspirin, and looked up at the snowy edge of a cloud far above me.

The voices on the other side of the hedgerow got closer and I hunkered deeper under the sumacs and the balm of Gilead trees. There must have been a whole row of the trees, which is real unusual. I tried to quiet my breathing by chewing a twig. In the shade I could smell myself, the sweat from work in the sun and running, and the raw smell of fear and pain from the stings. My sweat dripped all over the soft leather handbag. It was the most expensive leatherwork I had ever seen. Every seam was rounded and the stitching was concealed. It was leather made for royalty.

At first I didn't see anything inside but a compact and lipstick, some keys to a Mercedes and a bottle of perfume. There was a wallet with credit cards in the slots but I didn't find but thirty dollars in the bill compartment. I started to throw them all out in the weeds, but that seemed disrespectful, though I couldn't explain why. The woman was dead and wouldn't need her purse again. There was a driver's license that identified her as a resident of Coral Gables, Florida. I pushed aside the little bottle of mouthwash, the cellophane-wrapped peppermint candies, a couple of unmailed letters, and was about to give up when I saw the zipper almost concealed under a flap of shiny lining. I unzipped the pocket and felt inside. I touched edges that seemed stiff and sharp as razor blades. I got my finger around the packet and pulled it out. There was a wad of folded bills, brand-new bills, some twenties, some fifties, and some hundreds. It was the old woman's stash for her vacation in the mountains. The bills were starched with newness, the green and black inks printed in biting freshness, with some serial numbers and seals in blue. What fine cloth money is, I thought. There must have been over three thousand dollars in the folded pages. They were like a new printed book, every page pretty. I stuffed them in my pocket, deep so they wouldn't fall out.

All my pockets were full of bills and jewelry. If I found anything else I'd have to stuff it in my underwear, though that was danger-ous for it might fall out. Better to stuff money in my boots. I took the red bandanna off my hand and tied it around my right arm. It probably wouldn't work, but if anybody stopped me I could claim I was a volunteer fireman.

There were shouts from the direction of the crash. The firetrucks wailed and somebody was on the bullhorn again. I could see lights flashing through the hedgerow. "Clear the area, the area must be cleared," the voice echoed across the fields and back from barns. A patrol passed on the other side of the ditch not more than fifteen feet away. They could see me if they looked close. "Whatever we get we will divide up," one of the men was saying.

I had to think fast. If I was stopped by the firemen they would just take everything I had found. There were too many of them, and they would claim I was looting, or resisted arrest or something. If I was caught by the sheriff or one of the troopers, they would either take what I had or beat me up with their clubs, or both.

I chewed on the spicy twig in my nervousness. I used to do that when I was crouched down hiding from my brother, or waiting for the enemy to move or fire. It seemed to help. The medicine smell of the balm of Gilead woke me up a little from my worry. There was something about the smell of the bark that reminded me of soft drinks like root beer or Dr. Pepper. I wished I had a cold drink. If I ever got out of there with my money I would celebrate with a case of cold Pepsi.

"This is the U. S. Marshal," a voice said over a loudspeaker. "All who don't leave the site will be arrested. It is a Federal offense to loot an airplane crash."

There were shouts and more sirens arriving. A truck horn blasted for a full ten seconds. I waited until the firemen had gone on fifty or seventy-five feet on the other side of the ditch, and then I laid the purse down and stood up. The blood must have drained out of my head because it felt like a shadow had passed over everything. I waited for a few seconds to focus my mind. The stings ached worse than ever, but the headache had gone.

There was nobody in sight and I started walking to the east toward the Dana Road. I figured it was safer if I stayed away from the new highway where all the trucks and cars had converged. I would try to get back to the place we had been working before anybody else did. If I got back soon enough I could put my money in my lunchbox and nobody would ever see it. That's what Bishop the bulldozer driver did when he uncovered a mason jar of money on the pasture hill down at the south end of the county. When they first started building the highway, he cut into a bank and a fruit jar rolled out, a quart stuffed full of twenties. He got off the dozer and emptied the jar inside his shirt then threw the jar away. Wouldn't anybody know he got the money except one of the Ward boys saw him. But when the Ward boy told the foreman and they asked Bishop he said he hadn't seen any money, and he showed them his empty shirt. He had already moved the money to his lunchbox and thermos. Wasn't long after that, maybe three months, till he bought a store and fruit stand over near the line and quit driving the bulldozer.

I walked fast as I could without seeming to hurry. A hurry will draw suspicion. I was about a quarter of a mile from the end of the orchard when I saw the red and tan sheriff's car coming down the middle of the grove with all its lights flashing. At the same time I heard the chopper again. I don't know who spotted me first, the patrol car or the helicopter, but the next thing I heard was the bullhorn in the sky, "Hey you there, in the hardhat, stop."

I kept going for a few steps and the bullhorn blasted again. "Stop there or I'll shoot." I could hear the patrol car whining through the apple trees toward me. The chopper came in closer and its wind hit me like a slap. "Halt there," the voice in the sky said. "You're under arrest."

I wondered if they had seen my bulging pockets. I had to think quick. The haulroad was too narrow for the chopper to land in, but the sheriff's car would run me down in a few seconds. I had to do something or lose everything. The chopper wind smacked at my face.

I dove into the brush and rolled under some sumac bushes. Then I crawled on my elbows through the blackberry briars. The grit cut into my skin. I hadn't crawled like that in years. A moccasin snake plunged into the ditch ahead of me. The water was cloudy with chemicals and moss. I threw down my hardhat and slid in after the snake, and was going to head east, the way I had been running. But

I changed my mind and started back the other way, toward the creek. I crawled as fast as I could until the sheriff's car stopped, and then I backed in under some honeysuckle vines and listened.

"Right in front of you," the loudspeaker from the chopper said.

The deputy who got out of the car looked like he had never been out of air conditioning. His shirt was starched and ironed to his back and shoulders. He walked to the brush and peered into the hedgerow. "He went right in there," the voice from the helicopter said.

I wished I had something to darken my face. There was a good chance my skin would shine right through the honeysuckle bushes. I sunk low as I could, almost to my nose in the water. There was green paste thick as pancake batter floating on the surface. I squeezed my lips to keep water out.

"Look right there," the loudspeaker boomed. The wind from the blades shook the leaves of the balm of Gilead trees and trembled the surface of the water. If the chopper came in lower it might blow the vines aside and expose me.

The deputy parted the sumac bushes and looked into the ditch. He looked like he was afraid ticks and chiggers and snakes and spiders would attack him. He never took his sunglasses off, otherwise he would have seen me for sure. He looked at the water and paused, and I was certain he had seen me. I could feel the ditch water soaking into my pockets among the wadded bills. Luckily money won't melt. The ditchwater was warm as a mud puddle. But the money still felt cool.

"Look to the left," the voice on the bullhorn said.

The deputy peered past the sumac bushes and took out his gun. He must have seen my hardhat. "Come out or I shoot," he said. I pushed back under the vines far as I could. He fired twice and sent the hat skipping into the ditch.

"Look to the left," the voice from the chopper said again. They had seen me running that way and guessed I would continue in that direction. I waited until he had gone forty or fifty feet, and then I slid out of the honeysuckle vines and began crawling on my side through the ditch scum. I didn't have to worry about noise because of the chopper, but if I came out in an open place they would spot me. The chopper hovered just above the deputy.

Another snake slid off a limb, unwinding like a corkscrew, and disappeared into the cloudy water. I'd heard snakes have trouble biting in water because they can't brace themselves to coil and strike. I hoped that was right. The ditch was full of bottles and cans and all kinds of trash. Everything was covered with a slimy coat of silt. Everything felt like mucus. I could have made it out of sight except there was this burlap erosion dam across the ditch, the kind we're required by law to put around construction sites. They don't do any good but they're supposed to catch the dirt washing into ditches. The burlap was almost rotten and covered with leaves and dried mud. But it wouldn't tear. I had no choice but to climb over it.

If I stood up they could see me through the hedgerow. The deputy was about a hundred feet away, and the chopper right above him. I hesitated for a moment, but realized I didn't have much time. If they didn't find me in that direction they would come back looking in the other.

I stood up slowly and bent across the dam, and just as I was swinging over the voice from the chopper blasted, "Look over there, look over there." I had taken my chance and failed. I was going to have to run for it as best I could and hope they didn't shoot. I wheeled myself over the burlap and started running, but out of the corner of my eye I saw these two boys come out of an orchard row lugging a big suitcase between them. They looked like farmboys, maybe fourteen or fifteen, barefoot and without shirts. They started running back into the orchard and the deputy took after them. "No use to run boys, no use to run," the voice from the chopper said.

I knew that was the best chance I would have, so I dropped back into the ditchwater and crawled on my hands and knees for another hundred feet. There were sirens and horns and screams and loudspeakers from the site of the crash to my left. It sounded like hundreds of people had gathered there now. I couldn't go in that direction, and I couldn't go east to the Dana Road. I had no choice but to head toward the creek, and then to the highway construction.

After crawling another hundred yards I climbed out on the bank and started running. I crossed the haulroad dripping on the scorched weeds and darted into the apple trees. My pants were heavy with wetness and the wet bills weighed in my pockets, but I dashed from tree to tree. I didn't know if the helicopter could see me, but I couldn't pause to find out. I ran like I used to as a kid through the orchard, throwing myself forward into every stride, thrusting my chest out and pushing the edge of the world ahead of me.

As I ran I thought how cool my wet pants were in the wind, and how cool the money in my pockets was even where the wet cloth pinched. I passed a sprayer covered with white chemical frost and swung around it.

It was about a mile to the new road, but I could make it in a few minutes. Another half mile and I would be home free.

Thomas Glave

The Final Inning

From *The Kenyon Review*

AND WHETHER OR NOT Duane had really made a beauti-
ful or no *fly* corpse or not with all of his fingernails and fierce
teeth intact beneath the lid of that closed coffin, and why the fuck
his mother had just had to wear that shitcolored crushed-velvet or
whatever it was tacky suit (to match her just-as-tacky crushed-
velvet also shitcolored hat with that old cheap-looking Saint Patrick's-green fake daffodil on it), and if it was true that Uncle Bran-
don McCoy had made a goddamned fool out of himself again by
crying like a big old droopingass baby in front of all those people
instead of acting like a grown (old broken-down) man should even
in the midst of all that grief for the fallen brother, and what it was
exactly somebody had said to the minister (Reverend Dr. Smalls,
old pompous fire-and-brimstone drunkass) about going on and eating up all the (greasy-nasty, Cee-Cee had said) greens so that there
wasn't none left for nobody, not for *nobody,* honey—when it was all
over and they were all over it and just dying to get home and take
off heels and pantyhose and loosen up bra straps and what not,
those things, they all agreed, weren't even really the issues: by then
they just wanted to leave it all behind (especially what had happened in the church) and get back to where they were now, which
was back in Tamara's house in that most northeastern (and inacces-
sible, the black people who lived there cursed and praised) Bronx

neighborhood, Sound Hill; in her living room, with the heat on because it had gotten even colder, hadn't it, she said, and the television on too because it always was and like always now was showing some dumbass sitcom about two high-yellow girls as usual who couldn't even keep their trashy-looking hair straight, do you believe the shit they were putting on TV these days, Jacquie said, but it couldn't get no worse than that other show about that black family that was all doctors and what not, Cee-Cee said, cause I ain't never seen nobody like that acting like all we got is fly furniture and no problems, did you?—Nicky said; and all of them, even Jacquie's husband Gregory sitting off real quiet in the corner with two-year-old Gregory Jr. asleep on his knee and the *Sports Illustrated* open on the side table in front of him, said they hadn't, and laughed. Laughter out of and into sound and pulse as sharp or strained as anything else they might be feeling or making out and maybe even that one-half of one percent better.

The sad occasion had been over, more or less, for a few hours—ever since they'd all laid Duane away in the hard late-autumn earth of Saint Raymond's out by Whitestone, beneath the watchful distrusting eyes of the fastidious-when-it-came-to-Negroes grounds-keeping Italians (most of whom felt they themselves had pushed *this far* and even farther into the merciful hands of the Virgin in order to escape those colored hands stretched out today in grief and unbelieving fury to the hardedged sky—would the colored people even want heaven, too, now that they'd taken over everything else?). The main after-burial get-together was still going on at Miss Geneva Mack's—in the Valley, near the church used by some Sound Hill people, where the service had taken place—but after a few too many minutes of gossip that didn't interest anybody, kids who *weren't* cute, if only you knew, Ma'am, and just about enough senior citizen smalltalk of Mylanta and bloodclots and how it would come to us all someday and Lord, what a tragedy it was that such a fine young man had met the Savior so early but he sure had gone on up to Him with a beautiful-looking coffin, praise Jesus!—the five of them plus Gregory Jr. had piled easily enough again into Gregory Sr.'s car the same way they had on the way to the church. A little respite was in order now that they had done with the Saint

Raymond's part of it that everybody hated but for decency's sake couldn't miss, since all present had wanted to appear duly respectful, you know, the way you should for someone like Duane whom almost everyone had loved in spite of *that* (yes, *that,* but still, you had to have some feeling for the dead, didn't you?). Last regards had been paid at the cemetery to Duane's mother and stepfather (still in a severe state of shock after what had happened); Cee-Cee and Nicky and Tamara had finally been pulled away from chatting with the Reverend, who had proved inconsolable despite his drunkenness: It wasn't none of it his fault, what had happened in church, he shouldn't even worry about it, they'd said, although everyone knew that if the old alcoholic nigger had put the whiskey *behind* his shelf instead of all out front *on* it for a change none of the disgraceful shit today would have happened. Now, back in Sound Hill, they were all tired and cold and disgusted and just flat out, that was all. Tamara had put on the lima beans, Cee-Cee was helping with the rice and Jacquie was trying to season the meat in that kitchen that was looking more nasty to her today than ever before because (yes, Tamara was her friend, but, well, speak the truth before God, girl, she thought) she had seen not one but two roaches about which she would be sure to tell Gregory later. But then petty shit like that didn't matter so much now after such a sad occasion, with everybody talking and the TV blaring and the 40s of Olde English out on the living-room table and Tamara looking for her house shoes and her husband Kevin still not back with their kids Jaycee and Cassandra from Mrs. Shirley's: watching football with Mrs. Shirley's Harry after the funeral, now wasn't that some shit? she said; all the others except Gregory sucked their teeth and shook their heads. The house was still too damn cold, right down there on the Sound, after all, but the principal shit was Duane and *those others* too, still on everybody's mind after what had happened.

"Cause, girl," Tamara was saying to any one of them except Gregory, popping a halfcooked lima bean into her mouth and spitting out the skin, which she never ate, into the sink, "Lemme tell you. I ain't never think I'd live to see no shit like that. You know—"

"Word. You!" Cee-Cee said, pushing Jacquie out of the way to stand in a corner over the rice. The best corner, in fact, for affecting officiousness while nudging surreptitiously out from her behind the underwear that insisted on catching up in it beneath the folds of that stiff mourning dress she hardly ever wore.

"A damn shame. That's all that was," she said and lifted the lid off the rice pot to stir the water.

"What was?" Jacquie said, swaying to nobody's rhythm. "Why you holding your face over the pot, Cee-Cee? You think we want your makeup all in the rice?"

"Bitch, don't try it. You the one"—she replaced the lid on the pot and managed easily enough to rub her backside against the stove-door handle and there, she was free again—"you the one put on so much damn makeup couldn't nobody see that pimple on your chin you so de*ter*mined to try and hide—"

"Who you calling a bitch? Me and your grandmother."

"Your funky ass. Don't be talking bout my grandmother. She could—"

"Now what y'all fussing about? Tamara, this food is not even ready." Nicky strolled into the kitchen on long legs not quite hidden beneath the most elegant-looking black wool pantsuit all of them had ever seen and would have done more than kill to have. She had already had some of the Olde English, finally had found her cigarettes, and now with the contentment of the smooth dark cat that always lolled somewhere in the marshy fields of her eyes slowly began to pull in sweet soft drags of a Newport.

"I forgot his name already," Jacquie said. "After he got up there and dissed everybody I wouldn't even want to—"

"Dissed? That's what you gone call it? *Dissed?*" Cee-Cee stretched out three fingers toward Nicky's cigarette in a gimme-one gesture. "That shit wasn't even about no dissing. That was just goddamn disrespecting blasphemy, that's all. I wish it hada been me sitting up there with Duane's mother. I woulda knocked the shit outa him first and put a foot in his ass second."

"*OK.*"

"Y'all come on and sit in the living room," Tamara said, wiping her hands on the curtains over the kitchen window. "One thing I can't stand is sitting up in the kitchen talking bout dead people while food be on the stove." And I can't stand Nicky with her nasty self putting no damn cigarette ashes in my sink neither, she thought but didn't say either as she pulled one more lima bean out of the pot and this time pulled the skin off her tongue before she flicked it off into the sink.

"Y'all still going on about what happened in the church?" Gregory said, looking up from the *Sports Illustrated* and over the head of his sleeping son just long enough to give Jacquie an appreciative glance before he returned to a photograph in the magazine that had caught his eye. The look was returned with another, deeper one, which could have passed between them comfortably enough then as only one edging of that almost unbearable love she possessed not only for the man whose gaze mirrored the silent ponderings and longings of her own (and whose lashes, like those arcing humming-birds they yearned to become in dreams, nightly fluttered over the comforts her body offered that the dreams did not) but also for their child spread in smallish sleep across her husband's broad thighs. The child did not yet bear Gregory's unmistakably solitary look, which to her eyes had always spoken either of too many winding rivers already walked by the soul or the hands' constant reaching for what the ten fingers could not provide. Any or all of it might have worried or pleased her at the same time; speculations aside, they missed the look she gave him just then. Like so many others who knew them, distinct but distrusted, only occasionally acknowledged other versions of themselves, they rarely looked far enough into those interiors that were both theirs and hers, the here-and-always silty brew and the joy, the source of which none of them (through choice or necessity or the simple desire for safety, however they imagined it) had ever plumbed, had ever wanted to plumb. Their attention for the moment was anyway, as almost always, scattered: between the TV (they turned it off, they wanted music, it would go better with the Olde English) and Cee-Cee's Don't be mean girl, I gave you five cigarettes last week to Nicky's I know you did cause I gave you *six* the week before so now I guess you could go out and get you a pack, but then finally handing one over as the marshes wavered to stillness-accord in her eyes (Cee-Cee didn't never buy no cigarettes but still that was one of her main home girls), and Tamara putting on some Aretha and doing a jerky, rhythmless "white girl" dance to the first song that made them all laugh again, none of them had time to notice the new little things like that distant ticking sound in Gregory's voice when he spoke, or how hard up tighttight his right hand was gripping his little boy's small soft baby-shoulder.

"Lemme take him, Greg," Jacquie said. "I need to put his ass in the bed."

"You could put him right upstairs, girl," Tamara said. "Ooh, I love this song!"

"He all right. I got him," Gregory said, shifting thighs.

"Anyway, like I was saying," Cee-Cee said, exhaling a cloud of smoke and rolling her head back to rest it on the back of the couch where the three of them sat across from Gregory—Tamara was dancing—"I ain't never seen no shit like that neither. All in the church! And you know Duane's mother was through."

"Not just his mother," Jacquie said. "You ain't see Mr. Jackson?"

"I did," Tamara said.

"We *all* did, honey," Cee-Cee said. (The cigarette was sweet, the smoke was floating over her tongue, and *Breathe it in,* she thought, just like:) "—that old man got up and started *screaming,* honey. 'You will not say these things about my son! You will leave this church now! Get out of God's house!' *Honey . . . ?"* She raised her head and looked out at them with both arms stretched out along the sofa back—the easy, lazy stance they all associated with her.

"I thought I was gone fall out myself," she said.

"We all was," Tamara said, shaking on to the chorus. "How could you not? I mean, now, that was wrong—"

"Damn right."

"—it was, you know? I mean now how you gone sit up in church at somebody's goddamn funeral and bring out all kindsa shit—"

"That probably ain't even true," Jacquie said.

"Well, I don't know bout all that. But I'm saying how you gone get up there and do that shit when ain't nobody even want your white-looking ass up there in the first place?"

"He wasn't white," Gregory said. "The dude that got up and spoke? He wasn't no white. But I wish y'all would *stop—*"

"Lookded white to me," Cee-Cee said, chugging.

"Aw, girl, he did not. You gone sit there black as me and tell me you can't tell a—a half-breed when you see one? Come *on,*" Tamara said. She came and sat down on the floor next to Jacquie and looked up briefly at Nicky, who the entire time had remained silent and still behind the marshes, on her second glass.

"Hmmph. Half-breed. Somebody's business." Cee-Cee pronounced the words with particular contempt, as if describing someone who habitually shit on the only good side of his mother's bed. "See . . . that's why. Breeding, honey. Wouldn't no real black person do some shit like that."

"I don't know," Jacquie said. "A whole bunch of them stood up when he asked everybody to stand."

"Yeah," Tamara said. "The faggots did."

"Well, they was all faggots."

"Like I said," Cee-Cee came in again, "wouldn't no *real* black . . ."

"On *that* side of the church," Tamara said. "In the back, thank God. All sitting in a group. You see that shit?"

"You know we did," Cee-Cee said, putting out the cigarette.

"Faggots and bulldaggers. Ain't that some shit? With their hair all shaved off and zigzagged and earrings and nose rings—"

"Nasty. Probably all boggered up."

"That's how that shit spreads," Cee-Cee said.

"Girl . . ."

"—and *car*rying on—"

"Why y'all gotta keep talking about it?" Gregory said, shifting again and fastening his grip on his son and again staring down and out at that something anything not there but there.

"Why not? A goddamn freak show," Cee-Cee said, leaning forward. She snatched another cigarette out of Nicky's pack on the table, lit it that fast and exhaled two river-colored smoke streams from angry nostrils.

"Why the fuck not?" she asked again, turning to Gregory and then away and over to Tamara stretching her legs out on the rug.

Now it was her turn for the Olde English. Aretha was crooning out that very oldie *Who's Zoomin Who?* and Tamara's lips were there with her and her hips too, lacking the grace but filled with the intent.

"It wasn't all that, Cee-Cee. You got a real problem when it comes to . . ." It was the first time Nicky had spoken since they had left the kitchen. The marshes in her eyes had filled with the afternoon light of that other place quite clearly known only to her: the heavy sunset color of drowned fields descending beneath those lashes, a small space of enclosed time hours, even light-years, beyond the chilly Sound Hill late afternoon.

"It wasn't even all that," she said.

"What you mean?" Cee-Cee said.

"I *mean,* you got a problem."

"What kinda problem?"

All eyes in the room drove toward the marshes and stopped there.

"I mean . . . like, you . . . you don't like them."

"Them who?"

"You . . . well . . . umh . . . homos." (But oh no, now, she thought, she could be stronger than that with the Olde English, she thought, braver and maybe even—)

"Gay people," she said.

"Well—" Cee-Cee was facing the marshes directly. They were deeper than they had ever appeared before. They had in fact, without warning or comfort, given way to that untracked country which, even for those who thought (or had dared to think) they had always known the easiest way in—that simple road, the things you said or didn't, the half-smiles and the sliding glances, right?— confounded even the most scrupulous eye on the way back out into the farther brown that signaled both the marshes' end and the deeper waters' beginning.

"Well, no, I guess I don't—" (but it was all getting in her way, all around. Was that why her own voice suddenly sounded so—? And what was there just beyond those marsh-reeds pulling her out into—? The quick chill before that unknown whatever, nothing else and nothing noble, either, hurled her back onto firmer ground)

"—like no fucking faggots, girlfriend. Not up in no damn church. Not all up in somebody's goddamn funeral. Not calling nobody out when . . . —you acting like there's something to like. You gone sit up there in this house in Sound Hill with Duane dead and buried over in Saint Raymond's and his mother and Mr. Jackson over in Co-Op—"

"I know where we at."

"Ooh, yeah, Cee-Cee, Nicky *knows* where she at," Jacquie said and poked Nicky in the ribs, cause why we gotta go into all this now? she thought, feeling suddenly the surge of an unwelcome river rising up around their feet—it might have been the strangeness of panic, or anything else which had the all-knowing eyes of recognition but no comforting or settled-in name. The other woman smiled and slapped away her hand but they all knew that meant nothing. "Y'all know Miss Nicky ain't got just one but *two* men up on Gun Hill Road . . ."

"You stinking ho," Nicky said, almost laughing. "Liar!"

"—one name Billy and the other this Puerto Rican dude who ain't got shit in his pants to satisfy nobody—you know them Ricans just swear they all that"—they were all laughing easily enough now and the two were half-wrestling where they sat until Nicky let out a scream of half-real enough-now as Jacquie pulled at the weave that had cost eighty-five dollars at Jonay's up on White Plains Road and which, even in play, she wasn't about to have anybody mess up after the rain that afternoon had almost reclaimed it for free.

"Liar. Liar." (Straightening up and straightening out the hair, and Jacquie smiling in a relief wide enough for all: the river had returned to its proper place, wouldn't rise up and . . .). "You one ho and a half, honey. You gone go and bring in all you *think* you know about my business—"

"You said it wasn't true. Don't want nobody to talk about your business, baby? Don't have none then."

"Like you."

"May-be," Cee-Cee came in again. "But I'ma tell y'all one thing. When I die ain't *nobody*"—she leaned forward suddenly, the lioness in her jaw—"ain't nobody gonna drag my shit all out in the street in no church. You know what I mean?"

"Not like how they did Duane, you mean," Nicky said. "Poor old Duane," she said, more quietly.

"Word! And you know"—Cee-Cee lowered her voice to the confidential tone—"I got to say, when he got up there and started to speak I got scared. I'm telling y'all, I thought I was gonna pee on my dress."

"Wouldn't be the first time," Jacquie said.

"Shut up."

"What you was scared of? That one of em was gone jump up and bite you?" Nicky snorted.

"On the titties, probably," Jacquie said and laughed over in Gregory's direction. He returned a weak smile. "So put on some Luther 'ready, Tamara. I don't want to hear no more 'retha's old fat ass."

"I was just gone do that."

"I knew they wasn't gone *bite* me." Cee-Cee was going on. "But I'm saying—I'm saying—"

"You thought Duane's mother was gone get up there and smack the shit outa him," Jacquie helped.

"Exactly. You said it!"

"Well, she didn't."

"Nope. Just sat there screaming and crying."

"So did everybody else," Tamara said.

"Why y'all gotta keep going on and on about this damn funeral?" Gregory put in again. "I just can't stand—"

"Aw, shut up. Your own Aunt Hattie almost had a damn heart attack."

"That's cause she ain't used to people talking about—talking about—"

"Faggots," Tamara helped this time. Luther's croons did not quite cover Nicky's and Gregory's flinches.

"Faggots." He heard the word—

(—but it had flown up against his cheek where he sat almost but not quite motionless holding his son: holding him *faggots* and caressing him the word searing his flesh and thinking   )

(:—again? thinking but didn't want to now oh no but yes of those places, parks: alleyways: redlit (bloodlit) bars: fuckrooms/

darkrooms and those piss-streets too he knew had known and: but
no. Hadn't been him there. Had never been him among the ghosts
and the searchers and the lonelyones, walking: looking: stroking
and sliding, taking in: going in *now give it to me tight tighttight;*
—never him back there but somebody else   one of the ghosts: :a
spirit: :a dream or someotherbody fucking else in the moment
and moments there *lonely* and so he? the someotherbody sucking a
pair of thighs or a bootstrap with lace so that he?—had wanted
remember aw shit now to go down to that part the belly or the *aw yes*
and travel it, Jesus: hold it or him the whole thing body and go to
the feeling, Jesus: kissing and stroking and holding and take it and
aw fuck Jesus yes and ***:—*faggots* but naw don't be calling them
that now naw but OK *sucker* and *punk* call them that: wandering
again on those streets with the the the: *Faggots.* He. Who had been
unhappy and. Had wanted to wander, kiss manflesh. Find. Jacquie
but then can't tell Jacquie.—wandering again and *he'd been so scared!*
because yup one time he had kinda sorta without words told Duane
about all of it, everything, parks; bathrooms; movies and the:—
Duane who had understood kind of, Duane like a brother down
homie who wouldn't never say nothing to nobody, DuaneDuane
dead now and:—so now? he being Gregory who could? or couldn't
go on with this kinda shit much more Jacquie could? or couldn't lie
much longer Jacquie or keep on pretending to want to be with her
like that when no he didn't really want to and honest to God one
time thinking about Duane and *notsafe* and at the funeral shit-
scared cause maybe one of them would have *known* or thought
maybe could tell? he Gregory was a little *that way,* was close to
them. Close to them, living as he did up there in Co-Op City
nearby Sound Hill and Baychester and Gun Hill with a family but
who still no goddamnit fuck it all would not couldn't ever stick up
for their faggot asses nor get into it when the homies was beating
up on them; would not (couldn't) claim his hidden name among
them and the shared desire, anger, simply to be allowed to live and
be: not near his family, he thought; not with them, he thought.
Holding his little baby boy. Jacquie nearby. Not with them. Never.)

"You see what I mean?" Jacquie was saying. "You could talk to
the nigger till you dead in the face and he just go right on acting

"Told *you?* When?"

(Yes, he thought, the God's honest truth, he had told her, Nicky, but why? did you have to tell her or anybody up here Duane? why? couldn't you keep it downtown with all them downtown faggots (—:don't call them that:—) that came up to the funeral? why?)

(—But had *had* to, Duane had said: They were all his family and friends, weren't they? Had always loved him (they said), would always care for him (they said), wouldn't they? Hadn't become like whities who dissed their own at the drop of a hat, had they? Ooh but they didn't want nobody to know you had it, Duane. When they heard you had it said Yup serves his ass right cause you *know* he got it from hanging out with them nasty old white boys Village faggots downtown too much and: that's why you was *funny* they said: even now they won't stop talking about it and Nicky was saying)

"Yes, he did. Said he thought his mother mighta said something. Yes, he did. Coupla months ago. Oh yes he did."

"You lying!" Tamara said.

"Girl, you ever see me up in here lying?"

"His *mother?* Ain't that some shit? I ain't even know she knew!"

"Hell yeah she knew." Nicky turned the marshes toward her cigarettes, lit one and sat back, closing her eyes for a moment. The Olde English had begun to feel reckless in her veins, as it had in everybody's.

"She just didn't want to say nothing, that's all," she said.

"Um-hmm. But see—I'm sorry—I can't blame her," Tamara said.

"I can."

"What you mean?" Cee-Cee said. Luther was still singing.

The marshes opened again and turned—flickered, ever so slightly—toward Gregory. They were black as the night now descending, revealing only the shape of small scurrying things before the moon's glide.

"Because"—(her voice soft as the marsh-darkness he didn't turn his head to see, shimmying out toward him as if seeking a partner for that step-and-feint they might both have recognized on some other night—the most elusive, most interlocking dance of all) "—because, y'all . . . —they was gone bury him with—with a *lie*. Can you imagine?"

"Imagine what, girl?" Tamara said.

"She buggin," Cee-Cee said—but she was sitting very still.

"Naw, I ain't buggin. I know just what I'm saying. It's like—he lived his whole life— . . . see, y'all don't know, y'all didn't know Duane the way I knew him."

For the first time Gregory turned toward the marshes and felt their sweep of memory and night-knowledge shawl down over him through the silence. Luther sang no more.

"—the way he used to talk about how hard it was being so— outside the family and everything—"

"What you mean?" The new anxiety in Cee-Cee's voice could have built easily enough to agony someplace else: the simple shame of crucial words unspoken, the fearlatch left undone. He heard with them and knew—or thought he knew.

"What you saying, Nicky?" Cee-Cee went on and was leaning forward, almost on her feet. "He wasn't outside the family. All them people—his mother and Mr. Jackson and his Aunt Gracie and Sheila—that girl that got pregnant with Marcus—"

"She did? Get outa here."

"—they all loved him," Cee-Cee would not stop. "How you gone say he was outside the family when you saw the way everybody was crying and carrying on when they brought him in? Does that sound like somebody outside the family to you? Does it, Tamara?"

Tamara remained silent, a headshake saying neither yes nor no.

"Does it, Greg?"

(—holding his son verytight on his lap, tighttight like back in the church, and sitting; staring; at that very too-shiny coffin; he, sitting there senseless, staring but not believing (no!) that what had been Duane was *in there* ninety pounds lighter than what Duane had used to be: that ain't even you in there, he had thought, O my God: not even no you with all them purple marks on your face (:the coffin had been closed:) and your hands with them purple marks on them and up on your chest too O my God Duane even on your eyes and in your mouth and you skinny like a damn rail with your hair all funny too (chemotherapy, radiation, drugs: had made what had been hair into—*that?*) O my God Duane: remembering and holding still on his lap tighttight his son not even you   *wasn't even no you* he had thought

—Jacquie's shoulder pressed tight into him but she wouldn't cry, he'd thought, she wasn't no crying type: knowing he would much later. Yes, God. With his face pressed into that warm hot full space between her breasts, sobbing like a damn baby: that wasn't no Duane, he had half-wept silently at the cemetery into her softwarm body, Duane didn't die he didn't, just like Duane's mother screaming MY BABY MY BABY in the church and carrying on with all them others screaming *No, Jesus* to Jesus who didn't never listen. All of them sitting up and frozen, hands flying up to heaven when it had happened. The faggot)

"—got up outa his place, honey," Tamara was saying.

(—*his place* in the back where all of them had been asked or no, told) to sit and who invited them anyway? Jacquie had asked him later but he couldn't answer that: wondering if the *I don't know* in his eyes behind the grief and the pain and so much else she didn't have no idea about had been good enough for her:—but then it was like the faggot who had been crying with the rest of them had looked dead straight at him Gregory sitting there holding his son on his lap next to that strong-looking serious woman Jacquie his wife and Gregory Jr.'s mother: had been as if the faggot had recognized something or maybe had Duane told him something about the men, Duane, about the blackmen and the brownmen and the whitemen who had done him, Gregory, shared fuckheat and wanting-someone-for-whatever-heat in all them dark places (:holding his son tight, tighttight   Don't hold me so tight, Daddy, Greggie Jr. had cried out over the cries of the women with the sound of that light autumn rain falling over the church:)—had the faggot walking up there to the pulpit seen that in his eyes? the wanting and the searching and the? seen it? and gone on to push aside the minister and in his black leather jacket and jeans and boots wearing goddamn Lord Jesus not one earring but four and looking out at him and everybody past the minister who began to shout Sit down boy this is a funeral where you think you at as he the faggot began to say   )

"'You're killing us! With this silence! You won't stop, you keep on killing us!'" Tamara said, almost laughing, imitating—

(—just like that he thought, seeing it yet again, still holding his son tighttight: the one they had called a halfbreed, lightskinned, who even talked white like them trying-to-be-white downtown niggers on the West Side and the East Side and in the Village, that one: starting to shout from the pulpit with his back turned to the choir and all eyes looking at him in had it been disbelief disgust? hate? or the rage of *We oughta kill that fucking faggot right now. Kill his motherfucking faggot ass. Outside the church or in it. Right here. Anywhere.* Or had those downturned mouths and pressed lips finally been feeling with the outrage and hatredscorn that more unavoidable discharge of loss: the need to spew out with the screams and shouts what the hands and heart couldn't contain, the eyes not witness and live: that their very same adored Duane Taylor Clayton Ross was laying up there with his hands you couldn't see folded over his chest all hidden beneath the wood and flowers and his mother and stepfather screaming over him and screaming even more when the faggot began to shout and you could see them everybody going from one to the other   )

the faggot remember (:don't call him that:)

the others: everybody

and my name *(then louder)* my name is JAMES MITCHELL SCROGGINS and no you won't make me SHUT UP cause I'm PROUD to be here today as a GAY friend of DUANE'S and a *(shouting over the rage)* HUMAN BEING GODDAMNIT just like DUANE WAS TOO and

They: thinking: everybody yes with hands up in the air over hats and balding heads: hands fluttering to the top of the church and O my God Lord Sweet Jesus what is happening God who is this boy standing up there where's the minister well why don't you stop him what kinda going on is that and (faggot shit: growls: sissy

now why won't you SAY IT
he died of AIDS of AIDS
(Lord God the screaming
remember how their eyes looked
everybody shouting SIT
DOWN WHERE YOU
THINK YOU AT SIT
DOWN) say it AIDS we all
KNOW IT because I know
some of you know I HAVE
THIS DISEASE TOO and I
took care of him so I know
many of you KNOW ME and
what you're doing today is
WRONG WRONG Duane
wasn't ASHAMED of it
either but all of you people
YOU'RE KILLING US you
won't STOP you keep right
on KILLING US like you
didn't even want us to come
today to SAY GOODBYE to
our friend our LOVER and
then we came but you made
us wait out in the COLD
RAIN and then SIT WAY IN
THE BACK BACK OF
THE CHURCH: how can
you KEEP ON DOING
THIS: when is it going to
STOP: now how can you
bury him and say you LOVE
HIM and not say one word
about how HE LOVED
OTHER MEN   he loved all
of us and WE LOVED HIM
Yes he had AIDS   it

shit: abomination: growls) O
Jesus   Jesus   Jesus! No my
son ain't no homosexual no
my cousin ain't no faggot no
my nephew didn't have no
damn AIDS the devil's disease
don't you say that in this
church and O you you
filthy:—and the screaming
and the children Mommy
who's that man and look: O
God Almighty the women the
ladies crying and the men
their nostrils flaring and
saying muttering growling We
should kick his motherfucking
mulatto-looking ass and
getting ready to do it too: but
then you could see some
people thinking from what
you could see in their eyes the
way their heads nodded soft
and slow and the ladies' dark
eyes so dark revealing that
way showing so much so little
under those tacky hats their
eyes saying only in part You
speak the truth up there boy
but O God O Jesus but still
you speak it all the same
because it's all true all of it:
under three hats three ladies
in particular nodding Yeah we
sure do know how he died
but ain't nobody saying
nothing cept "a long illness"
and that boy is right

KILLED HIM we us here
now we should SAY IT SAY
IT you're trying to IN him
I'm bringing him OUT again
for God's sake please I'm
asking you for once won't you
just SAY IT SAY IT

The faggot continuing   Jesus

:—I want all of you now who
were proud of Duane as a
proud out open GAY MAN
to stand up WITH ME
STAND   for a moment of
silence STAND

rightright: could even be my
grandson my godson or: but
something and no it can't
keep going on because He the
One knows don't He: knows
the truth about all of it and if
we sitting right here with the
dead boy's mama and can't
even speak the truth now so
damn late in the day when
are we ever gone speak it and
now just think think about it
what in the hell kinda going
on is that?

He had said
Stand
(the last inning   the inning was over)
   "Yes, he did, honey," Tamara was saying—and every face there
was attendant, looking or unwilling to look into that slow yet sudden shock of memory. "Asked us all to stand *up*. In the church.
'Which one a y'all *proud* a him? Stand up!' "
   (—and everybody back there in pain, he thought. Crying. Eyes
closed. Hurt by the truth. The *truth* truth. Couldn't take it. Not
about nobody like you Duane. They all could take the truth about
everything else but: about knocked-up teenagers, crackhead sons,
numbers-running uncles, raped nieces, drive-by shootings, mixed-
race marriages, retarded cousins, rat-filled projects, shitbigoted
Koreans, pigfaced skinheads, African famines, Chinese massacres,
psycho Jamaicans, right wing terrorists, sellout nigger judges, even
white-trash serial killers: but not about nobody they cared about
supposed to be black and strong like you was Duane but with that
faggot shit: what to them was whitefolks shit, another sick nasty
fuckedup white thing like that nasty old AIDS, just like nasty
whitefolks, not for no black man we know and Jesus have mercy

Jesus don't want to talk about it never. Not to kiss another man, rock to slow dreams between his hips. Lay across his dusky thighs, smell his dusk, his musky parts in the hands; a palm to those musk-dusky parts moistened by the mouth. Not to love nor touch nor hold nor look him in the face and *see*. Never. Not one of our own. Not in the church. Too many rivers to cross. And specially not one a *them* telling your business about how he *loved* you and how you had *it* and how Jesus Savior he *had it* too. Couldn't take it. *I* couldn't take it, Duane. Can't.)

"I can't neither, Tamara," Jacquie was saying—a hint of that something of outrage or shame clouding into the same storm in all their eyes that was now descending not as cool easing rain but as that same old and loathsome bitter ash, weed: what would linger there long after the storm's eye and the parched brown field always beneath it, always so untended, had gone. It was there, from within those separate and gathered storms and the ash, that they sensed what she, out of that silence, suddenly knew—that he whom she loved, still holding on his broad lap their son, was (but for how long? and why?) in flight heavy with purpose and sadness away from her—from all of them.

(—because the faggot had wanted to show out, that was all, he thought: say No, *This* was Duane who died a *that thing*. That thing he Gregory knew he didn't have. *Did not have it*—:)

"—so then, y'all," Nicky's voice, still soft, full of the evening that had crept down from beneath those lashes, "see, Jimmy went back—"

"Jimmy! Jimmy!" Cee-Cee and Tamara shouted at the same time. "You—you know him?"

"Jimmy. James Mitchell Scroggins. Who got up. Yeah, Jimmy. I know him"—so softly, like music!—and looking straight at him. Penetrating, parting him. His hands on his son. Tighttight.

"How'd *you* know him?" Jacquie asked, moving her feet back. The river was rising again.

The other woman didn't answer. Her eyelids were drooping down. She settled herself back on the sofa. Stretched out her legs again as if the living room had once more become that which it could no longer be—comfortable, that was all, with nothing more than the smell of cooking rice and lima beans drifting in to them from the kitchen.

"I don't think y'all really want to know," she said from the twilight. "Do y'all?"

"Don't play, girl. Say what you got to say."

So alongside or even above their pursuit of something reckless, aloft, she spoke. "He used to be over there all the time," she said, very softly.

"Who? Not—"

"Jimmy. James."

"Over in—"

"Duane's apartment, Jacquie. Right on over there in Co-Op. The same one."

(Hearing the tiredness in her voice, he thought. Thinking as she was of that time of catheters and blood and—)

"He used to go over there, you mean?" It was Cee-Cee again, beginning to grasp the vaguest sense of it except for what was passing in silence between Nicky and the man seated there holding so tighttight his child-son on his lap: understanding even that, maybe, the heavy falls behind the silence cast over what did not fit, what could not ever be imagined to fit, there.

"I guess"—Nicky, sitting up with that startling abruptness they would all later remember; Nicky all at once fierce; the marshes afire, the dry storm ignited, swirled into their midst—"I guess if y'all had gone over there more often y'all woulda seen him. Y'all woulda seen him holding Duane up in his arms like he was a little baby or I don't know what. Kissing up on him even with them purple spots all on his face. Telling him he loved him, he loved him so much and all kindsa shit. Wiping the shit outa his ass—"

(Holding his son. But Jesus don't let her go off on them. Jacquie getting ready to get up and *sit down Jacquie* and Tamara looking like she want to curse somebody out now please Nicky don't say no more girl)

"Nicky." Tamara's voice rang out not-calm-but-calm, crackling the incipient warning ice. "Don't be talking that kinda shit in here, girl. You see we all just come from a funeral and I don't *think*—"

"—and him holding him"—implacable, in the deep river dark

now beyond the marshes—"—holding him, Tamara—where you going, Jacquie?"

"You see we got food on the stove, don't you? Kevin and them'll be back soon from—"

"Sit your behind down." More than the hint of a snarl.

"Girl . . . see, now, I know you must be buggin. This ain't even your damn—"

"Sit down." Leaning forward very far; the eyes very bright; the storm-fire running wild. "Y'all don't want to hear it. We sitting up in here talking bout faggots this and faggots that. Talking shit. Tamara, don't you open up your face to say nothing to me."

"I ain't say shit to you. But I'ma tell you now—"

(Holding him.   Verytight.   Tighttight.)

"You ain't gone tell me nothing. Y'all can't say shit to me cause—word, the whole time Duane was sick I ain't never seen not *one* a y'all up in his house. Not to stop by and visit. Not even to call. So now y'all can sit up in here talking bout faggot so-and-so but when the shit was down y'all couldn't even *visit* the motherfucker. I ain't never seen not *one* a y'all. Not one!"

"Hold on, girl!"

"I don't know who she think she talking to like she crazy. She—"

"You, Cee-Cee." Nicky got up to stand over her. The other woman's angry face didn't turn away from the possible smack it anticipated—if smack were to come, it would be easier to take than that acid-wash of the truth, the little jump-up truths or the greater wordless one, from which it had already turned long ago like the rest of them.

"I'm talking to you. And you, Tamara. And you, Jacquie."

"Don't put me in it."

"In it? You already in it. You don't even know how much you in it." Not looking at him. "You just as bad as everybody else, running your mouth *after* he's dead talking bout his *life*style and carrying on, but word, Jacquie, I ain't never seen your black ass neither when he had to have that old nasty catheter up in his chest. Y'all can talk a whole lotta shit, but what the fuck y'all really know about faggots? You ever kiss one?"

"Nicky!" But too late. Much too late. She had jumped way past what they would have once called their own innocence. It was only then that they saw that, like all those others who inhabited their eyes, she had in fact never been innocent, had never had any use for it, as, differently, they had never been either but did. They couldn't pull her back now, or even—especially—themselves.

"I'm telling y'all now"—swaying over Cee-Cee—"—y'all don't know nothing cause y'all didn't wanna know. I was going up there every day. Oh yes I was. Every damn day and I saw what y'all so busy calling faggots." Not looking at him. "Taking care a him. Jimmy. Cause didn't nobody else do it. Not even—not even his *mother*."

"Nicky—"

"Not even that bitch. You know she came by there two days one time and ain't never come back. And Mr. Jackson ain't never come. Guess maybe they couldn't take looking at all them faggots."

"Nicky . . ."

"Reverend Smalls didn't neither. Miss Cee-Cee, where was you at that whole time?"

(Her power. Fascinating him. Terrifying him. He couldn't speak. Could only stare the way he had stared in church. But now even his face was gone. He had left only a pair of hands to hold on to things, a clenched asshole to relieve the icy lead in his bowels, a pair of legs with which he could run. Runrun away from her voice saying)

"—so don't say shit, Jacquie, cause I *heard* Duane say—Tamara, don't you walk outa here!"

"I ain't going no place, girl. But you are."

"You damn right. When I get ready. You listen. I heard him say, on his *death*bed, 'Nicky girl, don't let Mama and them tell no lies. They gone try to change it and say I died a something else. I know she gone try cover it up,' he said. And she did. Everybody did, tried to, til the one y'all keep calling the faggot, who got a *name,* by the way, in case y'all forgot, his name is Jimmy, James M. Scroggins—"

Tamara had already retrieved Nicky's coat from the hall closet and then that fast (not hardly fast enough, they would say later) was in front of her with it and then—since even that didn't work—

thrust it full force into those furious arms and jerked her own head
back toward the front door.

"You got five seconds to get outa here," she said.

"Or what? You gone throw me out? Bitch, ain't nobody scared a
you. Just cause *your* man fucks every ho up and down the Valley—"

"Get out! Get the fuck out!"—and there would have been a fight
then for real if Cee-Cee hadn't sprung up and separated them and
with Jacquie's help (who hadn't wanted to go near the crazy bitch,
she would say later, but she hadn't been able to stand one more
minute of all that goddamned cursing in front of her baby boy and
her husband) got her to the front door and out into the dark cold
Sound Hill evening with that constant breeze off the Sound more
chilly tonight that carried her words down to Noah Harris's and
O.K. Griffith's and the Walkers and the Goodmans and God
knows even as far away as Pelham Parkway and Baychester: just
get that lowclass uglymouthed bitch the fuck outa my house,
Tamara was screaming, with Gregory Jr. awakened by all the commotion crying Mommy and then Daddy and Jacquie screaming
back Shut up at the baby because Nicky had almost punched her in
the mouth on the way out, shouting as she went that didn't none of
them know what a *real* faggot was or a real man neither since it
was what they'd called the faggots who'd kept Duane alive as long
as they had, and y'all bunch a bitches was as bad as the worst kinda
crackers, and now quiet as y'all wanted to keep it (except there, for
so many curious faces had begun to peek out from behind curtains
and from over awnings along Sound Hill Avenue) everybody in
Sound Hill *and* Baychester *and* the Valley knew Tamara's Kevin
had picked up that nasty VD last summer from that old broken-
toothed crackhead Jamaican ho up on White Plains Road, and
wasn't it true that Cee-Cee's brother Jervis had gotten another one
a them Puerto Rican bitches pregnant, cause everybody knew that
yellow nigger didn't never date no black girl, and all a that wasn't
even the real shit to what she *could* say but she knew at least one
person there had loved Duane and anyway she had promised the
dead she wouldn't never tell nobody's secret that shouldn't be
told—looking back at Gregory once more with a last fire which

scorched him to crucible ash on the spot, a moment of fiery intelligence from which he would never, for the rest of his nights and days in and out of that company and others, recover. It was only after they closed the door on all that outrage and pain (and then became aware of their own gliding up the smooth back of their necks, gathering spit at the swallow-point in their throats, bristling on to the ever-so-delicate eyebrow's curve) that they realized that what could serve as distraction-relief and the greatest tragedy of all had actually occurred: the lima beans had burnt black, what had been the rice had scorched, and not two but three enormous roaches had gotten into the meat and ruined it, ruined it, ruined it, Tamara began to cry, her sisters standing all around with their faces hidden within those sudden useless cages of their hands—a flock of fragile birds clustered for safety beneath that lingering storm and every other yet to come, descending.

—Up, upup the stairs. Feeling all the light and shadow in the universe flying about him; holding onto his baby boy who had fallen asleep again on his shoulder at the end of all *that;* nobody wanting to mention Duane's name; nobody wanting to follow up on what had been said; nobody wanting to—; then he had slipped away with his child and begun to climb the stairs, *time to put my baby boy to bed for real* he'd thought and would do now *cause I can do that much and maybe even a whole lot more,* he'd thought, *I got that kinda courage, enough for everybody*—now at the top of the stairs, almost believing his own nervechatter as he thought again too of how that night—fuck yes, that night—he would nuzzle into that space always there between her breasts: always there, warm, dark, rich, deep, for him, he thought; where he could without fail find just enough of himself and know that she would always offer that shared part of the inner life to him without complaint or anger, without inquiry, without demanding too hard what she still thought he, even as far as the sheathed truth stripped naked and lean, could give: once somebody gave up their soul to you, he thought, you could always go back to that part of them where it was safe: that was true, he thought, opening the guest bedroom door, feeling his child pressing into him: that space would always be there for that smaller version of himself, he thought, prayed, and was, at least tonight, wasn't it?—smiling that not happy but weary smile as he listened to Jacquie and the others downstairs fussing; thanking something deep within himself for still being able to feel within and without that offered no-questions part of her, as he felt again the rise within of the stranger, the he-without-face or name, placeless, loose, as the grief began to settle over him again: for Duane; grief for whom he had loved, he thought, remembering, grief . . . For all of them.

Duane who was with him now. Scolding him. Hovering. Admonishing him as he lay the sleeping child down on the star-patterned quilt made by Tamara's Aunt Gannell. His right hand beginning to stroke his baby's sleeping cheek as, lowering his face to that other, his left hand folded the broad blue quilt-thickness over the child, who smiled just then as if even from so far away in that dream-forest of tall dandelions through which he was now walking with two tiger-mamas, he felt the long passionate protective kiss his father's mouth and eyes and entire body bestowed upon him. *With him now:* that presence, you, Duane?—that (he couldn't be imagining it, he thought) put a consoling arm about him. *But don't worry,* he mouthed out soundlessly to the darkness, *I ain't gone bring home nothing to make her sick, Duane.* Those deeper eyes watching him in the dark; admonishing, sorrowful. *Aw shit, Duane, you know I just let em suck on me a little no more. Well no the truth like you know sometimes a whole lot more.* Lowering his eyes before the ghost or whatever it was watching, waiting; then bending over his son whom he knew then more than ever he would defend from everything. Everything, Duane. Even you. You the dead and . . . But now too much to remember, he thought, too many names, faces, things to take in, forget, release . . . so go on now. Leave. Go on, now, get out! . . . and then the thing, whatever it was or once had been, sorrowful, longing, mute and invisible as every other fallen body in that infinite outer and inner world, vanished into the darkness, and with that vanishing he knew it would appear no more.

Jacquie's footsteps on the stairs he thought. Thinking (knowing? more than ever? praying) he didn't need Duane nor nobody to tell him what was right nor how to take care of his own family. How to protect them and himself and everybody. Didn't need no ghost to tell him nor no faggot screaming up in no church neither. I'm the one, he thought, the main one up on it, he thought; sensing Jacquie slip through the door behind him as she came up and squeezed a hand deep into the exhausted sunken field of his left shoulder. Before she sat down next to him on the bed for what he knew would be the beginning of a long something-or-other between them, a meeting of lips and lipstick, he pressed the covering in more tightly around Gregory Jr. and thought with some surprise *He's mine   I made him I ain't never gone let nobody not nobody hurt him.* (She'd begun to massage his neck, he'd begun to give himself over to her, and aw yes, girl, all right, now. Yes.) Not nobody. Not no vicious gossip nor what nobody says. I'ma keep y'all safe from that, he thought. As sure as he knew his name and who he was. (He had always known his name, he thought, who he was.) Keep them very safe from ghosts and secrets and redrooms filled with:— *it wasn't safe,* some other ghost had once hissed into his innermost parts: *notsafe notsafe. Wasn't safe that time,* another had said, *who wants to be safe?*—keep them secure from all that and much more, he thought, lowering the grief-veil in his eyes as he gave what remained of him, the closures and the fells, into her openings: I got it all under control right here, he thought, stroking she who was with him now alive, Jesus, amen, yes: the other hand caressing his child: knowing now for all time in that darkness that this silence and shadow were *it,* where they had always lived, would continue to live: where he would keep them with every power possible, *safesafe:* now there and falling back into the dark above the world where the dead and the ghosts slept and rose, walked, searching: his hands there now clasping them the living and the flesh and the protected hot blood to his chest tight tighttight, for that time and ever after shielded from that outer world of lies, safe from other people's eyes, he thought. Safe from the truth.

Deborah Eisenberg

Mermaids

From *The Yale Review*

GOOD? NOT GOOD?" Mr. Laskey said. "What do you say, girls?"

"Kiss kiss," Alice said, making two spoons kiss, and Janey was just staring rudely into space, so it fell to Kyla (as it had all day) to make things all right. "It's perfect," she assured Mr. Laskey, and, true, the old-fashioned gleam and clatter, the waitresses in their pastel uniforms, the glass dishes with their ice-cream spheres, the other little groups of wealthy tourists and even New Yorkers, all of this would be exactly what her mother was back home picturing.

Spring vacation had been hurtling down toward Kyla for weeks and weeks, at first just a fleck troubling the margin of her vision, then closer and larger and faster until it smashed into place, obliterating everything that wasn't itself, and Kyla's mother was dropping her off at the Laskeys', where they were waiting for her, and Mrs. Laskey was smoothing Janey's dress and giving little Alice a hug, and for one fractured and repeating moment Kyla was saying goodbye to Richie Laskey, and then the car door shut Kyla in with Alice and Janey and Mr. Laskey, and Mrs. Laskey and Richie were waving goodbye, and Alice began to cry at the top of her lungs, as though she were being snatched away by killers. "Oh, grow up, Alice," Janey said.

The airport was gray and shiny, like a hospital where Kyla was to be anesthetized and detached hygienically from home. A corridor of shiny gray time sucked her in along with Janey and Alice and Mr. Laskey, and then the crowd in which they were to be conveyed away compressed itself into the tube of the airplane.

"You get the window seat," Janey said to Kyla. "You're the guest."

Seven days, Kyla had thought; seven days before she could go home, seven days of being the guest, seven days of having to have a good time—even though she was with Janey Laskey. "That's okay," she said. "Take it if you want it."

"You take it," Janey said. "I've been on lots of planes before. I get to go on planes all the time."

Kyla looked around for Mr. Laskey, but he was already settled into the seat across the aisle from Alice, and one of the stewardesses was leaning over him, laughing and laughing, as he told a joke about a fox and a bunny rabbit. And Kyla would have taken the window seat then (because someone should show Janey she couldn't always get away with that sort of thing) but the thought of her mother's pleading look intervened, so she just shook her head and sat down, thunk, where she was.

Janey shrugged. "Okay," she'd said, squishing her porky rear end past, to the good seat, "I guess some people don't like it. Some people are scared to look out the window." She opened the big book she was carrying and squinted down at it, following the print with her finger; her thin hair, the color of cardboard, drooped forward; obviously she should be wearing glasses.

Poor Janey. "What's your book about?" Kyla asked.

Janey jumped slightly. "Oliver *Twist?*" she said, and looked at Kyla. "Is about orphans."

"*Sor*-ry," Kyla said.

Air whooshed through some little spouts above them, the lights flickered, and a heartless angel's voice instructed them to strap themselves in.

No, Kyla thought. No no no no no. She closed her eyes; the gravity of her will flowed around the seats and into the little compartments: *The plane was growing heavier and heavier*—it would sit, the plane, heavy with her will; darkness would come; someone would open the door, and they could all go home. But for one instant there was a flaw in her concentration—or was it in her sincerity? Her will was flicked aside like an insect and the plane rose, through a great roaring.

The stewardess returned to make a big fuss over Alice. "Kindergarten, *already?*" she sang out, amazed, to Alice, who confirmed this with a gracious nod. The stewardess straightened up, twirled a bit of stray hair around her finger and tucked it back into place, smiling brilliantly at Mr. Laskey. Janey stared at her with loathing and then turned to the window.

"Guess what you can see from up here," Janey turned back to say to Kyla. "You can see the bodies in the lagoons."

"There are no bodies in the lagoons," Kyla had said firmly, for Alice's benefit, but Alice was playing happily with the safety instruction card, like someone who has no troubles in the world.

"They look just like mermaids, except they're face up," Janey said. "Their hair floats, and their legs are green and slimy."

"Don't," Kyla said.

"Eleven-year-old Courtney Collier disappeared from the mall at ten o'clock this morning while her mother was buying a new tie for Mr. Collier," Janey said. " '*Courtney was a beautiful little girl,*' authorities said. '*We're totally positive it was a sex crime.*' "

Seven days; seven more days. Minus the three hours and fifteen minutes between getting from the Laskeys' house to wherever it was they were now. Minus this second. Minus this second. Kyla leaned across Janey to see: Naturally there were no dead girls. You couldn't even see the lagoons—all you could see were clouds.

Now most of that seven days was over with. Sunday night Kyla had settled into the room she was to share with Janey and Alice, with the blue carpet and the alien blue-flowered wallpaper, and she'd carefully put her clothing into a bureau drawer or hung it on the hotel's heavy wooden hangers—how strange it looked on those hangers in that big, dark closet that smelled like wood and furniture polish and very faintly of other people, though nobody in particular. Then she and Janey had to play Brides with Alice to calm her down and they had all gone to sleep.

"I want you girls in bed early," Mr. Laskey had said, "except on the nights we've got tickets. And there are going to be some serious naps around here. Agreed? The days will be pretty strenuous, and I don't want to arrive back home with three little zombies. Now. I'll be right next door, but I'm looking forward to a little stress-reduction myself, and you have an entire hotel staff downstairs at your disposal. Kindly take advantage of that unusual fact. If you need anything, Donald will be at the concierge's desk every afternoon and night."

And it *had* been . . . strenuous. On Monday evening they'd gone to a restaurant with waiters in tuxedos, where Kyla had worn the new party dress her mother had gotten her for the trip, and Tuesday night she'd worn the dress again, when Mr. Laskey let them stay up late and they'd gone to a show with poor people who were singing and dancing. And yesterday evening they had gone to another amazing restaurant, in Greenwich Village, where everyone—all the waitresses and all the customers—looked like models. And during the days they'd gone to the Empire State Building and the Planetarium and the Statue of Liberty and the Museum of Natural History and various other museums (which Janey claimed to enjoy) and they'd walked in the big, dirty, interesting park with the little fringe of silver buildings at the edges, and they'd gone in a horse-drawn carriage, and had taken a boat around the whole island, and along with all that there had been a revolving display of fascinating delis and coffee shops and people you couldn't believe had even been *born,* and the long, sludgy naps in the sad blue room where it seemed Kyla had been living with Janey and Alice forever.

So now there was only tonight and then Friday and then Saturday, and on Sunday they'd get back in the plane, and on Monday morning Kyla would wake up in her own bed and all the big blank obstacles that at one time had been between her and home would have dissolved into a picture she could remember for her mother at breakfast.

Of course, at the time something was happening, you didn't know what it was like. At the time a thing was happening, that thing was not, for instance, *New York*. *New York* was what her mother was at home picturing. The place where you actually *were* was a streetcorner with wads of paper in the gutter, or it was standing there, facing the worn muzzle of the horse that had pulled your carriage, or it was sitting in front of a little stain on the tablecloth. *It* really wasn't *like* anything—it was just whatever it was, and there was never a place in your mind of the right size and shape to put it. But afterwards, the thing fit exactly into your memory as if there had always been a place—just right, just waiting for it.

On Monday morning, she would be home. She would be telling her mother over breakfast all about *New York*. And Kyla would know—because she'd be remembering it—just what *New York* was *like*. But today was the biggest obstacle so far. She was so tired that her body kept forgetting to do things in its usual way—even to sit in its chair properly, and Alice was easily upset, as though the nightmares that had plagued her all night long were rustling and hissing at her feet. And Janey was behaving . . . *abominably,* so Kyla had to be extra careful about everything. "It's just perfect," she said.

"Yes, this, girls, is New York as it used to be," Mr. Laskey said. "Genteel, clean, gracious . . ." He sighed. *"Oh, where are the snows . . ."*

Janey rolled her eyes.

It was preferable, Kyla thought, when Janey just *said* whatever horrible thoughts were in her mind. Otherwise they just leaked out and dripped all over *your* mind. . . .

"Try to have a wonderful time, darling," Kyla's mother had said. "And make sure to remember everything for me." And she looked at Kyla so sadly and sweetly.

Her mother was far away now. And tiny, standing there and peering through a dark distance for Kyla. Oh, why did her mother look so sad? Why? *Kyla* knew: because of her, because she had made her mother feel bad. She had made her mother feel—and this was a fact—as though she had forced Kyla to go on this trip against her will. And now, there was her mother, tiny and fragile across the miles, straining anxiously, as if Kyla had become lost right in the field of brilliant stars that at home shone so sparsely and coldly and far away.

Mr. Laskey raised his hand in the air to summon a waitress. "We'll see if the ice cream is as good as it used to be," he said.

"When Grandfather Laskey used to bring you here," Janey intoned.

Mr. Laskey hesitated. "Yes, Jane . . ." he said seriously, as though Janey had brought up some interesting point (but soon, Kyla thought, and her insides felt odd and sparkly, Mr. Laskey was going to decide to get angry), ". . . when Grandfather Laskey used to bring me to New York—"

"—on business!" One of Alice's spoons said enthusiastically to the other.

Janey snickered.

"Put those spoons down, Alice," Mr. Laskey said. He signaled again for a waitress. "It's not nice."

Alice dropped her spoons on the table and put her hands over her face. "Aha," Mr. Laskey said as a waitress appeared. "There you are."

The waitress smiled unhappily around the table. "What pretty blue eyes," she said to Alice, who was peeking skeptically through her fingers.

The waitress turned to Kyla first. She would be supposing, Kyla thought, that Kyla was one of them—that she belonged to the handsome man who only had to raise his hand in the air to bring over a waitress. Kyla, and not Janey. Because no matter how much Mrs. Laskey paid for Janey's clothes (plenty, Kyla's mother said), Janey always looked as if she'd been dressed out of some old lady's trunk. Yes, the waitress was smiling in such a kind and unhappy way—she must be admiring Kyla's soft brown hair, the dainty little skirt and sweater her mother had chosen for her at Baskin's. The waitress herself was not pretty at all. Although that, of course, made no difference. Just, it was what Kyla could feel Janey thinking. "I'm sorry," Kyla said. "I haven't decided."

"So what can I get you, doll face?" the waitress asked Alice.

"What will it be for Alice?" Mr. Laskey said.

"Ice cream for Alice," Alice confided huskily to the waitress.

"Yes?" Mr. Laskey said. He smiled at the waitress. "Are you sure? Or do you want cinnamon toast?"

Alice looked at Mr. Laskey uncertainly. "Cimona . . . ," she began, and halted warily.

"Do you know, Alice," Mr. Laskey said, "that this is one of the few places on the planet, along with our hotel, that still has cinnamon toast on the menu?"

He looked at the waitress, who made a little giggle and then looked surprised at herself. "That's right," she said.

Mr. Laskey tugged a lock of Alice's soft hair. "She's been eating nothing but cinnamon toast since we got to New York," he said. "Haven't you, Alice?"

Alice appeared briefly puzzled, then nodded vigorously.

"Good old Alice—sucking up to everyone as usual," Janey remarked, in some neutral area between audible and not audible.

Mr. Laskey's expression wavered, then settled down. "And what's your pleasure, Kyla?" he said. "Decided yet?"

This was always a terrible moment, and it was one that occurred about three times every day. Her mother had told her to be especially careful not to order the most expensive thing on the menu, but it didn't seem that the price of something was what Mr. Laskey was particularly thinking about.

She shook her head, watching him.

"Well, I'm having a hot fudge sundae," he said. "Why not join me?"

She felt herself beginning to blush. "Okay," she said.

"Good girl," he said, and Kyla tossed her hair back.

"Alice . . . Alice . . . ," Alice began.

"Chill out, Alice," Janey said.

"You want cinnamon toast, sweetheart," Mr. Laskey said.

"Oh," Alice agreed cheerfully.

"Janey?" Mr. Laskey said.

Janey turned to him with the look she could make that was as if she were gazing at something on the other side of a person.

"A promise is a promise," Mr. Laskey said. "Would you like a hot fudge sundae, too?"

Janey continued to stare at him as red waves came up into her face. "Fruit salad," she said.

Mr. Laskey looked down at the table as if it were an old, old enemy. "I'd like the fruit salad, *please,*" he said.

A promise is a promise. And what it was that had been promised—Kyla had been there; she had heard it—was *anything we like.*

It was a night she'd had to sleep over at the Laskeys'.

"I hate going to the Laskeys'," she'd said.

"Well, where will we put you, sweetie?" her mother said. "Because you've had too many sleepovers at Ellen's lately."

Kyla hesitated. "Could we call Courtney?" she said.

"Oh, no, sweetie," her mother said. "I don't think so, do you?"

"Why not?" Kyla said.

"Well, we don't really know the Colliers very well, do we? We can't ask them for favors."

Favors, Kyla thought; was she a "favor"?

"Besides, we don't really know what kind of people they are."

Kyla looked at her mother. "They're nice," she said.

"I'm sure they are, sweetie," her mother said. "But, no."

"Why do I have to sleep over at anyone's?" Kyla said.

"Oh, because," her mother said. "I'm going out to dinner with a friend."

"But—" Kyla said. "So why can't I just stay home by myself? Until you've eaten dinner?"

"And what would you do for dinner?" her mother said.

"I could have something," Kyla said. "From the microwave. Just like I do when you work late."

Her mother stroked her hair. "Just *as* I do."

"Why not?" Kyla said.

"Well, darling—" her mother smiled gently. "Because I need time to see my friends just as you need time to see your friends."

But the point was, Kyla thought, she didn't need time to see her friends. All she and her friends had was time—time and time and time. Waiting through the long, dull afternoons, the whole funnel of Kyla's memory, playing upstairs with the dolls or games or trading cards they'd been given to play with, doing each other's hair, pretending Brides or Baby or Shopping just like Alice did now, pretending—there was nothing else to do—that they were pretending, until it was time to come back down for milk and cookies or for one of them to be taken home. Waiting to understand the point of the dolls or games they'd been presented with, waiting for the afternoon to turn into night or for Sunday to turn into Monday, or for August to turn into September, or for nine years old to turn into ten and ten to turn, heavily, into eleven. Waiting alone in front of the television for the long evenings to fall away. Staring at the screen as if they were staring through periscopes for land, and in the dim evening rooms, the world, the distant world—which was what they must be waiting for—approached, welled into the screens, and the evening fell away in half-hour pieces. And then, finally, there was bed, and another long day had been completed. "What friend do you need time to see?" Kyla said.

"Stand up straight, darling," her mother said. "You don't want to look like Margie Strayhorn, do you? Doctor Loeffler."

Dr. Loeffler—Kyla stared. Dr. Loeffler had come over the week before and filled up their pretty living room, which he was much too big for, and her mother had made Kyla sit there for no reason at all. And the whole time—while Kyla looked at the shiny black hairs on the backs of his hands—this Dr. Loeffler had had a little smile, as if something were funny, or ridiculous. "You were planning this!" Kyla said. "Why didn't you tell me before? You knew you were going to do this!"

"Darling," her mother said with a breathless little laugh. "What do you mean?"

A tear had squirted into each eye, and yet the thing that Kyla meant, which had been so clear the instant before, was gone—simply gone—as if a hand had materialized and closed around it. "I don't like Dr. Loeffler," she said.

"Sweetie," her mother said, and no trace of the laugh was left, "you mustn't be so severe—you only met him once. Dr. Loeffler's a very fine man—He's only forty-two years old, and he's the head of the entire division of internal medicine at Hillsdale."

"Only forty-two years old," Kyla said.

"Don't be such a *cross* old thing," her mother said happily. "Besides, maybe the Laskeys will give you spaghetti again."

The Laskeys had not, however. Instead, there had been some sort of meat with a strange dark sauce and a fancy name.

"How was everyone's day?" Mr. Laskey said—which was what he said first thing every time Kyla had ever had dinner at the Laskeys'. He looked around the table. "Richard?"

Richie raised his serious dark eyes and then lowered them again. "Fine," he said.

"Yes?" Mr. Laskey said. He waited, his fork in his hand.

Dinner had only begun. Soon Mrs. Laskey and Janey and Alice would be crying and shouting, and then there would be after dinner, when Kyla would have to play with Janey, and then there would be morning, when she'd have to play with Janey yet again, before her mother came for her.

"Biology was interesting," Richie said. "We're studying the wheat rust cycle."

"Very good," Mr. Laskey said. "And what about calculus? Didn't you have a test the other day? I never heard how that went."

"That's a third-year class," Mrs. Laskey said. "Isn't it enough that—"

"It went fine," Richie said. "I got an A."

Mr. Laskey nodded. "There you go," he said. "You see?"

Chew slowly, one of Kyla's teachers had said once. *Your stomach has no teeth.* But what she was chewing, she thought, was the body of an animal, with blood cooked into it.

"And track?" Mr. Laskey said.

"Okay," Richie said.

A silence rose separately from Richie and Mr. Laskey and consolidated.

Richie was so . . . dignified, really, was the word, Kyla thought. Everything about him was clean and dignified. Even the way he ate—as if food were clean, as if all the frantic things your own animal's body did with it, with even the body of other animals, was just clean and ordinary.

"*Alice*—" Mrs. Laskey said, and the block of silence over the table became porous and dissolved.

"I came in ahead of Nelson Howell today," Richie said.

"What did I tell you," Mr. Laskey said.

"—You don't have to kill it, Alice," Mrs. Laskey said. "It's already dead."

"I did my report on Native Americans today," Janey said loudly. "Miss Feldman said it was the best report."

Kyla glanced inadvertently at Richie.

"Mother," Richie said, "Jane's prevaricating again."

"I am not!" Janey said. "It was really interesting. In lots of tribes the girls—"

"Pre . . ." Alice began, scowling quizzically at Mr. Laskey. "What does—"

"Absolutely nothing, Alice," Mr. Laskey said. "In this case."

"In *lots* of *tribes* the girls bleed and they go out to little—"

"*Not* at the table, Jane," Mrs. Laskey said.

"Janey made it up?" Alice said.

"No," Mr. Laskey said. "Yes."

"They *do*," Janey said. "They—"

"You heard your mother," Mr. Laskey said. "Not at the *table*." He turned to Kyla. "And what about you? Did you do a report today, too?"

"I did mine last week," Kyla said. And then, because it looked like Janey was about to erupt again, "It was about ballet dancers."

"Bal*let* dancers," Mr. Laskey said. He dipped his head as if he were tipping a hat.

"Bal*let* dancers," Janey said. "Yeah, wow, bal*let* dancers. Well, throw *you* a bone."

Mrs. Laskey snorted.

"Now," Mr. Laskey said. "Who wants more of this excellent . . . This . . . Kyla?"

"No, thank you," Kyla said.

"The child eats nothing," Mr. Laskey said admiringly. "She will vanish into thin air."

"More for Alice!" Alice shouted, flinging herself at the serving plate.

"Alice," Mrs. Laskey said, "kindly restrain yourself—look what you've done to your father's tie."

"Plus guess what, Alice," Janey said. "Your table manners make us all puke."

"Jane," Mrs. Laskey said warningly, "Alice—"

"Incidentally," Richie said. *Incidentally,* Kyla thought. "Scott Ryerson invited me to go skiing with him and his family over spring vacation."

"I want to go, too—" Janey said.

"Oh, were you invited as well, Jane?" Mr. Laskey said.

"Mother," Janey said. "Why does Richie always get to do everything?"

"Nobody said anything about—" Mr. Laskey said.

"But Alice and I never—" Jane said.

"Stop that this instant," Mrs. Laskey said. She turned to Alice, who was plucking at her. *"No,"* she said. "And I am not going to ask you one more time to behave."

Mrs. Laskey's fury was always like a gun pointing at the table; it made you tired, Kyla thought, waiting for it to go off. Her own mother never raised her voice, and she was always kind and patient. Everyone knew how patient she was. Lots of people said it was why (and the other people said it was because) she was such a good nurse. But that was frightening, too. No matter how angry Mrs. Laskey got, it was better than the look of disappointment her own mother got when Kyla did something wrong. Because when people got angry, they were angry and then they stopped being angry, and it was something that went from them to you. But when people were disappointed in you, it was something that went from you to them. You did something to them. It was as if you had made a hole in them, or had gotten a spot on them that could never be taken away.

"Where do Scott's people ski?" Mr. Laskey said.

"See, Mother?" Janey said. "Mother, don't you—"

"Jane," Mrs. Laskey said. "If I don't get—"

"All right," Mr. Laskey said, and everyone stopped talking.

"Yes," he said, quietly. "Fair enough. Janey, your point is well taken. And has given me an excellent idea: Rich will go skiing over spring vacation, I will take you and Alice to New York, and your mother—your *mother* will have one entire week of peace, all to herself."

Mrs. Laskey put down her fork. "Excuse me?" she said. Richie continued his pristine eating. "Correct me if I'm wrong," Mrs. Laskey said, slowly, "but weren't you just in New York?"

"On business," Mr. Laskey agreed pleasantly.

"And now you propose to go right back," Mrs. Laskey said.

"Not *right* back," Mr. Laskey said. "No."

"May I please be excused?" Richie said.

"You may," Mr. Laskey said. "In the future, please do not interrupt."

"I'm sorry," Richie said.

"Apologies accepted," Mr. Laskey said.

"And when did you become so enamored of New York?" Mrs. Laskey said. "The last time you and I were there together, *hellish sewer,* I believe, was what you. . . . It's a filthy place, and you loathe it, and you are now proposing to go right back and expose the girls to it, for what reason I cannot—"

"*As* you know—" Mr. Laskey overrode her "—As you *know,* Carol, the events of my childhood upon which I look back with the greatest affection are those trips I took to New York with my father. As you know, I consider those excursions to be the single most meaningful experiences of my childhood. It was during those trips that I felt closest to my father and learned to honor his values. . . ."

Mrs. Laskey was staring at him incredulously. "His *values,*" she said. She picked up her glass of water and drank until, to Kyla's amazement, the glass was empty. "I should go with you," she said. "That's what I should do."

A long, long look, arcing between Mr. and Mrs. Laskey, was pierced by a rising wail from Alice.

"Alice—" Mr. Laskey said. "What's the matter, sweetheart?"

Alice put her head on the table as though it were about to be chopped off. "It's all right, darling," Mrs. Laskey said. "You're just tired."

"Soon to bed," Mr. Laskey said. "But first, what's for dessert? What kind of ice cream do we have back there? Ice cream, Kyla?"

"No, thank you," Kyla said, because before you knew it, you could turn into a clump, like Janey.

"Yes, please, chocolate," Janey said.

"There's some fruit for you," Mrs. Laskey said. "Remember those five pounds."

"Daddy—" Janey said.

Mr. Laskey glanced at Janey; his glance held and sharpened. "Your mother has spoken," he said.

"And *you* can take it easy, too," Mrs. Laskey said. "I don't want to get a phone call from New York telling me you've dropped dead in your hotel room."

"I don't want to go to New York," Janey said suddenly.

Mr. Laskey took Janey's wrist and Kyla heard her quick intake of breath. "You cannot have it both ways, Jane," he said. "You cannot complain that Rich has privileges and then behave like a prima donna yourself. Of course you want to go to New York. We'll have a wonderful time, if you'll just stop this nonsense." He released her wrist and patted her hand. "We'll treat ourselves like royalty. We'll do anything we want and have ice cream whenever we want. A trip to New York City! Isn't that ideal? Ideal, girls? Ideal, Alice?"

Upstairs in her fancy bedroom Janey had more toys than anyone, a whole closet stacked with games and toys, and dolls, too. She was *spoiled,* Kyla thought, and that was a fact. But the only things she ever wanted to do was play Scrabble or read one of her great, thick books. Or worse, talk.

"My Great Aunt Jane who I was named for," she said, "used to have a mansion in New York. She had a lot of famous paintings, that you see in books, and jewels. Unfortunately she passed away, or I'd get to stay there when I go to New York."

"What happened to all her stuff?" Kyla said. Oh, why was she doing this? Encouraging a person who couldn't help lying was worse than *being* the person. "How come you don't have it?"

"Because unfortunately," Janey said, "her husband gambled it all away. At the . . . gaming table. So we'll have to stay at a hotel, like the Plaza, or the Carlyle. But places like that are all right."

"Do you stay at those places a lot?" Kyla said.

"Well, not just actually," Janey said. "But whenever my parents go anywhere, they always write me letters about it and bring me back . . . mementos. When they went to San Francisco this fall they brought me back a whole huge suitcase full of presents."

"That's nice," Kyla said. She stood up and stretched. "I don't feel like talking any more."

"So what?" Janey said. "Neither do I. I want to read my book."

And then, in the morning, of course there was Scrabble. Kyla could see Richie out in the front yard with John Hammond and then, finally, her mother's car.

"My mother's here," she said. "I'm going down."

"Relax," Janey said. "She'll call up for you when she's ready. We've got time for one more game at least."

"You're cheating," Kyla said.

"Cheating!" Janey yelped.

" 'Sosing' is not a word," Kyla said.

"It is, too," Janey said. "It means to send an S.O.S. Besides, you have to say something when the person does it."

"I'm not playing any more," Kyla said.

She wandered down to the living room where her mother was talking to Mrs. Laskey.

"Good morning, sleepyhead," Mrs. Laskey said.

"Hello there," her mother said, as Kyla leaned on her arm. "Have a good time?"

Kyla nodded.

"We'll go in just a minute, sweetie," her mother said, "but first I want to talk to Carol a bit. Now, run on back upstairs, quick like a bunny."

Kyla freed herself from her mother's careless arm and wandered out to the hall, where she inspected Mrs. Laskey's collection of little crystal animals.

"I *saw* him get the idea," Mrs. Laskey was saying. "I saw it happen. And then he hauled in this load of horse shit about his father—his father's *values*—as vile an old swine as ever lived. What a genius Dick has for exploitation! He exploits his children, he exploits his poor old dead disgusting father . . ."

"Well, Carol," Kyla's mother said carefully, "you have been dying for a break. And this is the . . . . And besides, he probably does want to spend some time with—"

"Dick?" Mrs. Laskey snorted. "That's very funny, Lorraine."

"Well, that's what I mean," Kyla's mother said, encouragingly. "After all, it's not something he does very often."

"And poor Janey," Mrs. Laskey said. "That poor kid is a born stooge. She was so *cute* when she was little. Of course, he simply adored her then. Now, there's nothing the poor child can do to—"

"She just needs friends," Kyla's mother said. "If she just spent more—"

Oh, no! Kyla thought.

But fortunately Mrs. Laskey had interrupted. "The worst thing," she was saying, "is you can see the man operating from a mile away."

"Well," Kyla's mother said, "of course this is a side of Dick I never—"

"*And* it's compulsive," Mrs. Laskey said. "He doesn't even know he's doing it. Do you know, I actually used to feel flattered by it?"

"Still," Kyla's mother said, "it is a wonderful opportunity for the girls. I only wish Kyla could—"

The little glass owl Kyla was examining almost slipped from her hand, but Mrs. Laskey had interrupted again.

"I used to feel flattered that he would expend so much energy just to manipulate me," she said. "That's how pathetic I was. That's where my self-esteem level was. But then I realized he was expending the same amount of effort manipulating everybody. He can't just *buy* a quart of milk, he has to get the store to *sell* it to him. But he's really got me over a—I'd just love to call him on this, but I don't dare give him a reason to—"

"No, no," Kyla's mother said. "At this point, I don't think you want to do anything to—"

"*New York,*" Mrs. Laskey said. "All those filthy people from God only knows where. . . . I just wonder how long this has been going on."

"Carol," Kyla's mother said. "I'm really serious. I really don't think it's prudent to jump to any . . . And besides, it's bound to be a wonderful learning opportunity for the girls. I only wish I could give Kyla an opportunity like this. And if anyone deserves a little time to herself, you know it's you."

Mrs. Laskey sighed loudly, and for a moment—since nothing else was happening—Kyla wondered if she could go back into the living room to get her mother. But then Mrs. Laskey laughed. "So, speaking of duplicitous sons-of-bitches," she said, "how was last night?"

"Why do you have to do it?" Ellen had said.

"I don't *have* to . . . ," Kyla said.

"You *want* to go on spring vacation with Janey Laskey?" Ellen said.

It was already the end of February. Snow from a recent storm still covered the ground and lay along the branches, and the sky was a glassy blue. But Kyla could feel spring marshaling strength right behind winter's fortifications.

"I feel sorry for her," Kyla said.

"I feel sorry for her, too," Courtney said.

"Well, I feel sorry for her, too," Ellen said. "When she's not around. But it's really hard to feel sorry for her when she is around."

"She's troubled," Kyla said.

"Kyla—" Ellen looked at her. " 'She's troubled.' "

"Besides," Kyla said. "I get to see New York."

"New York's great," Courtney said. "I used to get to go all the time. It's the worst thing about moving here."

"We'll probably stay at the Plaza or the Carlyle or someplace like that," Kyla said.

"I still don't see why your mother's making you do it," Ellen said.

"She *isn't*," Kyla said. She looked at Ellen in bewilderment. Oh. Of course. *Ellen was jealous.* "She just wants me to be able to go to all the museums and the ballet and that stuff. And Mrs. Laskey's her friend. . . ."

"Kyla's mom is so sweet," Courtney said dreamily, and Kyla looked at her with gratitude; she was so pretty, sprawled out on Ellen's bed. The prettiest girl in school, and she was *their* friend— Kyla's and Ellen's. Her short blond hair fluffed out evenly, like a dandelion. Her blue eyes—lighter than the sky—reflected nothing.

"But why does your mom like Mrs. Laskey so much?" Ellen said.

"Ellen," Kyla said.

"They have bags of money," Courtney said. "They have a big, huge money bin in their basement, my dad says."

"I think Mrs. Laskey's crazy," Ellen said. "My mother doesn't like her at all."

"My mother feels sorry for her," Kyla said. And then she said the thing she was never supposed to say, not about anyone, or was even supposed to know. "She used to be in the clinic where my mother works."

"I bet she takes pills," Courtney said. "You know the way she's all puffed up?" She studied her fingernails and frowned. "Mr. Laskey's handsome, but I'd hate to be married to him. They came to my parents' cocktail party last week, and Mr. Laskey and Peter Nussbaum's mother were flirting away like crazy."

"Really?" Ellen said.

"Mr. Laskey was flirting with everybody," Courtney said.

Kyla looked at her. Flirting. Flirting, actually, was when you . . . "What was he doing?" she asked.

"Just . . ." Courtney said, "just nothing. He was flirting. He was flirting with my mother, too. I bet he flirts with your mother."

"No he doesn't," Kyla said, and her heart veered.

"Rich Laskey is nice, though," Ellen said.

"Rich Laskey?" Courtney said. "Rich Laskey is *gorgeous*. But you know what? He looks exactly like Mr. Laskey, actually."

Ellen and Kyla looked at her. "Yikes," Ellen said. "That is so *strange*. . . ."

Outside, the air was as clean as an apple, and the crystal branches were glittering. Kyla shut her eyes, to keep Mr. Laskey's face from

Richie's, but the two merged unpleasantly. "I'm sick of sitting around," she said. "Let's go outside."

"It's cold," Courtney said. She shifted on the bed and sighed.

"What should we do?" Ellen said.

All around them were Ellen's toys and games. The television sat, opaque, in the next room. Dark, Kyla thought, but still seeing—still receiving everything that was happening. You could turn it off, but that only meant that *you* couldn't see, behind its darkness, what it was seeing. Sometimes at night, when you had to turn it off to go to sleep, you could feel the world seeping out from the blocked screen—the hot confusion of laughter, the footsteps pounding like a giant, besieged heart, and the squealing tires, the eruptions of gunfire and fearful pictures you couldn't help staring at before they vanished, and people at desks, smiling as though you'd imagined all the rest of it—rising up on all sides of you, staining the walls and the evening with the smells of blood and perfume and metal, staining the helpless moments before sleep, and your dreams, and the tattered edges where you broke through into morning.

"I know what we can do," Courtney said. She propped herself up lazily on an elbow. "One of us can pretend to be Richie Laskey."

How nice it would be to be at home, Kyla thought, in her own room. With the soft darkness outside and her mother right downstairs. . . .

Ellen was looking at Courtney strangely. "How do you mean?" she asked.

Then Kyla turned to Courtney, too, and her heart veered again.

"It's easy," Courtney said. "I'll show you."

"Okay," Ellen said.

The sounds of Ellen's mother moving around downstairs were fantastically loud in Kyla's ears.

"We'll take turns," Courtney said.

"Okay," Ellen said again.

Kyla heard Ellen speak, but she couldn't take her eyes off Courtney.

Courtney was watching her. "I'll be Richie," Courtney said. The clear blue silence of her eyes was like the silence of a clock. "Kyla first." She held out her hand. "Okay?"

□ □ □ □

"Why do I have to go to New York with the Laskeys?" Kyla said.

"You don't have to, darling. Of course." Kyla's mother looked surprised. "I didn't realize you were so upset about it. I was just so astonished when the Laskeys offered—it's extremely generous of them. Of course, I knew Carol would be so happy if Janey had a friend along, but I only accepted because it seemed like such a wonderful opportunity for you."

If her mother knew that Janey lied all the time and used words like *buns,* and *piss,* and even worse things, she might not think the Laskeys were so wonderful. And if she only understood how Janey really treated her when she came over to their house for dinner—that blank *yes, thank you, no, thank you*—You could feel exactly what Janey was thinking, that Janey was thinking about Kyla's mother as if she were the maid.

"I know Janey isn't your favorite person," her mother said.

"I hate Janey," Kyla said.

Her mother waited for a moment. "I know Janey isn't your favorite person," she said again. "But your kindness to her means so much. I'm very grateful, and I know her mother and father are, too."

"I feel sorry for Mrs. Laskey," Kyla said.

"For Carol?" Kyla's mother looked at her with amusement. "Carol's one of the most fortunate women I know. She's just as capable as anything—you don't remember that house when the Fosses owned it. *And* she has the means to enjoy her life, which is very important, darling, as I think you'll find one of these days, though, of course, there are other things that are more important, aren't there. And she's so *attractive.* I happen to know she hasn't done a thing to her face. You're very unusual, darling—most little girls would want to be just like her."

"I'd hate to be married to Mr. Laskey," Kyla said.

"Would you, darling?" Her mother laughed a little. "Well, fortunately, that's nothing you have to worry about. But it could be worse, you know. Dick is demanding, I suppose, and you could say he's a selfish man—or self-involved—but he's cultured and he's broadminded and he's attractive and he's energetic and he can be loads of fun. And he's certainly a good provider. All in all, he's what I'd call a good catch."

Kyla looked around at the pretty living room. Didn't her mother even like it? It was so much sweeter than the Laskeys' big white glassy house, with all its ugly paintings and statues—*sculptures*. "Wasn't my father a good catch?" Kyla said.

Kyla's mother stroked Kyla's hair. "Your father's a very fine man," she said. "He has a kind and generous heart, like you. He just . . . lacks ambition. I suppose it's a good quality to be content with things as they are, but not when you're the father of a young child. It used to—" She stopped, and laughed a regretful little laugh. "The fact is, your father and I just never really belonged together. Although—" she smiled at Kyla "—if we hadn't been together, I wouldn't have you, would I, darling? And speaking of you, what do you want to do this afternoon?"

"Stay here," Kyla said.

"Oh, darling. It's Saturday. You can't just stay in and mope around all day. Isn't there any special thing you want to do? Don't you want to call Ellen?"

"No," Kyla said.

"Or Courtney?"

Kyla shook her head.

"Don't you like your friends any more?" her mother said. "You haven't seen Ellen or Courtney in so long."

Kyla leaned against her mother's coolness.

"Don't *cling,* darling," her mother said. "You're getting much too big."

Kyla jumped away. What if her mother were to see what she herself had seen only this morning, in the mirror, for the first time? She was getting big. It was possible, after all, that she would get those legs that bulged out. Or the horrible little stomach that Judy Winner's sister got when she went into high school. Little things seemed to be happening to her face, too. In the mirror that morning, it had looked as if someone else climbed into her face during the night and was stretching it out into their own. And where was *her* face going? The face that her mother loved? She turned away.

"All right, darling. Please don't sulk." Her mother sighed. "You don't have to go to New York. I just want more in the way of advantages for you than I ever had—I want you to have an exciting life."

"But your life *is* exciting," Kyla said. She stared at her mother. "Isn't it, Mother? Isn't it? Your life isn't boring. Isn't your life exciting?"

"My darling," her mother said, and Kyla saw that there were things happening to her face, too. "My good, kind little girl."

"Janey," Mr. Laskey said, "just eat that nicely, please, like an adult. If you didn't want fruit salad you shouldn't have ordered it."

"Want fruit *salad,*" Janey said. "I didn't want to come on this *trip.*"

"That's not how I happen to remember it," Mr. Laskey said.

"I *wanted* to go skiing with Richie," Janey said.

"When, like Rich, you are fourteen," Mr. Laskey said, "and when, like Rich, you have a friend whose parents own a condo in Vail, then, like Rich, you may go skiing."

"When, like Rich, I am a boy," Janey said.

The waitress loomed hopefully. "How is everything?" she said, looking at Mr. Laskey.

"Just fine," Mr. Laskey said irritably. Then he seemed to remember who she was, and smiled. "Everything just as good as it used to be." He nodded commendingly.

"Well, that's nice," the waitress said. She appeared to be waiting for him to say something more.

Janey cast a small, contemptuous smile at her fruit salad, but Alice burst into tears.

"What's the matter now, Alice?" Mr. Laskey said.

"Anything we want," Alice announced belligerently.

"You have what you want," Mr. Laskey said, looking bewildered.

"What do you want, Alice?" Janey said. "Just calm down and tell me."

"You said you wanted cinnamon toast," Mr. Laskey said.

"No!" Alice roared. She pointed at Kyla's sundae. *"That."*

Mr. Laskey sucked in his cheeks and stared at his own sundae.

"Miss? Miss?" he called. "One more hot fudge sundae, please. For the young lady."

Alice's noisy tears were absorbed into the general cheerful clatter of the restaurant. But it was amazing, Kyla thought, how loud the voices of little children were. Whether it was joy or sorrow or terror, you could hear them screeching blocks away. Not just Alice, though she did seem prodigious, but all little children. It was nature, probably; it was nature that made Alice loud and it was nature that made Alice cute. Nature made little children helpless, but nature protected them, too, with loudness and cuteness. Kyla herself had probably once been able to produce sounds just like Alice's, and she'd never even noticed! And now, no matter how much she might want to let out a howl that would bring the whole neighborhood running, there wasn't a chance of it. Because the minute people struggled to get a bit free of nature, and could begin to take care of themselves, the point was, they stopped being loud, and they stopped being cute.

"All right, now," Mr. Laskey said as the waitress put an enormous hot fudge sundae in front of Alice. "Does everybody have what he or she wishes? Is everybody happy?"

"You bet, pal," Janey said.

"Jane," Mr. Laskey said. "Are we having some kind of problem today?"

Janey held his gaze for a moment and then looked away. "No," she said.

"You're sure," Mr. Laskey said.

"Yes," Janey said.

"Because," Mr. Laskey said, "if there is a problem, maybe you'd like to tell me what it is so we can clear it up right now."

"There isn't," Janey said.

"Isn't what?" Mr. Laskey said.

"Isn't a problem," Janey said.

"What was that?" Mr. Laskey said. "I didn't hear you."

For a moment Janey didn't speak. "There isn't a problem," she said finally, in a low, dead voice.

"That's my girl," Mr. Laskey said. "All problems forgotten. Now—" He looked at his watch. "We'll go back to the hotel for a three o'clock nap, then we'll get up at five thirty, and at six forty-five we'll have had our baths and be ready to go. Everybody with me?"

"I'm with you," Janey said. "You mean we have to have a two-and-a-half-hour nap."

"Aha," Mr. Laskey said. "Another mathematician in the family."

"A two-and-a-half-hour *nap?*" Janey said.

"No!" Alice said in alarm. "It's ideal!"

"You're confused, Alice," Janey said.

"On the contrary," Mr. Laskey said. "Do you know what an adult is? Jane? An adult is someone who's learned to delay gratification. We're going to the ballet tonight, and we're going to have a very late night. In short, this is nonnegotiable. But the question is, we have time for one quick activity before our nap, so what do we all want to do?"

"We all want to go to the children's zoo," Alice said.

"We all want to go to the Museum of the American Indian," Janey said.

"Kyla?" Mr. Laskey said.

"Either's fine with me," Kyla said. *She* just wanted to go home.

"Well," Mr. Laskey said, "we were just at the Museum of the American Indian yesterday. Besides, it's very, very far away—I'm afraid it's impracticable."

"It's only one thirty," Janey said. "We have time."

"Let me be the judge of that," Mr. Laskey said.

"But it's only one *thirty,*" Janey said.

"I think we all heard you," Mr. Laskey said. "And *I* said, let me be the judge of that."

"Children's zoo, children's zoo," Alice chanted.

Mr. Laskey peered at Alice. "Are those dark circles I see?" he said. "Didn't you sleep well last night?"

"No," Alice said nonchalantly.

Mr. Laskey looked at Janey. "What does she mean?" he said.

Janey and Kyla looked at each other. "She had nightmares," Janey said. "She kept me and Kyla awake all night."

"Is this true?" Mr. Laskey said.

"Janey wouldn't let me call mommy," Alice said.

"Did you want to wake mommy up?" Janey said fiercely. "Is that what you wanted, Alice?"

Alice hung her head, and large tears began to form in her eyes. "No," she said in a little voice. Though actually, Kyla thought, Janey was no mathematician at all—it wouldn't have been much past ten at home when Alice first woke them.

"What upset you, Alice?" Mr. Laskey said. "Was it the museum yesterday? Was it the Indians?"

"You weren't there," Alice said. Her shoulders were bowed and she stared at her melting sundae, tears sliding from her wide eyes. "The pond was there, and ice was on it, and it opened up, and you were thin air."

"I'm here, sweetheart. It was just a nightmare. I'm right here."

"That's what I told her," Janey said. "I told her it wasn't real."

"I was—" Mr. Laskey began. Then he looked at the wall, as if something had suddenly appeared there. "Jane," he said, "I'm proud of you. I'm gratified that you took responsibility and stayed calm."

Janey stared straight ahead; amazingly, it looked as if she was about to cry.

"And you know what?" Mr. Laskey said. "I have a thought. I think what we should do before our nap is to get Mommy a present. Isn't that a good idea?"

Janey and Alice nodded soberly.

"We'll get Mommy a present to show that we're thinking about her and to congratulate her for having two such good girls. Now, I'm just going to make a phone call, and when I come back Alice will have finished her sundae and we'll march along."

"We'll call Mommy?" Alice said, still furrowed and dubious.

"We'll call Mommy when we're all together," Mr. Laskey said.

"When . . . ," Alice said, and shook her head slowly.

"When we can be all together at the phone in the hotel," Mr. Laskey said.

Well, it was true; Janey, of all people, had taken responsibility last night. There had been no alternative. When Alice awakened for the second time, rattling as if in the grip of a high fever, and could

not be consoled, Kyla had said to Janey, "Should we get your father?"

"I don't know," Janey said. "Daddy said if we needed anything
we should ask Donald."

Alice, in a damp heap, continued to sob. "But what do we
need?" Kyla said.

"Hmm," Janey said. She and Kyla looked at each other.
"True. . . ."

"Daddy Daddy Daddy Daddy," Alice screamed.

"Be quiet, Alice, *please,"* Janey said. "You're going to wake up
everyone in the hotel."

"Daddy—" Alice screamed again, at an increased volume.

"All *right,"* Janey said. "I'll get him."

But she was not able to rouse him either by knocking on his door
or—when Kyla located a plastic card that told you how to call the
other rooms—by telephone.

Kyla could hear her own heart pounding, or maybe it was
Janey's, as they both snuggled against Alice on the little cot. What if
Mr. Laskey had actually had a heart attack? What if he was lying
there dead in the next room?

"Hey, Alice, let go," Janey said. "I'm going downstairs to get you
a cup of hot milk, and then you're going to sleep."

Janey put her coat over her nightie and went out the big wooden
door of their room, and Kyla remembered that there were many
other people, in many other rooms, all around them. Beyond the
sad blue flowers on the wallpaper, in fact, millions of people, who
couldn't help them at all, slumbered on in the twinkling city. At
least Alice was still cute, lucky for her; Kyla thought of the new
plainness spreading like an illness through her own face. *Don't
cling,* her mother had said. "Do you want to play something, Alice?" she said, when Alice grew quieter. "Do you want to play
Baby?"

Alice hiccuped. "No!" she shrieked.

And then Janey had returned, with, in fact, a big mug of hot
milk. "Here, Alice," she said.

Alice accepted the mug and held it out to Kyla. "Baby drink,"
she said, and hiccuped again.

"Stop that, Alice," Janey said. "You drink that yourself. Pronto. Donald made them put honey in it for you, wasn't that nice? So I want you to say thank you to him the very next time you see him."

Janey sat down stiffly and looked out the window while Alice drained her milk with gulps and sighs and, finally, a little belch.

"Donald said nothing can wake him up when he's asleep," Janey said. "He said once there was a burglar in his apartment and his roommate screamed and called the police and the police came and he slept through it all."

Kyla nodded, though Janey was still looking out the window.

"Lucky Richie," Janey said.

"For sure," Kyla said. And then it was as if Janey had lifted a curtain, and what was there—and had been there all along—was Richie. But Richie blending back and forth with Mr. Laskey— blending with Mr. Laskey helplessly because she had done something to him. She had done something to him, with Ellen and Courtney; she had let something happen to Richie.

The next morning when they got up and got dressed, Janey was still frozen slow and pale. But then there was Mr. Laskey, reading his newspaper at the breakfast table, just as always. "Daddy's here!" Alice observed superfluously. Janey paused; Alice scampered ahead to the table, and Janey went right into the cross mood that had lasted her all day.

"There," Mr. Laskey said when the bracelet they had all—including Kyla—chosen for Mrs. Laskey was put into its beautiful little velvet box. "I think Mommy's going to be very happy with that."

And no wonder, Kyla thought—delicate strips of gold, flashing with stars. It wasn't fair—it would look so much prettier on her own mother. And her mother deserved it, which Mrs. Laskey did not, and her mother would have been so much more grateful to have it. Kyla could just see her mother's face, radiant with surprise and love, if Kyla could present her with just such a little velvet box.

Mr. Laskey raised his hand in the air again, and this time what appeared was a taxi. They all climbed into the back seat quickly enough—Kyla landed a bit sideways between Janey and the door— but when Mr. Laskey gave the address of their hotel, the driver shook his head in disgust. "You'd be better off walking," he shouted over the loud fuzz of his radio. "The whole East Side is a nightmare."

"Thank you for your concern, sir," Mr. Laskey said. "But we'll keep the taxi. It's a good fifteen blocks, and the little girls are tired."

"You're absolutely positive," the driver said. He turned down his radio. "In three more blocks we're not going to budge."

Mr. Laskey smiled. "I understand, sir," he said. "But what do you suggest? We're too tired to walk, and our hotel's on the East Side."

"I suggest, sir," the driver said, "seeing as you're determined not to walk, that you move to the West Side."

"Ha, ha, ha," Janey said.

"Because furthermore," the driver said, "once I get into this shit I'm not going to be able to get out."

"I'll bear your difficulties in mind, sir," Mr. Laskey said.

"It does me good to hear you say this," the driver said, "because in a situation like today I starve."

The cab, which had been hurtling from side to side, causing Alice to turn a delicate green, was indeed slowing down almost to a standstill. "It costs me more to hire the fucking car on a day like this than I can make."

"I will, as I've said, sir, bear that in mind," Mr. Laskey said. "Jane, human beings do not lead difficult lives for your personal amusement. Our driver is understandably anxious, but once we get past the bridge traffic everything will be fine."

But within one more block they had entered a solid mass of honking horns in which Kyla's fatigue seemed to entrap her like amber. And after a time Mr. Laskey leaned forward. "What's the problem, driver?" he said. "We haven't moved for twenty minutes."

"What's the problem?" the driver said. "The problem is we aren't moving. Or, wait—you mean to ask what's *causing* the problem."

"That was my intention," Mr. Laskey said. A pulse had begun to throb in his forehead. "Yes."

The driver turned around and stared at Mr. Laskey. "Oh, hey—" he said, and struck the side of his head with his palm "—I get it! From which, ah, *planet* do you folks hail?"

"Perhaps you'll be so kind . . . ," Mr. Laskey said.

"With pleasure," the driver said. He turned the radio up savagely, but it was almost impossible for Kyla to hear through the static and the honking what it was saying. There was an apartment building, somewhere near their hotel, and there were policemen—

"Who?" Janey was yelling over all the noise. *"What did he do?"*

" 'Who?' " the driver yelled back. " 'What?' Incredible. Every radio station in the city. Every television network in the universe. More blood per cubic foot than the siege of Stalingrad. Where are you from, folks, seriously now—New Jersey?"

"Tell me, tell me, tell me!" Janey was shouting.

"This is not important, Jane," Mr. Laskey said.

"Not important," the driver said. "Right. Not important. Well, of course it's not important. You types really stick together, don't you? Sure, if the guy's rich enough, if the guy's handsome enough, if the guy remembers what kind of mineral water each of his patients drinks, it's just not *important* if he bludgeons his wife to death with a floor lamp, is it? It's not *important* that he pulverized her."

"I don't think this is strictly—" Mr. Laskey began.

"Oh, pardon," the driver said. "I have the honor of addressing a gentleman of the law, I'll wager. It's been *alleged* that this guy liquified his wife; it's been *alleged* that the neighbors waded in through body parts; it's been *alleged* that he fled, dragging his poor little child with him, to his girlfriend's apartment where the cops later found a sweater, all gunked up with hair and blood that allegedly matches his wife's; and now it's being alleged that he's up on the roof with this kid and he's—"

"Sir, I do not think—" Mr. Laskey said, and Alice began to cry.

"Nothing's going to happen to you, Alice," Janey said. "No one cares about you."

"That's right, Alice," Mr. Laskey said. "Nothing's going to happen to any of us."

"Oh, hey—" The driver turned around. He looked into Alice's eyes and took her hand. "Hey, I'm sorry, darlin'. It's going off, right now." He turned the radio off. "Click, right? No more depressing stories."

"Sir," Alice said, and rubbed her cheek against his hand.

Mr. Laskey sighed. "Alice, sweetheart," he said, "let the man drive."

"Why did he do it?" Janey said. "Daddy?"

"We'll never know, Jane," Mr. Laskey said. "Normal people can never penetrate the mind of a sick individual." He rolled down his window and thrust his head out.

"The wife was trash," the driver said. "What do you want to bet? A slut. A nag. A gold-digger. All the same, he should've just divorced her."

"Girls—" Mr. Laskey looked at his watch. "—I'm afraid it would be a great deal faster to walk at this point."

"Hey, listen to this guy, kids!" the driver said. "The original rocket scientist. *It would be faster to walk!* When do you think Mr. Wizard got a chance to perform the calculations? Say—" he turned around with raised eyebrows "—how's *right here* for you folks?"

"Do we get to pat the goaties?" Alice said as Mr. Laskey opened the door.

"Alice," Janey said, "you're confused again."

Mr. Laskey handed the driver a bill. "Here you are, sir. I sincerely hope this will recompense you for your time."

"And *I,* sir—" the driver dropped the bill into the gutter "—sincerely hope *this* will encourage *you* to reinsert your patronizing shit back up your butt, where it came from."

"The second we get inside," Mr. Laskey said as they straggled up the steps to the hotel, "I want you to get yourselves upstairs—It's way past three. Way, *way* past three," he added, shaking his head ominously. "And I want you to wash those hands. Alice's especially."

"Her hands are clean," Alice said loftily. "She washed them after lunch."

"That was after lunch," Mr. Laskey said. "You've touched God knows what since."

As they stepped inside the hotel, five or six young men in uniforms—bellboys and desk clerks—swiveled away from a small television on the front desk. Their eyes, brilliant with excitement, dimmed immediately into courteous greeting. "Hello, Mr. Laskey," one of them said. "Horrifying, this business, isn't it?"

"Horrifying," Mr. Laskey said, glancing at his watch irritably. "Come *along,* girls."

"Oh, Mr. Laskey—" Donald disengaged himself from the group and hurried over.

"What's that?" Mr. Laskey frowned back at Donald.

Donald hesitated.

"Yes?" Mr. Laskey said. He paused, looking at his watch again, and Alice bumped into his leg.

"That is," Donald said, "Miss Shawcross was here for you. I'm afraid she just left."

"Didn't she get my message?" Mr. Laskey said.

"I don't know, sir," Donald said.

"My mother's on the phone?" Alice said.

"Shut up, Alice," Janey said.

Alice tugged Mr. Laskey's sleeve. "Janey said, 'Shut up, Alice,' " she reported.

"Be quiet, Alice," Mr. Laskey said. "But I left her a message at her office. Didn't she get it?"

"I don't know, sir. She didn't say."

Alice sat down suddenly on the carpet.

"Your dress, Alice!" Janey exclaimed. "Get off your butt. Mother would kill you!"

"My mother would kill *you,*" Alice said, but she scrambled to her feet, swatting at her rear end.

"How are my girls?" Donald said. "Imaginations cooler in the light of day?" He winked at Janey, who gazed serenely at a point on the other side of his head.

Mr. Laskey appeared to wake from a trance. "Don't we say hello to people who say hello to us?" he said.

"Ah, Stan—" Donald said, and one of the uniformed men wrenched himself away from the TV screen to open the door for a man with a briefcase, and the blaring of horns entered the lobby.

"This is the damnedest business," Mr. Laskey said. "God damn it."

"Horrible, sir," Donald said. His eyes flicked eagerly toward the TV. "Incredible what a human being can do, isn't it?"

"You can play with your toys, Alice," Janey said. "You don't have to just lie there."

"Yes, I do," Alice said. "It's nap time." A large tear trickled from each eye.

"What's the matter?" Janey said. "Are you afraid to fall asleep? Are you afraid of having another nightmare?"

"I want to go home," Alice said. "I want to see Mommy. I want Billy and the big rope."

"Is she all right?" Kyla said. "What does she mean?"

"Oh, nothing," Janey said. "She gets Billy Jacobs to tie her up."

"I don't feel well," Alice said. She rolled over into her pillow.

Kyla looked at Janey. "Should we get your father?" she said.

"No," Janey said. "She's playing. Are you playing, Alice?"

"Yes," Alice said mournfully. "I'm playing Disease."

"Nurse—" Janey said. "The patient in bed number one has a horrible disease. She needs a sleeping potion."

"Right away, Doctor," Kyla said, and poured a glass of water in the bathroom.

Alice fell asleep before she even finished her water, and Janey picked up the big book she'd brought along, but Kyla looked at the dark TV screen. "Don't you want to see what's happening?" she said.

"No," Janey said. "I'm reading."

Kyla stood up and looked out the window. But of course there was nothing to see except tall apartment buildings, where everyone would be watching television to see what was happening. And below, nothing but stalled traffic stretching on and on, lines of cars like strands of colored beads. Lots of blue and green and black, more yellow, not so many red. . . . If there were fewer than fifteen red, it wouldn't happen. If there were more than fifteen. . . . The steely hand on the child's shoulder, the caress of metal against soft hair, the entire universe exploding in her skull, vanishing into thin air. The entire universe exploding—the universe—how many times was Kyla going to have to see it? To hear it? *"Please* let's turn it on," Kyla said. "Just for a second."

"No," Janey said. "I don't want Alice to wake up. I don't want Alice to freak out again. My father said we should rest, because we're going to the ballet tonight. My father's the one who's paying for this hotel. My father's the one who paid to bring you along."

"I know," Kyla said.

"Stuff like this happens all the time," Janey said. "Even at home. There was this person at home, in fact, who was a famous judge, but his wife was a secret drug addict, and he was afraid someone would find out. So one day he said, 'Goodbye, dear, kiss kiss, I'm going away on a trip to get lots of presents to bring home to you, and I'll be back in a few days.' So he drove his car down the street and waved to all the neighbors and he put a plastic bag over his clothes so he wouldn't get blood on his tie, and he snuck back. Lucky for him, it was the coldest winter in a hundred years, and there were icicles hanging from all the trees and houses. So he opened the door and dragged his wife outside and snapped off the biggest icicle he could reach and he stabbed it into her stomach stab stab, and there was splash splash blood all over the place and his wife tried to scream but she was dead. And then the judge snuck back to his car and drove to the airport and flew away. And the next day the sun came out and all the blood and the murder weapon melted into the ground."

"So how did they catch him?" Kyla said.

"How should I know?" Janey said, and turned back to her book. "Nobody, ick, talks about it, obviously."

From down below the soft tumult rose gently, like the sounds of a beach, Kyla thought, when your eyes are closed. What was going on out there? What was happening? Everybody else could see. Donald could see, and the taxi driver and the waitress would be somewhere by now watching, and all the people in all the other rooms of the hotel and in the little buildings out the window, and Miss Shawcross, and far away, in the mountains, Richie was watching—Richie was watching helplessly—and across the body-choked lagoons, Mrs. Laskey and Ellen and Courtney were watching, and her mother and Dr. Loeffler, twisting together on the sofa, were watching, their blood pounding and their eyes shining—

No—her mother was alone, pale, sitting bolt upright and trembling for the poor little child, *not* with Dr. Loeffler, that was what *Janey* thought; Kyla sprang up and turned on the television. ". . . to de-lethalize the situation—" a voice was saying. Janey reached the dial before the picture even came on, but Alice was awake already, and crying. "Thanks, Kyla," Janey said. "Thanks a lot, old buddy."

"I'm sorry—" Kyla said.

"Where's Daddy?" Alice roared. "Where's my daddy?"

"Hush, Alice," Janey said, curling up beside her on the cot. "Daddy's asleep in the next room."

But Alice had begun to scream. "Should we get your father?" Kyla whispered. "Do you think we should go get your father?"

"Our father's asleep," Janey said. "Our father's resting. Our father's asleep in the next room, and he doesn't want to be bothered, and plus, she's going to get over it."

Susan Fromberg Schaeffer

The Old Farmhouse and the Dog-wife

From *Prairie Schooner*

HE SAT AT THE TABLE, his head in his hands, and thought about what, over the years, he had done to the house. He was wearing blue jeans and an old plaid shirt. The blue jeans had been washed so many times they were soft, like flannel, and faded almost to white over the knees and the crotch. The rim of the pant legs, where they brushed against his leather boots, were beginning to fray. He fingered the sleeve of his shirt, which was soft and thin, thinner than a summer shirt, and remembered how stiff it was when his wife bought it for him, how stiff and bright, although now it had faded until the red plaid design was barely discernible, and when he stood back from the mirror to take himself in, the shirt was rose-colored and vaguely patterned. As time passes, he thought, things become softer. Look at the shirt, look at the jeans, look at his skin, look at the clapboards on the porch, the wood so soft you could push a pencil point into them. At what point would he grow too old to make the repairs on this house himself?

The man who came in winter to plow the road to the house still called it the big white farmhouse, although of course now it was smaller, because in the years he had the house, he had torn down the barn and the screened-in porch that ran the length of the two front parlors. His wife had been against these demolitions. She would take out the pile of old photographs displaying the original owners of the house swinging from their hammocks on the small porch in front of the kitchen, or sitting on their fancy chairs in front of the large porch. She was particularly fond of one postcard that showed an automatic sprinkler, something the owners had evidently invented themselves. They were there in the background like shadows while in the foreground, water, caught in the act of falling, suspended itself in a rain of silver beads over the whirling metal arms attached, somehow, to the thick garden hose. *It works!* read the message on the back of the card. *Look at this handwriting, how spidery it is!* his wife said. *And the ink, this color purple. I believe they made the ink themselves!*

The house was built in 1780, and for this reason his wife was against making any changes, as if, should the first owners come back, they would not recognize the place and begin to reproach her. He suspected her, moreover, of having a religious faith in the rightness of old things simply because they were old, and when he accused her of this, she had nothing to say in her own defense, and so he knew he was right, not that she liked to argue. When they first married, she would argue about everything, or so it had seemed to him, but after they had been married some years, she would shake her head when something saddened her and go about her business, humming. When she was displeased with him, she said nothing, but somehow, whenever he entered a room she had a task that took her somewhere else. If he came into the kitchen and she was baking, she had to attend to the clothes on the line outside. If he followed her behind the house to the clothesline, she remembered the pies in the oven, dropped her clothespins into the little twig basket, and hurried back inside. It was like pursuing a nervous cat, and eventually he stopped. He knew when he was forgiven because when he entered a room, she stayed where she was.

He was tearing boards away from the barn walls one day when his wife came out and stood behind him. "Don't stand there like a guilty conscience," he said to her. "Take up the old nails."

When he had stripped the planks from the walls, the barn stood there, its slate roof varnished with dew. Now that the clapboards were down, you could see through the barn to the hills in back of the house. "Someone coming along wouldn't know if it was going up or coming down," he said. His wife made an odd, choking noise and gathered up a handful of the old nails. They were long and thick, with oddly shaped heads. "I know you think if something's been standing a long time, that's reason for it to go on standing forever," he said. When he turned to look at his wife, she was gone. He saw her going through the kitchen door, back into the house.

In those days, he was fond of saying that life was a struggle. The weather was against you, the bank was against you, and your own children were against you. He felt genuine pity for the barn swallow who every year built her nest over the kitchen door, and in the late spring when he got up and went out and saw the nest filled with gaping, squawking beaks, he would shake his head in commiseration every time. It made sense to try and even the odds. If the barn came down, there would be no more climbing up on the roof to nail down loose shingles, no more climbing up there in the winter to shovel off the roof which, under the weight of fallen snow, was threatening to collapse. If the big porch came down, there would be no need to climb out the bedroom window and shovel off that roof, no need, in the spring and summer to jack up the porch roof and repair the rotted floorboards. *What you can get rid of, that you should get rid of,* he said, quoting his father.

Of course while they had a horse and a cow the barn had to stand. In exchange for two loads of gravel from the gravel pit up the road above the house, a man in the village gave him an old red cow and he took it, thinking it might give a little milk, and if not, he would slaughter it and cook it into stew. The cow, which promptly became his wife and children's pet, gave so much milk the sound of churning was heard day and night, the buttery overflowed with butter and cheese, and the children's cheeks rounded. In those days, they often paid bills with cheese and milk and fresh-baked bread. In those days, too, cars were less reliable than you would like them to be, and his children always arrived at the school in the horse drawn sleigh, and not only his children, either, but the children of other families who were stranded in cars stuck in snow-drifts along the roads. In those days, the barn was steamy with the breath of the cow and the horse and the pigs and the heat from the wood stove, and the smell of the bales of hay. In those days the barn had a use, but when it had no use, he began to tear it down. It seemed to him obvious that useless things ought to be torn down and it annoyed him that this was not only unclear to his wife, but was the source of discord between them.

He sat in the old kitchen in front of the old kitchen table and worked on his drawing of the house as it looked when he first saw it. They had been looking for a place for two years when he drove over the little bridge, turned right, and saw the big white farmhouse smack in the middle of its eight acres. "This is it," he said. From the porch of the house, there was no other house in sight. The thick trees on the bank of the creek hid the road from view, although in winter when the leaves fell, they would be able to see passing cars and the old white house across the road.

His wife observed that the house was a wreck, that its roof leaked, its walls were rotten, and you had to hop from floorboard to floorboard unless you wanted to wind up in the cellar, which was no more than a hole cut in the ground and lined with stones. Inside, the house was cut up into many tiny rooms, some not much larger than cupboards, but he said he could knock down the walls and install wood stoves and put up chimneys and in six months the house would be warm enough to live in while he continued to work on it. His wife stood on the porch, and the cool breeze blew the smell of fallen pine needles toward her, and an enormous stand of lilacs was in full, aromatic bloom.

"One thing," said his wife. "I want a nice bedroom. I don't want to sleep in a half-finished room." He promised her a nice bedroom and they bought the house outright. The owner was glad to get rid of it. There were sinkholes in back of the house, where the water ran off from the hills behind. Probably the previous owner saw the house as a responsibility he was happy to have off his hands.

His drawing of the house had progressed, was, in fact, almost finished, when he heard the sound of a car's motor outside the house. He got up, stiffly, and walked through the open kitchen door onto the screened-in porch. His old dog, Ruff, heard him get up, lifted his head, sniffed the air, and lay back down. "You are a useless animal," he said to the dog.

A brilliant green Dodge was idling on the curved drive that wound around the lilac bushes, its nose pointed at the house. The sun glared on the windshield so that he couldn't see the driver, but a white-shirted arm came through the open window and opened the car door from the outside. He stayed where he was, watching. The driver got out, reached down and rubbed his knee, then looked up at him, smiling. "I was hoping for a drink of water," he said. Still smiling, he held out a silver canteen. It glinted in the blinding sun.

The farmer stood on the porch and looked at the car, thinking, Once I had a car like that. It was a 1950 Dodge. Everything about it was familiar, its curved swelling shape, its rounded bottom, its divided windshield. "How does it run?" he asked the stranger.

"It runs fine, but it eats gas," the man said. Everything about him was thin. His gray hair was thinning. "Until I get where I'm going, I don't have a nickel to spare," he said. "Every penny goes for gas and oil."

"I'll get you some water," he said, walking down the steps and over to the car. The thin man was about to hand him the canteen when loud, frantic barking erupted from the back seat. "Got a dog?" he asked the thin man.

"Well, not exactly," the stranger said.

Before he could say anything, Ruff erupted into loud barks on the porch.

"My dog thinks it's a dog," the farmer said. He could feel the smile leaving his face, but the thin man was smiling more intensely than ever. His teeth, he saw, were bright white, the color of brand new kitchen sinks. If his wife were still here, he thought, she'd say, Why doesn't he just wear a sign saying, *I paid a lot for these teeth*? A man with teeth that white, he thought, has something to hide.

"I could use some cold water," the thin man said. "My name's Fred."

"Fred," he said. "What about your dog? You want some water for your dog?" He moved toward the back seat of the car, but the man moved in front of him. When the stranger turned back to him, he tripped over Ruff, a big old shepherd, and as he righted himself, the farmer moved quickly and looked through the window into the back seat of the car. "My God," he said. "That's no dog."

"Well, I never said it was a dog," Fred said.

In the back seat of the '50 Dodge was an unkempt woman, very thin, her bones showing everywhere, her gray hair long and wild. She was up on her hands and knees, crouched down, her nose almost against the glass, crouched and growling as if she were a dog.

He moved away from the car and a few steps away from Fred.

"What's this, now?" he asked him.

"Don't get excited," the thin man said, his eyes on him. "Nothing to get excited about."

He thought about his rifle, behind the kitchen door. If this man Fred had a gun in the glove compartment, he could take it out and shoot him in the back as he walked back to the house.

"She must be hot in that hot car," he said.

"Oh, she is hot," the man said edgily. "Hot and thirsty. How about that water?"

"I'll get it and come out," he said, and turned to walk into the house. When he got to the porch, he turned, expecting to see the thin man pointing a gun at his back, but the man's head and shoulders had been swallowed by the back window and the blackness inside the car. Ruff was sitting on the grass behind the thin man, his head tilted to the left, as if he were trying to hear better. He took down his rifle, walked to the kitchen sink, and filled the canteen. As he passed, he looked at the picture he had drawn of the house, but in the picture, the house looked deserted and unreal. Once it had been a stagecoach stop. He should try drawing the stagecoach in front of the house. The drawing needed something to bring it to life. He walked across the porch and back outside. The thin man was extricating himself from the back of the car, wiping sweat from his forehead.

"That gun isn't a real friendly thing," Fred said.

"It's got nothing to do with you," he said. "There's a woodchuck tearing up the shed floor."

"A woodchuck," said the thin man. "Well, a lot of people start seeing woodchucks after they look into that car."

"You kidnapping her or what?" he asked, the rifle still under his arm.

"A man doesn't have any call to kidnap his own wife," the thin man said.

"She's your wife?" he said. "She looks older."

"She always did look older," the thin man said, "but after she fell ill, she looked a lot older. The doctor said it happens. When they're sick that way, they hold their faces stiff, and their faces freeze that way."

"She's sick or she's crazy?" he asked, moving closer to the car. When he was near enough to the window to see his face reflected in it, the crouching woman rose up on all fours and began snarling, then barking ferociously.

"A little bit of both, I guess," the thin man said.

He looked over his shoulder at the thin man who felt edgy but not dangerous. The farmer had been a hunter all his life. He thought he knew when an animal, man or beast, was threatening. This man wasn't threatening, not this minute, although he knew he could be. The farmer turned away from him and thrust his head suddenly against the car window. At this, the crouching woman jumped up, pulled her teeth back, and began barking like a mad-dened, chained dog. He turned to the thin man.

"She knows who she is?" he asked the stranger.

"Well, I couldn't say," the man said. "She clearly thinks she's a dog and she clearly thinks it's her business to protect me. She always was a protective kind of woman."

He looked from the thin man who stood with his hands thrust deep and tight into his jeans pockets and back to the '50 Dodge. A hot wind picked up the elm branches and dropped them down. An elm in front of the house was diseased. "I want it to last as long as we do," his wife once said, and after that he paid the tree surgeon his exorbitant yearly fee. From the look of things, the tree was going to outlast him. He thought again of the old stagecoach that used to stop in front of the house, and for the first time thought about the original owner of the house and what misgivings he must have had each time the coach stopped and let out its load of strang-ers, any one of whom could be a thief, a murderer, or worse.

"Where do you sleep at night?" he asked the man. "In the car?" The thin man nodded. "I guess you don't want to answer questions," he said. The thin man smiled a tight, wry smile. He held tight to the silver canteen of water. "The streams around here are good and clean, you know," he told the stranger. "You can drink from them and not worry about anything."

"Yes, well," said the thin man. Now that he had his water, he seemed ready to go.

"At night it drops down very cold. Well, since last Monday it's been dropping down very cold. I came home last night and already there was smoke coming out of chimneys."

"It's a nice smell, that wood smoke," the thin man said.

"Not so nice when you're chopping the wood, though," he said. "Look. My hands are full of splinters."

"Your wood's all chopped?" the stranger asked.

He thought about the wood in the shed, stacked from floor to ceiling, stacked against all the walls, six or seven cords. Since his wife died, what did he have to do but chop wood?

"Look," he said to the thin man, "you could stay here the night, but you'd have to tie up—"

"Tie up the dog. Sure," the thin man said. "She likes being tied. You should see her, how she curls up and lies around my feet."

"Well, I wouldn't have gone so far as to call her a dog," he said.

"She's not yours," the thin man said flatly.

"Why don't you come in now and have a sandwich?" he said. He looked nervously at the car.

"Oh, she eats anything," the thin man said. "I'll put her on her leash."

"You put her on her leash and bring her in," he said.

They were sitting in the kitchen, eating buttered frankfurter rolls and drinking bottles of beer. He had quieted Ruff, who lay under his chair, his ears down, his nose pointed in the direction of the woman whose feet and arms were tied together. She lay peacefully on the floor next to her husband who, every now and then, reached down and handed her a piece of buttered roll. He fed her piece by small piece and she took each one gently and chewed it up. After she swallowed each piece, he said, "Good girl, Martha," and the woman would tilt her head of grayish blond hair and look gratefully up at him, although at times her eyes looked spiteful.

"This is a nice house you have here," the thin man said, looking around. "You did a lot of work on it?"

"It was rotting when we got it," he said. "But the original beams were good, under the floor and under the roof, so little by little, I did it over. Those wide planks on the floor? They're from the old barn. I sanded them down after I pulled the barn down. The beams in the ceiling? The original beams. Can you imagine the trees, how tall they were then? How many oxen it took to pull them back through the snow?"

"I know these old houses," the thin man said. "A jumble of tiny rooms. You can see clear from one end of the house to the other in here."

"That's my work," he said. "I told my wife, 'We have a wood stove, we have all the wood we need, if we get rid of the walls, we can heat the whole house with no trouble for no expense at all.'"

"I bet she didn't like it," the thin man said, handing down a bit of buttered roll. The wild-haired woman took it between her teeth, chewed it and swallowed it.

"She said, 'Who wants to sit on a couch and look at the kitchen sink,' but after a time she saw I was right. Easier to clean, easier to heat. Do things the easy way, that's my motto."

"She died long ago?" the thin man asked.

"Five years this April," he said. "She sat down on the couch, picked up a book, made a funny little noise, and then she sort of slid against the arm rest. She's buried out there in the back, way out back, under those two big willows."

"You changed anything in the house since then?" the thin man asked. The woman on the floor lifted her head and growled slightly.

"Well, I added a few more dirty dishes to the sink," he said.

They sat in silence. The thin man's index finger began tracing the geometric design which bordered the enamel-topped table. "This is a nice table," he said. "Real old-fashioned. When I was a boy, my father did sums on a table like this, right on the table with a black crayon, and when he was finished, he took a damp rag and wiped the table down."

"Two thousand and fifty little knife marks," the farmer said. "All the times she cut up vegetables or meat or dough on this table top. Thousands of tiny scratches, but you have to look to see them." He saw it was getting dark and got up to turn on the light over the table.

"It's wicked dark outside for five o'clock," the thin man said.

"It's going to storm," the farmer told him. "I always feel it along my skin, the way it lies there, like a knife blade you took out in the sun."

"I hope it doesn't storm," the thin man said. "It frightens the dog. Once she broke a table, trying to hide herself under it. Some dogs are afraid of thunder, you know. They don't flinch at guns, but thunder, that's something else."

"She's not a real dog," the farmer said and then was sorry he said it.

"If it storms, I'll have to tie her up hand and foot and put a blanket over her," the thin man said. "It's for her own good." He looked around the kitchen and from it to the parlor where a gray couch and two gray velvet chairs surrounded a pink flowered rug. "Sometimes when a person dies and you don't change a thing, you're keeping the house like a monument to them. Sometimes it means you really loved that person. Sometimes it means the opposite altogether. 'This was your house, this was how you wanted it, now you're gone, I'm never going to be bothered with it again,' that's what you're saying."

"If it's going to storm, maybe you should take her out to the bathroom," he said. "Before the lightning starts."

"Oh, she can use the indoor plumbing," the thin man said. "She remembers how to do that."

"Sometimes I wonder how well the house is grounded," he said. "I don't like to sit on a toilet in a thunderstorm."

"I'll take her now," said the thin man. He untied the woman's feet and led her off. Before they entered, the woman turned, looked at him and growled.

I can think of one hundred good reasons why I shouldn't have let him in the door, he said to himself. Outside the trees sighed, just as his wife would have sighed if she were there.

When he returned, they began to talk. The thin man talked mainly about his wife, how one day she had begun to grow forgetful. For instance, she would put down her pocketbook and search the house for it when all she had to do was stop and think what she had been doing when she first came back in. Then it got worse. He would come home and find her going from room to room, looking for the pocketbook, and there it was, swaying from her wrist. Of course, he said, all that wasn't too bad, but when she forgot to turn off the burners on the stove, or when she put a pot on and forgot to turn down the fire and the stew boiled over and the grease caught fire, well, then she was a plain hazard. The doctor said, hire a helper, and he hired one, but she got away from her and they found her trying to wade across a river in the middle of December and when they got her out of the ice water, she had a three-inch gash in her foot, so the doctor said it was time to put her away, and he was thinking about putting her away when she got it into her head that she was a dog, and she'd been a dog ever since. But he didn't have the heart to put her in some asylum, so he took her with him in the car, and when it was warm enough, they went from place to place sleeping in the Dodge, and when it was cold, they headed out to the little island on Maine where she grew up and where they still had a little house. In the winter they were the only ones there so no one came out and asked questions. You know how it is in these small towns, he said. If you want to be left alone, they leave you alone. Every so often, he said, he sat Martha up in a chair at the window when the postman went by, so the man saw her sitting there. Half the people in the shore villages were recluses for one reason or another, so they thought nothing of it. Probably they thought she didn't come out because at her age she was afraid of the ice, slipping on it and breaking her hip. The towns were full of old people who only came out when the ground was smooth and dry and otherwise stayed inside playing solitaire and watching television. You only need one experience going out for wood and falling and lying there and waiting all day hoping someone will find you and then you don't want to go out anymore. You move the woodpile indoors, you don't care what it looks like. Everyone up there has a TV dish, he said. They have to. They have nothing else to do. And the funny part is, he said, it seemed to him that every other house had a member of the opposite sex: first a widow, then a widower, then a widow, and so on down to the last house on the street, and it didn't seem to occur to any of them to double up. A whole line of sad arks, he said, just one of a kind in each one and the name of each animal out there on the front stoop or the mailbox, like the name of the particular kind of animal it was. If he were a free man, he said, he wouldn't waste time moving in with someone else.

"I never gave it much thought," he told the thin man.

"Well, Martha here, she used to say that a happy widower wasn't much of a compliment to his dead wife, because, if he'd been happily married, he'd want to be married again. You did say that, didn't you, Martha?" He reached down and patted the woman's head. Just then, thunder crashed and shook the house, Martha raised her head toward the ceiling and began howling. "She'll never eat her franks and beans now," the thin man said.

"Well, you must have had one of those happy marriages, that's obvious," he said. "To go to so much trouble to keep her with you."

"Oh, we weren't happy at all. Never were. Always snapping at each other, always disagreeing. I was restless, always wanted to go back out to sea, and she'd say, 'Then go!' and throw a shoe after me, well, it got to the point that the children knew if they heard something hitting the wall and then falling down that I wanted to go back out and she was against it, so I never did go, but I never did stop complaining and she never did stop trying to prevent me. So that's how it went on, until this happened. 'I am your cross to bear.' She used to say that. 'I am your cross to bear.' "

"But how do you know she's sick?" he asked the thin man. "Maybe she's plain crazy and a doctor in one of those places could do something for her."

"I took her to doctors," the thin man said. "They said she had that aging disease, but whatever she had, there was nothing they could do for it, so I thought, well, we stuck together this long, she was a faithful wife, I owe her this much."

He shook his head.

The thin man saw it and said, "I know what you're thinking. You don't know if you could do it. That's right. You don't know. If anyone had asked me, four, five years ago, what would I be doing now, I'd have told them I'd lock her up and throw away the key and live the life of Riley. Well, maybe I am living it. Anyway, I can't do otherwise."

The storm was right over their heads now and the lightning flashed and crackled and lit up the kitchen appliances, once white, but spray-painted yellow when his wife, looking through home-making magazines, decided her kitchen looked too much like a hospital. He hated yellow. Yellow was the color he liked least in the world, but he knew better than to suggest painting the cabinets and refrigerator blue. "Blue is a terrible color," she used to say. "When you have it indoors, what can it look like but a poor imitation of the sky?"

Now when the skies rumbled and crashed, the walls of the house shook. He was not afraid. The house had stood this long. It would continue to stand after he was long gone.

The thin man was covering his howling wife with a blanket. Ruff stood up, his big paws on his knees. The dog was frightened by the woman on the floor, howling like an animal. Ruff was not frightened by storms.

The night wore on in this way, the two of them drinking beer, eating franks and beans, or bacon and eggs, or buttered rolls, the thin man untying his wife when the storm died down to take her to the bathroom, then tying her up again. Finally, by morning, the sky was clear and he said, "You must be worn out. Up over the shed there's a bedroom at the head of the stairs on the right. Go get some sleep." The thin man untied his wife's legs and led her, yelping and growling, up the shed stairs after him.

By morning the sky had cleared and the storm was over. He went out into the shed and started up the mower and began mowing the three acres he and his wife had kept cleared in front of the house. The triangular stretch between the road and the bank of the creek, which his wife had claimed as a flower garden, had long ago overgrown itself with weeds and small scrub trees and he never started up the mower without casting a guilty look at that unattended patch. The grass was still wet and it was slow going, but at least he'd made a start. The neat swath he carved out in front of the lily beds under the house windows would taunt him until he brought the rest of the lawn to the same state of grace. He had just cut the motor when the man came out of the house.

"The wife's tied up upstairs," he said. "She can't do harm."

The two of them stood still, looking at one another, then out across the meadow to the mountains, soft and green in the still misty light, breathing in the smell of wet, cut grass and taking in through their skin the cool glassy feel of the freshly washed air.

"Have some breakfast?" he asked the thin man, who said, "I don't mind if I do."

He cooked bacon and eggs and toasted bread on the oven grill because after their third toaster had broken down, his wife said the best bread didn't fit in them anyway; she was tired of pulling bread out piece by piece and finally turning the toaster upside down to shake out the last broken pieces and crumbs, and why waste money on a toaster when they could make toast just as well in their wood cook stove which was always on anyway. He himself liked bread crisped in a toaster, where it came out having a purer taste than bread from the oven, which inevitably tasted smoked and redolent of whatever meal had last been baked inside that black cavity, but he had respected his wife's wishes while she was alive, and he supposed he was respecting them still. When she was alive it had always been a question of money, where the next two cents was coming from, but now that she'd died and the price of land had gone so astronomically high, all he had to do was sell off part of his acreage, and he'd never miss it. He never even saw it anymore, it was too much trouble to borrow a horse and ride up there, and he'd lost his nerve for the snowmobile ever since his neighbor took his up a mountain trail, ran out of gas, and was clawed by a cougar, probably after he froze. Probably he never knew he was clawed by a cougar, but still. Well, if he sold off even a small part of his land he'd be a rich man and wasn't that something, that he'd finally gotten to a place where he had no need for money at all?

As he toasted the bread, he spoke of this to the thin man, although he omitted any mention of how much land he had, and how, if he sold it, he could be a rich man, because he could hear his wife saying, "Don't talk about money to people unless you want them to cut your throat." She had strong opinions on everything, his wife, and whenever possible, she enforced them on everyone else, a strong woman altogether, although not strong enough to last as long in this world as he had.

The thin man said he'd better go up to get his wife. "She'll be ready for her visit to the water closet and in the morning she's always hungry as a horse," he said, and disappeared upstairs.

He took out the butter, put it on the counter in the square of sunlight to let it soften, and turned over the bread on the baking tray in the oven. Some things were nice about women as they aged, he thought. For one thing, you could take them for drives without stopping at every gas station and asking the attendant for the key to the washroom because they were never so frantic about anything as they were about getting blood on their skirts. He stood there, smiling, thinking of the high excitement on the highway while everyone in the car strained for the sight of a gas station or a rest stop while his wife sat next to him, white and immobile and panic-stricken. For their children, these panics were funny, but not for his wife, a member of what their oldest girl called The Clean Generation. "You think this is funny, but it is not," his wife told their daughter. "Wait until it happens to you." And this would strike them as the funniest thing of all, and while he hunted for the next garage with bitten lips, the children whispered to one another in the back and roared with laughter. "From now on," said his wife, "when it comes to those days of the month, I stay home."

The thin man tied a rope to his wife's ankle and then to a leg of the table. "She won't run off now that she's familiar. She won't cause trouble at all," he said.

He set out three plates and dished out the scrambled eggs, the bacon and the toast. He had a large container of homemade applesauce left him by the woman across the creek, and filled a large blue and pink-striped ceramic bowl, and set that down in the center along with the two-gallon bottle of milk. He had to lift that bottle with two hands because of the arthritis in his wrists.

"I guess once she was a good housekeeper," he said, looking

down at the woman on the floor, who was growling up at the table. The thin man lowered a full plate to the floor, whereupon the growling stopped.

"She was terrible, the worst," the thin man said. "My mother, when she came, used to say, 'You look before you let anyone in here because if that person is from the Board of Health, they will condemn this house surely as I'm standing here.' I went into our bedroom one day looking for her and I didn't see her anywhere and I searched the house and I was about to go call the police when she came walking out the bedroom door. The bed was so heaped up with things I never saw her sleeping there. And once she picked up a load of laundry and threw it over the railing from the second floor and it let out a yowl and what did she do? She'd thrown down the laundry and the family cat. Well, she never knew the cat was in there, of course, it was such a mess. Of course you think I'm exaggerating. I'm not embroidering a thing. When the boys moved out, we had to close off their rooms. They were filled from floor to ceiling with trash. Not just used clothes and toys. Dishes, cups, forks, everything. When I tried to clean it out, she'd get upset and start ranting. The boys, when they called up, they'd ask, 'How many rooms you got left now?' We had this beautiful greenhouse-sun porch combination I built with my own hands, but we couldn't use it, it was so filled with trash, and then she had two dress racks set up in the living room so she could sort out her things, but she never did, so they stayed there permanent, until I sold the house. We didn't get much for it, neither, because how could we? Most people opened the front door and beat it back to their cars."

"So she was a good mother," he said, buttering a piece of toast and turning it this way and that, as if it mattered which corner he bit into first.

"Terrible," the thin man said. "She had no patience at all, not in the early years when they woke up crying at night, and then, when they got bigger and got into bigger troubles, she had so much patience you wanted to kill her. They'd come home at one in the morning, two in the morning, and I'd be out driving around, and she'd say, 'They have to take care of themselves sooner or later,' and go back to her painting. After the youngest was four years old, she said, 'That's enough cooking,' and she never cooked a meal again. She was a real trial in the house, I can tell you."

Painting! Then she was an artist! So that was why he had put up with her! He'd said as much.

"Oh, she was real talented," the thin man said, "but even then I should have known there was something not right. All she painted was dogs. If she saw a nice dog in the village, she'd go plead with the owner as nice as you please, her hair all washed, wearing her best dress, until they'd let the dog stay with us until she finished the picture. I don't know how many rugs we ruined because of those dogs, since, naturally, they wanted to go home and didn't like it in a strange house with this woman who was always hollering at them to sit still."

"You have any of those paintings?" he asked the thin man, who said, Yes, he had a few folded up in the trunk of the car. "Folded up?" he asked, and the thin man said yes, the best thing about them was how easy they were to transport because they were painted on the best quality velvet. Well, the thin man said, they used to look upon the paintings as an investment, because after all they did bring in money.

"People bought them?" he asked the thin man, who said, Oh, yes, she sold most of the portraits. You'd be amazed at how sentimental people were about their pets. For years they made a pretty good living off those paintings, but then things began to go wrong. Well, first they went wrong in the paintings, and then they went wrong in real life. But it was a shame about the paintings, because while they were going well, there was always money for fixing the roof or getting a rebuilt engine for that Dodge out there.

The farmer wanted to know what had gone wrong with the paintings.

First of all, the thin man told him, she gave up velvet and began painting on wood. And not just any wood. It had to be wood with lots of cracks in it, and the planks he cut down for her had to be wide planks, so he was always looking for a barn about to come down. And then the dogs! Well, you could recognize who the dog was supposed to be, at least for a while, but sometimes the dogs' flanks were covered with fish scales, and sometimes the dogs had wings springing from their dog collars and even bigger wings springing from their sides, and sometimes their tails were curved and curled and ended in snake heads. And that was just the beginning, the thin man said, picking up another piece of toast. After she started ruining the dogs, she couldn't stop and she'd paint a wingless dog with the face of the postmaster or the owner of the general store or the local minister, and then there were dogs with saints' faces and halos over their pointed ears, and dogs with horns and devils' tails, but always with faces of people in town. "So," said the thin man, "everyone was insulted, and everyone said it wasn't very neighborly of her, and if that's what she thought of them, then she could just go shop in another store, and then I had all the shopping to do and everything else as well, and it wasn't long after that she forgot to turn off the gas and went off wandering into town and getting on buses and when the bus came to its last stop, she just sat there because she didn't know what she was doing on the bus or who had put her on. So," he said, taking another bite of his toast, and picking up his mug of milk, "that's how we got from here to there."

"You have any of the paintings she did on wood?" he asked the thin man.

"Some idiot from the city came and took them all off," the thin man said. "He said, 'I'll give you a hundred dollars for a hundred paintings. That's fair enough,' and I said 'Done,' because how could we take them in the Dodge anyway and whoever bought the house, he'd only use them for firewood. He seemed happy to get them. A New Yorker probably. My cousin, he runs an antique shop, he says you can always recognize them. When they see something they want, they pick it up and carry it around the shop with them as if some big bluejay would fly in the window and make off with it, but country folk, they put the thing back down and walk far away from it so you won't think they're interested. But I saved some of the nice ones on velvet, to remind me, because I guess one of these days I'll miss that house. I have one on burgundy velvet—that one's a dalmatian—and one on black—that one's a French poodle. They're the most artistic."

"I saw an article somewhere about paintings of dogs with human faces," he said. "In a paper in here somewhere. Maybe I burned it up. But if I didn't it's in that basket."

"It's something I don't need to see," the thin man said. "It will only remind me."

"Dogs with people's faces in some museum," he said.

"You're fixing over that bedroom at the top of the stairs?" the thin man asked. "You need any help? To tell you the truth, wouldn't mind another night in a warm bed. I can't stretch out these legs in the back seat of that car."

He said he wouldn't mind the company and he could use some-one to help with the sheetrock for the ceiling and besides that, he was opening up the wall near the door and he knew his wife put things in there behind that wall the last time he paneled the room, souvenirs, things to let the next owner know who lived here, like a time capsule, that's how she thought of it.

Shortly thereafter, he was prying loose the sheetrock from that wall. The thin man crouched behind him. His wife lay in the middle of the room, her head resting on her thin arm. When a car or truck passed by on the road on the far side of the creek, she would raise her head and growl slightly, look first at her husband, then at him, and lie back down. "Well," he said, sitting back on his heels, "this is it."

On the other side of the sheetrock was a flat, oblong box. He took it out, opened it, and saw it was filled with photographs. The topmost were snapshots of his children and of the house. Beneath were copies of the first photographs of the house, when it still had its barn and its two front porches. He handed these back to the thin man, who looked through them.

"Houses are full of ghosts," the thin man said.

"Not this house," he said. "I never felt this house was haunted."

"That's because your wife kept these pictures and gave them a place," he said. "She did them an honor."

Probably he is crazy as a bedbug too, he thought, traveling as he does with this—and then he hesitated because he didn't know how to say it—*dog-wife?*

Still, he could see it, he could see it happening. Already he was used to the woman lying on the ground, growling like a dog. Already he liked feeding her bits of buttered bread from the table. He liked filling the plate for her and watching her eat as if she'd never seen food before. This wasn't affection. This was growing used to something. You grew used to it, you grew fond of it, pretty soon you thought you loved it. He saw clearly, saw it so fast and so vividly, it was as if it had already happened, that if the man and his growling dog-wife stayed on, the two men would compete for the attention of the mindless woman on the floor. They would push one another at the table, hustling to see who could get her plate ready first. In a few weeks, in a month, whoever was first to stroke her wild hair would be glared at by whoever was still sitting with his hands on the table. Proximity was everything. Whoever said that familiarity bred contempt, that person had never lived in an empty house, alone except for the creaking of the floorboards and the walls, contracting and expanding in the heat, sighing and squeaking like something half-alive, night after night. No, what familiarity bred was familiarity, the biggest part of love.

He took out another box: three pairs of tiny shoes, the first pair each child owned. The leather had discolored and cracked and the laces looked brittle. His fingers moved slowly over these shoes before he handed them behind him to the thin man. A small doll, what the children used to call a Grandmother Moses doll, an old black typewriter whose keys stood up in the shape of a fan. She had used that typewriter, but what had she ever written? Some letters back to her family in Ohio. But maybe she'd written other things, things he didn't know about, letters to other people. "Well," he said, "I guess that's it," thinking, not much to show for fifty years of married life, when his eye caught sight of something farther in. He edged carefully in between the strips of molding toward the thing farther back, and finally his shoulders and then his body were through, but when he pushed back behind the wall of the house, his body shut out the light. His hands retained the memory of the object and closed on it and he knew immediately that his hand had closed on something once made of skin and bone. He carefully lifted the object and began working his way back out through the hole in the wall.

"Well, look at that," said the thin man. "A cat skeleton." On the floor, his wife growled but did not stir.

"That's Daisy," he said. He held the cat in both hands like a precious object. The thin man watched him, saying nothing. A great silence fell over the house, and present time slid away like a decal washed from a wet window and outside it was thirty years ago and his wife, slender in her rose-printed house dress, seemed to drift above the mowed meadow grass, her hands to her mouth, calling *Daisy! Daisy! Come on, Daisy! Time to eat, Daisy!* Then she would stop, stand stock-still, and lower her hands, place her hands on her hips and stare out into the meadow, looking for the cat. He watched from the kitchen where it was cool and hopeless, knowing she would not find the cat. Probably, he thought, the cat had been caught by raccoons and never made it back. He saw his wife turn back toward the house, wave helplessly in the direction of the kitchen window, her hand moving up and down with an odd, floaty motion, as if it were made of fabric, as if it had become a surrendering flag. She began drifting, rose pattern and all, under the floating clouds, in sight of the brook in which clouds floated, back toward the white house, floating in the middle of the green green sea of the meadow.

"She is gone," said his wife.

"The raccoons," he said again.

"I don't believe it was the raccoons," she said. "I don't believe she is really and truly gone."

"Well, eat something," he said.

"Eat something. That's your answer to everything," said his wife. Still, she chewed absently on a piece of leftover doughnut. After awhile, she stood up and looked out the window, where, of course, there was no sign of the cat. "Sometimes, when you lose something, you're relieved," she said. "Other times, you say to yourself, 'I've lost a little piece of my soul.' And you tell yourself, 'It's just a little piece.' But one little piece and then another and then another and one day there's nothing left."

"It's only a cat," he said.

"Yes. Well," said his wife, fixing him with a look that always frightened him, as if to say, If you were a piece of wood, you'd have more reason to exist on this planet, on this part of the planet where I myself exist.

"My wife loved this cat," he said to the thin man. "When it was gone she never really believed it went away."

"They're always right," the thin man said. "Always. They speak in riddles like the Sphinx."

"She didn't know where the cat was," he said. "If she'd known, she'd have torn down the walls."

"What are you going to do with that cat?" the thin man asked him, and he said he guessed he'd put it back where it was. Or maybe he'd take it out and bury it next to his wife, deep, deep, so that nothing could come along and dig it up.

"Which is it?" the thin man asked. He said he didn't know. He supposed it would depend on how much energy he had when he got around to it.

"You kept this house up real well," the thin man said, and he told him he had no choice: his wife was always after him to fix this and that.

"When we first came here," he said, "people used to call this the house with the pink walls, because of the insulation, you know. Once I got the insulation in—in those days it came in pink rolls— then I felt finished. We were warm enough, there was a lot to do out in the barn and all around, so I forgot about the walls. But she said she was tired of these pink filaments all over everything, and besides, she'd long ago picked out wallpaper and why couldn't she have walls like everyone else? So eventually I got it done. But you look around, you'll see there's always something left undone, like the floorboards where you slept last night. They're mostly painted, but then there are stretches of unpainted wood because a bureau used to stand there and I thought, Why move the bureau? So she used to say, that was my signature, something left undone. And usually she'd follow after me and finish the thing up, but not always.

They stopped talking then and began to work on the room. When they were finished, they looked like ghosts, so thoroughly were they covered in plaster dust, and then they went down to the creek, leading the man's wife on her rope, and the three of them bathed until they were clean. They sat on the bank of the creek and let the sun dry them out.

"I guess you loved her," he said to the thin man, who looked at his dog-wife, and said, "No, I didn't love her in the old days, but I love her now." He began beheading the purple clover near his left hand. "But you," the thin man said, "you must have loved her."

"She always made me feel I was in the wrong," he said.

"But you loved her," the thin man insisted.

"I guess I did," he said. "But at night, I had this habit. I used to like to come out and look at the stars and see if they'd moved any since I last looked at them, dropped down the sky, or whatever they do. And she'd always say, 'Shut the door. The heat is escaping.' And I used to laugh at her. 'The heat is escaping!' When it was always too hot in that house, even in the coldest, open winters because of those wood stoves! And the idea of the heat *escaping!* As if it were something alive that spent its time plotting to get out! So you know what happened. After awhile, I stopped going out to look at the stars and the heat couldn't escape. I used to think about the heat, locked up in the house with no hope until spring. I used to laugh at her about it. But she'd just look at me and think what an impractical man I was. A male flibbertygibbert, that's what her mother called me, whatever that meant."

"Well," said the thin man, "I guess I'd better be getting on if I want to get to Maine tomorrow night." He jiggled the rope and his wife got up on all fours and began crawling to the house. "Stand up," he said, and the dog-wife got up and walked stiffly toward the old Dodge. "It was a nice break in the journey," he said. "We're much obliged to you."

After the man and his wife had gone, he went in and cleaned up the kitchen. Then he went up to the room over the shed and put the skeleton of the cat back where he found it. He replaced the other objects where he had found them. This was a simple matter because the dust had settled around them and when he disturbed them, they left their outline on the unpainted wooden floor. Then he sat back and proceeded to talk to his wife, who, for one reason or another, seemed at that moment to be inhabiting the house.

"Helen," he said, "this life is a mysterious thing. Can you tell me why he is traveling the countryside with that dog-woman?" Outside, the wind sighed in the trees and he took this for an answer. "And you, after all those years of dissatisfactions, you weren't really dissatisfied with me, nor was I with you. 'You can't let them know how important they are to you.' I heard you telling that to Emily the night before she married and I thought, 'Shut up, woman! That is the worst advice I ever heard!' But of course Emily is happy with her husband.

"Still, I want to know why that man sticks with that dog-wife. Why is it no one can know the most important things? Was it accommodating and accommodating that led to love, or was it love that gave you the patience to adjust and shift until you hardly recognized the person you became? Poor Daisy here, dying inside the wall, trying to get back to you and you're out there, scouring the countryside, nailing up reward notices to trees and stores! I want to know: we felt so much for one another. Was it love? We spent a life together. We were married longer than some people live, but that's not the same thing. Or is it the same thing? Tell me. I want to know."

Nothing disturbed the silence in the house. He picked up the piece of sheetrock, cut to fit over the section of wall behind which his wife had hidden the objects precious to her. There was no photograph of him, none of her. Perhaps she thought those photographs belonged to him, that they would keep him company for the rest of his life in this empty house. But what should he do with the skeleton of the cat? He put the sheetrock down and decided to work on another wall. There was no reason he couldn't leave this task for last. Besides, he wasn't ready to nail in the three small pairs of shoes.

He thought that he had loved his wife best when they were first married, least when their children began to grow, and most when the children left home and she had little use about the house. Of course she cooked and cleaned for him, but she was no longer a mother, could no longer be a mother—she was too old. He loved her most when she was least necessary.

Outside, he could hear the wind lifting and dropping the great elm branches, stirring with a low moan through the pines they had dug up in the forest. Once they were only seedlings they had dug up in the forest and seen disappear beneath the first, shallow snow. Now the pines were so tall their shadows covered the meadow in the afternoon and licked at the wooden steps leading up to the screened-in porch. The white birches shook their shimmery leaves in the late afternoon light like spangles, like sequins on his wife's dress when she dolled herself up for weddings and christenings, and he looked at the wall and could see the birch leaves as clearly as if he were looking at them through a window, as if the walls and the lathing and the beams had suddenly become utterly transparent. And he saw the dust around the curved roadway blown up into the air by a brisk wind, an autumn wind, although sometimes you got winds like that early in August, it all depended, and if the wind blew the dust just right, it hung in the air for an instant and caught the light, and each dust particle shone like pure gold. And then he saw himself carrying the lawn furniture out from the shed and setting it up in front of the house even though there was still snow on the ground, because in country where the winters lasted so long, you wanted to take advantage of every second of summer, and then, when the leaves began blowing across the meadow from the bordering trees, he saw himself carrying the furniture back into the shed, hosing down the plastic cushions and leaning them against the house walls to dry. These must be the things that mattered, he told himself, carrying the furniture out every season, carrying it back in as the season changed, his wife standing on the porch steps watching and smiling, saying nothing, or watching from the kitchen window, smiling and not even waving, but there was no need for a wave. And he stood still, looking through the wall, and there was his wife, kneeling on the grass, holding her trowel, planting tulip bulbs and crocuses and irises and lilies, and every year when she came back in, she would brush off her skirt and say, "That is my act of faith," because who without faith would plant bulbs in the winter that did not come up until spring? And he would lean against the barn door and watch her and smile even when he didn't know he was smiling, but when she dug her lily beds she was the sun that reaches you in the deep pine woods when you believe no light can ever reach down to that deep place where you are.

Lilies and weeping willows, she was so partial to them that he used to tease her and say there was nowhere on the property you couldn't lie down and fold your hands over your chest and call the photographer to take a picture of you beginning your last, deep sleep. These, he thought, were the things that signified something to human beings. These were the things you remembered, not what you thought, at the time, you would remember, all those things you squirreled away into albums and keepsake boxes, so that now when you looked at them, all you could ask yourself was why on earth you had kept them. Even the children, who were now gone: how rarely he thought of them. And when he did, he remembered them as the small, bright beings they were when they first arrived home, wrapped in their flannel baskets, set safely in their bassinets. Then years had passed and what had they become? Just three more grown-ups. It was a mystery, what you remembered and what you did not, what mattered to you and what did not.

All his life he had tried to get things down to their simplest, easiest forms and so he had torn down the barn and the long front porch. He thought, now, he had been foolish. Now he wished there were unnecessary things for him to look after. It occurred to him that the unnecessary things might be the things one truly loved.

In the distance, a dog howled, and another took up the cry, and then another, until you would think every house in the valley had someone breaking in through the back door. Perhaps, he thought, he should get a new dog, a big dog—he liked big dogs—that would last as long as he did. Well, he didn't want to ask for more than that. You had to be reasonable.

The wind, as if it were getting the last word, as if it were his wife's voice, sighed and sighed again in the many, great trees.

Patricia Elam Ruff

The Taxi Ride

From *Epoch*

JIMMY WENT OVER to the dialysis clinic at Howard Hospital three times a week. He had to sit for four hours at a time hooked up to a machine with all them needles in his arm. One of the boys would take us over there in the morning and I'd stay until it was time for him to go on the machine. I'd go to the cafeteria, get my tea and drink it with him while we waited. Sometimes Jimmy wanted me to read Maya Angelou out loud and I'd do that, too. His eyes was startin to go bad from sugar diabetes, but he said he liked the way wrote-down words sounded when I said them. While he was on the machine all he did was watch TV.

When Jimmy first started goin to the clinic I used to stay all day with him, but the boys could see it was wearin me down (my pressure kept goin up and I couldn't rest much as I needed). They decided I should go on home stead of waitin there; one of them would bring Jimmy back after they got off work.

After the nurses came to hook Jimmy up, I'd leave and walk to the bus stop. Weather had got real cold and I'd have to take the scarf from my neck and wrap it round my hat to keep the wind from biting my ears. I'd get my coat buttoned almost to the top but then I could feel that arthritis kickin up again, making my fingers act like they wasn't mine. Bus took me down Florida Avenue to West Virginia Avenue. Sometimes I'd get lucky and somebody'd take pity on me, I guess, and give me a seat. (It ain't like it was when I was growin up—my mama woulda beat my hindpots if I didn't jump up and give my seat to an elderly person.) When I did get a seat, my feet'd be so tired from standin, they'd like to cry when I finally sat down.

I was standin out there waitin for the bus on one of them real cold days when I could see my breath. I started thinkin bout Jimmy to take my mind off the cold. I wondered if Jimmy was ever gonna be hisself again. Seem like so much of the old Jimmy was already gone that it'd be a mighty far ways for him to come back. The old Jimmy used to stay up late talkin to me, bout his dreams for us and the world. He used to say come retirement we was gonna travel all around, go back to places he'd been when he was in the war. Like Paris, France and a village in Italy where he said they got streets so small only two people can walk down them at a time. He described the places so good I felt like I'd be able to find my way around once I got there.

Before retirement had a good chance to impress us, though, Jimmy started gettin sick. The sick Jimmy didn't do much talkin, seemed to take too much effort. Them legs of his that liked to dance on the weekends became full of pain and slow-movin; his skin that used to shine from smilin withered up and turned the color of ashes. I knew he was getting close to dyin. It would be specially on my mind when I was watchin him sleep. He used to sleep hard as a rock and snore somethin awful with his eyes shut tight. But them sick days, seem like he was half-expectin to die every time he went to sleep—the way he kept his eyes open a crack. Only the white part showed and it made him look like he was on the way to see his Maker.

I'd touch his arms or his chest gentle-like, just to let him know I loved him and he'd try to wink at me the way he used to but instead, it just looked like he was blinkin. Then he'd usually start talkin some mess bout gettin with the boys so he could get his papers straight. That way I wouldn't have no burdens when he was gone. And I'd tell him it didn't matter bout all that, I just didn't want him to leave me. Then he'd get quiet again and sad lookin and go on to sleep.

One of my days was twin to the next. I don't care much for the mess they got on television—too much cussin and killin and people half-naked so I'd read my books and my newspaper until Oprah came on—most of the time I can stomach her show. Then I'd cook dinner. By that time Latrice would be home from school and soon, Edward or Lance would bring Jimmy home. After dinner Jimmy'd sit in front of the television and fall asleep there most likely. I'd help him get in bed. Most nights I'd fall asleep after I started readin again, but sometimes I'd need to make myself a hot toddy. Them days, I got real acquainted with lonely.

A young girl with two babies came and stood next to me at the bus stop. It was all I could do not to tell her to cover the baby's face up from the cold and wipe the other one's nose. Snot looked like it'd been there since the days of Methuselah. My boys, Lance and Edward, keep tellin me not to say nothing to strangers nowadays—specially the young ones. And they right. I don't know what's got into some of them teenagers but they just plain crazy. Read in the paper the other day bout a poor seventy-five-year-old woman (same age as me) who told one of them young girls she should stop slappin her child around. Next thing you know the girl done punched the old woman. Well, you don't have to tell me twice. When I saw this young girl at the bus stop I just held my tongue and told myself: it ain't that bad. Just a young girl who don't know what she doin.

The girl, tired of waitin I guess, started tryin to flag down a taxi. There was one taxi man who was always around drivin folk to and from the hospital and he used to ask me all the time did I need a ride. Sometimes he'd say, "Ain't gonna charge you today, ma'am," but I never took him up on it. I was thinkin, I wish he woulda asked me today, that's how cold it was. Anyway, he drove up when the young girl put her hand in the air. He musta read my mind, too, cause he rolled down the window and said, "Mighty chilly out, ma'am." I looked around every side of me to make sure he wasn't talkin to somebody else. When I seen he was talkin to me, I thought about how I only had enough money for the bus and I didn't want to be nobody's charity case. I just wrapped my arms around myself and said, "No, sir, thanks for askin, though."

Well, next thing you know that man got out the taxi and came over to me. Now he ain't a young man, mind you. I don't think a young man would give a damn. This was a well-seasoned man (the way Jimmy was fore he got sick) wearin a raggedy but respectable sportscoat and tippin his hat to me. "The hawk's out here today, ma'am. I don't want it to get you so I'll take you where you got to go. No charge."

My cold feet overtook my pride and I sat up front next to him cause the young girl was in the back with her two squealin babies. We dropped her downtown at the paternity and child support place on G Street. I thought bout changin to the back seat when the girl got out but that's all I did was think bout it. He had some of them beaded seat covers up front. Them things feel like a miracle on your back; leave the imprint on your clothes, though.

He took one hand off the steerin wheel and extended it to me. "Name's Alonzo Murphy, ma'am. D.C. born and bred." And he gave an uphill laugh along with his name.

I took his hand in my glove without looking at him cause I didn't want him to take his eyes off the road. "Helen Jones," I said. "You any relation to the Murphys belong to Israel Baptist up on the hill?" I held my purse on my lap, gave me somethin to do with my hands.

"Could be," he said. "Most of my people gone from here, though and I don't do much church-goin. But could be. Had a white lady in here the other day, looked at my hacker's license and said her father-in-law name Murphy, too. I told her same thing—never know, could be some relation." He let out that rich laugh again.

"What the white woman say to that?"

"Well, she didn't have too much to say. She was just tryin to make conversation at first, I guess, and when I said we might be related it got a little uncomfortable for her."

I told him where I was goin when I realized he hadn't asked.

"You in a hurry?" he said, slow as beans cookin in a crockpot.

I thought for a minute. I looked at his hands, brown as a paper bag, restin on the steerin wheel while we was stopped at a red light.

His fingers were thick and knotted; hard-workin hands but with a kindness to them. His hands reminded me of my daddy who picked tobacco for most of his life. I noticed he wasn't wearin no weddin ring. I twisted mine around and around, rubbin my finger back and forth cross the small diamond Jimmy had saved so long to get.

I looked at Murphy's eyes, too, when he asked the question. Tired eyes, with specks of red in them. Truthful eyes that don't try to hurt nobody.

Murphy had one of them green air fresheners in the shape of a tree hangin off the cigarette lighter and it smelled just like a pine cone. You could hear the heat hummin along with the soft music station on the radio. It was a nice change from the rap songs the kids play on the bus that set your head to poundin. Somethin told me wasn't no call to be scared, Alonzo Murphy wasn't no serial killer or rapist. For one thing, he was too old to be one. I glanced at him again from the corner of my eye. He was singin along with the radio tune, his hat tilted to the front of his head like Frank Sinatra. The way his beard seemed to smile along with his mouth set my mind at ease.

"I ain't in no hurry," I said, unbuttonin my overcoat. I surprised myself but there wasn't nobody or nothin home waitin for me, that's for sure, so I was only tellin the truth.

Murphy drove around, pickin up passengers and pointin out sites in between, even though I told him I had lived in D.C. for most of my life, too. We talked bout things I hadn't thought bout in a long time, from black people tryin to bleach their skin to Adam Clayton Powell, Jr. "Folk couldn't understand why he married that Hazel woman. Thought she was just too dark for him. But that woman was a looker, I'll tell you. She was a real looker." Then I felt him lookin at me. "I hope you don't mind me sayin so, but you could almost pass for her twin."

My face felt feverish and my eyes were jumpy. I didn't know what to say. The only men I talked to, other than Jimmy, was Mr. Washington cross the street, Preacher Wilkins, the deacons at church and my boys, who sometimes pass for men.

But I let Murphy drive me around for a couple of hours and

didn't think nothin more bout it. Acted just like I was sposed to be there when he picked up and dropped off passengers. I noticed how Murphy could conversate with anybody. He joked with some of the businessmen bout the stock market and which football teams did what over the weekend, he discussed the President's European trip with somebody from the Russian Embassy, and he talked numbers with two ladies we picked up near Rhode Island and Brentwood, coming from a church meeting. The next people he picked up was a man and woman couldn't hardly keep they hands off each other, just kept gigglin, smoochin and gettin on my last nerve.

Murphy drove through Northeast, tellin me he had lived for awhile in the Parkside projects, which used to be off Benning Road, but don't exist no more. He had a buddy who lived in some other projects and they was always arguin bout which had the most broken windows and the worst reputation. We was laughin and then Murphy got serious, makin creases come in his forehead. "We was poor as dirt back then," he said, "but we wasn't comin apart at the seams the way we is now. As a people, you know what I mean? We wasn't killin each other, that's for damn sure."

I felt an excitement growin in me because the way the conversation was headin reminded me of how Jimmy and I used to talk about things. It had been so long since somebody was interested in my opinion (all Lance and Edward wanted to do was tell *me* what to do, like they the parent). I told Murphy bout my seventeen-year-old granddaughter Latrice (Edward's chile Jimmy and me raised) who been to more funerals in one year than I been most of my life (cept for now when my friends is dyin off like flies). "What you think gonna make all this violence stop?" I asked him.

"More whuppins," he said just like that. "Young people nowadays don't whup they kids way they did when we was comin up. My mama would beat us for what we was thinkin about and damn near kill us for what we did. If these kids got more beatins at home, they wouldn't be actin like they do out here on the street. I wish I had me one big long hose to whup all of them."

"Ain't that simple," I said. "You can't just beat kids. You gotta talk to them. I'm tellin you what I know. I wish I'd talk to my own more and beat them less. Kids today got more things to face than we did. I believe they scared and they got a lot to be scared of."

"Like what?" Murphy seemed impatient.

"Like this crack cocaine, this AIDS, all these guns and killin. I read in the paper the other day bout eleven-year-old kids plannin they own funeral. They ain't got no business thinkin bout stuff like that."

The love-birds in the back of the cab interrupted us to say we was approachin they destination. Murphy slowed down near a three-story building, collected his fare and let them out. "I don't know," he said when he started to drive again. "Sometimes I think there's too much thinkin and figurin out bout problems. We didn't waste a whole bunch of time on thinkin. I know my mama and daddy didn't. You did wrong, you got beat, you learned your lesson. That was that."

We kept on talkin and Murphy kept on drivin and pickin up "fares" as he called them. I was wonderin bout why he wanted to give me a ride in the first place but I figured maybe underneath his smilin, he was just lonely like me. He had a smooth way of drivin so I didn't even feel all the bumps in the street, way I do when I'm ridin with my boys. He said he been drivin a taxicab since he dropped out of high school. "Same one?" I asked. He caught on that I was tryin to be smart and let out a short laugh. Somethin told me to check my watch and sure enough it was time for one of the boys to be bringin Jimmy back home. "Mr. Murphy," I said. "I gotta be goin home now. My husband be comin home from the clinic any minute." Murphy looked at me good, studyin me.

"What's the matter with him?"

"Oh, his liver and his kidneys ailin him. He goes over to the hospital to get hooked up to the dialysis machine. Plus he got sugar diabetes and high blood pressure. Been that way for awhile now. Doctors givin him another year they said." I started buttonin my overcoat back up.

"Doctors get on my nerves with that talk. Don't nobody got the right to say how long somebody else got in this world, I don't care who they is. If they ain't God." What he said impressed me and I nodded my head. "Where'd you say you live at?" he asked.

I told him I lived on Trinidad off West Virginia Avenue and started tryin to give directions. He waved me off with his hand and drove straight to my house by a route I never woulda thought of. My house needed paint and roof work, the walk was crumblin and the yard was crowded with tools, broken furniture and old appliances Jimmy meant to do something with one day. I felt kinda shamed bout it when we pulled up. "Been thinkin of sellin, getting somethin less tiresome," I said quickly. "Can't take care of it all myself."

"I thought you mentioned some boys back aways? Why can't they do it?"

"They grown. They got they own places and I'm just lucky they take they daddy to and from the hospital I guess."

Murphy nodded. "Well don't worry bout it. It looks just fine. Who said everybody got to have a picture perfect house, huh? Yours here got . . . character."

I extended my hand to say goodbye and offered to pay him. Silly, cause I didn't have no money and had already told him so. He didn't say nothing, though, just waved me off again. I started to let myself out but he touched my arm to stop me and came around to open the door like a gentleman's sposed to. When I took his hand to balance myself climbin out I looked up and saw Edward at the window. Murphy was sayin somethin about me takin a ride again. "When you got sick folks life ain't always easy and you might need a break sometime." I didn't answer cause the look on Edward's face was worryin me; just thanked him and went on in the house.

Jimmy was propped up in his chair watchin a game show. I kissed his cheek before takin off my coat and scarf. Edward stood next to the hall closet with his arms folded, watchin me. "Mama, where you been?"

I stepped into my bedroom slippers which I keep near the radiator so they'll be nice and warm. I ignored that chile cause I didn't like what I heard in his voice.

Edward has always been my most difficult chile. He has something called dyslexia but we didn't know it back then and he was frustrated somethin awful in school and played hooky a lot. Seem like Jimmy was always beatin him but it didn't do no good. That's why I ain't for all that beatin no more. Anyway, Edward dropped out of high school and got a job baggin groceries. He messed around with drinkin and drugs and all that goes with it; had to go to court a couple of times but I prayed hard over that boy. He took some night classes and we found out about the dyslexia. That helped him a lot. Gave him some hope. Boy got a steady job now at a parkin lot downtown and got his own place. Course in the meantime he had Latrice by a gal who was on that stuff and me and Jimmy had to raise her. Edward spends time with her, though, gives us money sometimes and he buys her school clothes and whatnot so I ain't complainin.

He took Jimmy's sickness hard though, I guess cause he and Jimmy was mad at each other for so long. When Jimmy got sick they didn't have time to be mad no more but it didn't seem like they had enough time to make up neither. Edward started up drinkin again as a result. That's why I wished he hadn't seen me with Murphy that day.

I fixed me a cup of hot tea and sat at the kitchen table just thinkin about my day, goin back over it again and again, tryin to taste it. Edward followed me in there. "You late, Mama. You wasn't even here when Daddy got home. How you think he feel?"

"I'm sorry, Edward."

"Well, where you been? Shoppin? Visitin? Huh? Mama, I'm talkin to you!" He was shoutin at me, with his hands stretched in front of me on the table, twitchin. I smelt the liquor every time he opened his mouth. "And what was that taxi man doin talkin to you so long?"

"Nothin, Edward. There ain't no reason for you to be so upset. I had some errands to do and the man gave me a ride home. That's all."

"Ain't no dinner cooked or nothin. You always got catfish on Friday, Mama. Somethin ain't right." Edward shook his head, still wearin that troublesome expression, but there was somethin sad mixed in with the mad.

Latrice came downstairs and asked her father bout all that yellin. He don't like her to know he been drinkin so he had to get himself together and he left me alone. I went out to the living room and sat down with Jimmy. "I ain't fixed nothin to eat yet," I said. "You hungry?" I knew he hated the food in the hospital cafeteria and was always glad to be home for dinner. His drooping eyes were almost closed when he nodded. I noticed the bones in his face seemed to be right at the edge of his skin. It gave him a helpless, pleading look. A look I didn't like seein in him. I would have given half the days the Lord has left for me to get my old Jimmy back.

The picture of me and Jimmy when we got married was on the mantel in the living room and I focused on it, amazed that I had been in the company of another man even for a few hours. In the picture Jimmy had on his army uniform and I was wearin the dress my mama created from scraps of material left over from the dresses she made for white women. I was holdin a bouquet of wildflowers. I stared at the picture, trying to remember that Jimmy. He was standing so straight, makin him seem taller than the 5'8" he was. In the photograph I was gazin into his eyes, under a spell from that powerful grin he had. I remembered the way he used to dance with me on the tops of his shoes, tryin to teach me to jitterbug, his legs bendin every which way, too quick for me to catch on.

When I got up, Edward came and sat down with Jimmy to watch the news. Latrice was on the phone—her favorite spot. I cooked up what I had in the refrigerator and tried not to think bout my ride with Alonzo Murphy.

Jimmy slept through most of the weekend. He woke up a few times, ate and went to the bathroom but he said he wanted to stay in the bed. On Sunday when I came back from church he was still sleepin. I called Lance to come over cause I couldn't wake him and I got scared. Lance shook him hard. "I ain't dead?" was the first thing Jimmy said when he finally woke. That night he sat down and went over his papers with the boys like he'd been talkin bout so that told me somethin.

Lance acted like wasn't nothin different in his life. He always been that way. Mr. Cool and Calm. Even as a little chile, when he got beat he wouldn't never cry. Edward be screamin so loud I used to think the neighbors gonna call the social workers on Jimmy. Ain't it somethin how children born from the same parents and so close in age (eleven months apart) could turn out different as night and day? Lance married, got a nice stable home life, good government office job, no kids, and don't raise his voice to his parents. But he trouble me in other ways, cause I know when you keep so much in you can get ulcers and such. I ask him questions all the time. He say, "Don't worry, Mama. I'm all right."

After the weekend was over, Jimmy went back to the clinic like regular. He asked me to read something to pass the time. I read him some of Miss Maya Angelou; I keeps her in my purse. I think she's a mighty fine writer cause she makes me feel as if me and her been places together. I put my readin glasses on and started in with Miss Maya's *All God's Children Need Traveling Shoes*. Jimmy smiled every once and again and said, "Ummhmm" a couple of times so I know he liked what I was readin him.

One of the nurses came in and said the doctor would like to speak to me. They had three or four different doctors that used to tend to him. They nice enough but they all seem to act like I couldn't comprehend what was goin on with Jimmy, so they didn't have no need to try to explain it. That riled me something else. Anyway, one of the lady doctors was in the waitin room when I got there. She sat me down and spoke gentle and soft in a slow whisper voice, like she was sharin a secret with a chile.

One thing I find with white people is no matter how many times you seen them or talked to them, they always act like it the first time. Somethin bout the way they look straight through you like you transparent; their words don't stick, just touch you lightly, then gone. She wasn't no different. "I'm sorry to have to tell you this. But we think that . . . your husband doesn't have much time left. We would like to hospitalize him from here on so that we can monitor him much better and do everything we can to make him comfortable." Her jump-around eyes got wide while she waited for me to answer.

I told her no. I could take care of Jimmy fine at home and besides, Jimmy didn't want to die cooped up in no hospital. Who would? She asked me wasn't it a burden to bring him back and forth three times a week. I told her sure, it was a pain in the rear, but that comes with life. She too young and white to know that yet,

I guess, but I watched my mouth, I didn't tell her so. She talked a little more, askin me if I wanted her to discuss it with my sons. I didn't even answer that. Then she finally said it was my decision. Which, course, I already knew. Mine and Jimmy's.

When I left there that mornin, my stomach wasn't settin right. I guess havin the doctor tell me Jimmy's time was gettin closer rattled my nerves. For her to tell me face to face meant it was more than just my thinkin or feelin. I took my time walkin to the bus stop, hopin I could get my stomach to act right before I had to mix it with all them smells be on the bus.

Well, lo, and behold, Murphy's taxi was waitin at the bus stop. Lord, he just don't know, I thought. He was wavin at me and smilin. I got in the front even though wasn't nobody in the back. "Good afternoon. What you doin here?"

He turned the radio down. "Thought I'd see if you needed a ride today. I remembered this was bout the time I picked you up Friday. But I wasn't sure if you'd be back today or later in the week." He looked at me, liftin one eyebrow. "You look a little perturbed. Did I do the wrong thing?"

"No, no," I said settlin in the seat. "It's just . . . Jimmy's doctor told me today that it won't be long and I guess it gettin to me."

"Well, sure. Course it would. I'm sorry. That's got to be some kind of somethin to hear. Look, I'm givin you my number in case you need anythin. Never know." He started writin and then handed me a piece of note paper folded in half.

I wanted to ride around with him again but thought better of it. "I think it'd be best if I waited for the bus. Thank you anyhow, Mr. Murphy." I unfolded the paper and looked at his scratchy handwritin. I put my hand on the door and started to get out.

"Call me Alonzo, please. Is it all right if I call you Helen?"

I nodded without lookin up.

"Tell you what. I'll take you straight home. You already in here, no sense in you goin back out in the cold. How often you up at the hospital, anyway?"

"I come Monday, Wednesday and Friday."

"Well, I'll make you a promise. Monday, Wednesday, Friday, I'll be right here waitin on you. I'll take you straight home or you can ride around with me till it's time. Whichever, whatever. How's that?" He hadn't even pulled off or nothin. We was just sittin there. I wasn't sure what to think about this offer. My first reaction was to say yes, thank you Jesus. No more freezin my toes off, besides the fact I liked conversatin with the man. But it was a scary feelin. Been so long since I thought about any man other than my Jimmy, to tell you the truth, I really didn't know how to act. Murphy seemed to understand what my hesitation was about cause he turned to me and said, "I ain't tryin to upset you or nothin. I just see you got a situation that could be better and I got a way of making it a little better. That's all there is to it."

"I don't know," I said.

Before he took me home, we drove over to the wharf cause he said he wanted some catfish. "You ain't tasted no catfish till you tasted mine," he said. "Used to fish myself till I got arthritis in my arm." I told him I know all bout arthritis. Murphy gave me some of the catfish, sayin he only had himself to feed. When he dropped me off I thanked him for everything: the conversation, the catfish, and most of all—for takin my mind off my sadness.

He got out, of course, and came around to let me out. Fore I had a chance to take stock of anything, Edward came up on us, like a storm, and started pushin on Murphy. "What you think you doin with my mama, you ol' joker?" Murphy looked startled and almost fell over on top of me. He backed up and stood up straight, brushin his hands over his jacket. I got out by leanin on the door handle. I could see Edward's liquor-stoked eyes heatin up. "Ain't you got no decency, Mama? Your husband's on his deathbed and you out there gallivantin with this ol' . . ." Edward raised his hand again.

I reached out and tried to stop him. "Edward, calm down. You don't know what you're sayin. Mr. Murphy is just tryin—"

Edward cut me off. "Tryin to what? Tryin to figure out if you got any money comin once Daddy dies! And you fallin for it, you should be ashamed. I'm ashamed for you. Ashamed to call you my mother!" He glared at me, veins threatenin to press through his forehead. He shoulda been cold cause he wasn't wearing no coat.

"Watch how you talkin to your mama, young man," Murphy said in a gentle tone.

Edward looked like he was gonna push him again or hit him but just then Lance's car pulled up behind Murphy's taxi. I said, thank you, Lord, to myself. "Lance!" I yelled. When I realized I was shakin all over, I started cryin.

Lance rushed over to us and asked what was goin on. Edward was talkin loud and glarin at Murphy. "Brought Daddy home early today cause they called me and said he was feelin weak. Get home—she ain't even here. Your mother been runnin around all day with this . . . bum while Daddy sittin up there dyin!" He pointed toward the house. We all turned and Jimmy, lookin small as a chile, was in his wheelchair watchin us through the storm door.

Lance glanced at me. "Mama?" I shook my head and wiped my eyes with my gloves. Lance put his hand on Edward's shoulder. "Edward, go on inside with Mama. You handled it fine, man. I'll take it from here." He took Murphy's elbow, saying, "Maybe you should leave now," and they moved away from us. Edward, poutin, went ahead of me, through the gate and up the walk.

I could hear Murphy sayin, "I didn't mean no harm at all." I looked back at them. It seemed like Lance and Murphy was talkin peaceful, and so some of the tightness went out of my chest.

Jimmy said he was having shortness of breath and the doctors wanted to keep him but Jimmy didn't want to stay. He told me he was sleepy and didn't even want no dinner; just a bath. I ran the water and Edward helped get him in the tub. Edward wasn't talkin but at least he wasn't yellin no more. I put some of my bubble bath in the water, sat on a low stool and started bathin Jimmy. Edward went on out. "Do it feel nice?" I asked Jimmy. He nodded but he was lookin awful weary. "What's wrong, sweetness?" I said. "Somethin painin?"

"Nothin new," he said, real slow and his voice sounded gravelly, like he had marbles in his mouth. "I sure wish Edward would stop drinkin. I don't want to have to worry bout none of y'all after I'm gone."

"Watch you talkin bout? Where you goin?" That's what I always said when he talked like that. Lance poked his head in the door and asked if we needed help. I told him no. But he didn't go away; I could feel him listenin at the door.

"I'm roundin the corner, Helen," Jimmy said. "We got to face it. It's right up on me now and I guess I'm ready. My mind and my body is sure tired." He lifted his brown, wrinkled hands out of the water and stared at them, turning them over. "Wonder what it'll be like not to reach cross and touch you no more or wake up to the sun in my eyes. Ain't nobody alive who can tell me bout it, though, is there?" He talked more that night than he had in a month. "I ain't scared no more, Helen. Just the other day I got a comfortable feelin that it's gonna be okay. I know it ain't bad what's about to happen to me. Even left me with the impression it might be good." We both laughed till he started coughin up blood.

"Listen, Helen," he went on after I wiped around his mouth. "I don't know if I told you lately how much you mean to me." I began washin his back cause I didn't know what to say. He brought my hand down and clasped it inside his. "Of all the joys in my life, over these years, you the most important one. I just wish I coulda taken you to France and Italy like we always talked bout. I just wish I had a little more time." I moved closer and put my arms around his neck and just laid my head next to his. We stayed that way for a few minutes.

I let the drain plug out. He put one tremblin hand on my shoulder and the other on the pole the boys put around the tub. Lance came into the bathroom and helped me get Jimmy out. I heard Lance sniffle and I looked up at him, catchin sight of bold tears on his face. Shocked me so, I almost let go of Jimmy. I ain't seen Lance cry since he was a baby and I'm his mama.

While we were takin Jimmy to the bedroom, he muttered to Lance, "Ain't no call for tears now. Don't want to spoil a perfect record, do ya?" (Jimmy musta been thinkin same way as me.) Lance cracked a smile and he and Jimmy hugged for the first time in a good while. I sat on the bed next to Jimmy, puttin lotion on him, rubbin it good into all his creases. I gave him a massage at the same time until my finger bones began achin. He sighed cause of how good it felt I guess. "It ain't but six o'clock," I said to him while I fluffed the pillow behind his neck.

"That's all right," he said and turned out the lamp next to the bed. I went out and cooked up Murphy's catfish for me, Latrice and the boys.

Jimmy died later that night in his sleep. Boys was long gone by then. I sat in the rockin chair beside him till the sun came up.

The rest of that week I felt like somebody's robot; people just told me what to do and I did it. Food and folk came and went. Preacher Wilkins gave a powerful sermon at Jimmy's funeral on Saturday. He called Jimmy a "champion of life." Said he always did his best and never complained. That was mostly true. I sat up front—Edward on one side of me, Lance on the other. Next to Lance was his wife, Geraldine and then Latrice, lookin like a grown woman in one of Geraldine's black dresses.

After the scripture readin Latrice recited a poem she wrote about Jimmy back in eighth grade. I cried a lot. It came from way deep inside me, a place I didn't even know about, and shook my whole body. Everyone kept lookin at me and handin me tissues.

We walked out of the church behind the casket holdin Jimmy. Edward held onto my arm as if he were keepin me in check. All the faces I passed were blurs of dark color. By the time I got in the family car I had stopped cryin but I felt a big empty space spreadin, like a stain, inside my chest. A space I was scared might never get filled up again.

The cemetery was the hardest part. Preacher Wilkins was mercifully short-winded, though. People took flowers out the funeral wreaths brought from the church and placed them on top of Jimmy's casket. Someone handed me a rose. I laid it where I thought his heart would be. I promised myself I would leave him with a smile. It was hard but I did.

We all started walkin back toward to the roadway where the family car was parked. That's when I saw Alonzo Murphy standin near an evergreen tree. He nodded at me and tipped the hat he held in his hand. It dawned on me that I hadn't gone to the clinic on Wednesday or Friday like I said and he had probably been there waitin. I wanted to go over and thank him for comin but I just went ahead and got in the limousine. I looked out the window and saw Lance walkin toward Murphy. They shook hands and Murphy gave Lance one of his slow, easy smiles.

"Who's that man?" Latrice wanted to know.

"Nobody special," I said. "Just an old friend." Lance came soon after and joined the rest of us in the family car.

Carol Shields

Mirrors

From *Prairie Fire* and *Story*

WHEN HE THINKS about the people he's known in his life, a good many of them seem to have cultivated some curious strand of asceticism, contrived some gesture of renunciation. They give up sugar. Or meat. Or newspapers. Or neckties. They sell their second car or disconnect the television. They might make a point of staying at home on Sunday evenings or abjuring chemical sprays. Something anyway, that signals dissent and cuts across the beating heart of their circumstances, reminding them of their other, leaner selves. Their better selves.

He and his wife have claimed their small territory of sacrifice, too. For years they've become "known" among their friends for the particular deprivation they've assigned themselves: for the fact that there are no mirrors in their summer house. None at all. None are allowed.

The need to observe ourselves is sewn into us, everyone knows this, but he and his wife have turned their back on this need, said no to it, at least for the duration of the summer months. Otherwise, they are not very different from other couples nearing the end of middle age—he being sixty, she fifty-eight, their children grown up and married and living hundreds of miles away.

In September they will have been married thirty-five years, and they're already planning a week in New York to celebrate this milestone, five nights at the Algonquin (for sentimental reasons) and a few off-Broadway shows, already booked. They stay away from the big musicals as a rule, preferring, for want of a better word, *serious* drama. Nothing experimental, no drugged angst or scalding discourse, but plays that coolly examine the psychological positioning of men and women in our century. This torn, perplexing century. Men and women who resemble themselves.

They would be disinclined to discuss between them how they've arrived at these harmonious choices in the matter of playgoing, how they are both a little proud, in fact, of their taste for serious drama, proud in the biblical *pride* sense. Just as they're a little proud of their mirrorless summer house on the shores of Big Circle Lake.

Their political views tend to fall in the middle of the spectrum. Financially, you might describe them as medium well off, certainly not wealthy. He has retired, one week ago as a matter of fact, from his own management consulting firm, and she is, has always been, a housewife and active community volunteer. These days she wears a large stylish head of stiffened hair, and he, with no visible regret, is going neatly bald at the forehead and crown.

Walking away from their cottage on Big Circle Lake, you would have a hard time describing its contents or atmosphere: faded colors and pleasing shapes that beg you to stay, to make yourself comfortable. These inviting surfaces slip from remembrance the minute you turn your back. But you would very probably bear in mind their single act of forfeiture: there are no mirrors.

Check the medicine cabinet in the little fir-panelled bathroom: nothing. Check the back of the broom cupboard door in the kitchen or the spot above the dresser in their large skylighted bedroom or the wall over the log-burning fireplace in what they choose to call "the lounge." Even if you were to abuse the rules of privacy and look into her (the wife's) big canvas handbag you would find nothing compromising. You would likely come across a compact of face powder, Elizabeth Arden, but the little round mirror lining most women's compacts has been removed. You can just make out the curved crust of glue that once held a mirror in place.

Check even the saucepans hanging over the kitchen stove. Their bottoms are discolored copper, scratched aluminum. No chance for a reflective glimpse there. The stove itself is dull textured, ancient.

This mirrorlessness of theirs is deliberate, that much is clear.

From June to August they choose to forget who they are, or at least what they look like, electing an annual season of non-reflectiveness in the same way other people put away their clocks for the summer or their computers or door keys or microwave ovens.

"But how can you possibly shave?" people ask the husband, knowing he is meticulous about such things.

He moves a hand to his chin. At sixty, still slender, he remains a handsome man. "By feel," he says. He demonstrates, moving the forefinger of his left hand half an inch ahead of the path of an imaginary razor. "Just try it. Shut your eyes and you'll see you can manage a decent shave without the slightest difficulty. Maybe not a perfect shave, but good enough for out at the lake."

His wife, who never was slender, who has fretted for the better part of her life about her lack of slenderness—raged and grieved, gained and lost—has now at fifty-eight given up the battle. She looks forward to her mirrorless summers, she says. She likes to tell her friends—and she and her husband are a fortunate couple with a large circle of friends—that she can climb into her swimsuit and walk through the length of the cottage—the three original rooms, the new south-facing wing—without having to look even once at the double and triple pinches of flesh that have accumulated in those corners where her shoulders and breasts flow together. "Oh, I suppose I could look down and *see* what I'm like," she says, rolling her eyes, "but I'm not obliged to take in the whole panorama every single day."

She does her hair in the morning in much the same way her husband shaves: by feel, brushing it out, patting it into shape, fixing it with pins. She's been putting on earrings for forty years, and certainly doesn't require a mirror for that. As for lipstick, she makes do with a quick crayoning back and forth across her mouth, a haphazard double slash of color. Afterward she returns the lipstick smartly to its case, then runs a practiced finger around her upper and lower lips, which she stretches wide so that the shaping of pale raspberry fits perfectly the face she knows by heart.

He's watched her perform this small act a thousand times, so often that his own mouth sometimes wants to stretch in response.

They were newly married and still childless when they bought the cottage, paying far too much, then discovering almost immediately the foundations were half-rotted, and carpenter ants—or something—lived in the pine rafters. Mice had made a meal of the electric wires; ants thronged the mildewed cupboards. Officially the place had been sold to them furnished, but the previous owners had taken the best of what there was, leaving only a sagging couch, a table that sat unevenly on the torn linoleum, two battered chairs, a bed with a damp mattress, and an oak dresser with a stuck drawer. The dresser was the old-fashioned kind with its own mirror frame attached, two curving prongs rising gracefully like a pair of arms, but the mirror it had once embraced was missing.

You would think the larceny of the original owners would have embittered the two of them. Or that the smell of mold and rot and accumulated dirt would have filled them with discouragement, but it didn't. They set to work. For three weeks they worked from morning to dusk.

First he repaired the old pump so they might at least have water. He was not in those years adept with his hands, and the task took several days. During that period he washed himself in the lake, not taking the time for a swim, but stopping only to splash his face and body with cold water. She noticed there was a three-cornered smudge of dirt high on his forehead that he missed. It remained there for several days, making him appear to her boyish and vulnerable. She didn't have the heart to mention it to him. In fact, she felt a small ping of sorrow when she looked up at him one evening and found it washed away. Even though she was not in those days an impulsive woman, she had stretched herself forward and kissed the place where the smudge had been.

Curiously, he remembers her spontaneous kiss, remembers she had washed her hair in the lake a few minutes earlier, and had wrapped a towel around her head like a turban. She was not a vain woman. In fact, she had always mourned too much the failures of her body, and so he knew she had no idea of how seductive she looked at that moment with the added inch of towelling and her face bared like a smooth shell.

At night they fell exhausted into the old bed and slept as though weights were attached to their arms and legs. Their completed tasks, mending and painting, airing and polishing, brought them a brimming level of satisfaction that would have been foolish to try to explain to anyone else. They stepped carefully across their washed floorboards, opened and shut their windows, and seemed to be listening at night to the underhum of the sloping, leaking roof. That first summer they scarcely saw a soul. The northern shore of Big Circle Lake was a wilderness in those days. There were no visitors, few interruptions. Two or three times they went to town for groceries. Once they attended a local auction and bought a pine bed, a small table, and a few other oddments. Both of them remember they looked carefully through the domestic auction for a mirror, but none was to their liking. It was then they decided to do without.

Each day they spent at the cottage became a plotted line, the same coffee mugs (hers, his), the comically inadequate paring knife and the comments that accrued around it. Familiar dust, a pet spider swaying over their bed, the sky lifting and falling and spreading out like a mesh of silver on the lake. Meals. Sleep. A surprising amount of silence.

They thought they'd known each other before they married. He'd reported dutifully, as young men were encouraged to do in those days, his youthful experiences and pleasures, and she, blocked with doubt, had listed off hers. The truth had been darkened out. Now it erupted, came to the surface. He felt a longing to turn to her and say: "This is what I've dreamed of all my life, being this tired, this used up, and having someone like you, exactly like you, waking up at my side."

At the end of that first married summer they celebrated with dinner at a restaurant at the far end of the lake, the sort of jerry-built knotty-pine family establishment that opens in May for the summer visitors and closes on Labor Day. The waitresses were students hired for the season, young girls wearing fresh white peasant blouses and gathered skirts and thonged sandals on their feet. These girls, holding their trays sideways, maneuvered through the warren of tiny rooms. They brought chilled tomato juice, set a basket of bread on the table, put mixed salad out in wooden bowls, then swung back into the kitchen for the plates of chicken and vegetables. Their rhythmic ease, burnished to perfection now that summer was near its end, was infectious, and the food, which was really no better than such food can be, became a meal each of them would remember with pleasure.

He ate hungrily. She cut more slowly into her roast chicken, then looked up, straight into what she at first thought was a window. In fact, it was a mirror that had been mounted on the wall, put there no doubt to make the cramped space seem larger. She saw a woman prettier than she remembered, a graceful woman with high, strong cheekbones, deeply tanned, her eyes lively, the shoulders moving sensually under her cotton blouse. A moment ago she had felt a pinprick of envy for the lithe careless bodies of the young waitresses. Now she was confronted by this stranger. She opened her mouth as if to say: who on earth?

She'd heard of people who moved to foreign countries and forgot their own language, the simplest words lost: door, tree, sky. But to forget your own face? She smiled; her face smiled back; the delay of recognition felt like treasure. She put down her knife and fork and lifted her wrists forward in a salute.

Her husband turned then and looked into the mirror. He too seemed surprised. "Hello," he said fondly. "Hello, us."

Their children were six and eight the year they put the addition on the cottage. Workmen came every morning, and the sound of their power tools shattered the accustomed summertime peace. She found herself living all day for the moment they would be gone, the sudden late-afternoon stillness and the delicious green smell of cut lumber rising around them. The children drifted through the half-completed partitions like ghosts, claiming their own territory. For two nights, while the new roof was being put on, they slept with their beds facing straight up to the stars.

That was the year her daughter came running into the kitchen in a new swimsuit, asking where the mirror was. Her tone was excited but baffled, and she put her hands over her mouth as though she knew she had blundered somehow just presenting this question.

"We don't have a mirror at the cottage," her mother explained.

"Oh," the child replied. Just "Oh."

At that moment the mother remembered something she had almost forgotten. In the old days, when a woman bought a new purse, or a pocketbook as they were called then, it came packed hard with gray tissue paper. And in the midst of all the paper wadding there was always a little unframed rectangle of mirror. These were crude, roughly made mirrors, and she wasn't sure that people actually used them. They were like charms, good-luck charms. Or like compasses; you could look in them and take your bearings. Locate yourself in the world.

We use the expression "look *into* a mirror," as though it were an open medium, like water—which the first mirrors undoubtedly were. Think of Narcissus. He started it all. And yet it is women who are usually associated with mirrors: Mermaids rising up from the salty waves with a comb and a mirror in hand. Cleopatra on her barge. Women and vanity went hand in hand.

In his late forties he fell in love with another woman. Was she younger than his wife? Yes, of course she was younger. She was more beautiful, too, though with a kind of beauty that had to be checked and affirmed almost continually. Eventually it wore him out.

He felt he had only narrowly escaped. He had broken free, and by a mixture of stealth and good fortune had kept his wife from knowing. Arriving that summer at the house on Big Circle Lake, he turned the key rather creakily in the door. His wife danced through ahead of him and did a sort of triple turn on the kitchen floor, a dip-shuffle-dip, her arms extended, her fingers clicking imaginary castanets. She always felt lighter at the lake, her body looser. This lightness, this proof of innocence, doubled his guilt. A wave of darkness had rolled in between what he used to be and what he'd become, and he longed to put his head down on the smooth pine surface of the kitchen table and confess everything.

Already his wife was unpacking a box of groceries, humming as she put things away. Oblivious.

There was one comfort, he told himself: for two months there would be no mirrors to look into. His shame had made him unrecognizable anyway.

He spent the summer building a cedar deck, which he knew was the sort of thing other men have done in such circumstances.

She had always found it curious that mirrors, which seemed magical in their properties, in their ability to multiply images and augment light, were composed of only two primary materials: a plane of glass pressed up against a plane of silver. Wasn't there something more required? Was this really all there was to it?

The simplicity of glass. The preciousness of silver. Only these two elements were needed for the miracle of reflection to take place. When a mirror was broken, the glass could be replaced. When a mirror grew old, it had only to be resilvered. There was no end to a mirror. It could go on and on. It could go on forever.

Perhaps her life was not as complicated as she thought. Her concerns, her nightmares, her regrets, her suspicions—perhaps everything would eventually be repaired, healed, obliterated. Probably her husband was right: she made too much of things.

"You remind me of someone," she said the first time they met. He knew she meant that he reminded her of herself. Some twinned current flowed between them. This was years and years ago.

But her words came back to him recently when his children and their families were visiting at Big Circle Lake.

The marriages of his son and daughter are still young, still careful, often on the edge of hurt feelings or quarrels, though he feels fairly certain they will work their way eventually toward a more even footing, whatever that means.

He's heard it said all his life that the young pity the old, that this pity is a fact of human nature. But he can't help observing how both his grown children regard him with envy. They almost sigh it out—"You've got everything."

Well, it's so. His mortgage is paid. There's this beautiful place for the summer. Time to travel now. Old friends. A long marriage. A bank of traditions. He imagines his son and daughter must amuse their separate friends with accounts of their parents' voluntary forswearing of mirrors, and that in these accounts he and his wife are depicted as harmless eccentrics who have perhaps stumbled on some useful verity which has served to steady them in their lives.

He longs sometimes to tell them that what they see is not the whole of it. Living without mirrors is cumbersome and inconvenient, if the truth were known, and, moreover, he has developed a distaste in recent years for acts of abnegation, finding something theatrical and childish about cultivated denial, something stubbornly willful and self-cherishing.

He would also like to tell them that other people's lives are seldom as settled as they appear. That every hour contains at least a moment of bewilderment or worse. That a whim randomly adopted grows forlorn with time, and that people who have lived together for thirty-five years still apprehend each other as strangers.

Though only last night—or was it the night before?—he woke suddenly at three in the morning and found his wife had turned on her light and was reading. He lay quiet, watching her for what seemed like several minutes: a woman no longer young, intent on her book, lifting a hand every moment or two to turn over a page, her profile washed out by the high-intensity lamp, her shoulders and body blunted by shadow. Who was this person?

And then she had turned and glanced his way. Their eyes held, caught on the thread of a shared joke: the two of them, at this moment, had become each other, at home behind the screen of each other's face. It was several seconds before he was able to look away.

Christine Schutt

His Chorus

From *Alaska Quarterly Review*

THE GIRLS had their own version, of course, which they told, calling her by his name for her, Margaret, saying, "Margaret, we knew your brother. He wasn't bad." Then what? she wondered, and Margaret came upon them again as she had come upon them. Long days, taking the washed streets home from work, Margaret had come upon them, the girls and her brother, bunched under the portico of the night-abandoned embassy, all shiny blacks and chains before a match, another match illumined their sprung faces—surprise!—or else they did not see her, and they argued. Margaret had heard their girl voices in the muffle of the huddle, asking, "Share, will you, please? I'm cold." In the unhinged season this had been, already dark, when the wind off the river rolled barrels down the promenade and banged the padlocked gates of shut-up shops. "Coming home?" Margaret had asked him, and her brother had answered, rolling his shoulders to say, "I don't want it—fuck off, you mother!"

The brother was a shrug, a glance, a long, stooped back, rough hair belted in notched garbage ties—and gone before he was gone: This was Margaret's version. She told anyone at all about the resinous stains on his fingers, the slept-in folds of his shirts. The jeans he wore so long unwashed were oily with his dirt. No coat, no socks, shoes curled witchy and split at the seams, her brother at the lip of things—the door, the curb, the dock—was licking at the fogged face of his kiddie-face watch.

Do you know what time it is? If she could only ask her brother again—do you have any idea what time it is? Margaret folded laundry, pinching at her collar bath towels still warm yet coarse against her chin. What else was there to do? she asked. Margaret told the girls, "I waited up for him at night. I washed the floors." From upstairs came Martin's calling, "Margaret, look at the time!"

Four, five, six in the morning when the sky pearled and others, early wakeful, moved, she guessed as she did, to hoard the spangled outlook, Margaret did not care by then that her brother's bed was empty. "Not one of you girls in it," she said, "and I bet you thought I didn't know, but he told me."

On the nights he did come home, he spoke of the girls. Crouched in the collaspe of his bed, he gave his version of the girls to Margaret. How their hands brushed over the new hair under his arms—as though it were high grass and they walking through the field of him. "My brother," she said, "he told me what happened some nights after you abandoned the abandoned embassy." The sucked-down candies he proffered on his tongue. The brother was talking and Martin was calling "Margaret!"—when who was this Margaret? She sometimes forgot herself with the boy—the boy huffing on his watch and scolding, "Fuck Martin! Margaret, it's me who needs you."

She told the girls, "I had no babies of my own."

And another time, when they would speak to her of him, she asked the girls, "He did tell you about us, didn't he?"

"Yes, yes, yes, yes, yes," the girls said, which made her wonder then what her brother might have said about her.

He might have said Margaret was his mother, even when their own was alive and making a living at night. He might have described a sister of stout and rounded back, despite that she was young; she was working. She was working dirty jobs in dirty clothes—for him. For him she was broiling cheap cuts done for dinner. For him she bargained; for him she wrote: "Please excuse this lateness. He wasn't feeling very well. He didn't mean it. He didn't know. He didn't understand."

The ways she thought to love him! Draping towels over his bent head at the mouth of the steaming pot—to help him breathe when he was croupy—such was her mothering. Margaret was the person he thought first to see when they picked him up for thieving. She never made him promise to quit his ways, but listened to him promise he would try to be better—especially around Martin—no more stripping through the kitchen, drying himself with his shirt. He would not cough when Martin was talking or in the man's presence snipe at her for money. The rinds and open cartons behind the milk—sometimes even a plate, fork and knife crossed over it—empty dispensers and unexpected bills, late-night lockouts and bust-up girls: There would be, the boy promised her, no more surprises.

Was that how he thought to tell the girls it was among them—a sister, a brother, a brother-in-law—in a strip of rooms made smaller if the brother had company?

Because, she told the girls, she was not so old as to forget some sensations; she recognized the knock of the bed and the yeasty smell of yearning. Her brother's broken, coaxing voice—she knew the sound of that: his *please* and *won't* and *will you.* The sore places near his lips and his lips, so split and glossy, were some of what it was about him—must have been—that made the girls say yes, grind their heels against his back, ask, "Doesn't this hurt, what I am doing?"

"No, no, no, no, no," the girls insisted. "We were not like that," and they didn't call her by her married name, but spoke familiarly. "Margaret," they said, and they described her brother as sullen. They had seen him elbow clingy girls, seen him shawled against the chills, seen him counting his money. The way he left the bathroom with his beery piss unflushed in the unseated bowl, the girls laughed to tell it, although Margaret had seen it, too. Suddenly, the brother was leaving his mark in the rooms through which he passed.

"No," she said. "He wasn't such a beast as that." He spent time uptown on the high grounds of the garden with the scrolly gates. "He could be sweet," Margaret told the girls. "He was not indifferent to his surroundings." He looked at trees, at how in spring the

new leaves were so many of them spiked. He had his places—that
much she said she knew. He sometimes went for drugs. "But,
Lord," she said, and looked hard at the girls, "we all of us sometimes need it."

The grassy smell of him come home on an evening when the sky
stayed white, Margaret remembered him with blades of grass
pressed against his back and with muddy, open shoes. He brought
home a smell of something she had forgotten, with Martin in the
broad bed crying out, "Margaret!"

Of course, there were resentments, she explained, Martin's version of things, what he called "assaults by that punk-mouthed
brother of yours," then added, "Yours the family with the fuckedup genes—lucky you can't pass them along."

"My fault," Margaret said to the girls, hands cupped between her
legs. "My fault he was my brother. I could not scold him. I liked to
kiss him instead. I liked to rub my thumb along his front teeth, sit
in his room and watch him sleep." In sleep, his body was newly
heavy and unmarked—breath fluttering the hollow of his neck. She
said, "I was meant to see him, but not like that."

"No, no, no, no, no," Margaret cried, but when the girls appeared confused, she said, "Remember who saw him last."

Late night or early morning, the hallway narrowed to a tunnel in
the light from the end where he stood. He was returned but about
to leave. His loose clothes undone confused her, but his sideways
moves she understood. She had experienced before the unexpected
charge of his unexpected smile, the hands lifted as in blessing:
good-bye, good-bye!

But wait!

She had been waiting for him; she was awake, brushing aside
other versions of his story—the one with the coroner's instruments
or the one where the heart gave out softly, and she pointed to that
place on herself.

"My brother's heart," she told the girls. "I have heard its tricked
beat. I have kept him company here," Margaret said, and she
opened the door for the girls to see his bedroom, the sheeted windows and the cutouts, things tossed, tented or on a tilt—in some
ways just a boy's room, no matter what was written on the wall.

Impossible to make out anyway, his aggressive urban scrawl, his tag—whatever was his name—he wrote it where she walked from work past the diplomatic row, the promenade, the padlocked buildings. His bullying design was everywhere she looked.

His face, too, his wounded face—the bruised hollows of his eyes and his eyes so thickly lashed and sleepy—was the first version of his face Margaret saw. Here the skin's imperfections, summer-oiled and overwrought, were more pronounced than in the colder seasons when confronted with the smallness of his face behind a scarf. Outside, or on the way outside, the brother's skin was close in winter, blown clear, cheeks a wind-scratched rouge. Yet she did not move to touch that face or the others that occurred to her out of order but up-to-date. Margaret told the girls, "Of the little boy he was, I remember less and less."

A swatch of baby hair—shades lighter—and the slatted cage that was his chest, veiny threading everywhere.

Nails soft enough to bite off.

A new body very clean.

Shoes.

Hands again.

The sweated valleys between his fingers, his fingers ringed at the knuckles—and then not—but squaring at the ends to an older boy's hands, drumming the kitchen counter.

"Hush that noise! You'll wake Martin," she scolded, then asked, "What is it you want?"

The brother grinned his hungry face, the one he wore when the drugs wore off, and he propped himself against the cupboards. This face was a face she knew regardless of season—slack or sly, it was hard to tell—but his eyelids twitched and his speech slurred in its wavering volume of request. "Do you still—" he began.

"Still what?" she asked. "What?" She could not understand! "What is it you want?" she asked this brother again and again. "What is it?"

When anything, she told the girls, she would have given him anything—and he knew this.

He was spoiled.

"Yes, yes, yes, yes, yes," the girls said. They said, "Margaret, we've been there."

"But he didn't answer," Margaret said. "That time he was in my arms—flat out on the floor I found him and pulled him up against my knees—his mouth stayed shut."

"This was in the living room," Margaret said.

"I have his watch. I took it off. I thought, What the fuck does it matter to you? Look at all this stuff of his I've got," and she started opening his drawers—beer caps, rubbers, cans of spray paint. "Can you imagine," she told the girls, "the bony rattle of the cans at night and Martin hollering for him to quit!"

"You must have known this about my brother," she said, "surely," and she threw away a plastic bag, burnt matches, some kind of stuck-on candy.

"Yes," the girls said. "Yes and no."

"We knew him first from the yearbook. We guessed his long smile was to cover up his teeth. We thought we would like him, and we did."

"He found us names," the girls told her—okay-sounding gang names from unflattering sources, from defects like moles or stutters.

"Spider was mine," a dark girl said. "Can you guess from where he got it?"

But he was affectionate, the girls told her. He seemed hardest on himself—wedging his narrow body in any narrow space. He said he wasn't smart.

"You are!" the girls had told him. "You only have to learn how to work!"

Margaret said, "I remember his crying. He woke me with his crying—how many times?"

"Yes," they said, yes to what she tossed before them: the pink and yellow bodies of the skin magazines, sticky tubes of jelly. "He only told us he was sad," the girls said.

"What for?" Margaret asked. "What was ever denied him?" Margaret said, looking past the girls to see if she could see his knotted chest and arms and shoulders in his furious abandon— shoving, shoving himself against a loose shape whose head knocked against the headboard of the bed. The noise! The noise! The old masturbator from next door, crying out, he couldn't stand it, Margaret; he couldn't stand this fucking boy!

He was a boy.

He woke with his hands between his legs.

He cried out, "Is there anything to eat?" Doors slammed, or else he slunk past in his tired clothes. The light was afternoon light or later—and cool. All day he slept; skin flakes flew up when his sheets were tossed, also fingernails, hair—his hair was anywhere, as was the glass imprinted with his ghostly mouth.

"All this talk about this boy," she said to the girls, when he was just a boy, who lived, a brother with his sister and his sister's husband—in odd arrangement—but who did not these days?

Rick Moody

Demonology

From *Conjunctions*

T HEY CAME in twos and threes, dressed in the fashionable Disney costumes of the year, Lion King, Pocahontas, Beauty and the Beast or in the costumes of televised superheroes, Protean, shape-shifting, thus arrayed, in twos and threes, complaining it was too hot with the mask on, *Hey, I'm really hot!,* lugging those orange plastic buckets, bartering, haggling with one another, *Gimme your Smarties, please?* as their parents tarried behind, grownups following after, grownups bantering about the schools, or about movies, about local sports, about their marriages, about the difficulties of long marriages, kids sprinting up the next driveway, kids decked out as demons or superheroes or dinosaurs or as advertisements for our multinational entertainment-providers, beating back the restless souls of the dead, in search of sweets.

They came in bursts of fertility, my sister's kids, when the bar drinking, or home-grown dope-smoking, or bed-hopping had lost its luster; they came with shrill cries and demands—little gavels, she said, instead of fists—*Feed me! Change me! Pay attention to me!* Now it was Halloween and the mothers in town, my sister among them, trailed after their kids, warned them away from items not fully wrapped, *Just give me that, you don't even like apples,* laughing at the kids hobbling in their bulky costumes—my nephew dressed as a shark, dragging a mildewed gray tail behind him. But what kind of shark? A great white? A blue? A tiger shark? A hammerhead? A nurse shark?

She took pictures of costumed urchins, my sister, as she always took pictures, e.g., my nephew on his first birthday (six years prior), blackfaced with cake and ice cream, a dozen relatives attempting in turn to read to him—about a tugboat—from a brand new rubberized book. *Toot toot!* His desperate, needy expression, in the photo, all out of phase with our excitement. The first nephew! The first grandchild! He was trying to get the cake in his mouth. Or: a later photo of my niece (his younger sister) attempting to push my nephew out of the shot—against a backdrop of autumn foliage; or a photo of my brother wearing my dad's yellow double-knit paisley trousers (with a bit of flair in the cuffs), twenty-five years after the heyday of such stylings; or my father and stepmother on their powerboat, peaceful and happy, the riotous wake behind them; or my sister's virtuosic photos of *dogs*—Mom's irrepressible golden retriever chasing a tennis ball across an overgrown lawn, or my dad's setter on the beach with a perspiring Löwenbräu leaning against his snout. Fifteen or twenty photo albums on the shelves in my sister's living room, a whole range of leathers and faux-leathers, no particular order, and just as many more photos loose, floating around the basement, castoffs, and files of negatives in their plastic wrappers.

She drank *the demon rum,* and she taught me how to do it, too, when we were kids; she taught me how to drink. We stole drinks, or we got people to steal them for us; we got reprobates of age to venture into the pristine suburban liquor stores. Later, I drank bourbon. My brother drank beer. My father drank single malt scotches. My grandmother drank half-gallons and then fell ill. My grandfather drank the finest collectibles. My sister's ex-husband drank more reasonably priced facsimiles. My brother drank until a woman lured him out of my mother's house. I drank until I was afraid to go outside. My uncle drank until the last year of his life. And I carried my sister in a blackout from a bar once—she was mumbling to herself, humming melodies, mostly unconscious. I took her arms; Peter Hunter took her legs. She slept the whole next day. On Halloween, my sister had a single gin and tonic before going out with the kids, before ambling around the condos of Kensington Court, circling from multifamily unit to multifamily unit, until my nephew's shark tail was grass-stained from the freshly mown lawns of the common areas. Then she drove her children across town to her ex-husband's house, released them into his supervision, and there they walked along empty lots, beside a brook, under the stars.

When they arrived home, these monsters, disgorged from their dad's Jeep, there was a fracas between girl and boy about which was superior (in the Aristotelian hierarchies), Milky Way, Whoppers, Slim Jim, Mike 'n Ikes, Sweet Tarts or Pez—this bounty counted, weighed and inventoried (on my niece's bed). Which was the Pez dispenser of greatest value? A Hanna-Barbera Pez dispenser? Or, say, a demonic *totem pole Pez dispenser?* And after this fracas, which my sister refereed wearily *(Look, if he wants to save the Smarties, you can't make him trade!),* they all slept, and this part is routine, my sister was tired as hell; she slept the sleep of the besieged, of the overworked, she fell precipitously into whorls of unconsciousness, of which no snapshot can be taken.

In one photograph, my sister is wearing a Superman outfit. This from a prior Halloween. I think it was a *Supermom* outfit, actually, because she always liked these bad jokes, degraded jokes, things other people would find ridiculous. (She'd take a joke and repeat it until it was leaden, until it was funny only in its awfulness.) Jokes with the fillip of sentimentality. Anyway, in this picture her blond hair—brightened a couple of shades with the current technologies—cascades around her shoulders, disordered and impulsive. *Supermom.* And her expression is skeptical, as if she assumes the mantle of Supermom—raising the kids, accepting wage-slavery, growing old and contented—and thinks it's dopey at the same time.

Never any good without coffee. Never any good in the morning. Never any good until the second cup. Never any good without freshly ground Joe, because of my dad's insistence, despite advantages of class and style, on *instant coffee.* No way. Not for my sister. At my dad's house, where she stayed in summer, she used to grumble derisively, while staring out the kitchen windows, out the expanse of windows that gave onto the meadow there, *Instant coffee!* There would be horses in the meadow and the ocean just over the trees, the sound of the surf and *instant coffee!* Thus the morning after Halloween, with my nephew the shark (who took this opportunity to remind her, in fact, that last year he saved his Halloween candy *all the way till Easter, Mommy)* and my niece, the Little Mermaid, orbiting around her like a fine dream. My sister was making this coffee with the automatic grinder and the automatic drip device, and the dishes were piled in the sink behind her, and the wall calendar was staring her in the face, with its hundred urgent appointments, e.g., *jury duty* (the following Monday) and *R & A to pediatrician;* the kids whirled around the kitchen, demanding to know who got the last of the Lucky Charms, who had to settle for the Kix. My sister's eyes barely open.

Now this portrait of her cat, Pointdexter, twelve years old—he slept on my face when I stayed at her place in 1984—Pointdexter with the brain tumor, Pointdexter with the Phenobarbital habit. That morning—All Saints' Day—he stood entirely motionless before his empty dish. His need was clear. His dignity was immense. Well, except for the seizures. Pointdexter had these seizures. He was possessed. He was a demon. He would bounce off the walls, he would get up *a head of steam,* mouth frothing, and run straight at the wall, smack into it, shake off the ghosts and start again. His screeches were unearthly. Phenobarbital was prescribed. My sister medicated him preemptively, before any other chore, before diplomatic initiatives on matters of cereal allocation. *Hold on, you guys, I'll be with you in a second.* Drugging the cat, slipping him the Mickey Finn in the Science Diet, feeding the kids, then getting out the door, pecking her boyfriend on the cheek (he was stumbling sleepily down the stairs).

❑ ❑ ❑ ❑

She printed snapshots. At this photo lab. She'd sold cameras (mnemonic devices) for years, and then she'd been kicked upstairs to the lab. Once she sold a camera to Pete Townshend, the musician. She told him—in her way both casual and rebellious—that she didn't really like The Who. Later, from her job at the lab, she used to bring home *other people's pictures,* e.g., an envelope of photographs of the Pope. Had she been out to Giants Stadium to use her telephoto lens to photograph John Paul II? No, she'd just printed up an extra batch of, say, Agnes Venditi's or Joey Mueller's photos. *Caveat emptor.* Who knew what else she'd swiped? Those Jerry Garcia pix from the show right before he died? Garcia's eyes squeezed tightly shut, as he sang in that heartbroken, exhausted voice of his? Or: somebody's trip to the Caribbean or to the Liberty Bell in Philly? Or: her neighbor's private documentations of love? Who knew? She'd get on the phone at work and gab, call up her friends, call up my family, printing pictures while gabbing, sheet after sheet of negatives, of memories. Oh, and circa Halloween, she was working in the lab with some new, exotic chemicals. She had a wicked headache.

My sister didn't pay much attention to the church calendar. Too busy. Too busy to concentrate on theologies, too busy to go to the doctor, too busy to deal with her finances, her credit-card debt, etc. Too busy. (And maybe afraid, too.) She was unclear on this day set aside for God's awesome tabernacle, unclear on the feast for the departed faithful, didn't know about the church of the Middle Ages, didn't know about the particulars of the Druidic ritual of Halloween—it was a Hallmark thing, a marketing event—or how All Saints' Day emerged as an alternative to Halloween. She was not much preoccupied with, nor attendant to articulations of loss nor interested in how this feast in the church calendar was hewn into two separate holy days, one for the saints, *that great cloud of witnesses,* one for the dearly departed, the regular old believers. She didn't know of any attachments that bound together these constituencies, didn't know, e.g., that God would *wipe away all tears from our eyes and there would be no more death,* according to the evening's reading from the book of Revelation. All this academic stuff was lost on her, though she sang in the church choir, and though on All

Saints' Day, a guy from the church choir happened to come into the camera store, just to say hi, a sort of an angel (let's say), and she said, *Hey Bob, you know, I never asked you what you do.*

To which Bob replied, *I'm a designer.*

My sister: *What do you design?*

Bob: *Steel wool.*

She believed him.

She was really small. She barely held down her clothes. Five feet tall. Tiny hands and feet. Here's a photo from my brother's wedding (two weeks before Halloween); we were dancing on the dance floor, she and I. She liked *to pogo* sometimes. It was the dance we preferred when dancing together. We created mayhem on the dance floor. Scared people off. We were demons for dance, for noise and excitement. So at my brother's wedding reception I hoisted her up onto my shoulder, and she was so light, just as I remembered from years before, twenty years of dances, still tiny, and I wanted to crowd-surf her across the reception, pass her across upraised hands, I wanted to impose her on older couples, gentlemen in their cummerbunds, old guys with tennis elbow or arthritis, with red faces and gin-blossoms; they would smile, passing my sister hither, to the microphone, where the wedding band was playing, where Bob would suddenly burst into song, into some sort of reconciliatory song, backed by the wedding band, and there would be stills of this moment, flash bulbs popping, a spotlight on her face, a tiny bit of reverb on her microphone, she would smile and concentrate and sing. Unfortunately, the situation around us, on the dance floor, was more complicated than this. Her boyfriend was about to have back surgery. He wasn't going to do any heavy lifting. And my nephew was too little to hold her up. And my brother was preoccupied with his duties as groom. So instead I twirled her once and put her down. We were laughing, out of breath.

On All Saints' Day she had lunch with Bob the angelic designer of steel wool (maybe he had a crush on her) or with the younger guys from the lab (because she was a middle-aged free spirit), and then she printed more photos of Columbus Day parades across Jersey, or photos of other people's kids dressed as Pocahontas or as the Lion King, and then at 5:30 she started home, a commute of forty-five minutes, Morristown to Hackettstown, on two-laners. She knew every turn. Here's the local news photo that never was: my sister slumped over the wheel of her Plymouth Saturn after having run smack into a local deer. All along those roads the deer were up-ended, disemboweled, set upon by crows and hawks, and my sister on the way back from work, or on the way home from a bar, must have grazed an entire herd of them at one time or another, missed them narrowly, frozen in the headlights of her car, on the shoulders of the meandering back roads, pulverized.

Her boy lives on air. Disdains food. My niece, meanwhile, will eat only candy. By dinnertime, they had probably made a dent in the orange plastic bucket with the Three Musketeers, the Cadbury's, Hot Tamales, Kit Kats, Jujyfruits, Baby Ruths, Bubble Yum—at least my niece had. They had insisted on bringing a sampling of this booty to school and from there to their afterschool play group. Neither of them wanted to eat anything; they complained about the whole idea of supper, and thus my sister offered, instead, to take them to the *McDonaldLand play area* on the main drag in Hacketts-town, where she would buy them a Happy Meal, or equivalent, a hamburger topped with *American processed cheese food,* and, as an afterthought, she would insist on their each trying a little bit of a salad from the brand new McDonald's salad bar. She had to make a deal to get the kids to accept the salad. She suggested six mouthfuls of lettuce each and drew a hard line there, but then she allowed herself to be talked down to two mouthfuls each. They ate indoors at first, the three of them, and then went out to the playground, where there were slides and jungle gyms in the reds and yellows of Ray Kroc's empire. My sister made the usual conversation, *How did the other kids make out on Halloween? What happened at school?* and she thought of her boyfriend, fresh from spinal surgery, who had limped downstairs in the morning to give her a kiss, and then she thought about *bills, bills, bills,* as she caught my niece at the foot of a slide. It was time to go sing. Home by nine.

◻ ◻ ◻ ◻

My sister as she played the guitar in the late sixties with her hair in braids; she played it before anyone else in my family, wandering around the chords, "House of the Rising Sun" or "Blackbird," on classical guitar, sticking to the open chords of guitar tablature. It never occurred to me to wonder about which instruments were used on those AM songs of the period (the Beatles with their sitars and cornets, Brian Wilson with his theremin), not until my sister started to play the guitar. (All of us sang—we used to sing and dance in the living room when my parents were married, especially to *Abbey Road* and *Bridge Over Troubled Water.)* And when she got divorced she started hanging around this bar where they had live music, this Jersey bar, and then she started hanging around at a local record label, an indy operation, and then she started *managing a band* (on top of everything else), and then she started to sing again. She joined the choir at St. James Church of Hackettstown and she started to sing, and after singing she started to pray— prayer and song being, I guess, styles of the same beseechment.

I don't know what songs they rehearsed at choir rehearsal, but Bob was there, as were others, Donna, Frank, Eileen and Tim (I'm making the names up), and I know that the choir was warm and friendly, though perhaps a little bit out of tune. It was one of those Charles Ives small-town choruses that slips in and out of pitch, that misses exits and entrances. But they had a good time rehearsing, with the kids monkeying around in the pews, the kids climbing sacrilegiously over that furniture, dashing up the aisle to the altar and back, as somebody kept half an eye on them (five of the whelps in all) and after the last notes ricocheted around the choir loft, my sister offered her summation of the proceedings, *Totally cool! Totally cool!,* and now the intolerable part of this story begins—with joy and excitement and a church interior. My sister and her kids drove from St. James to her house, her condo, this picturesque drive home, Hackettstown as if lifted from picture postcards of autumn, the park with its streams and ponds and lighted walkways, leaves in the streetlamps, in the headlights, leaves three or four days past their peak, the sound of leaves in the breeze, the construction crane by her place (they were digging up the road), the crane swaying above a fork in the road, a left turn after the fast-food depots, and then into her parking spot in front of the condo. The porch by the front door with the Halloween pumpkins: a cat's face complete with whiskers, a clown, a jack-o'-lantern. My sister closed the front door of her house behind her. Bolted it. Her daughter reminded her to light the pumpkins. Just inside the front door, Pointdexter, on the top step, waiting.

Her keys on the kitchen table. Her coat in the closet. She sent the kids upstairs to get into their pajamas. She called up to her boy-friend, who was in bed reading a textbook, *What are you doing in bed, you total slug!* and then, after checking the messages on the answering machine, looking at the mail, she trudged up to my niece's room to kiss her good night. Endearments passed between them. My sister loved her kids, above all, and in spite of all the work and the hardships, in spite of my niece's reputation as a firecracker, in spite of my nephew's sometimes diabolical smarts. She loved them. There were endearments, therefore, lengthy and repetitive, as there would have been with my nephew, too. And my sister kissed her daughter multiply, because my niece is a little impish redhead, and it's hard *not* to kiss her. *Look, it's late, so I can't read to you tonight, okay?* My niece protested temporarily, and then my sister arranged the stuffed animals around her daughter (for the sake of arranging), and plumped a feather pillow, and switched off the bedside lamp on the bedside table, and she made sure the night light underneath the table (a plug-in shaped like a ghost) was illu-mined, and then on the way out the door she stopped for a second. And looked back. The tableau of domesticity was what she last contemplated. Or maybe she was composing endearments for my nephew. Or maybe she wasn't looking back at my niece at all. Maybe she was lost in this next tempest.

Out of nowhere. All of a sudden. All at once. In an instant. With-out warning. In no time. Helter-skelter. *In the twinkling of an eye.* Figurative language isn't up to the task. My sister's legs gave out, and she fell over toward my niece's desk, by the door, dislodging a pile of toys and dolls (a Barbie in evening wear, a poseable

Tinkerbell doll), colliding with the desk, sweeping its contents off with her, toppling onto the floor, falling heavily, her head by the door. My niece, startled, rose up from under covers.

More photos: my sister, my brother and I, *back in our single digits,* dressed in matching, or nearly matching outfits (there was a naval flavor to our look), playing with my aunt's basset hound—my sister grinning mischievously; or: my sister, my father, my brother and I, in my dad's Karmann-Ghia, just before she totaled it on the straightaway on Fishers Island (she skidded, she said, *on antifreeze or something slippery);* or: my sister, with her newborn daughter in her lap, sitting on the floor of her living room—mother and daughter with the same bemused impatience.

My sister started to seize.

The report of her fall was, of course, loud enough to stir her boyfriend from the next room. He was out of bed fast. (Despite physical pain associated with his recent surgery.) I imagine there was a second in which other possibilities occurred to him—hoax, argument, accident, anything—but quickly the worst of these seemed most likely. You know these things somewhere. You know immediately the content of all middle-of-the-night telephone calls. He was out of bed. And my niece called out to her brother, to my nephew, next door. She called my nephew's name, plaintively, like it was a question.

My sister's hands balled up. Her heels drumming on the carpeting. Her muscles all like nautical lines, pulling tight against cleats. Her jaw clenched. Her heart rattling desperately. Fibrillating. If it was a conventional seizure, she was unconscious for this part—maybe even unconscious throughout—because of reduced blood flow to the brain, because of the fibrillation, because of her heart condition; which is to say that my sister's *mitral valve prolapse*—technical feature of her *broken heart*—was here engendering an arrhythmia, and now, if not already, she began to hemorrhage internally. Her son stood in the doorway, in his pajamas, shifting from one foot to the other (there was a draft in the hall). Her daughter knelt at the foot of the bed, staring, and my sister's boyfriend watched, as my poor sister shook, and he held her head, and then changed his mind and bolted for the phone.

After the seizure, she went slack. (Meredith's heart stopped. And her breathing. She was still.) For a second, she was alone in the room, with her children, silent. After he dialed 911, Jimmy appeared again, to try to restart her breathing. Here's how: he pressed his lips against hers. He didn't think to say, *Come on, breathe dammit,* or to make similar imprecations, although he did manage to shout at the kids, *Get the hell out of here, please! Go downstairs!* (It was advice they followed only for a minute.) At last, my sister took a breath. Took a deep breath, a sigh, and there were two more of these. Deep resigned sighs. Five or ten seconds between each. For a few moments more, instants, she looked at Jimmy, as he pounded on her chest with his fists, thoughtless about anything but results, stopping occasionally to press his ear between her breasts. Her eyes were sad and frightened, even in the company of the people she most loved. So it seemed. More likely she was unconscious. The kids sat cross-legged on the floor in the hall, by the top of the stairs, watching. Lots of stuff was left to be accomplished in these last seconds, even if it wasn't anything unusual, people and relationships and small kindnesses, the best way to fry pumpkin seeds, what to pack for Thanksgiving, whether to make turnips or not, snapshots to be culled and arranged, photos to be taken—these possibilities spun out of my sister's grasp, torrential futures, my beloved sister, solitary with pictures taken and untaken, gone.

EMS technicians arrived and carried her body down to the living room where they tried to start her pulse with expensive engines and devices. Her body jumped while they shocked her—she was a revenant in some corridor of simultaneities—but her heart wouldn't start. Then they put her body on the stretcher. To carry her away. Now the moment arrives when they bear her out the front door of her house and she leaves it to us, leaves to us the house and her things and her friends and her memories and the involuntary assemblage of these into language. Grief. The sound of the ambulance. The road is mostly clear on the way to the hospital; my sister's route is clear.

I should fictionalize it more, I should conceal myself. I should consider the responsibilities of characterization, I should conflate her two children into one, or reverse their genders, or otherwise alter them, I should make her boyfriend a husband, I should explicate all the tributaries of my extended family (its remarriages, its internecine politics), I should novelize the whole thing, I should make it multigenerational, I should work in my forefathers (stonemasons and newspapermen), I should let artifice create an elegant surface, I should make the events orderly, I should wait and write about it later, I should wait until I'm not angry, I shouldn't clutter a narrative with fragments, with mere recollections of good times, or with regrets, I should make Meredith's death shapely and persuasive, not blunt and disjunctive, I shouldn't have to think the unthinkable, I shouldn't have to suffer, I should address her here directly (these are the ways I miss you), I should write only of affection, I should make our travels in this earthly landscape safe and secure, I should have a better ending, I shouldn't say her life was short and often sad, I shouldn't say she had her demons, as I do too.

Contributors' Notes

LEE K. ABBOTT's sixth collection of stories, *Wet Places at Noon* is forthcoming from the University of Iowa Press in 1998. His fiction has appeared in *The Georgia Review, The Atlantic Monthly, Harper's,* and many other literary periodicals. When he's not living three miles west of Lincoln, New Mexico (pop. 62), he directs the MFA Program in Creative Writing at Ohio State University in Columbus.

"The story arises out of my fascination with—okay, my obsession for—knowing how our crooked kind deals with the extraordinary that itself rises up almost daily to bedevil us. I like the whomp the unexpected makes. Better yet, I like what comes next, after the dust clears."

JOHN BARTH is the author of nine novellas, two collections of essays, the National Book Award–winning novella series *Chimera,* and two volumes of short stories—including, most recently, the series *On with the Story.* He is Professor Emeritus in the Writing Seminars at Johns Hopkins University and a fellow of both the American Academy of Arts and Letters and the American Academy of Arts and Sciences.

"I once asked a scientific colleague to help me calculate in how many directions and at what speeds we're moving when we're sitting still. These calculations, along with other things, suggested the story 'On with the Story.' On with the story?"

ARTHUR BRADFORD is twenty-seven years old and lives in Austin, Texas. He has received a Wallace Stegner Fellowship from Stanford and a James Michener Fellowship from the Texas Center for Writers. "Catface" is part of a longer series of stories.

"I am a big fan of Denis Johnson's book *Jesus' Son,* and also Richard Linklater's film *Slacker.*

"Some parts of this story are real. I've had some pretty weird housemates. Although I never actually lived with a catfaced person, I did often see a man at the library here in Austin who had very catlike facial features. I thought, 'I wonder if people call him Catface.' Later on I got to know him and discovered this was not the case.

"When I was living in San Francisco, I met a woman in the park who claimed to have some puppies back in her apartment. I followed her over there to see them, at her request, but when we reached the doorway she suddenly decided I should not come inside. She said, 'I don't think this is such a hot idea.'

"My keen writer's sensibility told me that there must be a fascinating story behind this odd behavior."

CAROLYN COOKE was born on Mount Desert Island in Maine and now lives in Point Arena, California, with her husband, poet Randall Babtkis, and their two children. Her fiction has been published in *The Gettysburg Review, New England Review, Puckerbrush Review,* and *The Paris Review,* and also appears in *The Best American Short Stories for 1997.*

"I wrote this story after my great-uncle died. He was ninety-two and interesting in the New England way—he saw the world as perfectly unforgiving. At his funeral I said he had loved glaciers and skiing, but inside I dwelled on other, less suitable details for a dirge. For my tenth birthday, for example, he gave me a Kraft cheese. Another detail: A few days before he died, I drove him on an errand. We passed over some shadows from a maple tree and he clutched his cane (he was nearly blind) and yelled, 'Damn it, Cabbie, you just ran over a bicyclist!' There was genuine irritation in his voice, but no suggestion that we should stop. That tone interested me, irritation as a condensed form of horror or deep feeling. These were poor points for a eulogy, but through them I began to understand certain old man things. Eventually an old man spoke convincingly to me, although he was not my great-uncle. He began with the gift of the cheese."

KIANA DAVENPORT is a *hapa-haole,* of native Hawai'ian and Anglo-American descent. She is the author of four novels, most recently

Shark Dialogues (Plume Penguin, 1995). Her short fiction has appeared in *Seattle Review, New Asia Review, Hawaii Pacific Review, New Letters, Story,* and many other journals and anthologies.

"I lived near a river-station on the Sepik River in Papua New Guinea. One day a young girl came to me. 'Please help me,' she said. 'I want to become a modern woman.' 'The Lipstick Tree' is her story. Indigenous women have become the conscience of the Pacific, fighting nuclear testing and dumping, mass tourism, and mining. In the forefront of the struggle are the women of Papua New Guinea—doctors, lawyers, engineers.

"But in the mountain villages and river hamlets across this vast island, there are still women denied education, literacy, women crippled from spousal abuse, women even worked to death. In despair, some commit suicide. Some become *breakaways,* running off to large towns and cities. For those who succeed, becoming domestics, nurses, even teachers, the price is often devastating. Renouncement by their tribes, loss of culture, family, place. Each time I return to Papua New Guinea, I search for the girl in 'The Lipstick Tree.' "

ANDRE DUBUS: "I live in Haverhill, Massachusetts, have six children, have published nine books and am working on a book of essays. From time to time, I have been blessed with grants and awards that have paid my bills: two Guggenheims, two NEA awards, a MacArthur Foundation Grant, and the Rea Award for the short story.

"I received the seed for 'Dancing After Hours' when one of my daughters, who was about ten, said to me: 'What if someone were named Drew?' Several things happened at once: In my mind I saw the name Drew Purdy; I saw a quadriplegic friend of mine in his motorized chair; I saw him riding into a town; and I saw the line: *Drew Purdy rode into town in a motorized chair.* I gestated for years, thinking for at least a year that my protagonist would be a male bartender who was impotent. Then I learned that a man cannot be made impotent by an accident unless he is paralyzed, and that the other causes of impotence are medication or psychological. So I made my protagonist a woman who believes she is homely. I wanted someone who felt insulated. Then I started the story."

DEBORAH EISENBERG: "My most recent collection of stories is called *All Around Atlantis.*

"I live in New York City and I teach at the University of Virginia, but I grew up in the Midwest, and I was sent off to a boarding school in Vermont. I flew over an area not far from our house called

The Lagoons. The mystery of the word, the rigid proprieties of the suburb I came from, the killers I divined roving insatiably through the vast landscape beneath me, and my exile from a hostile and familiar childhood into a hostile and foreign adulthood all evidently rolled up into a ball and came bouncing back cheerfully into this story."

MARY GAITSKILL is the author of one novel and two collections of short stories. Her work has appeared in *The New Yorker, Harper's, Esquire, Best American Short Stories 1993,* and in many other anthologies. She is currently teaching creative writing at the University of Houston.

" 'Comfort' is about two people who want decency and kindness but who are unable to respect or understand each other's way of trying to find it. The beauty of each is hidden from the other—but to me the story is in the way the man is straining to make out the woman's silhouette in the dark."

THOMAS GLAVE's work has most recently appeared in *Children of the Night: The Best Short Stories by Black Writers 1967–Present* (Little, Brown), *Men on Men 6: Best New Gay Fiction* (Penguin), *The Kenyon Review, His 2: Brilliant New Fiction by Gay Men* (Faber & Faber), and *Soulfires: Young Black Men on Love and Violence* (Penguin), and is forthcoming in *Callaloo*. A former Fellow of the Fine Arts Center in Provincetown and the NEA/Travel Grants Fund for Artists, he is currently pursuing graduate studies at Brown University.

"I wrote 'The Final Inning' because, for years, I had wanted very much to read it. I thought that someone, somewhere, surely must have already written it, but it appeared no one had, so I did. Wrote it desiring to see something in which black people—particularly black gay people, more deeply invisible amongst the invisible—were taken seriously; were not trivialized, dismissed, or reduced to caricature or to the insults of literary minstrelsy. Wanted a story, in short, about *familiar* people, who—like other human beings, with whom black and gay people are often not equated—lived, loved, hoped, thought, and died.

MARY GORDON's novels have been bestsellers—*Final Payments, The Company of Women, Men and Angels,* and *The Other Side*. She has published a book of novellas, *The Rest of Life,* a collection of stories, *Temporary Shelter,* and a book of essays, *Good Boys and Dead Girls*. She has received the Lila Acheson Wallace-Reader's Digest Writer's Award and a Guggenheim Fellowship. She is a professor of English at Barnard College. Her most recent book, *The Shadow Man,* a memoir, was published in May of 1996.

"In some mysterious way 'City Life' was influenced by the voice of Jean Stafford, whose work I was reading intensely at the time I wrote it. It reflects that fascination—where avidity can turn to paranoia—that a New York apartment dweller has about her neighbors."

MATTHEW KLAM studied writing at Hollins College. He has received fellowships from the Fine Arts Work Center in Provincetown, Massachusetts, St. Albans School, and American University, and has taught at The Hill School and Stockholm University in Sweden. His work has appeared in *The New Yorker, Shankpainter,* and *The Washington Post Magazine.* "The Royal Palms" is part of a collection of stories to be published by Random House.

"The story didn't take any work and wrote itself—truly, no sweat—and that's annoying. Once I stuck the opening scene onto the situation, the one couple and the sexy couple, I was rolling. It seemed obvious and funny to me from the beginning and I had a draft in about two weeks. That's why what occurs is so simple. Despite the breakdown between the narrator and his wife, the tension is between the two men—that was the file name for it in my computer, MEN. That's how guys like this express their sexual attraction, by involving the other guy in his problems in a way that is essentially intimate—rather than by doing each other. Nothing about the story is real, except for Diane's excuse that she can't have sex because she has a fat ass, and the way Joanie grins at everything, good and bad, which a friend of mine does, and the whole opening, I ripped that off, and the way Rick gets the money, though I can't figure out who that could be."

IAN MACMILLAN has published four books, the most recent of which is *Orbit of Darkness* (HBJ, 1991). His short story collection *Light and Power* (Univ. of Missouri Press) won the 1979 Associated Writing Programs Award. He has made seventy-five appearances in literary and commercial magazines including *Yankee, The Paris Review, The Iowa Review,* and *The Missouri Review,* and has been reprinted in *Best American Short Stories* and *Pushcart Prize* volumes. He has lived in Hawaii for the past thirty-one years, teaches fiction writing at the University of Hawaii, and is fiction editor of *Manoa: A Pacific Journal of International Writing.*

"Although I have lived in Hawaii all these years, I still write stories set in Upstate New York, where I spent my adolescent years. I refer to these as 'cows and chainsaws' stories, of which I have written probably forty or fifty. The idea for 'The Red House' came about while I was sitting watching TV with my wife and two daughters, who were home from college on the mainland for vacation. It was a simple 'what if' proposition in which I pictured a boy from that somewhat depressed and remote region of Upstate New York I was once so familiar with. What happens when a semiliterate boy with access to a television set stumbles into the recognition of the power of words?"

RICK MOODY is the author of the novels *Garden State, The Ice Storm,* and *Purple America,* and a collection of stories, *The Ring of Brightest Angels Around Heaven.*

"There are few things I've written that I would rather talk about less than 'Demonology.' Had I more to say on the subject, I would have said it."

ROBERT MORGAN has published nine collections of poetry and four books of fiction, most recently the novel *The Truest Pleasure,* which *Publishers Weekly* listed as one of the best books of 1995. His stories have appeared in many magazines, including *Epoch, The Southern Review,* and *South Dakota Review.* A native of western North Carolina, he has taught at Cornell since 1971.

"When a jetliner crashed near Hendersonville, North Carolina, in 1967, a friend of mine who was working on a nearby interstate highway, described watching bodies fall out of the sky and onlookers rushing to the bodies. He did not admit looting the bodies himself, but I knew there was a story there. Twenty-five years later, I found this narrator and wrote 'The Balm of Gilead Tree.'"

ALICE MUNRO grew up in Wingham, Ontario, and attended the University of Western Ontario. She married, moved to Vancouver and Victoria, became the mother of three daughters, and with her husband opened the well-known bookstore Munro's Books. She has published seven collections of stories—*Dance of the Happy Shades, Something I've Been Meaning to Tell You, The Beggar Maid, The Moons of Jupiter, The Progress of Love, Friend of My Youth,* and *Open Secrets*—and a novel, *Lives of Girls and Women.*

Among her awards are three Governor General's Literary Awards—Canada's highest; the Lannan Literary Award; and the W. H. Smith Award, given to *Open Secrets* as the best book published in the United Kingdom in 1995. Her stories have appeared in

The New Yorker, The Atlantic Monthly, The Paris Review, and other publications, and her collections have been translated into thirteen languages.

Alice Munro and her second husband divide their time between Clinton, Ontario, near Lake Huron, and Comox, British Columbia.

"What did I know first about this story? A man and woman disposing of her lover's body. This happened on an island off the B.C. coast—they put him in his own boat and towed him out into open water (into Desolation Sound, actually, which is a bit too much for a story). The sudden switch from sex to murder to marital cooperation seemed to me one of those marvelous, unlikely, acrobatic pieces of human behavior. Then the lover got transferred into a car, and it all went on in Huron County, and the boys got into it, and their families, and Enid, who took over the story as insistently as she took over a sickroom. And there is the boat, still, waiting by the bank of the Maitland River."

PATRICIA ELAM RUFF has written for *Essence, Emerge,* and the *Washington Post* and provided commentary for National Public Radio and CNN. Ms. Ruff, who holds J.D. and M.F.A. degrees, lives in Washington, D.C., and is currently completing a novel. Her story "The Taxi Ride" was also selected for inclusion in *New Stories from the South: The Year's Best, 1997.*

"I rarely take taxis but one day my car was in the shop, my feet hurt, and I hailed one. The driver was an older gentleman accompanied by an older woman who sat up front with him. I immediately noticed that there was something very comfortable and caring about their relationship. Whether they were talking or silent, they were constantly communicating. During the brief time I was in their presence, I became aware of the romance and love they shared even though there was no physical touching between them. The experience was quite magical and I had no choice but to go home and try to write a story about it."

GEORGE SAUNDERS's fiction has appeared in *The New Yorker, Harper's, Story,* and other magazines. Two of the pieces in his collection, *CivilWarLand in Bad Decline* (Random House, 1996) received National Magazine Awards. He teaches in the Creative Writing Program at Syracuse University.

"I have now written three utterly false paragraphs about 'The Falls' and have decided to be a party-pooper and simply say that I don't very much like to write about my stories and am not any good at it. Instead, I'd like to use this space to thank the O. Henry editor and jury for putting out this book, which I think is a force for good in the literary world, and for including my story in it."

SUSAN FROMBERG SCHAEFFER has published ten novels and one collection of short stories, *The Queen of Egypt.* Many of her stories have been anthologized. She is the recipient of a Guggenheim Fellowship and has won the Lawrence Award for Short Fiction, The Edward Lewis Wallant Award, and the Friends of Literature Award, among others. Last year, she received an award from the University of Chicago for outstanding career achievement. Her second book of poetry, *Granite Lady,* was a National Book Award nominee.

" 'The Old Farmhouse and the Dog-wife' appeared literally out of nowhere. A friend had said that any description of any event can lead into a story. To test this theory, I wrote down the following sentence: 'A car drove up to the house.' The rest of the story promptly followed. I think this story, if not all my stories, hatch in what I call 'empty time,' the time when I appear to be doing nothing, or more irritatingly to bystanders, seem to be staring into space. Probably, there is no such thing as empty time for a writer. If you are a writer, you *will* write. There is no escaping it. That, at least, has been my sad experience."

CHRISTINE SCHUTT lives and teaches in New York City. Her first story collection, *Nightwork,* was published by Knopf in 1996. She has published stories in many small magazines, including *Alaska Quarterly Review,* in which "His Chorus" first appeared.

" 'His Chorus' was inspired by what I only dared glance at then, a dark figure in just such a portico, a student I might have had or a son."

CAROL SHIELDS: "I grew up in the American Midwest and have lived in Canada for the last forty years. I've written poetry, plays, and novels, coming later, with a great shock of pleasure, to short fiction. Currently I am Chancellor of the University of Winnipeg.

"Like the couple in the story, I once spent a month without looking into a mirror, and I still remember the stunned surprise of meeting my image after an enforced separation—*can that woman really be me!* I suppose most of us think of mirrors as providing a daily reality check; without them we drift into a new and perhaps freer sense of ourselves."

JURORS

LOUISE ERDRICH is the author of *The Beet Queen, Tracks,* the National Book Critics Circle Award winner *Love Medicine, The Bingo Palace,* and *Tales of Burning Love.* Other books include *Baptism of Desire: Poems* and a children's book, *Grandmother Pigeon,* and the novel *The Crown of Columbus,* cowritten with Michael Dorris. In 1987, she was an O. Henry Awards First Prize Winner and she also had a story included in *Prize Stories 1985: The O. Henry Awards.*

THOM JONES is the author of the short story collections *The Pugilist at Rest* and *Cold Snap and Other Stories.* His fiction has appeared in *The New Yorker, Playboy, Harper's, Esquire, GQ,* and *Buzz.* In 1993, he was an O. Henry Awards First Prize winner.

DAVID FOSTER WALLACE is the author of the novels *Infinite Jest* and *The Broom of the System,* the story collection *Girl with Curious Hair,* and *A Supposedly Fun Thing I'll Never Do Again,* an essay collection. His fiction and nonfiction have appeared in *The New Yorker, Playboy, Harper's, Paris Review, Esquire,* and *Story.* Wallace has received the Lannan Literary Award, the Whiting Award, a MacArthur Foundation Grant, and was a 1989 O. Henry Award winner.

50 Honorable Mention Stories

ALEXANDER, ELENA, "Sic Transit," *Bomb,* No. 57
Aboard a train bound for Cologne, an English-speaking German eavesdrops on a conversation between an American woman and her boorish lover, an egotistical painter.

ALTER, STEPHEN, "Confluence," *Denver Quarterly,* Vol. 30, No. 3
A man returns to Jawalaghat, in northern India, to throw his father's ashes in the confluence of the Bhulganga and Alsi rivers, where they once fished when he was a boy.

ANSAY, A. MANETTE, "Neighbor," *Epoch,* Vol. 44, No. 2
A father and husband becomes fascinated by a single woman living next door whose untended garden imposes on the order he is trying to maintain on his own property.

BARRETT, ANDREA, "The Mysteries of Ubiquitin," *Story,* Summer 1996
A ten-year-old girl falls in love with her parents' friend, an entomologist. The girl grows up to be a renowned scientist herself, and she and the entomologist become lovers.

BAXTER, CHARLES, "The Cures for Love," *DoubleTake,* No. 4
A classicist whose boyfriend has left her, seeks consolation in Ovid's *Remedia amoris.* Following the author's advice, she seeks refuge in the bustle of a public place: O'Hare Airport.

BEAL, DAPHNE, "Azure," *American Short Fiction,* No. 21
A precocious girl lives with her older brother and their eccentric English mother in a house once attached to a palace in Katmandu.

BOYLE, T. CORAGHESSAN, "Rapture of the Deep," *The Paris Review,* No. 136

> Narrated by Jacques Cousteau's on-board chef, Bernard, who, tired of being at sea, tries to foment a mutiny by serving terrible meals and emptying the wine overboard.

BUSCH, FREDERICK, "Timberline," *The Georgia Review,* Vol. XLIX, No. 4

> On the eve of his forty-fifth birthday, a man walks out of his Greenwich Village apartment, fetches his car from the garage, and heads north. While driving, he recalls a mountain hike he took with his father when he was eight years old.

CARLSON, RON, "Oxygen," *Witness,* Vol. X, No. 2

> A young man takes a summer job delivering medical oxygen in Phoenix and becomes emotionally entangled with one patient and sexually involved with the daughter of another.

COTTLE, BRENT, "Rijstafel," *Mid-American Review,* Vol. XVI, No. 1

> The adventures of two young Americans serving as Mormon missionaries in the Netherlands.

DICKINSON, CHARLES, "Colonel Roebling's Friend," *The Atlantic Monthly,* September 1995

> New York City in the 1870s and '80s. A Union veteran wounded at Vicksburg takes a job working on the Brooklyn Bridge and ends up disabled as the result of a severe case of the bends from time spent in the caissons beneath the river.

DIEDRICH, STEVE, "The Transfer of Grief," *Boulevard,* Volume 11, No. 3

> An unrepentant underachiever, dope smoker, drinker, liar, and bisexual with a pregnant wife learns that his brother-in-law, whom he once had sex with, is dying of AIDS.

DIXON, STEPHEN, "The Miracle," *StoryQuarterly,* No. 32

> A woman suffering from a debilitating disease experiences a miraculous one-day remission when her husband, half-mockingly, prays for her to get well.

DONER, DEAN, "The Comfort of This World," *The Hudson Review,* Vol. XLIX, No. 2

> After the sudden death of his wife, just before they were set to retire, a man takes an apartment in Manhattan and searches for meaning in museums, galleries, theaters, and concert halls.

ELLISON, RALPH, "I Did Not Learn Their Names," *The New Yorker,* April 29, 1996

Depression era setting. A black man riding the rails on his way to school to study music meets a white couple on their way to visit their son in prison. Evocative, posthumously published sketch shows a young writer's future promise.

ELY, SCOTT, "The Angel of the Garden," *The Gettysburg Review,* Vol. 9, No. 4

A disabled Vietnam vet whose only work is shooting feral cats on a property in the Mississippi Delta, loses his job when the owner's cousin, an alluring young woman, moves in and traps the cats humanely.

EVENSON, BRIAN, "The Polygamy of Language," *Conjunctions,* No. 26

A man kills two polygamists in search of "the solution to the problem of all possible languages."

FALCO, EDWARD, "Ax," *North Dakota Quarterly,* Vol. 62, No. 4

A young man returns to a university after a semester away, having fled an uncomfortable situation, the aftermath of which he must now confront.

FROMM, PETE, "Lifesaving," *Vignette,* Vol. 1, Issue 4

A man who has saved a mother and child from a burning boat wreck does not think himself a hero. Others do, including his initially skeptical wife and an attractive coworker.

GILBERT, DAVID, "Remote Feed," *Harper's,* July 1996

A CNN film crew assigned to the Galapagos Islands to cover the First Lady's visit is still in shock from an assignment in Bosnia where the on-camera reporter they worked with suddenly died.

GLASSBERG, ROY, "Rifka, a Cracked Record," *Manoa,* Vol. 8, No. 1

In Warsaw, just before the Nazi invasion, a Jewish group weighs their alternatives for escape, with the help of an eccentric old woman and a young American thug.

GOODMAN, ALLEGRA, "The Four Questions," *Commentary,* April 1996

A middle-aged couple, more culturally Jewish than religious, attends a Passover seder with their four college-age children, one of whom is born-again Orthodox, another of whom brings a Christian girlfriend.

HELPERIN, MARK, "Last Tea with the Armorers," *Esquire,* October 1995

Set in Israel in 1972. An unmarried holocaust survivor in her thirties, living with her aging father, meets a new immigrant from Australia.

HWANG, CHANG, "Little Beauty's Wedding," *Story,* Winter 1996

Mr. Un, who sells the preserved bodies of dead young women in remote Chinese villages, places the corpse of a young prostitute, Little Beauty, with a wealthy couple, to be "wed" to their dead son so he will have a wife in the next life.

LA SALLE, PETER, "The McClanaghans," *The Literary Review,* Vol. 39, No. 1

A group of twelve-year-old boys enter the house of a neighbor away on vacation and maliciously trash it. The entire story is told in a single run-on sentence.

LAWSON, DOUG, "Elephants," *Sycamore Review,* Vol. 8, No. 1

A truck driver crashes his rig as the result of a hallucination: an elephant charging toward him. His two sons, who live with their mother and new husband, visit him in the hospital.

LEE, MARIE G., "Artificial Light," *American Voice,* No. 39

A young woman, born in Korea but adopted by American parents, returns to Korea for a language and culture class. She and a half-Caucasian classmate sneak onto a U.S. military base in search of her father.

MCGRAW, ERIN, "Daily Affirmations," *The Georgia Review,* Vol. XLIX, No. 3

The author of a self-help/recovery book goes to visit her parents over Christmas to help her mother, who has a broken ankle, only to have her own progress toward recovery undone.

MARIE, LYNN, "One Step from Doing," *The Antioch Review,* Vol. 54, No. 1

A black twelve-year-old girl who has been sexually abused, and has also experienced consensual sex, yearns to remain a child. She lives with a kind uncle, for whom she feels an undertow of inappropriate sexual attraction.

MEIROSE, JIM, "Fair Night," *Oasis,* Vol. IV, No. 2

It's Sunday morning and a young girl asks her parents to take her to the fair, as promised. Her parents bicker over breakfast. Told from the child's and the family cat's points of view.

MILLER, ALYCE, "Several False Starts and a Rough Connection," *American Short Fiction,* No. 22

Two women with the same lover await the man's arrival at Newark Airport, unbeknownst to one another.

MOORE, HAL, "The Burning Heart," *Manoa,* Vol. 8, No. 1

A man has an attack of what he perceives to be heartburn and collapses on his way to the toilet. His soul flees his body and he sees his wife, daughter, and son gather around his fallen body.

MOSLEY, WALTER, "Marvane Street," *Story,* Spring 1996

A paroled killer living in a shack and earning his living by boxing groceries takes a troubled young man under his wing.

NELSON, ANTONYA, "Loose Cannon," *Prairie Schooner,* Vol. 70, No. 1

A young woman in the throes of a breakdown takes refuge with her shiftless brother, who lives in an abandoned church in New Mexico without a car or telephone.

NOVAKOVICH, JOSIP, The Enemy, *The Sun,* Issue 252

A Croatian marries an American woman jilted at the altar, who turns out to be a Russian emigree from a noble family. Their brief union produces a child.

OATES, JOYCE CAROL, "The Affliction," *Bomb,* Fall 1995

A successful artist in his seventies reveals his secret: He makes his art from the products of his affliction, strange parasites beneath the surface of his skin.

POVERMAN, C. E., "Deer Season," *Ontario Review,* No. 44

A man and woman, lovers, bicker over the man's planned hunting trip. He goes nonetheless and gets caught in a snow storm while retrieving a deer he has killed.

REILLY, GERALD, "Leaving St. Caspar's," *Image,* No. 14

A priest whose speech is impossible to understand—through an unfortunate combination of a heavy Irish brogue, a lisp, and a stutter—attempts to effect a cure through the use of subliminal tapes.

RIOS, MIGUEL, "Gravity's Angel," *Wascana Review,* Vol. 30, No. 2

A man who, with his wife, sold their newborn baby, has the boy, now five and brain damaged, returned to him one night outside a bar he frequents and must decide what to do with the strange creature.

SEAMON, HOLLIS, "Gypsies in the Place of Pain," *Calyx,* Vol. 16, No. 2

The mother of a very sick boy living in a children's hospital in New York encounters a group of gypsies who have brought in a girl with a severe kidney infection.

SHISHIN, ALEX, "Mr. Eggplant Goes Home," *Prairie Schooner,*
Vol. 70, No. 2

A mean-spirited and alcoholic Japanese professor of English, whose
wife has written all of his papers on Hawthorne, goes home to his
ailing mother in the small village where he was raised.

STERN, DANIEL, "The Passion According to Saint John, by Johann
Sebastian Bach: a story," *New Letters,* Vol. 62, No. 3

A high school symphony conductor stopped for speeding tells the
arresting officer that he was inspired by Bach's The Passion According to Saint John. The born-again officer misinterprets this to mean
the man was inspired by Jesus.

STOLLMAN, ARYAH LEV, "The Adornment of Days," *Southwest
Review,* Vol. 81, No. 1

A young and brilliant composer takes up residence in his recently
deceased grandfather's Jerusalem apartment to write an opera about
a false messiah.

STUCKEY-FRENCH, ELIZABETH, "Junior," *The Atlantic Monthly,*
April 1996

A teenage girl, accused of trying to drown a little girl in a public
pool and sent away by a judge, is rescued by an eccentric aunt.

TAGATAC, GERONIMO G., "Ten Degrees North," *Writers' Forum,*
Vol. 21

A Vietnam vet is haunted by the ghost of a Viet Cong soldier he shot
and driven to madness by these visions.

TUNG, PALO, "One for Ma," *New Orleans Review,* Vol. 22, Nos. 3
& 4

A woman returns to China with her Americanized children to visit
her husband's eccentric, tradition-minded family.

UPDIKE, JOHN, "The Cats," *The New Yorker,* December 9, 1996

A man left to straighten out his dead mother's affairs and sell her
Pennsylvania farmhouse tries to figure out what to do about the
numerous cats remaining on the property.

WILSON, ROBLEY, "California," *The Iowa Review,* Vol. 25, No. 3

A young woman returns to Iowa for her father's funeral and revisits
the site where a UFO supposedly landed when she was a child. She
recalls her father's visit to her in California, when he experienced an
earthquake and she discovered he was dying.

YACHIMSKI, PATRICK, "Asylum," *DoubleTake,* No. 2

A young man committed to a mental hospital befriends a hairless, toothless oddball who recites the same speech, word for word, over and over again.

ZAFRIS, NANCY, "Swimming in the Dark," *The Missouri Review,* Vol. XIX, No. 2

A Japanese flight attendant, in Rome for a layover, takes an interest in a boisterous group of Americans trying to dispose of the ashes of their friend.

Magazines Consulted

Entries entirely in boldface and with their titles in all-capital letters denote publications with prize-winning stories. Asterisks following titles denote magazines with Honorable Mention stories. The information presented is up-to-date as of the time *Prize Stories 1997: The O. Henry Awards* went to press. For more complete information, contact individual magazines or visit our Web site at:

http://www.boldtype.com/ohenry

Magazine editors who wish to have their publications added to the list of those consulted and to have the stories they publish considered for O. Henry Awards may send subscriptions or all issues containing fiction to the series editor at:

P.O. Box 739
Montclair, NJ 07042

Please note this address is only for correspondence from magazines. All other correspondence should be sent to Anchor Books.

African American Review

Stalker Hall 213
Indiana State University
Terre Haute, IN 47809
Joe Weixlmann, Editor
web.indstate.edu/artsci/AAR
*Quarterly with a focus on African
American literature and culture.
Averages one short story per issue.*

Agni

236 Bay Street Road
Boston University Writing Program
Boston, MA 02115
Askold Melnyczuk, Editor
www.cais.net/aesir/fiction/AGNI/
Biannual.

Alabama Literary Review

Smith 253
Troy State University
Troy, AL 36082
Theron Montgomery, Chief Editor
Published annually.

Alaska Quarterly Review

University of Alaska Anchorage
3211 Providence Drive
Anchorage, AK 99508
Ronald Spatz, Executive Editor

Amelia

329 "E" Street
Bakersfield, CA 93304
Frederick A. Raborg Jr., Editor
Quarterly.

America West Airlines Magazine

4636 E. Elwood Street, Suite 5
Phoenix, AZ 85040–1963
Michael Derr, Editor
*Inflight magazine with occasional
fiction.*

American Letters and Commentary

850 Park Avenue
Suite 5B
New York, NY 10021
Jeanne Beaumont, Anna
Rabinowitz, Editors

American Short Fiction*

University of Texas Press
Journals Division
Box 7819
Austin, TX 78713–7819
Joseph E. Kruppa, Editor
journals@uts.cc.utexas.eduwww.
utexas.edu/utpress/journals/
jasf.html
Quarterly.

The American Voice*

332 West Broadway
Suite 1215
Louisville, KY 40202
Frederick Smock, Editor
Triannual.

American Way

P.O. Box 619640
DFW Airport
Texas 75261–9640
Chuck Thompson, Senior Editor
102132.711@compuserve.com
www.americanair.com/away
*American Airlines' inflight
magazine. Published twice a
month, with one story per issue.*

Another Chicago Magazine

Left Field Press
3709 North Kenmore
Chicago, IL 60613
Barry Silesky, Editor & Publisher

Antietam Review

7 West Franklin Street
Hagerstown, MD 21740
Susanne Kass, Executive Editor

The Antioch Review*

P.O. Box 148
Yellow Springs, OH 45387
Robert S. Fogarty, Editor
Quarterly.

Apalachee Quarterly

P.O. Box 10469
Tallahassee, FL 32302
Barbara Hamby, Editor

Appalachian Heritage
Besea College
Besea, KY 40404
Sidney Saylor Farr, Editor
Quarterly of southern Appalachian life & culture.

Ascent
English Dept.
Concordia College
901 8th Street S
Moorhead, MN 56562
W. Scott Olsen, Editor
Triannual.

Atlanta Review
P.O. Box 8248
Atlanta, GA 30306
Daniel Veach, Editor & Publisher
Biannual.

The Atlantic Monthly*
77 N. Washington Street
Boston, MA 02114
C. Michael Curtis, Senior Editor
www.TheAtlantic.com

Baffler
P.O. Box 378293
Chicago, IL 60637
Thomas Frank, Editor-in-Chief

Bellowing Ark
P. O. Box 45637
Seattle, WA 98145
Robert R. Ward, Editor

Black Warrior Review
University of Alabama
P. O. Box 862936
Tuscaloosa, AL 35486–0027
Mindy Wilson, Editor-in-Chief
Biannual publication.

Blood & Aphorisms
P.O. Box 702, Station P
Toronto, Ontario
M5S 2Y4, Canada
Dennis Block, Michelle Alfano, Fiction Editors
fiction@interlog.com
www.interlog.com/~fiction
Quarterly.

Bomb*
New Art Publications
594 Broadway
New York, NY 10012
Betsy Sussler, Editor-in-Chief
editor@bombsite.com
www.bombsite.com

Border Crossings
Y300–393 Portage Avenue
Winnipeg, Manitoba
R3B 3H6 Canada
Meeka Walsh, Editor
Canadian magazine of the arts.

Boulevard*
4579 Laclede Avenue
Suite 332
St. Louis, MO 63108–2103
Richard Burgin, Editor
Triannual. Note new address.

The Briar Cliff Review
3303 Rebecca Street
P.O. Box 2100
Sioux City, IA 51104–2100
Tricia Currans-Sheehen, Editor

The Bridge
14050 Vernon Street
Oak Park, MI 48237
Jack Zucker, Editor
Biannual.

Buffalo Spree
4511 Harlem Road
P.O. Box 38
Buffalo, NY 14226
Kerry Maguire, Associate Editor
Buffalo, New York–area quarterly arts magazine.

Button
Box 26
Lunenburg, MA 01462
Sally Cragin, Editor & Publisher
"New England's tiniest magazine of poetry, fiction, and gracious living."
Biannual.

Buzz
11835 West Olympic Boulevard
Suite 450
Los Angeles, CA 90064
Marilyn Bethany, Editor
www.buzzmag.com
Stylish Los Angeles monthly
occasionally publishes fiction
under the banner "L.A. Stories."

Callaloo
English Dept.
322 Bryan Hall
University of Virginia
Charlottesville, VA 22903
Charles H. Rowell, Editor
www.muse.jhu.edu/journals/
cullaloo
A quarterly journal of African
American and African arts &
letters.

Calyx*
P. O. Box B
Corvalis, OR 97399–0539
Editorial collective
calyx@proaxis.com
www.proaxis.com/~calyx
Triannual journal of art and
literature by women.

The Carolina Quarterly
Greenlaw Hall CB #3520
University of North Carolina
Chapel Hill, NC 27599–3520
Rotating editorship
Triannual.

Chariton Review
Truman State University
Kirksville, MO 63501
Jim Barnes, Editor
Biannual.

The Chattahoochee Review
2101 Womack Road
Dunwoody, Georgia 30338–4497
Lamar York, Editor
Quarterly.

Chelsea
P.O. Box 773
Cooper Station
New York, NY 10276–0773
Richard Foerster, Editor
Biannual.

Chicago Review
5801 South Kenwood Avenue
Chicago, Ill 60637–1794
David Nicholls, Editor
humanities.uchicago.edu/
humanities/review/
Quarterly.

Christopher Street
P.O. Box 1475
Church Street Station
New York, NY 10008
Tom Steele, Editor
Monthly with focus on gay issues.

Cimarron Review
205 Morrill Hall
Oklahoma State University
Stillwater, OK 74078–0135
E. P. Walkiewicz, Editor
Quarterly.

City Primeval
P.O. Box 45637
Seattle, WA 98145
David Ross, Editor
Quarterly publishing "Narratives of
Urban Reality."

Colorado Review
Colorado State University
English Dept.
Fort Collins, CO 80523
David Milofsky, Editor
Biannual.

Columbia: A Journal of Literature
and Art
404 Dodge Hall
Columbia University
New York, NY 10027
Rotating editorship
Biannual.

Commentary*
165 East 56th Street
New York, NY 10022
Neal Kozodoy, Editor
103115.2375@compuserve.com
*Monthly, politically conservative
Jewish magazine.*

Concho River Review
English Dept.
Angelo State University
San Angelo, TX 76909
James A. Moore, General Editor
Biannual.

Confrontation
English Dept.
C. W. Post Campus of Long
Island Univ.
Brookville, NY 11548
Martin Tuck, Editor-in-Chief

CONJUNCTIONS*
Bard College
Annandale-on-Hudson, NY
12504
Bradford Morrow, Editor
www.conjunctions.com/lit
Biannual.

Crazyhorse
English Dept.
University of Arkansas at Little
Rock
Little Rock, AR 72204
Ralph Burns, Editor
Biannual.

The Cream City Review
University of Wisconsin-Milwaukee
P.O. Box 413
Milwaukee, WI 53201
Rotating editorship
www.uwm.edu/People/noj/tccr/
  tccrhome.htm
Biannual.

Cut Bank
English Dept.
University of Montana
Missoula, MT 59812
Allyson A. Goldin, Lary Kleeman,
Editors-in-Chief
Biannual.

Denver Quarterly*
University of Denver
Denver, CO 80208
Bin Ramke, Editor

Descant
P.O. Box 314, Station P
Toronto, Ontario
M5S 2S8 Canada
Karen Mulhallen, Editor

Descant
English Dept., Texas Christian
University
Box 32872
Fort Worth, TX 76129
Neal Easterbrook, Editor
Biannual.

DoubleTake*
1317 W. Pettigrew Street
Durham, NC 27705
Robert Coles and Alex Harris,
Editors
dtmag@acpub.duke.edu.
www.duke.edu/doubletake/
  index.html
*Beautifully produced quarterly
devoted to photography and
literature.*

EPOCH*
251 Godwin Smith Hall
Cornell University
Ithaca, NY 14853–3201
Michael Koch, Editor
***Triannual. This year's O. Henry
  Award–winning magazine.***

Esquire*
250 West 55th Street
New York, NY 10019
Erica Mansourian, Associate
Literary Editor
Summer reading issue.

Event
Douglas College
Box 2503
New Westminster, British
Columbia
V3L 5B2, Canada
Calvin Wharton, Editor
Triannual.

Fiction
English Dept.
The City College of New York
New York, NY 10031
Mark Jay Mirsky, Editor
www.ccny.cuny.edu/Fiction/
fiction.htm
All-fiction format.

The Fiddlehead
University of New Brunswick
P.O. Box 4400
Fredericton, New Brunswick
Canada E3B 5A3
Don McKay, Editor
Quarterly.

The Florida Review
English Dept.
University of Central Florida
Orlando, FL 32816
Russel Kesler, Editor
Biannual.

Flyway
203 Ross Hall
Iowa State University
Ames, IA 50011
Stephen Pett, Editor

Folio
Literature Dept.
The American University
Washington, DC 20016
Cynthia Lollar, Managing Editor
Biannual.

FOURTEEN HILLS
The Creative Writing Dept.
San Francisco State University
1600 Holloway Avenue
San Francisco, CA 94132–1722
Rotating editorship
hills@sfsu.edu
www.sfsu.edu/~cwriting/
14hills.html
Biannual.

Geist
1014 Homer Street #103
Vancouver, British Columbia
V6B 2W9 Canada
Stephen Osborne, Publisher
geist@geist.com
*"The Canadian Magazine of Ideas
and Culture."*
Quarterly.

THE GEORGIA REVIEW*
The University of Georgia
Athens, GA 30602–9009
Stanley W. Lindberg, Editor
Quarterly.

THE GETTYSBURG REVIEW*
Gettysburg College
Gettysburg, PA 17325
Peter Stitt, Editor
Quarterly.

Glimmer Train Stories
812 SW Madison Street
Suite 504
Portland, OR 97205–2900
Linda Davies, Susan Burmeister-
Brown, Editors
www.glimmertrain.com
Quarterly. Fiction and interviews.

Global City Review
Simon H. Rifkind Center for the
Humanities
The City College of New York
138th St. and Convent Ave., NY,
NY 10031
Linsey Abrams, Editor
*Nifty, pocket-size format. Annual
as of 1997.*

Good Housekeeping
959 Eighth Avenue
New York, NY 10019
Arleen L. Quarfoot, Fiction Editor

GQ
350 Madison Avenue
New York, NY 10017
Adrienne Miller, Assistant Editor
gqmag@aol.com

Grain
Box 1154
Regina, Saskatchewan
Canada S4P 3B4
J. Jill Robinson, Editor
grain.mag@sk.sympatico.ca
www.sasknet.com/~skywriter/
grain 25
Quarterly.

Grand Street
131 Varick Street
Room 906
New York, NY 10013
Jean Stein, Editor
www.voyagerco.com/gs/
Quarterly arts magazine.

Green Mountains Review
Box A 58
Johnson State College
Johnson, VT 05656
Tony Whedon, Fiction Editor

The Greensboro Review
English Dept.
University of North Carolina at
Greensboro
Greensboro, NC 27412
Jim Clark, Editor
www.uncg.edu/eng/mfa
Biannual.

Gulf Coast
English Dept.
University of Houston
4800 Calhoun Road
Houston, TX 77204–3012
Rotating editors
Biannual.

Gulf Stream
English Dept.
Florida International University
North Miami Campus
North Miami, FL 33181
Lynne Barrett, John Dufresne,
Editors

Habersham Review
Piedmont College
Demorest, GA 30535–0010
David L. Greene, Lisa Hodgens
Lumpkin, Editors
Biannual.

Happy
240 East 35th Street
Suite 11A
New York, NY 10116
Bayard, Editor
Off-beat quarterly.

Harper's Magazine*
666 Broadway
New York, NY 10012
Lewis Lapham, Editor
www.harpers.org

Hayden's Ferry Review
Box 871502
Arizona State University
Tempe, AZ 85287–1502
Rotating editorship
HFR@asuvm.inre.asu.edu
129.219.240.141/hfr/hfr.html
Biannual.

High Plains Literary Review
180 Adams Street
Suite 250
Denver, CO 80206
Robert O. Greer Jr., Editor-in-
Chief
Triannual.

The Hudson Review*
684 Park Avenue
New York, NY 10021
Paula Deitz, Frederick Morgan,
Editors
Quarterly.

Image*
P.O. Box 674
Kennett Square, PA 19348
Gregory Wolfe, Publisher & Editor
73424.1024@compuserve.com
A quarterly journal of the arts and
religion.

Indiana Review
465 Ballantine
Bloomington, IN 47405
Rotating editorship
Biannual.

The Iowa Review*
308 English/Philosophy Building
University of Iowa
Iowa City, IA 52242–1492
David Hamilton, Editor
www.uiowa.edu/~english/
iowareview
Triannual.

Iowa Woman
P.O. Box 680
Iowa City, IA 52244–0680
Rebecca Childers, Editor
Quarterly.

The Journal of African Travel-Writing
P.O. Box 346
Chapel Hill, NC 27514
Amber Vogel, Editor
Biannual. First issue, Fall 1996.

The Journal
The Ohio State University
English Dept.
164 West 17th Avenue
Columbus, OH 43210
Kathy Fagan, Michelle Herman,
Editors
Biannual.

Kalliope
Florida Community College at
Jacksonville
3939 Roosevelt Boulevard
Jacksonville, FL 32205
Mary Sue Koeppel, Editor
Triannual journal of women's art.

Kansas Quarterly/Arkansas Review
English & Philosophy Dept.
Box 1890
Arkansas State University
State University, AR 72467
Norman Lavers, Editor
Formerly Kansas Quarterly.
Resumed publication as a triannual in 1996.

Karamu
English Dept.
Eastern Illinois University
Charleston, IL 61920
Peggy Brayfield, Editor
Annual.

THE KENYON REVIEW
Kenyon College
Gambier, OH 43022
David H. Lynn, Editor
kenyonreview@kenyon.edu
Triannual.

Kinesis
P.O. Box 4007
Whitefish, MT 59937–4007
Leif Peterson, Editor & Publisher
Kinesis@Netrix.Net
Monthly.

Kiosk
State University of New York at
Buffalo
English Dept.
306 Clemens Hall
Buffalo, NY 14260
Rotating editorship
Annual.

The Laurel Review
English Dept.
Northwest Missouri State
University
Maryville, MO 64468
William Trowbridge, Editor
Biannual.

Literal Latté
Suite 240
61 East 8th Street
New York, NY 10003
Jenine Gordon Bockman,
Publisher & Editor
litlatte@aol.com
   www.literal-latte.com
Bimonthly.
Literary Review*
Farleigh Dickinson University
285 Madison Avenue
Madison, NJ 07940
Walter Cummins, Editor-in-Chief
TLR@fdu.edu
www.webdelsol.com/tlr
Quarterly.
Louisiana Literature
Box 792
Southeastern Louisiana University
Hammond, LA 70402
David C. Hanson, Editor
Biannual.
The Madison Review
University of Wisconsin
English Dept., Helen C. White Hall
600 North Park Street
Madison, WI 53706
Rotating editorship
Biannual.
Magic Realism
P.O. Box 922648
Sylmar, CA 91392–2648
C. Darren Butler, Editor-in-Chief
The Malahat Review
University of Victoria
P.O. Box 1700
Victoria, British Columbia
V8W 2Y2 Canada
Derk Wynand, Editor
malahat@uvic.ca
Quarterly.

Manoa*
English Dept.
University of Hawai'i
Honolulu, HI 96822
Frank Stewart, Editor
www2.hawaii.edu/onjournal
Biannual.
The Massachusetts Review
South College
University of Massachusetts
Box 37140
Amherst, MA 01003–7140
Jules Chametzky, Editor
Quarterly.
Michigan Quarterly Review
The University of Michigan
3032 Rackham Building
915 E. Washington Street
Ann Arbor, MI 48109–1070
Laurence Goldstein, Editor
Mid-American Review
English Dept.
Bowling Green State University
Bowling Green, OH 43403
George Looney, Editor-in-Chief
Biannual.
Midstream
110 East 59th Street, 4th Floor
New York, NY 10022
Joel Carmichael, Editor
*Monthly with focus on Jewish
issues and Zionist concerns.*
The Minnesota Review
English Dept.
East Carolina University
Greenville, NC 27858–4353
Jeffrey Williams, Editor
Non–Minnesota based biannual.

Mississippi Review
University of Southern Mississippi
Southern Station, P.O. Box 5144
Hattiesburg, MS 39406–5144
Frederick Barthelme, Editor
www.sushi.st.usm.edu/mrw/
    index.html
*Internet version publishes full text
stories and poems monthly, many
of which are not included in
regular issues of the magazine.
Among the top literary Web sites.*

The Missouri Review*
1507 Hillcrest Hall
University of Missouri
Columbia, Missouri 65211
Speer Morgan, Editor
www.missouri.edu/~moreview
Triannual.

Ms.
135 West 50th Street
16th Floor
New York, NY 10020
Marcia Ann Gillespie, Editor-in-
Chief
ms@echonyc.com
Focus on feminist issues.

Nassau Review
English Dept.
Nassau Community College
One Education Drive
Garden City, NY 11530–6793
Paul A. Doyle, Editor
Annual.

The Nebraska Review
Writers' Workshop
Fine Arts Building 212
University of Nebraska at Omaha
Omaha, NE 68182–0324
Art Homer, Richard Duggin,
Editors
www.unomaha.edu/~ahomer
Biannual.

New Delta Review
English Dept.
Lousiana State University
Baton Rouge, LA 70803–5001
Rotating editorship
Biannual.

New England Review
Middlebury College
Middlebury, VT 05753
Stephen Donadio, Editor
nereview@mail.middlebury.edu
Quarterly.

New Letters*
University of Missouri at Kansas
City
5100 Rockhill Road
Kansas City, MO 64110
James McKinley, Editor-in-Chief
Quarterly.

New Millennium Writings
P.O. Box 2463
Knoxville, TN 37901
Don Williams, Editor
www.mach2.com/books/williams/
    index.html
Biannual. Started in 1996.

New Orleans Review*
P.O. Box 195
Loyola University
New Orleans, LA 70118
Ralph Adamo, Editor
noreview@beta.loyno.edu
Quarterly.

The New Renaissance
26 Heath Road #11
Arlington, MA 02174–3614
Louise T. Reynolds, Editor-in-
Chief
jpagano@allegro.cs.tufts.edu
Biannual.

THE NEW YORKER*
25 West 43rd Street
New York, NY 10036
Bill Buford, Fiction Editor
wwww.enews.com/magazines/
   new_yorker
*Esteemed weekly with special
fiction issues in June and
December.*

Nimrod
2010 Utica Square
Suite 707
Tulsa, OK 74114–1635
Francine Ringold, Editor-in-Chief
Biannual.

96 Inc.
P. O. Box 15559
Boston, MA 02215
Vera Gold, Editor
Biannual.

The North American Review
University of Northern Iowa
1222 West 27th Street
Cedar Falls, IA 50614
Robley Wilson, Editor
nar@uni.edu
*Bimonthly founded in 1815.
Features short shorts.*

North Dakota Quarterly*
The University of North Dakota
Grand Forks, ND 58202–7209
Robert W. Lewis, Editor

Northeast Corridor
English Dept.
Beaver College
450 S. Easton Road
Glenside, PA 19038–3295
Susan Balée, Editor
Biannual.

Northwest Review
369 PLC
University of Oregon
Eugene, OR 97403
John Witte, Editor
Triannual.

Notre Dame Review
Creative Writing Program
English Dept.
University of Notre Dame
Notre Dame, IN 46556
Valerie Sayers, Editor
Biannual. Started in 1996.

Oasis*
P.O. Box 626
Largo, FL 34649–0626
Neal Storrs, Editor
Quirky quarterly.

Ohio Review
Ellis Hall
Ohio University
Athens, Ohio 45701–2979
Wayne Dodd, Editor

Ontario Review*
9 Honey Brook Drive
Princeton, NJ 08540
Raymond J. Smith, Editor
Biannual.

Other Voices
English Dept. (M/C 162)
University of Illinois at Chicago
601 South Morgan Street
Chicago, IL 60607–7120
Lois Hauselman, Executive Editor
Biannual with all-fiction format.

Oxalis
Stone Ridge Poetry Society
P.O. Box 3993
Kingston, NY 12401
Shirley Powell, Editor

The Oxford American
115½ South Lamar
Oxford, MS 38655
Marc Smirnoff, Editor
*John Grisham–backed magazine
with Southern focus.*

Oxygen
Suite 1010
535 Geary Street
San Francisco, CA 94102
Richard Hack, Editor

Pangolin Papers
P.O. Box 241
Nordland, WA 98358
Pat Britt, Editor
All fiction triannual.

The Paris Review*
541 East 72nd Street
New York, NY 10021
George Plimpton, Editor
www.voyager.com/PR/
Quarterly.

Parting Gifts
3413 Wilshire Drive
Greensboro, NC 27408
Robert Bixby, Editor
rbixby@aol.com
  users.aol.com/marchst/msp.html

Partisan Review
236 Bay State Road
Boston, MA 02215
William Phillips, Editor-in-Chief
Quarterly.

Passages North
English Dept.
Northern Michigan University
1401 Presque Isle Avenue
Marquette, MI 49007855–5363
Anne Ohman Youngs, Editor-in-Chief
Biannual.

Playboy
Playboy Building
919 North Michigan Avenue
Chicago, IL 60611
Alice Turner, Fiction Editor
editor@playboy.com
  www.playboy.com
Sometimes takes on literary sheen.

PLOUGHSHARES
100 Beacon Street
Boston, MA 02116
Don Lee, Editor
**www.emerson.edu/
  ploughshares/**
Well-known writers serve as guest editors.

Potpourri
P.O. Box 8278
Prairie Village, KS 66208
Polly W. Swafford, Senior Editor
Quarterly.

Pottersfield Portfolio
P.O. Box 27094
Halifax, Nova Scotia
B3H 4M8 Canada
Ian Colford, Editor
saundc@auracom.com
users.atcon.com/~saundc/
potters.html
Triannual.

PRAIRIE FIRE
423–100 Arthur Street
Winnipeg, Manitoba
R3B 1H3 Canada
Andris Taskins, Editor
Quarterly. "Literary immortality series" enables donors to be written into stories and poems.

PRAIRIE SCHOONER*
201 Andrews Hall
University of Nebraska
Lincoln, NE 68588–0334
Hilda Raz, Editor
Quarterly.

Press
125 West 72nd Street
Suite 3M
New York, NY 10023
Daniel Roberts, Editor
pressltd@aol.com
  www.paradasia.com/press
Quarterly. Premier issue Summer 1996.

Prism International
Creative Writing Dept.
University of British Columbia
Vancouver, British Columbia
V6T 1W5 Canada
Rotating editorship
prism@unixg.ubc.ca
www.arts.ubc.ca/crwr/prism/
  prism.html
Quarterly.

Prison Life
Joint Venture Publishers
1436 West Gray Street
Suite 531
Houston, TX 77019–4946
www.prisonlifemag.com
Magazine devoted to prison, prisoners, and prison-related issues. Publishes fiction written by inmates.

Provincetown Arts
650 Commercial Street
Provincetown, MA 02657
Christopher Busa, Editor
Annual Cape Cod arts magazine.

Puerto del Sol
P.O. Box 30001
Dept. 3E
New Mexico State University
Las Cruces, NM 88003–8001
Kevin McIlvoy, Editor-in-Chief
Biannual.

Quarry Magazine
P.O. Box 1061
Kingston, Ontario
K7L 4Y5 Canada
Mary Cameron, Editor
Quarterly.

The Quarterly
650 Madison Avenue
Suite 2600
New York, NY 10022
Gordon Lish, Editor
www.salzmann.com/gutter/#q
Publication interrupted.

Quarterly West
317 Olpin Union Hall
University of Utah
Salt Lake City, UT 84112
Lawrence Coates, M. L. Williams, Editors
Biannual.

Raritan
Rutgers University
31 Mine Street
New Brunswick, NJ 08903
Richard Poirier, Editor-in-Chief
Quarterly.

REAL
School of Liberal Arts
Stephen F. Austin State University
P.O. Box 13007, SFA Station
Nagodoches, TX 75962
W. Dale Hearell, Editor

Redbook
224 West 57th Street
New York, NY 10019
Dawn Raffel, Books & Fiction Editor

Rio Grande Review
Hudspeth Hall
University of Texas at El Paso
El Paso, Texas 79968
M. Elena Carillo, Editor
Biannual.

River Styx
3207 Washington
St. Louis, MO 63103
Richard Newman, Editor
Triannual.

Room of One's Own
P.O. Box 46160, Station G
Vancouver, B.C.
V6R 4G5 Canada

Rosebud
P.O. Box 459315 E. Water Street
Cambridge, WI 53523
Roderick Clark, Editor
Quarterly.

Salamander
48 Ackers Avenue
Brookline, MA 02146
Jennifer Barber, Editor
Biannual.

Salmagundi
Skidmore College
Saratoga Springs, NY 12866
Robert Boyers, Editor-in-Chief
Quarterly.

Santa Monica Review
Santa Monica College
1900 Pico Boulevard
Santa Monica, CA 90405
Lee Montgomery, Editor
Biannual.

Seven Days
29 Church Street
P.O. Box 1164
Burlington, VT 05042–1164
Paula Routly, Copublisher
Free Burlington, Vermont, area
weekly newspaper with
occasional fiction.

The Sewanee Review
University of the South
Sewanee, TN 37375
George Core, Editor
http:/www.sewanee.edu/sreview/
home.html
Quarterly.

Shenandoah
Troubador Theater, 2nd floor
Washington and Lee University
Lexington, VA 24450
R. T. Smith, Editor
Quarterly.

The Slate
P.O. Box 581189
Minneapolis, MN 55458–1189
Rachel Fulkerson, Chris Dall, etc.,
Editors
Not to be confused with
Microsoft's Michael Kinsley–edited
online 'zine. Ceasing publication.

Snake Nation Review
110 #2 West Force Street
Valdosta, GA 31601
Robert George, Editor
Triannual.

So to Speak
4400 University Drive
George Mason University
Fairfax, VA 22030–444
Rotating editorship
"A feminist journal of language
and art."

Southern Exposure
P.O. Box 531
Durham, NC 27702
Jo Carson, Fiction Editor
Southern@igc.apc.org
Sunsite.unc.edu/
Southern_Exposure
A journal of Southern politics and
culture.

Southern Humanities Review
9088 Haley Center
Auburn University
Auburn, AL 36849
Dan R. Latimer, Virginia M.
Kouidis, Editors
Quarterly.

The Southern Review
43 Allen Hall
Louisiana State University
Baton Rouge, LA 70803–5005
James Olney, Dave Smith, Editors
Quarterly.

Southwest Review*
Southern Methodist University
307 Fondren Library West
Dallas, TX 75275
Willard Spiegelman, Editor-in-
Chief
Quarterly.

STORY*
107 Dana Avenue
Cincinnati, OH 45207
Lois Rosenthal, Editor
All-fiction quarterly.

StoryQuarterly*
P.O. Box 1416
Northbrook, IL 60065
Diane Williams, Editor

The Sun*
107 North Roberson Street
Chapel Hill, NC 27516
Sy Safransky, Editor
Eclectic monthly.

Sycamore Review*
English Dept.
Heavilon Hall
Purdue University
West Lafayette, IN 47907
Rob Davidson, Editor-in-Chief
sycamore@expert.cc.purdue.edu
www.sla.purdue.edu/academic/
  engl/sycamore/
Biannual.

Tamaqua
Humanities Dept.
Parkland College
2400 West Bradley Avenue
Champaign, IL 61821–1899
Bruce Morgan, Editor-in-Chief
Biannual.

Tea Cup
P.O. Box 8665
Hellgate Station
Missoula, MT 59807
Rhian Ellis, Editor
Triannual.

Thema
Box 74109
Metairie, LA 70053–4109
Virginia Howard, Editor
For every issue a theme. Biannual.

Third Coast
English Dept.
Western Michigan University
Kalamazoo, MI 49008–5092
Theresa Coty O'Neil, Fiction Editor
www.wmich.edu/thirdcoast/
  index.html
Biannual.

The Threepenny Review
P.O. Box 9131
Berkeley, CA 94709
Wendy Lesser, Editor
Quarterly.

Tikkun
60 West 87th Street
New York, NY 10024
Thane Rosenbaum, Fiction Editor
TIKKUN@panix.com
*"A Bimonthly Jewish Critique of
Politics, Culture & Society."*

Time Out New York
627 Broadway, 7th Floor
New York, NY 10012
Susan Kelly, Books & Poetry
Editor
www.timeout.co.uk
*Weekly guide to New York City
entertainment. One special issue
with fiction to date.*

Treasure House
Suite 3A
1106 Oak Hill Avenue
Hagerstown, MD 21742
J. G. Wofensberger, Editor-in-
Chief
thpublish@aol.com
As of 1997, renamed VERB.
Published triannually.

TRIQUARTERLY
Northwestern University
2020 Ridge Avenue
Evanston, IL 60208
Reginald Gibbons, Editor
Triannual.

The Urbanite
P.O. Box 4737
Davenport, IA 52808
Mark McLaughlin, Editor &
Illustrator
"Surreal & lively & bizarre."

Urbanus
P.O. Box 192921
San Francisco, CA 94119–2921
Peter Driszhal, Editor
*Published "approximately 3 times
a year."*

Vignette*
P.O. Box 109
Hollywood, CA 90078–0109
Dawn Baillie, Editor
vignet@aol.com
*All fiction quarterly. Each issue
has a theme.*

The Virginia Quarterly Review
One West Range
Charlottesville, VA 22903
Staige D. Blackford, Editor

Wascana Review*
English Dept.
University of Regina
Regina, Saskatchewan
S4S 0A2 Canada
Kathleen Wall, Editor
Biannual.

Washington Review
P.O. Box 50132
Washington, DC 20091–0132
Joe Ross, Literary Editor
Quarterly D.C.–area arts magazine.

Weber Studies
Weber State College
Ogden, UT 84408–1214
Neila C. Seshachari, Editor
*Triquarterly interdisciplinary
humanities journal.*

Wellspring
4080 83rd Avenue North
Suite A
Brooklyn Park, MN 55443
Meg Miller, Editor/Publisher

West Branch
Bucknell Hall
Bucknell University
Lewisburg, PA 17837
Karl Patten, Robert Love Taylor,
Editors
Biannual.

West Coast Line
2027 East Academic Annex
Simon Fraser University
Burnaby, British Columbia
V5A 1S6 Canada
Roy Miki, Editor
www.sfu.ca/west-coast-line/
WCL.html
Triannual.

Western Humanities Review
University of Utah
Salt Lake City, UT 84112
Barry Weller, Editor
Quarterly.

Whetstone
Barrington Area Arts Council
P.O. Box 1266
Barrington, IL 60011
Sandra Berris, Editor
Annual.

Whiskey Island Magazine
University Center
Cleveland State University
1860 East 22nd Street
Cleveland, OH 44114
Rotating editorship
whiskeyisland@popmail.csuhio.edu
Biannual.

The William and Mary Review
College of William and Mary
P.O. Box 8795
Williamsburg, VA 23187
Forrest Pritchard, Editor
Annual.

Willow Springs
526 5th Street, MS-1
Eastern Washington University
Cheney, Washington 99004
Christopher Howell, Editor
Biannual.

Wind
P.O. Box 24548
Lexington, KY 40524
Charlie Hughes, Leatha Kendrick,
Editors
Biannual.

Windsor Review
English Dept.
University of Windsor
Windsor, Ontario
N9B 3P4 Canada
Alistair MacLeod, Fiction Editor
Biannual.

Witness*
Oakland Community College
Orchard Ridge Campus
27055 Orchard Lake Road
Farmington Hills, MI 48334
Peter Stine, Editor
Biannual with theme issues.

Worcester Review
6 Chatham Street
Worcester, MA 01609
Rodger Martin, Managing Editor
Annual.

Wordplay
P.O. Box 2248
South Portland, ME 04116–2248
Helen Peppe, Editor-in-Chief
Quarterly.

Writ
Innis College, University of
Toronto
2 Sussex Ave.
Toronto, Ontario
M5S 1J5 Canada
Roger Greenwald, Editor
*No longer publishing. Last issue
Fall 1995.*

Writers' Forum*
University of Colorado
P.O. Box 7150
Colorado Springs, CO 80933–
7150
Alexander Blackburn, Editor-in-
Chief
Annual.

Xavier Review
Xavier University
Box 110C
New Orleans, LA 70125
Thomas Bonner Jr., Editor
Biannual.

THE YALE REVIEW
Yale University
P.O. Box 208243
New Haven, CT 06250–8243
J. D. McClatchy, Editor
Quarterly.

Yankee
Yankee Publishing, Inc.
Dublin, NH 03444
Judson D. Hale Sr., Editor
*Monthly magazine devoted to New
England. Occasional fiction.*

ZYZZYVA
41 Sutter Street
Suite 1400
San Francisco, CA 94104–4903
Howard Junker, Editor
ZYZZYVAINC@aol.com
www.webde/sol.com/ZYZZYVA
*Triannual. West coast writers and
artists.*

Permissions